ON TARGET!

Eyes on his instruments, it seemed to Ecker they were plunging toward the desert in a vertical dive. The steepness of the descent was to give as rapid a loss of height as possible. The spiral minimized displacement and had an added advantage—it made them appear static for a brief moment on a radar screen before disappearing altogether. It was a dangerous maneuver, but Hohendorf and Bagni knew precisely what to do.

As they hurtled earthward, Bagni kept closely tucked in to the infrared image of the IDS that filled his head-up display. In the backseat, Stockmann was already programming the chameleon, the "intelligent" crystals in the special paint that was the self-altering camouflage system of the ASV Tornadoes.

Three turns, and it was time to level off. They settled at one hundred feet, switched off the radar height warning to minimize any radar broadcast and, at five hundred knots, streaked toward their target.

Also by Julian Jay Savarin

Trophy
Target Down!
Wolf Run
Windshear
Naja
The Quiraing List
Villiger
Water Hole

Published by
HarperPaperbacks

PALE FLYER

JULIAN JAY SAVARIN

HarperPaperbacks
A Division of HarperCollins*Publishers*

This is a work of fiction. The characters, incidents, and dialogues are products of the author's imagination and are not to be construed as real. Any resemblance to actual events or persons, living or dead, is entirely coincidental.

HarperPaperbacks *A Division of* HarperCollins*Publishers*
10 East 53rd Street, New York, N.Y. 10022

Cover illustration by John Berkey

First printing: March 1994

Printed in the United States of America

HarperPaperbacks and colophon are trademarks of HarperCollins*Publishers*

❖ 10 9 8 7 6 5 4 3 2 1

For the members of the "North Devon Air Force"
who turn fledglings into Hawks

For Oggy and Ken,
Hawkmasters

And very especially for
Carol . . . *polar bears?*

PRELIMINARIES

Moscow, August

"Humankind is a disease."

The speaker was dispassionate as he looked down upon the excited crowd in the square, beyond which the starbursts of fireworks lit the night sky. It was, he thought, like the frenzy of a pagan ritual; a sacrifice was being offered to appease the gods. His expressionless eyes, now and then briefly speckled by the intermittent flares of the firework display, seemed to hold dangerous secrets as he watched the fourteen-ton hollow statue of Feliks Dzerzhinsky, father of the KGB, being taken off its plinth.

"Look at them," he continued. "They think it's all over." He permitted himself a fleeting, grim smile. "It's only just beginning. Yugoslavia's taught them nothing."

KGB colonel Feliks Alexandrovitch Kurinin was watching the antics of his fellow comrades from the Lubyanka, the KGB headquarters. Three other officers, one each from the air force, the army, and the navy, stood with him. All were of equivalent rank. A high flyer, Kurinin had become a full colonel at the age of thirty-four. Though a few years older, his companions had themselves been no slouches in the promotion game. The oldest was only forty-four.

Kurinin was now thirty-seven. He watched as the statue was loaded, like so much garbage, onto the open back of a truck that had been positioned for the purpose. "*Sic transit gloria,*" he murmured. He'd always hated the thing anyway, considering it gross in the extreme. Kurinin did not possess the historical loyalty of the ideological warriors who inhabited the upper echelons of his service. He had little time for septuagenarian generals. Like poor old Feliks out there, their time was passing.

Kurinin was no liberal reformer, though he acted the part to the hilt, as did his companions. One was even an elected people's deputy. It was all part of the game plan, conceived long before there was a Russian parliament, running in parallel with the Supreme Soviet. Now that the failed coup was over and the witch-hunt was starting, it was time to shift into the next phase. Alliances among the various republics would be made, and broken, as the fragmented union tried to find a way out of its self-inflicted woes. Strong hands, and minds, would be needed to create a new central command to bring together a new, revitalized union. The lords of chaos, among whom he numbered those in the West whose vested interests lay in the dismemberment of the union, would not hold the field for long. When the inevitable ethnic and civil strife began to take its toll, those very people out there would cry for a return to the stability they were now so eager to discard. But all would be different. First they must suffer the consequences of their gadarene rush toward their blinkered perceptions of individual and national freedom.

The air force colonel, a fighter pilot, moved to the window and stood next to Kurinin. He was the elected deputy, and he had vociferously made his reforming zeal known in parliament. He had even been on international TV.

He stared down at the milling crowd. They had all been looking from separate windows. "What do they think they're doing?" He sounded amused.

"Getting rid of the old and bringing in the new." Kurinin's words had a sharp edge to them. "They believe the good times are just round the corner. Having heeded the siren's call, they can't see the path of chaos they have chosen. And as for the West, it can barely contain its glee and self-righteousness. It now wants to assuage its sense of guilt and self-preservation by handing out alms to us, the new international poor. We, a great nation, have been reduced to the status of beggars." The tone of his voice had grown harder. "But we are not helpless, nor ripe for the taking."

There was a suppressed fire behind his eyes as he surveyed his countrymen in the square that once had required written permission for entry. They knew so little. Among them mingled hand-picked personnel, ostensibly taking photographs of the great event. There were so many cameras and video units of the international press, all eager to record this particular twilight of the gods, a few extra would excite little interest. Many faces would be on photographic records for future attention.

Kurinin permitted himself another fleeting twitch of the lips. It could have passed muster as a smile, barely. Some of his own people, politically trustworthy, had even thrown Molotov cocktails at armored personnel carriers—after the crews, also politically sound, had first clambered out.

The old guard would be removed from positions of power, leaving room for young officers like him and his companions, supposedly fired by the spirit of reform and radicalism. Even those who were now in the forefront of what the West liked to call the second revolution would eventually be replaced. The coup would succeed, but not in the way everyone expected.

"And then," he went on softly, "we shall have control. The West has a few surprises to receive. It believes it has won, but in fact it will be bled by continuing demands for aid, more money, and economic refuge. We, on the other hand shall be leaner, fitter, and much stronger. Think of it." He gestured toward the square. "The engine of chaos. Our prime asset."

His companions turned in the darkened room to look at him, the pulses of light from the outside throwing dancing shadows upon their faces. Each was smiling tightly, dangerous men with apocalyptic visions. They had remained in constant touch when each had gone into a different branch of service, their shared political ideals owing their genesis to that time. Behind them was a small table with four glasses, filled with champagne. They went to the table, picked up the glasses, and drank a silent toast to each other; then Kurinin returned to the window, the empty glass still in his hand, while his companions placed theirs slowly back down upon the table.

He held up the glass to the feverish light coming in from outside. "Fragile," he began, as if speaking to the glass itself, "but whole. You know where you are with it. You can hold it to your lips, without fear of injury. You can drink from it . . . sustenance or poison." He let go of the glass suddenly. It crashed to the polished floor, shattering explosively and startling his watching companions.

He did not peer down at the fragments at his feet but, instead, kept staring out of the window. One booted foot trod with seeming absentmindedness upon some shards yet crunched them with slow deliberation.

"Now," he continued softly, "it is dangerous. Countless tiny pieces, each capable of doing injury. You may sweep up as much as you like, but there will always be one, or two, or three shards that will be missed in the cleanup . . . waiting for an incautious toe, or finger . . . to pierce, to poison, to infect. That, comrades, is the nationalism that has been unleashed upon the Motherland this night; because even Russia herself will suffer. And the West, watching smugly on the sidelines at the self-inflicted dismemberment of the union, may think itself safe and, in so doing, is making one of its gravest mistakes." Kurinin turned now, facing the others. "We . . . shall ensure it."

In the coming weeks and months, with the purge of the older officers of all the services, all four would be promoted to general rank or equivalent. As for Kurinin, the gutting of the KGB would, if anything, accelerate his own promotion.

JOSIS, Washington; February

JOSIS was not a place, but a special intelligence unit so small, very few people knew of it. In fact, its detractors, of which there were many, called its staff the invisibles. To them, the JOSIS people had a status of zero. With the high-tech success of the Gulf War, someone had come up with the idea of creating a specialized satellite intelligence unit, and the Joint Satellite Intelligence Service—JOSIS—was born, with an initial staff of fifty.

Then came the upheavals in the Soviet Union. Arms cuts became the flavor of the moment. Not unexpectedly, these newcomers were among the first to feel the cold wind of budget changes. The JOSIS staff was reduced to two members, until something more productive could be found to give them to do.

Major Chuck Morton, USAF, ex-F-16 pilot, walked into one of the two offices he commanded and sat at his desk in preparation for another boring day, most of which he would spend writing out yet another transfer request. He wanted to get back to flying. So far all his pleas had fallen on deaf ears.

Morton had suffered the misfortune of running out of fuel during a training mission over the Nevada desert, and though he had performed a classic dead-stick landing—bringing the aircraft safely down on a once only chance—he had been grounded by the subsequent court of inquiry. The court had not accepted Morton's assertion that a faulty fuel systems readout had led him to overestimate his fuel reserves. It was his job to monitor his fuel state at all times, triple-checking if necessary. He was found culpable of fuel mismanagement and was grounded indefinitely, it seemed. There were those who felt that his excellent airmanship in bringing back an expensive taxpayers' aircraft deserved some sort of medal. The inquiry board thought otherwise and posted him to JOSIS, where, apparently, they hoped he would stay forever.

The only ray of light in Morton's otherwise unrelievedly bleak world was Sergeant Macallister. Sergeant Mac, or simply Mac, as Morton normally addressed his subordinate, was a marine. Sergeant Mac was also a woman. But there was no fraternization, overt or otherwise. Mac was adept at nearly every hand-held weapon in the U.S. Marine Corps armory, worked out regularly at one of the Pentagon gyms, and she could drive an Abrams main battle tank with the best. On first discovering her service history, Morton had wondered what someone of her skills could possibly have done to merit burial in such a dead-end unit. Then a fellow officer had told him that at her previous unit, Mac had repulsed an advance from a senior officer by hitting him across the face. Unfortunately she had used her fist. The officer had been knocked out cold. Only the fact that the officer in question had refused to bring charges had saved her from a court-martial. Removal from her unit had been inevitable.

Mac breezed in. "Hi, Chuck. Writing another request for flying duties? You sure don't give up, do you?"

"Is there anything else to do around here?" He smiled at her sheepishly. He found the trim fitness of her figure attractive, and the short cut of her hair gave the unexpectedly soft outlines of her face a gentle beauty that was observed only after a second look. Those who knew no better suspected her of being muscle-bound. She wasn't.

She handed him a photograph. "This might interest you."

He took it skeptically. "Desert. What I really need is a picture of a patch of sand."

"See the section I've circled."

"More sand."

"Try this." She handed him something that looked like an eyebath. It was a loupe, a photographic magnifying glass.

He placed it on the encircled area and brought an eye close, like a jeweler inspecting a stone. "Still more sand. You should be a pilot. You've certainly got the eyesight; better than mine. I can't see what you mean."

"Oh, it's difficult, sure. But something's there. They've been clever."

Morton looked up at her. "They? What's all this, Mac?"

Mac gave a tight smile. "Come into my office, sir. I've got a computer enhancement on the screen. All will be revealed." She passed a hand through her blond crop.

"You don't want to say things like that," Morton joked as he left his desk to follow her out. "People might overhear and misunderstand."

They were in an empty and silent corridor. Mac looked about her theatrically. "No one here but us chickens. We're the forgotten ones, Chuck. An embarrassment no one knows what the hell to do with. Now come and look at this."

"Jesus!" Morton remarked softly as he stared at the computer enhancement. They stood close together, looking at the computer screen. "Are you sure of this?"

Mac tapped a few keys. "More definition, perhaps?" The image grew sharper. There was now no doubt.

Finally Morton spoke: "A missile battery, complete with radar and missiles, out there in the middle of nowhere? What the hell for? There's nothing to protect. The nearest village, never mind town, must be hundreds of miles away. Are you sure this photo's genuine?"

"The real thing all right, Major. Came in the batch this morning. I checked. The usual stuff they pass to us from the hotshot units. Stuff they don't think is of any use. They keep all the exciting shots of airbases, naval units, and ships, or of terrorist camps and so on. Nothing important normally comes our way. They missed this."

Morton was wary. "They wouldn't set us up, would they? You know what those jokers think of us."

She turned her head slowly, to look at him. Their faces were very close, bathed in the ghostly light of the computer screen. "I don't think so, Major. I think this is for real."

"Then how could they have missed it?"

She tapped the keyboard once more. A new photograph merged into the one on screen. The missile battery had disappeared.

"Is this the same area?" Morton asked.

She nodded.

"And what's the time lapse between shots?"

"Fifteen minutes."

"Fifteen!" Morton was surprised. "There should have been . . . several during that period."

"The satellite malfunctioned. It wasn't even supposed to be taking pictures of that area. I guess that's why they sent these to us."

Morton nodded slowly. "Yeah. They were having some fun, after all."

Mac straightened. "Sorry, Major. I guess it's pretty hard on you, being stuck down here."

He gave her a quick smile. "It helps having you here, Mac. I wouldn't want it differently."

A slight color came to her cheeks and vanished almost as soon as it had come. She cleared her throat. "So what do we do?" She pointed at the screen.

He stared at it. "Hanged if we do and hanged if we don't. What the hell. They can't ground me twice. Let's tell somebody."

The SR-71A Blackbird, high-speed, high-level reconnaissance aircraft brought out of semiretirement, seared through the night above the desert. Its mission was to comprehensively photograph the area accidentally surveyed by the malfunctioning satellite. Someone had taken Morton and Mac seriously enough to authorize the expensive mission.

Though the Blackbird had been publicly retired the year before, broad hints were being dropped of a superstealthy replacement—even more advanced than the F-117A Stealth fighter that had been so successful during the Gulf War—that was already operating; but there were some missions that the black ship was called upon to do. This was one such.

The two crew members, in their fully pressurized suits—virtual spacesuits—went through the routine of constantly checking and rechecking the aircraft's systems as its twin J58 ramjets hurled it through the night at three times the speed of sound. They were not worried about possible threats. At this height and speed, no possible hostile aircraft or missile could catch or harm them. It was therefore with some astonishment that the reconnaissance systems officer, sitting in his ejection seat hidden from the outside world behind the pilot, noted a fast-moving trace on the threat warning display.

"There's something up here with us!" he said. "And it's catching up!"

"*What?* You've got to be kidding."

"Would I kid at a time like this? Let's get the hell outta here."

They had been told that under no circumstances were they to continue the mission if interrupted. They were reluctant to abort but obeyed mission orders and headed back, increasing speed as they went. Whatever was pursuing them soon lost the race and disappeared out of sensor range.

They made it back to base without further incident, but minus the photographs.

In the JOSIS offices, Morton and Mac were stunned to be visited by a USAF general.

"My name's Bowmaker," the general said in greeting as they sprang to attention. "At ease." He inspected the offices while they hovered uncertainly. In the corridor, his aide, a smug-looking air force captain with shiny pilot's wings, glanced superciliously at Morton from time to time.

"So this is where they buried you," Bowmaker said to the two members of JOSIS. "And who discovered the anomaly in the photograph?"

"Sergeant Macallister," Morton replied.

"Major Morton, sir," Mac said at the same time.

Bowmaker looked at each in turn. "Commendable loyalty, but you can't have both spotted it at the same time."

"We did, sir," Mac insisted.

Bowmaker chose not to pursue it further. "All right. Well, it seems you two have stirred up something. The people who sent you the photos in the first place are feeling like . . ."

"If the general will permit, sir," Mac had the temerity to interject, "like assholes, sir?"

Morton held his breath. In the corridor, the smug captain stiffened like a gundog, waiting almost enjoyably for the explosion.

Unexpectedly, Bowmaker smiled. "Marines do happen to be blunt at times."

"Yes, sir!"

"Don't make a habit of it, Sergeant."

"No, sir!"

"But I agree with you."

"Yes, sir!"

"Major," Bowmaker went on to Morton, "you've got a good one here."

"I know it, sir. Sergeant Macallister's very good at her job."

"Well, you're both making people sit up and take notice. We ran a Blackbird mission over the suspect area. It got chased by a high-altitude bogey."

Morton's eyes widened. "You ran a mission on our say-so? And we were right?" He could hardly believe it.

"Well, Major, someone didn't want us to see what's down there. Sort of excites the interest even more, doesn't it?"

"It certainly does, sir."

"So how would you two like to work for me while this thing's running?"

Morton glanced at Mac, whose eyes said it all.

"*Yes, sir,* General!"

"All right. Take whatever you need. As of now, you're moving to new offices."

Morton and Mac grinned at each other.

In the corridor, the smug captain looked sick.

Night, the North African Desert, Two Days Later

The F-117A Stealth fighter prowled over the target area, its mission to do what the Blackbird had been unable to. Its pilot, though deployed to the Gulf region, had not flown in actual combat. Nevertheless, he had every confidence in his aircraft and was certain he could get in, do the job, and get out without being detected. The F-117A was invisible to contemporary radars. As far as he was concerned, whoever was down there was blind when it came to detecting his aircraft.

He therefore had only the briefest of warnings before a terrible explosion ripped apart the F-117A. As he died, the pilot was aware of a feeling of consternation. It was as if his Stealth fighter had been as vulnerable as any ordinary aircraft.

General Bowmaker strode into the newly acquired offices, his face grim, a look of shock in his eyes. Even the pair of stars on each shoulder didn't seem to gleam as usual. His aide, looking rather less than his normal supercilious self, was in furtive tow.

Morton and Mac stared at the general expectantly as they rose to attention. He waved absently at them, indicating they should resume their seats.

The new offices were a complete contrast to the old ones. Each of them had a semicircular console with a bank of computers that had access to the latest satellite intelligence information. They knew about the F-117A.

Bowmaker said, "All hell's broken loose. Suddenly people are looking at a multibillion-dollar project going down the tubes, leaving a black hole in our defenses. I've seen panic in some faces."

"If the airplane was acquired and shot down without the pilot knowing anything about it, sir," Morton began, "it means there's a fully operational antistealth radar already in use."

"That's what's scaring the hell out of everybody. Antistealth is supposed to be years away, perhaps decades."

"Looks like we were wrong about that, if it's what really happened."

"Yes," Bowmaker said grimly. "We've got work to do. You're on the move again. We're going to Europe . . . Britain, to be exact."

"Britain, sir?" This from the general's aide.

The general just stared at him.

The captain swallowed and looked hurt.

Bowmaker turned to Mac. "Sergeant, your record says you're good with a handgun. That right?"

Taken aback, she hesitated. "Sort of, sir—"

"Cut the crap, Sergeant," Bowmaker interrupted. "I haven't the time for false modesty. Are you good or not?"

She stared back at him without flinching. "I'm very good, sir."

"That's more like it," Bowmaker said. "And you, Major. I know all about your many requests for return to flying duty. If we get through this okay, I'll consider putting my weight behind your next request."

Morton felt a wave of gratitude. "Thank you, sir!"

"We're not there yet. However, I think you'll like some people I'll be introducing you to. As for you, Sergeant . . . Mac, isn't it?"

"Yes, sir." She was pleasantly surprised by the unexpected use of her shortened name.

"Well, Mac, I'll be authorizing a handgun for you to carry, under my orders. That's it, troops. Let's move."

Two Hundred Feet Above a Valley Floor, Wales

"What's that crazy German doing?" Hank Stockmann asked from the backseat of the Super Tornado as the aircraft banked steeply and a sheer wall of rock suddenly loomed close to the top of the canopy.

In the front, Nico Bagni made no reply as he handled the speeding aircraft with the light touch of a master.

"Nico?" Stockmann called. "You hear me?"

The aircraft banked the other way, just as steeply, as Bagni threaded twenty-five hurtling tons of expensive metal between the mountains.

"What he is doing," Bagni replied at last, "is trying to get away from us. And he is succeeding. Now don't speak. Let me concentrate."

"C'mon, Nico!" Stockmann urged. "Let's get him. Let's get him, man!"

"Shut up, Hank."

"Yup."

They were on a training mission, practicing air combat. For a while, Bagni, who was very good at it, thought he had been gaining the upper hand on Hohendorf and Flacht, who were in the lead aircraft. But Hohendorf was an excellent and wily pilot. Bagni knew that any moment now, the twisting and turning airplane up ahead, which seemed to be getting ever closer to the rushing ground, would do something unexpected and spectacular, then disappear from view. Hohendorf always had a few tricks up his sleeve. To make life even more difficult, helmet sights were not being used, so it was down to the normal head-up display, and the Mark One eyeball, which was all less fortunate fighter pilots had at their disposal.

Suddenly the darting shape leapt skyward, wings fully swept.

"Jeez," Stockmann said. "Look at him go! Why aren't we following?"

"I'm not falling for that trick," Bagni replied. "He'll do a high reverse and catch us right on the nose. A head-to-head missile shot; and as he will have created his own arena, he'll be waiting for our move. He's watching us already, from up there."

Bagni had judged correctly. As soon as he had cleared the mountains, Hohendorf had reduced speed. The Super Tornado's wings had moved to midsweep, improving maneuverability. As speed decayed rapidly, the wings continued to move until they were fully forward, maintaining flying integrity. Then, holding the aircraft steady, he gave a firm push on the left rudder pedal. The Tornado pivoted on its wingtip and was again pointing toward the mountains below.

But there was no expected sound of the missile seeker acquiring a suckered target.

"Nico's learning, Wolfie," Hohendorf remarked to his backseater. "He's not where he should have been."

"You've caught him out too many times," Flacht said, turning his head constantly, searching for the threat. "Now he's trying to catch you out."

"No chance," Hohendorf said. Already he had come out of the steep dive, but he was still heading downward, making for another valley. "Let's see how he handles this."

The world about the cockpit was suddenly dark as the Super Tornado plunged between two razorlike peaks and continued downward.

"Are we skateboarding today?" Flacht inquired. "Not that I'm worried, of course. It's just that the boss might be a little upset if we scratch his nice airplane."

"They're all his nice airplanes."

"Exactly."

When conversing between the two crew stations, they invariably spoke German to each other.

Hohendorf eased gently out of the descent and tore through the valley. The green glow of the readout on the head-up display gave a radar altitude of fifty feet.

"We're going to get complaints," Flacht warned.

"This valley is uninhabited," Hohendorf said. "It's clearly marked on the charts."

"Some hill walker might have seen us. 'Dear sir,'" Flacht went on, reading the imagined letter, "'one of your airplanes nearly took my head off last Sunday when I was out enjoying a quiet walk in the hills. I protest at this invasion of my privacy. I did not pay taxes et cetera, et cetera . . .' How was that?"

"Sounds about right. Ah-ha!"

Hohendorf's exclamation was accompanied by the missile seeker going crazy, its modulated tone sounding increasingly excited. Then it changed into a single, ominous sound.

"Fox Two!" he transmitted, indicating a short-range missile kill.

Bagni's aircraft had been silhouetted nicely as it had climbed to clear a peak.

"Goddamn!" Stockmann said in frustration as the hit tone confirmed the kill. "*Goddamn!*" he said again.

He had been keeping a good lookout but had seen nothing, either in the air or on the threat display. Hohendorf had cleverly used the mountains to mask his approach.

"Sorry, Nico," he apologized to his pilot. "I missed him. He must have gone way down. They probably could have got out and walked!"

"Not your fault, Hank," Bagni said calmly. He did not sound put out. "Axel is Axel. He always goes as near as possible to the edge. It was a good move. I should have expected something like that."

"Yeah," Stockmann agreed reluctantly. "But at least we made him work for it."

Stockmann was right. Throughout the entire flight, this was the only time Hohendorf had scored.

"Good fight," came a voice on their headphones. The second Tornado was now keeping station with them. "One day, Nico, you're going to get me."

"But of course," Bagni said.

The two aircraft, clear of the mountains, banked in tight formation and headed back to base.

November One Base, Moray Coast, the Grampian Hills, Scotland; Late February

"Hey!" McCann exclaimed. "Will you guys take a look at this?"

"What now, Elmer Lee?" Selby inquired with the world-weariness of someone who had been around McCann too long.

"Give me a break, will you, Mark? I'm not kidding here. Come see for yourself. You too, Wolfie and Axel."

"Do we have a choice?" Axel von Hohendorf asked hopefully.

"Nope."

"That's what I thought."

The other three men went up to where McCann was standing, prepared to humor him.

They were in the aircrew kitting room, with its paraphernalia of flying gear hanging neatly from seried lines of racks. Like bodies without skeletons, the G-suits and immersion suits, topped by visored helms with masks and dangling oxygen hoses, seemed to belong to alien life forms. In a way, they did; for without their protection, the frail human bodies of their various owners could not survive within the dangerous arena that was their working environment.

They stared at the wall that had so excited McCann.

Someone, it seemed, had been visited by the muse. McCann read aloud:

> I salute thee, pale flyer,
> As you flee through great valleys
> Of dark and shining white.
> I salute thee, pale warrior,
> And envy your scything wings
> And burning fire.

"Someone's been robbing Keats," he added softly.

"Badly, by the looks of it," Selby remarked. "And what do you know of Keats, anyway?"

"Oh, give me a break, will you?" McCann repeated. "And stop being so goddamned British. It's not that bad."

Hohendorf studied the graffiti. "A frustrated pilot. One of the ground crew?"

"I've got one closer to home," Selby said with a grin. "I carry him in the backseat every time I fly."

Which was certainly true. McCann had joined the U.S. Air Force with the express intention of making available to that august body, his—as he saw it—quite dazzling ability to fly airplanes. Unfortunately the USAF did not agree. Several hairy landings during training had served to convince them. He was offered the backseat in the vain hope that he would reject it and please everyone by giving up.

True to form, he had accepted and had confounded his instructors by becoming one of the best backseaters in the business. McCann was a mess on the ground, to some eyes. In the air, however, everyone had to admit he was a genius. And as a team, he and Selby made a deadly pair in combat, despite the sharp comments.

Only two other teams matched their standard: Hohendorf, with Wolfgang Flacht in the backseat and Nico Bagni, with Hank Stockmann III, a quietly dangerous U.S. Marine, as backseater. They were the top three of the November crews, and sometimes it was difficult to choose among them, though each of the six went about his business in very different ways.

McCann, a Kansas City banker's son and USAF captain, registered Selby's comment with equanimity and cheerfully ignored it. "You really think it's one of the ground crew?" he asked of Hohendorf.

"Unless it's you," Hohendorf said, straight-faced.

"Hah!" McCann snorted as he began to put on his kit.

They all took great care as they donned their outfits: the G-suits to help their bodies take the punishing forces of gravity during hard maneuvering; immersion suits over that, to enable them to survive in the cold waters should they need to eject; the life jackets over the lot, to keep them afloat; then the restraints, to prevent flailing arms and legs during ejection. Penalties were usually lost limbs with improperly secured restraints and death without the suits. They got their helmets and oxygen masks and were about to leave when a sergeant hurried in.

"Sorry, gents. Mission's scrubbed."

His words brought groans out of them.

"You've got to be kidding!" McCann said disbelievingly. "After trussing ourselves up like Thanksgiving turkeys?"

The sergeant looked at him sympathetically. "Sorry, sir.

Boss's orders. Two other crews have been given your slot. The wingco wants to see you all in briefing room alpha. Mr. Bagni and Mr. Stockmann are already there."

They stared at the sergeant, puzzled and curious at the same time.

"Nico and Hank?" Selby began. "Any idea what this is all about?"

The sergeant shook his head. "None at all, sir."

"Come on, Sarge," Selby prodded. "Nothing much around here you don't know about."

"Well . . . I don't know whether this has any bearing on it, but an American general—USAF—and some people have just landed in an executive jet. A Sabreliner."

Selby glanced at McCann. "They've caught up with you at last, Elmer Lee. They weren't carrying leg irons, were they?" he said to the sergeant.

The sergeant gave a hesitant smile, knowing all about Selby and McCann. "I wouldn't know, sir. Um, the boss would like you all to hurry, gentlemen."

"All right, Sergeant Heddon," Hohendorf said. "Thank you. We'll get on with it."

"Sir," Heddon said, and went out.

"So what do you guys think?" McCann asked, including everyone in the question as they began to remove their cumbersome gear. "Something special for us?"

Selby and Hohendorf looked at each other and said nothing.

McCann tried again. "Wolfie?"

"We will know soon," Flacht replied logically.

McCann decided to give up as the sound of moving thunder passed above them. "There goes our slot," he said, not glancing upward as he concentrated on removing the immersion suit.

Briefing room alpha had excited McCann's interest with good reason. It was *the* briefing room on Zero One squadron. Like a small lecture theater, it was used only for special purposes.

In flying overalls that bore the patches of the blue NATO four-pointed star on one shoulder and of the wearer's national flag on the other, they entered the room expectantly. Bagni and Stockmann looked up at them from leather upholstered chairs as they made their way to their seats.

Capitano Nico Bagni, formerly of the AMI—Aeronautica Militare Italiana—was the first to speak. "Any ideas?" he asked in general.

"Your guess is as good as ours, Nico." It was Selby who answered. "Did Sarn't Heddon come to get you two?"

Stockmann's brutal haircut would have identified him as a U.S. Marine anywhere. "Yeah," he replied to Selby's query. "Didn't say anything much."

"All we could get out of him was that a Sabreliner's dropped in with a USAF general and assorted staff aboard."

Stockmann's large, strong teeth gleamed at McCann.

"Don't say it," McCann warned. "Mark's already been there."

Stockmann shook his head. "Must be hell being so popular."

A powerful roar swept by above them, then the cadence altered suddenly.

"One coming in," Hohendorf remarked.

"A baby pilot on convex?" Bagni wondered aloud. "Or more visitors?"

The new hopefuls who came to the November base tended to find their skills rigorously tested on conversion exercises, to see whether they could hack it with the November mount, the Tornado F.3S Air Superiority Variant. Before they even arrived at the unit, they would have already been considered the best on their original squadrons.

"I say a nugget," Stockmann suggested, using the naval term for untried pilots.

"Nah," McCann said. "More visitors. I feel it in my bones."

"That's his head," Selby explained. "All bone. Doesn't really need a bone dome to protect that skull of his."

"And all because he can't live without me," McCann retorted.

Moscow, the Same Day

Newly promoted General Feliks Alexandrovitch Kurinin, KGB, studied the reports at his nice new desk in his nice new office and felt pleased with himself. The national and international news followed the trend he had predicted all those months ago. The so-called commonwealth of independent states was coming apart at the seams, and Russia herself was heading into danger. The savage price rises of January had merely served to make bad things worse, and the military, their five-thousand-strong congress of senior officers having made their true feelings known about what was being done to the armed forces, were now making the kinds of rumbles that should seriously warn the politicians.

"But of course," Kurinin murmured to himself, "they won't listen. Which is where we come in."

A diffident knock sounded on the tall doors to the office.

"In!" Kurinin called authoritatively.

A young colonel entered smartly. "The comrade generals are here, Comrade Kurinin."

"Thank you, Vladimir. Please send them in."

The colonel nodded respectfully and went out.

Kurinin stood up as the door opened once more and

the colonel ushered in three senior officers, then left and closed the door quietly behind him. Once on their own, all four broke into huge smiles and briefly hugged each other in greeting.

Valeri Ivanovitch Tikov, Ukrainian, air force general; Viktor Viktorovitch Selenko, Russian, naval commodore; and Igor Leonidovitch Garadze, Georgian with strong Russian ancestry, army general, were the other members of the group that had toasted each other the previous August.

Kurinin surveyed them in turn. "Well, I must say you all look good in your new ranks."

They studied his office pointedly. "And your new surroundings, Feliks Alexandrovitch," Selenko began, "they do you proud."

Kurinin went over to a highly polished drinks cabinet, took out a tray with four small glasses and a bottle of vodka upon it. He put the tray on a low table at which there were four comfortable chairs. He poured vodka into each glass and picked one up.

"Comrades," he said.

They went over, and each picked up a glass.

"To a new and powerful Soviet Union," Kurinin offered in a toast.

"To a new and powerful Soviet Union," the others repeated.

They drank the vodka in one gulp.

"Please take your seats, comrades," Kurinin said as they put down the empty glasses; when they had done so, he continued: "We've had an interesting few months. All that has happened so far has served to confirm the fears I voiced last August. The creation of this new commonwealth has merely intensified the squabbles. We are reduced to *bargaining* with our armed forces. Your contacts in the Black Sea fleet, Viktor," he said to Selenko, "how do they feel about what's happening?"

"In a word? Poisonous."

"This will never be resolved amicably, no matter what the politicians say. Memories are long, and within the year the other republics will be up to their necks in trouble. Valeri?" Kurinin addressed Tikov. "The air forces must be feeling the chill."

"They are, and they don't like it."

Kurinin turned to Garadze. "And you, Igor?"

"You saw what happened at the officers' congress in January. Did they seem like happy people to you?"

"They looked extremely unhappy. But none of this surprises me, nor you. Which is why we're here. Our late comrades, the general and Stolybin, were on the right track; but they were flawed personalities. Though they saw the route our Motherland was being led down, and though they attempted to do something about it, they made serious mistakes and paid the price. There are now many flawed personalities in the seats of power. Our task is to make certain they, too, pay the price, before we all pay for their stupidity.

"Igor and Valeri, I'm very impressed with the way you handled the American spy planes. My reports tell me they still have no idea what happened. Is the unit secure?"

"Very secure," Garadze confirmed. "Work continues unimpeded, and as the evidence shows, the system works."

"They will, of course, mount countermissions. We've given them plenty to worry about."

"We'll be ready. I would have preferred not to have shot down that Stealth aircraft. At least, not yet. I had hoped we could have kept the existence of our new radar a secret from the outside world a while longer; but they kept coming over. Something had to be done."

"We've been out there a long time," Kurinin said. "It was

inevitable that someone somewhere would do his job properly and spot something. It took them so long, however, we were able to virtually complete our trials before they knew anything was there. They still don't really know."

"Shouldn't we bring the unit back home?" Selenko suggested. "If the trials are complete . . ."

"Not all are complete," Garadze interjected quietly. "And besides, it is an enormous installation. Moving now would only give everything away. And I'm not sure we should risk bringing it back here as long as matters are the way they are at the moment. How do we know that some idiotic politician might not use it as a bargaining chip with the West? Someone might think it a good idea to make it part of an arms reduction package."

"Igor is right," Kurinin said. "It's safer out there in the desert. I expect you to give it secure air protection, Valeri," he added to the air force man.

"Count on it."

Kurinin turned once more to Garadze. "I'm sorry about what's happening in Georgia, Igor." He then looked at each in turn. "All our homelands are in danger. Armenia and Azerbaijan will continue to pulverize each other. In the Baltics, very serious trouble is brewing between our soldiers and the people of those republics. Sooner or later the soldiers will fight back. It is to be hoped that the West will not be so foolish as to even consider intervening, for its own sake. They have already made a mess of the Yugoslav business. Let us hope they have the wisdom to keep out of ours.

"As for the Ukraine"—Kurinin looked grim—"because of the trouble with the Black Sea fleet, and the forcing of our soldiers to choose allegiance . . . this could be the most serious confrontation of all. Valeri," he went on to Tikov, "you've got a brother with the unit, haven't you?"

Tikov nodded. "Yes. Anatoly. Afghan war veteran. He

serviced Su25's out there and was a sergeant when he got back. He's a lieutenant now, hard as nails. He commands a missile servicing and operating team."

"How does he feel about what's happening in the Ukraine?"

"He's a proud Ukrainian, but he hates this whole business. He believes totally in a unified command. You don't have to worry about him."

"Never thought I would. We'll need plenty like him before we're done. Part of our task," Kurinin went on, "is to cause dissension among our NATO and EC friends. They're doing it all by themselves, but a little encouragement of their nationalistic tendencies won't go amiss. You'd have thought they would have taken note of what is happening here as our own union splits asunder. Our top priority has to be the elimination of the November units, to prevent them developing the program into a fully cohesive NATO-EC force. Western Europe can become a formidable superpower. The best hope against that happening are those very nationalistic tendencies I've just mentioned."

"And how do we stifle the November program?" Selenko asked.

"We put constant pressure upon it. We discredit it, we sabotage it . . . we do anything that may prove inimical to its continuing existence. We are not alone in desiring its demise. In the West, it has many opponents, particularly among those seeking budget cuts. We can also rely upon their politicians to make the sorts of blunders that will get the program into trouble."

Kurinin stopped and smiled suddenly. "I'll give you an example of the sort of thing I mean. Germany, against the better judgment of the rest of the EC, has recognized Croatia and Slovenia. Think of the old memories that little faux pas has stirred up. What do you think would happen if we declared solidarity with the Serbs?"

They all stared at him. "Are we likely to do that?" It was the Georgian who voiced their thoughts.

"All things are possible," Kurinin replied. "If, despite our president's apparent support for Croatia and Slovenia, we were to offer to help strengthen Serbia's borders . . ."

"Surely not," Tikov began. "But the president has . . ."

"So?" Kurinin's eyes were baleful. "We have soldiers who are rotting in cold tents with time on their hands. They feel humiliated and would no doubt like some action, any action."

Selenko smiled uncertainly. "You're not seriously suggesting this, Feliks."

"At this moment, no . . . but I am pointing out the fluidity of the situation. Serbia and Croatia at each other's throats today . . . tomorrow, the Bosnian powder keg." Kurinin tapped at his temple. "The world's having nightmares about Sarajevo. Presidents come . . . and go. . . . Can you see the people of the fat Western nations being prepared to send their soldiers to die for a small Balkan country? Distractions, my comrades. We're creating distractions, while we retrieve our country from the hands of incompetents. Remember history.

"And don't think there are not people in the West who would prefer to see the old union return, though they would perhaps not admit this in public. More certainty, you see. They knew where they were. In that, at least, I am in accord with them. The way things stand, any idiot can trigger a hot confrontation without having first thought it through. I do not like battles that are not of my own choosing. Too many people ignore the lessons of history. The lessons of the Gulf War, for example, are not lost upon me, nor, I'm pleased to say, upon you. That is why our installation is so important, that nothing must hinder its farther development and eventual deployment. They have not stopped their Star Wars program, and the

November program is continuingly active. We have the Star Killer. Another drink, my friends, then tell me what the soundings are throughout the services."

While Kurinin was listening to what his fellow comrades had to say, in briefing room alpha at the November base Mark Selby and his companions came to attention as the door to the room opened.

Wing Commander Christopher Tarquin Jason, RAF, strode in, followed by his deputies Fregattenkapitän Dieter Helm of Germany's Marineflieger, and Tenente Colonello Mario da Vinci of Italy's AMI.

The waiting flyers stared as more people came through the door. Air Vice-Marshal Robert Thurson, in flying overalls, they already knew. The rest, the USAF two-star general Heddon had spoken of and his retinue, were total strangers. Jason mounted the small dais while the newcomers occupied all the seats in the front row.

Jason removed his peaked cap, wiped his forehead with the back of the same hand as if to erase the cap's indentation, and placed the cap on the lectern before him. "At ease, gentlemen," he began. "Please sit down. I apologize for keeping you waiting. The air vice-marshal's aircraft had to wait for a landing slot."

That explained the thundering cadence they'd heard earlier. The AVM, who enjoyed piloting his own Tornado—a standard F.3—liked to make stylish landings.

"I was right," McCann whispered hoarsely to Stockmann. "Visitors."

Stockmann did not make a response. His gaze had fastened upon the blond head of the sole woman, in civilian clothes.

Jason, however, had zeroed his own gaze upon McCann. "Yes, Captain McCann?"

"Uh . . . nothing, sir!" said McCann, who thought he had recognized the major who had come in with the USAF general.

The general glanced briefly round to do a visual ident on McCann.

"Thank you for coming," Jason began, as if the summons had not been an order. "Allow me to introduce our visitors . . . General Bowmaker, United States Air Force, whom you've never met but who has been of great help to us in the past."

The general nodded at them.

"His aides," Jason went on, "Major Chuck Morton, Captain Wilbur Raintree, also USAF, and Sergeant Helen Macallister, U.S. Marines."

Mac looked straight ahead respectfully, as was expected of her rank in a gathering that included heavyweight senior officers.

"Yo the marines!" Stockmann said eagerly.

"Thank you, Captain Stockmann," Jason cut in with quiet authority. "Now, gentlemen," he continued, "I have no doubt your minds are full of questions. General Bowmaker and the air vice-marshal, will be speaking to you about a little job that has been allocated to us. I'm certain we can handle it." He treated them to a fleeting ghost of a smile.

"Now why doesn't that make me feel so good?" McCann again whispered, this time taking care to keep his voice truly soft.

Anything else he might have wanted to say was terminated by the painful connection of Stockmann's elbow with his side. Jason appeared not to have noticed.

The wing commander was that exotic kind of person who seemed unremarkable yet who managed to command attention just by being there. A clean-shaven man of medium build and regular features, he had dark eyes that gave the impression he could turn the object of his gaze to stone if need be. Sandy hair, receding slightly at the crown and temples, seemed to add to his presence, and there was an air about him that clearly signaled he was in total command, even in the company of his superior officers.

"I'll now hand you over to General Bowmaker," he said, "who has some interesting things to say to you. General."

Bowmaker stood as Jason picked up his cap and stepped down from the dais.

"Thank you, Wing Commander." Bowmaker climbed the dais and turned to face his audience. "I'll come straight to the point. Someone has shot down a Stealth fighter, having first acquired it with a radar that's not supposed to exist."

The six flyers looked stunned.

"Holy shit," McCann heard himself say, realizing too late that his words had carried.

"My feelings exactly," Bowmaker remarked. "What I actually said at the time would burn your ears off. We have run recce missions, to no avail. We've got a very poor satellite photograph, but that only gives the approximate area. We have no precise location. Further, we have no idea of how many surface-to-air missile batteries are surrounding the . . . er . . . item. We need a fast, low-level reconnaissance mission to clearly identify this item . . . and then we're going to take it out." Bowmaker paused, waiting for his words to sink in.

They stared at him, then turned to look at Jason. The wing commander's eyes remained fixed upon the general. It was impossible to tell what his thoughts were on the matter.

"Why the hell doesn't he call it a target?" McCann commented, whispering for a third time to Stockmann.

"Perhaps he's trying to spare your feelings," the marine replied in a fierce whisper of his own. "Now can it!"

McCann stared ahead innocently, a faint look of injury upon his features.

"We nearly missed it," Bowmaker continued, "and only the diligence of Major Morton and Sergeant Macallister here brought its existence out into the open. For all we know, it has been at the site for several months. We did, after all, have other matters occupying our attention in the Gulf."

No one smiled. Bowmaker could not have received more attention from the November crews if he'd begged.

"Gentlemen, the F-117A is not supposed to be vulnerable to radar. That's the sole reason for its existence. If someone has created a system that lights this bird up like a Christmas tree, we've got a flying duck on our hands. Intelligence believes that this unit may well be the only one around, a prototype in the advanced stages of testing. The downing of the F-117A has proved it works. If that airplane is to be the last it ever shoots down, there's just one remedy. We take it out. That radar is your target, gentlemen." Bowmaker seemed to speak directly to McCann as he ended.

McCann wisely said nothing.

Bowmaker left the small platform, and Thurson took his place.

Thurson was a tall, slim man with the features of an aesthete. He had once been Jason's flying instructor and had loyally backed the wing commander throughout the long and difficult genesis of the November program. Despite two successful operational outings for elements of the unit that had involved the flyers now in the briefing room, the program's continuing survival was always a precarious affair. Ministerial ax wielders and their counterparts in the NATO and EC nations were never far from the door. Thurson was only too well aware that it would take a very slight excuse indeed to persuade the choppers to go to work. Everyone was on the hunt for a budget cut here, another there. Long-term thinking never seemed to come into it. Come an emergency, and the tools were not there with which to deal with it effectively. A lot of running around like headless chickens, usually followed by a cobbled-together effort, was par for the course. They never seemed to learn. No one was going to do that to the November program, not as long as he was around. It didn't necessarily mean Jason would always get his own way; even so . . .

With these thoughts chasing themselves in his mind, Thurson turned his attention to the three ASV crews before him. The mission would be dangerous. No point hiding that from them. He also knew the November unit had been selected because it was required yet again to prove the value of its existence. The accountants were always on the prowl.

Truth was, however, this was just the sort of thing the November program was meant to handle. He appreciated the irony.

"Like General Bowmaker," the air vice-marshal began, "I shan't beat about the bush. This will be a dangerous mission. However, you chaps have handled yourselves admirably in dangerous situations before. But every mission is different and carries with it its own subtleties and very special dangers. You will therefore be undergoing a rigorous training program and only when we're all happy about the results will the actual mission take place. As time is at a premium, the training period will of necessity be highly pressurized."

"You mean normal business, sir." It had to be McCann.

Thurson looked as if he were deciding whether to bite McCann's head off or to be kind. He chose kindness.

"Knew you'd see it my way, Captain."

Jason's neutral glance at McCann, however, spoke volumes.

"Wing Commander Jason has all the details," Thurson continued, "and he'll brief you fully. From time to time, Major Morton and Sergeant Macallister will be liaising with you. Finally, gentlemen"—his eyes raked them—"there is a total embargo on the mission, and the preparations for it. You will speak to no one not currently in this room about it. Those who need to know will be told by those authorized to do so. Each element will know its job. Yours is to prepare for and fly the mission. Thank you, gentlemen."

The air vice-marshal stepped down from the dais, and everyone stood up as he, the general, and his retinue, followed by Helm and da Vinci, left the room.

Jason, standing legs slightly apart, waited until the door had closed before turning to his crews. "Now you know," he said to them quietly. He looked at McCann. "What are we going to do about you, Captain?"

"Keep me, sir?"

"What are you? Some kind of pet?"

"I've got to feed him a banana in the back cage every now and then," Selby said.

Jason allowed himself one of his fleeting smiles before saying: "What the AVM said is true. This will be a dangerous mission. I picked you lot because I have every faith you can do it and come through. However, if anyone thinks otherwise, I won't hold it against him if he prefers not to participate. There are one or two of the other crews whom I believe have reached the right level of proficiency—"

"I do not believe there are others who will be able to handle this as well as we can, sir." The normally correct Hohendorf took the liberty of interrupting his CO. There was no boastfulness in the words. "As the air vice-marshal said, we have been under fire. We know how we'll react. A different crew would need to learn *during* combat. If the mission is as dangerous as we have been warned, I'd rather we went in instead of a green crew. I am not trying to be a hero, sir. It makes sense, that's all."

Jason studied each face carefully. "Does Axel speak for all of you?"

Each nodded.

The wing commander seemed to breathe a sigh of relief. "Thank you, gentlemen. Be back here in an hour. We'll start introducing you to your target." He put on his cap in preparation for leaving. "By the way, McCann, Major Morton seems to think he knows you from some-where. On the way here, I was giving the AVM and the general my crew selection for the job. The major appeared to think your name struck a bell. Another satis-fied customer, perhaps?"

"I'm innocent, sir," McCann said.

"Captain McCann, you're never innocent," Jason said with a straight face. "One hour, gentlemen." He strode out.

They all turned to McCann. "All right, Elmer Lee," Selby began. "What have you been up to?"

"Are you guys my friends or what?" McCann queried in his best injured tone.

"Or what," Flacht answered.

"I sure don't need enemies with you bunch around."

"Oh, but you do!" they crowed at him.

2

The Desert, Four Thousand Kilometers—About 2,500 Miles—to the South

Deep within the heart of the Sahara, Lieutenant Anatoly Tikov supervised a team working on one of the surface-to-air missile systems. It had been his team that had shot down the American Stealth aircraft, and they were currently looked upon as the aces of the base; most of the glory, though, had been showered upon Tikov himself. As the watch commander that fateful night, it was his alertness that had served to catch the covert reconnaissance aircraft unawares. The time from acquisition to the shoot could have been measured in fractions of a second.

But Tikov was not happy. He would have preferred it if the aircraft had flown on unmolested and unseeing. The whole reason for being in this godforsaken place was to remain undetected. Shooting down one of the Americans' prime air assets was the best way to attract unwelcome attention. It also ensured such attention would be forthcoming in the not-too-distant future. The act of shooting down an American aircraft was not something that would normally cause him to lose any sleep. It was just that there was the right time and place for everything, and this was certainly not it.

True, the entire complex was well hidden in deep silos and perfectly camouflaged, even from prying spy satellites. But the whole thing had been jeopardized by the on-site commander. No vehicles, missiles, or troops were supposed to be aboveground during the passage of an orbiting satellite. The location had been chosen precisely because it was routinely out of the areas of interest of such spaceborne cameras.

From his experience in Afghanistan, however, Tikov knew that satellites sometimes turned up where they were not supposed to, did not perform when they were meant to, and performed when not expected. It happened to Soviet machines. There was no reason to suppose American equipment was totally immune to malfunction.

As a precaution, he had first voiced his fears to his immediate superior, the captain in charge of three SAM teams. When nothing had happened, he went to the lieutenant colonel, the officer in charge of the entire battery of nine SAM teams. The battery commander took note of Tikov's comments but was annoyed that he had seen fit to go over the head of his captain.

Still no obvious changes in operating procedures were made. Frustrated, Tikov decided to go directly to the site commander. The colonel was even less pleased that a junior officer, one recently commissioned from the other ranks at that, had possessed the temerity to go over every superior's head. Instead of giving Tikov's warnings consideration, the colonel thought it best to bawl Tikov out. It did not help that Tikov was Ukrainian. The colonel himself had a brother in the services, a destroyer captain in the Black Sea fleet. He was outraged that the Ukraine had dared to ask members of the fleet to swear allegiance. In his anger, he chose to see Tikov's warnings as yet another Ukrainian affront, as if Tikov were really saying he knew better than his colonel.

When the recce flights had suddenly begun, the Ukrainian's vindication had merely increased the antipathy the colonel felt. The subsequent destruction of the Stealth aircraft, instead of earning Tikov an accolade from his colonel, had simply made the senior officer more embittered. An unreasoning hatred of Tikov grew from that.

Aware of this, Tikov decided from then on to keep a very low profile. Having a brother who was the air force general actually responsible for the aerial defense of the site made an already bad situation very much worse. As a result, Tikov did not report his warnings about the possible satellite overflights. He knew his brother would have acted severely toward the colonel, making it look as if the Ukrainians were throwing their weight about. Most of the personnel at the site were Russian, including the civilian scientists.

In the strictest military sense, he should still have made the report; but these were not normal times. No one was sure of what was going to happen to the armed forces. A mistake on his part could easily rebound upon his brother, general or no general. Generals could be unceremoniously sacked, no matter how high up the command ladder they had scrambled. Even the outside world knew it was happening.

The West must be laughing at us, he thought.

Tikov was certain a malfunctioning satellite had blown their cover, but he had no proof. His position did not allow him access to such information. He had merely been relying upon his own feelings. Afghanistan had honed his survival instincts. They were also warning him about the colonel. A former aircraft servicing NCO-turned-SAM team commander was no match for a full-blown colonel, and being Ukrainian in the current climate did not help, either.

A much earlier incident also caused Tikov some worry. Long before the site had been completed, a desert nomad astride a camel had blundered into a patrol of the troops who were part of the site's ground defense force. There could have been only one outcome. The nomad could never have been allowed to return to wherever he had come from, to blab about strange soldiers in the Sahara.

It was most likely that the man had become just another statistic on the long list of desert victims; but someone, somewhere, a relative or close friend, would remark upon his disappearance. And even if no one searched for him, it would be talked about. What was talked about could reach the most unlikely ears.

Not wanting further confrontation with the colonel, Tikov had kept those fears to himself. Besides, it was now much too late to do anything about it. For the moment, however, he was protected by the temporary glory of having destroyed the American aircraft. He was not just a Ukrainian, but an admired member of the Soviet forces. Under the circumstances, it was the best thing to be.

Moscow, the Same Day, Same Moment in Time

The three horsemen were leaving Kurinin's opulent office, each on his way back to his respective unit. Tikov was thoughtful.

Selenko glanced at him inquiringly. "You seem far away, Valeri. A problem?"

Tikov seemed to rouse himself. "Ah . . . no. Not a problem. I was just wondering why Feliks made no mention of the fact that it was my brother's SAM unit that shot down the American. He must have known. He's got his own people down there. Blowing a Stealth aircraft out of the sky is not exactly an everyday occurrence."

"Surely you don't think . . ." Garadze paused, giving Tikov a sideways glance. "Oh, no, Valeri. We are the four horsemen . . . indivisible. The future depends on us. You cannot believe Feliks has another agenda. He's very preoccupied. He has the lion's share of the load. If we fail, he takes the biggest fall."

"I suppose you're right," Tikov said after a while. "Still, I can't help wondering."

The others said nothing.

When they had gone, Kurinin summoned his colonel. "I want you to check out a file for me," he began as soon as the younger man had entered. "Tikov."

The colonel looked surprised. "The general, comrade?"

"No . . . no. Another Tikov. Lieutenant Anatoly Tikov. He's at the desert site."

The colonel was even more surprised. "The one who shot down the American aircraft? But . . ."

Kurinin raised a restraining hand briefly. "I know what you're about to say. I'm after something. Anything . . . an anomaly. Tikov, before he was commissioned, serviced Su25's in Afghanistan, frequently under fire. His team had the highest number of combat-ready aircraft on his squadron."

"Sounds like the man's a hero."

Kurinin's lips turned down fleetingly. "I know of another hero who flew for the same squadron. *That* 'hero' flew our only flying example of an advanced fighter prototype to the West. Luckily for us, it ended in pieces nearly four thousand meters down on the seabed."

"Ah," the colonel said, understanding. "Kukarev."

"Indeed. Kukarev. Unfortunately, he escaped with his life, which he is now presumably enjoying under a new identity, with plenty of American dollars to ease the pain of separation from his homeland. One day . . ." There was a controlled savagery in Kurinin's voice as he paused, clearly thinking of something he intended to have done in the future. "The late and unlamented Comrade Stolybin was involved in a plot to trap Kukarev and discredit the new NATO unit at the same time. As we know, he failed disastrously. The NATO unit gave Kukarev an escort, which was successful in destroying our chase fighters.

"Kukarev was not even shot down," Kurinin went on in disgust. "He ran out of fuel. That was it, Colonel. Only a lack of fuel prevented the aircraft from falling into Western hands. So don't tell me about heroes, or those who claim to have the Motherland's interests at heart while they work to dismember it." Kurinin's eyes fastened upon his subordinate. "Lieutenant Tikov was Kukarev's personal servicing crew chief in Afghanistan. Kukarev arranged to have him posted to the development unit where he flew the aircraft . . . and Tikov told *no one* . . . that Kukarev was planning to defect."

"If the comrade general will allow me . . . I know the case history. Tikov was thoroughly interrogated at the time. If anything, he felt betrayed. He was very angry with Kukarev. He had no doubts about Kukarev's soundness and trusted him completely. They had been under fire together. . . ."

"And you believe this makes someone politically sound? If anything, warfare tends to raise great doubts in the soldier's mind. Beware of heroes, Vladimir. Now go and find out about Tikov. There may be other things he has been reluctant to talk about."

If the colonel thought, as he walked out, that Kurinin might be trying to find a lever to use on General Tikov, he kept his thoughts to himself.

Was Kurinin already maneuvering for the top position?

The colonel shut the door quietly behind him. It was opportune to be so close to potential power. The Motherland was in desperate need of a strong hand.

The November Base, Scotland

Two sleek Super Tornado ASVs were lined up on the long wide runway that pointed itself toward the waters of the Moray Firth. On their fins were the identification letters N-02—NATO Zero Two—the second of the November squadrons. It said much for Jason's staying power that he was actually able to receive funding for the creation of the second squadron, and this unit was now well on its way to achieving full strength.

A stiffish breeze came off the firth, meeting the two aircraft on the nose. The headwind would make their already short takeoff capability even shorter. A sudden roar tore at the air as the pilots pushed the throttles into max dry on the brakes, then the aircraft seemed to lunge forward as the brakes were released simultaneously. A greater roar filled the air as throttles were pushed farther, into afterburner. Four tongues of blue white seared rearward. The aircraft streaked down the runway and in very little time, it seemed, were lifting off. Wheels came up and were tucked in quickly, then the ASVs stood on their flaming tails and fled into the cold February sky.

Soon a relatively hushed silence fell as the afterburners were cancelled. But the aircraft continued to accelerate upward. In moments they were out of sight from the ground.

In the VIP suite in the officers' mess, Jason listened to the takeoff. Bowmaker watched him interestedly. They were waiting for the air vice-marshal, who was briefing Jacko Inglis, the group captain in overall command of the entire base. Morton and Macallister were in the alpha briefing room, setting up for the next session.

Bowmaker said, "Don't worry. They won't close you down. We won't let them."

Jason turned almost guiltily. "Am I that obvious?"

"When a man believes in something as much as you do, worry comes with the territory."

"We've got the second squadron working up nicely, but"—Jason gave a shrug—"one can never tell these days. In the Royal Air Force, for example, whole squadrons are being mothballed; and that's *after* the Gulf War. There's no guarantee that some cost-cutting bureaucrat might not think it a good wheeze to lob the ax our way."

"As I've said, it won't be allowed to happen. Certainly not as long as the air vice-marshal's around. And I'm in your corner."

"It's appreciated, sir. I assure you."

"There is a payoff, of course."

"There always is. I expect it as a matter of routine."

Bowmaker gave a thoughtful smile. "You know, Wing Commander, you're not so far removed from McCann."

"God forbid!" Jason was horrified. "That undisciplined—"

"Oh . . . I wouldn't be too quick to distance yourself," the general interrupted mildly. "You're both mavericks in your own way. You both give higher authority a headache. I know, I know. McCann's sort of like an unguided missile, but he knows his job. Right?"

"Best backseater I've got. No doubt about it. That's why I put up with him."

"And you, Wing Commander, are the best shot this program has got."

"Are you saying, sir, that I'm being—"

"You were offered promotion to group captain, I believe."

Jason was surprised. "How do you know that, General?"

"The air vice-marshal. You refused the promotion. Why?"

Jason took his time before replying. "I felt I was not quite ready."

"Why?" Bowmaker insisted.

"Well, sir . . . er . . . I'm just not ready."

"Why?"

"You're making this difficult. . . ."

"I know I am. You going to answer me? . . . No? All right. I'll tell *you.* You did not take that promotion because you knew two group captains would not be left in the same command. One would have to go. You were afraid you would be the one. Posted upstairs . . . out of the way. What price the November program then? How am I doing so far?"

"More or less correct, sir," Jason admitted.

"As I said, a maverick. It so happens I like mavericks. They usually get things done, while the pussyfeet take the credit. Same old story throughout history. You bust your gut trying to get something done, and when it works, it's the guys who spent most of their time opposing you who take the prizes. See how nations praise their inventors, conveniently forgetting the tough time they gave them in the first place? How many inventions would you say you British have lost to other countries—mine included—in the last . . . say, fifty years, because there was no backing at home when it was needed?"

"I wouldn't dare hazard a guess," Jason replied uncertainly. "Quite a few, I suspect."

"Quite a *lot*," Bowmaker corrected in partial mimicry. "Quite a lot. You see, Wing Commander, it's the fate of the maverick. Again, as I've said, he gets things done, while the rest hang on to his shirttail, kicking and screaming no-no-no. Until it works. Then it becomes 'ours.' And you're not like McCann, the unguided missile. You're the kind that's more dangerous to the bureaucrat. The guided missile that's *also* a maverick."

"You sound like someone who's speaking from experience, General."

"No, Wing Commander. I'm not like you at all. I'm the other historical figure in this particular triangle . . . like the air vice-marshal. We're the fixers. We back the mavericks and stall the pussyfeet. The bureaucrats don't have that much love for us, either." Bowmaker grinned suddenly, with distinct relish. "Hell . . . somebody's got to kick butt now and then."

At that moment Thurson walked in. "Well, General," the air vice-marshal began, "is my wing commander attending to you?"

"Doing a good job," Bowmaker replied. "We had an interesting talk."

Thurson eyes tracked toward Jason. "Oh?"

"I gave him a history lesson. Jacko Inglis okay?" Bowmaker went on.

"Thoroughly briefed," Thurson replied. "He knows what's expected."

"Then it's time for the target brief." Bowmaker looked at Jason as he spoke.

Jason checked his watch. "Yes, sir. The car's waiting."

"Let's do it," Bowmaker said.

As they left the suite, Jason hung back slightly while the American general strode on ahead.

Thurson slowed his pace slightly. "Something on your mind, Christopher?"

"I'd like a talk before the briefing, sir."

"The general will be having a word with his people before we begin. We can talk then."

"Very good, sir."

Thurson hurried on to catch up with Bowmaker.

When they arrived at the squadron building that housed briefing room alpha, Bowmaker called his aides into an office that was assigned to him, to check their preparations for the brief. Jason took the opportunity to talk to the AVM about the subject on his mind.

"There's something I've got to mention, sir," he began.

"Go on."

"Flight Lieutenant Hamilton-Jones . . ."

"Young Caroline."

"Yes, sir."

"The last time we discussed her," Thurson said, "she had begun training on Hawks and vaguely entertained the idea of progressing to combat jets. And if I'm not mistaken, she even had a posting to a November squadron in her sights. Never happen, of course . . . despite the belief in some quarters that a couple of other young ladies might make it to RAF operational units." Thurson fixed the wing commander with a warning stare. "She hasn't applied, has she?"

"Er . . . no, sir."

"That's something, at least. What is the world coming to? Royal Air Force female combat pilots indeed."

"The Americans have got them, sir. Served in the Gulf."

"That's the Americans for you," Thurson commented, as if that said it all. "Mind you, they weren't on fighters."

"No, sir."

"Well? What about Flight Lieutenant Hamilton-Jones?"

Jason cleared his throat. "I've been following her progress, sir. She's good. I've visited the flying training school, and have been up with her once or twice. Very impressive."

Thurson's voice was calm. "Once or twice?"

"Three times, sir."

"I see."

"All properly arranged through channels."

"I'd expect no less. But there's more, I take it?"

"Yes, sir." Jason decided to give the AVM the lot at one go. "From time to time, aircraft from other units visit us . . . sometimes using us as a diversion airfield during an exercise, and sometimes for a short deployment, particularly if we have dissimilar air combat exercises. Flight Lieutenant Hamilton-Jones has been cleared for such a visit. . . ."

"Flying the Hawk?"

"Yes, sir. Though not for air combat practice, of course."

"And has this also been cleared with Jacko Inglis?"

"Yes, sir."

"And I take it you'll be making another flight with her . . . all perfectly done by the book."

"Yes, sir," Jason said for the third time.

"Whoever recommended this young woman for flying training, anyway?"

"I did, sir . . . with backing from you."

"Hmm," Thurson said. "Well . . . you appear to have everything covered. So what's the problem?"

"She'll be arriving during the training period for the mission. I'll cancel."

"Absolutely not! That's the one thing you must not do."

Jason waited, in some surprise, for the AVM to continue.

"Nothing changes," Thurson said. "Your routine will remain unaltered, and all schedules adhered to as normal. Her pending visit has been logged, I take it?"

"Of course, sir."

"Then leave it unchanged. Make your flight with her."

"This is an operational unit, sir. Schedules change all the time. We scrubbed that mission just a short while ago. . . ."

"I'm not talking about scrubbing routine training missions. I'm talking about altering *your* schedule. Nothing must be done to give any impression that a special operation is on the agenda."

"If you're thinking about security, sir . . ."

"I'm not questioning your unit's security arrangements, Christopher. I know you've got things properly sewn up. That double security fencing and the ancillary equipment that surrounds this place is a pretty tough nut to crack. Your airfield guards are on the ball; but that takes care of the physical, *observable* side of things. The people we're dealing with, to judge by what General Bowmaker has told me, won't waste time on security fences. That's for the less sophisticated players.

"The sort of people I'm thinking about will wait and watch for anomalies, for changes in the pattern that do not follow routine. The sort of bods who are in Charles Buntline's province. You do remember Mr. Buntline."

Jason nodded. "Yes, sir." He remembered very well indeed. Buntline was a shadowy type of civil servant whose real job Jason would much prefer to be ignorant about. However, Buntline had been involved in operations that had concerned the November aircraft. Buntline was all right, but on occasion . . .

"Both the Americans, and Buntline, have got teams of people already working on this . . . but *your* crews are our cutting edge. No one outside those who need to know must even suspect what we're up to. Here at November, all personnel already assume, because of the nature of the program, that the unit is engaged on tasks no one talks about. Maintain that level of interest, and no higher. Your flight with Flight Lieutenant Hamilton-Jones goes on as scheduled."

"Very good, sir."

"Is she really doing well?" the AVM asked with more than passing interest.

"Her flying is impressive. You'd be pleasantly surprised, sir."

"Nothing surprises me when a woman's got the bit between her teeth. Now they want our aircraft, too. Good God. It does not bear thinking about. Ah," Thurson went on before Jason could make comment. Bowmaker and his team were coming out of the office. "The general and his people appear to be ready. Let's join your gentlemen, shall we?"

At about the time that Thurson, Bowmaker, and Jason were on their way to briefing room alpha, Tikov paused in the act of entering his own staff car. The cars of his colleagues were parked nearby in the small courtyard of the Moscow building. A weak flurry of snow seemed to hang in the still, cold air. Earlier falls had been cleared and piled in a low border around the yard.

Not yet at his car, Selenko stopped and turned to look. "A problem?" he called.

For answer, Tikov walked over slowly. Garadze, who was already aboard his own vehicle, climbed out and joined them. They watched Tikov inquiringly.

"I was talking to the wife of a close friend yesterday," Tikov began in a quiet but tense voice. "These are people who not so long ago ate well, lived well, dressed well. Professional people. Now she stands in a line, waiting to get one of the food parcels that manages to get here from the West." His face grew dark beneath his cap. "Food parcels . . . airlifts with monitored distribution. They're rubbing our noses in it! Our medical people go on strike because they have no earnings. . . . I don't know about you, but this whole situation fills me with outrage. How could we have allowed our so-called fellow *comrades* to bring us down to this level? *How?*" he went on fiercely. "And now, even the Baltics, in the name of all that's crazy, think they can tell *us* what to do. They make *demands*. It's insane!"

Without another word he turned suddenly and went back to his car. He entered, and the driver shut the door firmly before climbing in behind the wheel. The engine whirred into life, and the car set off at speed.

Tikov touched a hand to his cap in a parting salute as it went past.

Garadze and Selenko stood uncertainly for some moments.

"A very angry man," Garadze murmured.

"We all are," Selenko told him.

"Yes."

"He's right, of course. It is insane."

"Then we had better do something about it," Garadze said as they turned to their cars. "And soon."

Briefing Room Alpha, November One

The lectern had been moved to one side, and sliding doors in the wall behind it were open, revealing a large screen with video/TV equipment just beneath it, a little above the level of the dais itself. To one side of the small platform, Morton and Macallister sat at a workstation with a computer keyboard set upon it. Mac was at the keyboard.

Just in front of the workstation was a low table upon which was the relief model of a desert landscape. There were various markings on the model.

Bowmaker stood at the lectern.

"The breakup of the Soviet Union," he began, "and the Gulf War have opened up a whole bunch of Pandora's boxes. We were victorious in the Gulf, but that little war, gentlemen, also showed the world what high-tech weaponry can do. Result . . . every kid on the block now wants some of those lethal toys and will pay highly to get them.

"We don't know precisely what's out there in the desert. We did not get our recce photos, and the satellite pictures were so poor, they were missed by everyone except Mac and Morton. The satellite, after all, was not supposed to have made that orbit, and there are none currently available. Too busy watching those little firefights that are springing up all over the place.

"The Soviet breakup has let loose a whole lot of disgruntled, highly skilled military and technical personnel with a lot of stuff to sell . . . to the highest bidder. It's open news that some of this has already been intercepted by various governments; but it is also realistic to assume that some *will* get through. The hope is that it will be low-grade, conventional stuff that will do damage mostly to those who use it and whatever opponent they're currently fighting.

"Because we don't know the nature of what's out there, we can't conclude who owns it. Perhaps it's for a client state, although I do not personally believe such advanced technology would be sold off. Perhaps it's being developed by a Soviet group who want the union back. There are many who do. Again, we don't know. Whatever it is, and whoever owns it, no prizes for guessing where the technology comes from, as it certainly isn't ours. We don't normally go around shooting down our Stealth fighters."

There were tight smiles on some faces, but not even subdued laughter.

"If they are selling to a client state," Bowmaker continued in a hard voice, "we cannot allow that to happen. This is a clandestine unit that has already taken out a highly advanced United States aircraft. The implications are obvious. Your job, gentlemen, is to take it out. We believe this radar to be the only one of its kind . . . so far. Let's make sure it stays that way.

"Someone screwed up and let us have a peek. A lucky break. Now we do a surgical job on it. You are the surgeons. And no collateral damage, please. Your target is well away from centers of population. Even so, watch where you place your ordnance. And now, Major Morton will take over. Major."

"Sir," Morton acknowledged, rising to his feet as Bowmaker left the dais to take a seat.

Morton stayed off the dais. Instead he stood to one side, looking at the screen as the lights in the briefing room dimmed.

"We've got a short piece of film for you," he said to his audience, "but first, here's something we were able to put together with the help of the computer. Great little machine. No bigger than the average PC, but run by a chip that won't be on the market for years, if ever. While everyone's been getting excited about high-speed 486's and 586's, this little baby's leapt several generations to the two thousand series. We call it the billennium chip—short for bi-millennium—and the speed's classified . . . even to me. But I suspect Mac knows it. It can't sing and dance . . . yet. Mac," he added in a cue to Macallister.

Her fingers worked at the keyboard, and the large screen came alive, showing a computer videographic version of the model on the table.

"We used data," he continued, "based upon the Defense Mapping Agency aerial charts of the region, some relief maps of the same place, the bad satellite photos, and a little guesswork. We mixed it all together in the computer and came up with this."

As Mac manipulated the keyboard, the computer image gave various views of itself: side elevation in full relief, displaying high ground and wadis; open stony desert; sand dunes; even roads and tracks. The computer then "flew" across the terrain at low level, giving the aircrew a good idea of what to expect.

Each was already working out in his mind various points of entry, transit, and exit.

The image changed to a God's-eye view and became static in a particular area, close to a mountain range with many depressions. They were narrow and looked very dangerous to fly through. A red disc appeared in a flat area. This was then enclosed by a red circle. From the central disk, nine red umbilicals spread out like equidistant tentacles to the circle and stopped when they touched it. Small red disks appeared at each touching point. Then the circle disappeared, leaving the main disk, the smaller ones, and the connecting lines radiating from the center.

"Based upon our limited information so far," Morton said as the image was frozen, "and on studies of other radar/SAM emplacements, we have assumed this defensive configuration. You'll note it follows the familiar star-shaped system favored by the former Eastern bloc and its allies and clients." He looked at the attentive aircrew. "We don't *know* that this particular setup follows the same pattern; but until we have better information, we'll treat it as such.

"Another reason is that it's a pretty lethal system. Get caught in it, and you could be dead meat."

Morton paused, as if waiting for his last words to sink in. In fact, he had glanced at Mac, who tapped at the keyboard. The image changed perspective and could now be viewed side on, with the added impression of what it was thought the whole construction looked like underground.

"I don't like being dead meat," McCann whispered to Selby. "Too many women still to love."

Selby glanced at him with faint disapproval. "Be quiet!" he hissed.

Morton glanced their way before continuing: "We believe, and again I must stress we don't *know* . . . that the belowground architecture could look like this. You'll see that each of the smaller disks houses one of the advanced SAM units in its own silo, with connecting tunnels to the central radar. We believe that a single high-explosive bomb down the throat of that radar is all it will require to take out the whole complex. The bomb will simply be a trigger, igniting underground explosive and missile fuel stores that will finish the job. Even if there are blast doors to the tunnels, the radar itself will have been destroyed and the SAMs, in any case, will be blind."

"Excuse me," someone said politely.

Morton paused to look.

"Why not use ALARM?" Bagni asked, meaning the air-launched antiradiation missile that took its cue from the target emissions and homed in on them. It also meant the weapon could be fired from a standoff range, reducing the risks of the aircraft taking hits from the irate defenders.

Morton gave a knowing smile. "Good question, but I'm afraid there are no comforting answers. Almost certainly this new radar is immune to any antiradiation missile currently in service. We don't know, but we'll assume it. If it isn't, then we've got another lucky break. It means there's a hole in their technology that we can exploit at a future date; but for the purposes of this mission, a bomb down their gullet is the only option."

"Great," McCann remarked in a not-so-quiet voice. "So which of us gets the short straw?"

Morton looked uncomfortable and glanced at Jason. "I . . . er believe the wing commander has the answer to that."

All three crews looked toward Jason, who did not look round.

"Er . . . Captain McCann," Morton said.

"Sir?"

"May I continue?"

"Of course, sir."

Even Bowmaker worked hard to hide a smile.

"Thank you," Morton said dryly to McCann, and turned back to the screen. "It is reasonable to expect that each missile position will also have ground troops for local defense." Using a remote to move a cursor in the shape of an encircled crosshair, he indicated each SAM unit. "Distance from SAM position to the radar is for the moment variable—from about one to three klicks . . . er, kilometers."

"We do understand the jargon, Major," the air vice-marshal said in a mild voice.

"Er, yessir!" Morton said, looking a little confused.

McCann grinned at his discomfiture.

"To . . . er, continue . . ." Morton paused, then regained his composure. "It's also possible there may be ZSU-23 triple A as additional defense. No need to tell you about the damage those things can do."

Though none had experienced it, they were well aware of the deadly four-barreled, rapid-firing antiaircraft weapon. Mounted upon a tracked chassis, it was capable of laying down a substantial curtain of fire from two kilometers out. With a firing rate of a thousand rounds per minute and microwave target acquisition, it was extremely dangerous to aircraft.

"So as to give you all the bad news at once," Morton went on, "I'd say it was a good idea to expect man-portable SAMs as well, quite possibly shoulder-launched. Now I'll show you a computer-enhanced video, made from the stills we got from the satellite. We've repeated the stills so that it looks as if a camera's hovered over the same spot. You'll be able to see the entire setup before it suddenly disappears . . . but . . . if you look for an imaginary circle, you'll just be able to make out some of the other SAM positions, at different stages of being raised or lowered."

They all watched the film in silence for some minutes before Morton ended the sequence. The lights in the room brightened. "Questions," Morton said, and seemed to be looking directly at McCann.

But McCann did not oblige. It was Flacht who spoke.

"Can you make it more difficult for us?"

There was a sudden explosion of pent-up sound that developed into uncontrollable chuckles, lending release to the tensions felt by the aircrew.

"Wha . . . *what?*" Morton was taken aback. Then he got the point and smiled ruefully. "Oh, I see. Sorry, gentlemen. I just tell it like it is. The job of the messenger."

"In the old days in China, they'd've have shot you," McCann informed him.

There were further chuckles, which died out as Jason rose to his feet.

"Clearly," the wing commander began, "there are no questions." He surveyed his crews. "Or perhaps there are too many," he added as if to himself. "All right, Major. I'll take over from here. That was a very good presentation. A job excellently done."

"Thank you, sir," Morton said, looking pleased. The screen went blank as he stepped down.

3

The lectern was back in its former position, and Jason stood at it.

"You've heard from General Bowmaker," he began to the flyers, "the air vice-marshal previously, and now, Major Morton. I can imagine the sorts of questions burning away in your minds. First, you're all wondering why talk to you about a ground attack mission. After all, you're fighter crews.

"To begin with, this is just the sort of operation that suits the November brief. As the general has already said, a surgical operation, with the minimum fuss . . . and *no* publicity. You won't be alone. There'll be backup systems working with you; some, you'll not even see. Right. I'm ready for questions."

"As the attack mission is to be flown by one of our crews," Hohendorf began, "who is it to be?"

"I thought I might give that to you," Jason replied

evenly. "You're the one with the greatest experience of the IDS Tornado, by virtue of your time with the Marineflieger. You'll of course be required to reconvert, to get to know the aircraft again." Jason gave a brief smile. "In case you're worried, your change of mount is strictly temporary. You've not lost your ASV. All right?"

Hohendorf nodded.

"And how do you feel about doing the attack?" Jason asked.

Hohendorf glanced at Flacht, who gave a brief nod in agreement. "We can hack it, sir."

"Ah," Jason said. "Not with Flacht, I'm afraid. Sorry, Wolfie," Jason added to an astonished and visibly upset Flacht. "I'll be needing you for something else. You'll be teaming up with an old friend for the mission," the wing commander continued to Hohendorf before anyone could comment or possibly raise objections. "It has been arranged for you to do your IDS training with your old unit in Germany, and your backseater will be Kapitänleutnant Ecker."

"Johann!" Hohendorf and Flacht said together.

"Indeed," Jason confirmed. "As Ecker was your old backseater, getting into the swing of things should not take long. Time is necessarily of the greatest essence."

"Why back to my old unit, sir?" Hohendorf inquired. "Why not a unit here in the U.K.?"

"In the first instance, it is more practical to send you there than to bring Ecker over. Second, you'll ostensibly be going on leave . . . visiting family, if you like. Take your young lady with you. Give it more authenticity, in case anyone's interested in your movements."

Hohendorf was aware of a glance from Selby when Jason mentioned "young lady." His fellow flyers all knew the person the wing commander was talking about: Morven Selby, Mark Selby's sister. Despite a relationship that was now moving into its second year, Selby was still very unhappy about it. Morven was Selby's only sibling. It did not help that Hohendorf was married, to an unfaithful wife who stubbornly refused to divorce him.

"Before you came to us," Hohendorf heard Jason say, "you had a well-deserved reputation for flying extremely low. You have used it to good effect both in Red Flag competitions with the IDS and in actual combat with the ASV. You'll be needing that ability more than ever for this mission.

"Mr. Flacht," Jason went on, "I'll be needing you here to work up to speed a pilot I shall be selecting to fly one of the escorting aircraft, with you in the back. The second escort will be flown by Selby and McCann. Bagni and Stockmann . . . you two gentlemen have got the first phase of the mission. You'll be flying the initial reconnaissance . . . low down, and very fast. An ASV is being specially kitted out for the purpose. In the period before deployment to the forward operating base, you two will get to know that airplane as well as the one you currently fly. And that's it for the moment. You'll be receiving further details throughout the training period. Any questions?"

Jason paused expectantly. But even McCann was silent.

"Very well," the wing commander said. "The code name for the mission is Pale Flyer." The aircrew stared at him. "Yes," he continued. "I've seen the poem. It was hidden by a small sign that has been taken down to allow the wall to be repainted. It's been there for some time, perhaps since November One was being constructed. I thought it rather appropriate." Then he added, "Thank you for coming, gentlemen. I shall be discussing the training program with you later. The target model will remain in this room, and Major Morton and Sergeant Macallister will be at your disposal for further target information, as and when it comes in."

Jason, the AVM, and Bowmaker and his aides remained as the flyers stood and began filing out.

Selby paused at the door to speak to Jason, who had walked up to see them off. "How long do we have, sir?"

"Three weeks at the most. Then the recce flight goes in."

A short while later, Thurson and Bowmaker left the briefing room.

As they walked along the short corridor to the office that had been allocated for their use, Bowmaker said: "The German crew did not like being split up. From what you've said about them, they're a solid combat team. Maybe it's not such a good idea to separate them, especially for something like this, which requires a very special coordination between the crew members."

"I'll admit when Jason announced the changes, I had my doubts," the air vice-marshal said as they entered the functional office and shut the door behind them. "But I trust his decision making. After all, every one of the aircrew has been chosen by him, after a particularly detailed study of the confidential files on each man."

Bowmaker lowered himself onto one of the two basic, general issue armchairs, while Thurson chose to perch on the edge of the plain desk.

"He made all the pairings," the AVM continued, "and so far has not put a foot wrong. Giving Hohendorf his old backseater on the IDS is a good move, for the purposes of the mission. God knows how he managed to persuade the Marineflieger to part with Ecker, even for the duration of this operation."

"Perhaps he promised to let them have Hohendorf back."

"Not a snowball's chance in hell. More than likely some-one would like to join the November units. Lots of changes going on at the moment over there. Many people might be taken off flying. Access to a November posting would be an ideal opportunity for someone who wants to continue in the cockpit . . . provided he can hack the entry, of course. Jason's very rigorous with his entry requirements."

"So you feel secure with his choices."

"Oh, yes. We shall have the best men for each job, Abe."

Abraham G. Bowmaker nodded slowly in agreement. "You trust your wing commander, and I trust *your* judgment. Hell of a thing, this Soviet breakup," he went on. "You know, there are those on our side of the pond who are beginning to wish the whole thing was back to its old self as the USSR. Knew where they stood. This splintering with the real possibility of all that hardware getting in God knows whose hands . . ."

"And what about your own thoughts on that little problem?" Thurson asked of the USAF general.

Bowmaker paused for thought. "Knowing what we now do," he began, "and what the entire world sees on its TV screens every night . . . the idea sure looks attractive. But then, hindsight always was a hell of a teacher."

"Useless, you mean."

"Exactly."

Sagrado, Italy, 1500 Local Time, the Same Day

In the small town forty kilometers north of Trieste and a mere five from the motorway that led there, a tough-looking man with cold eyes was waiting in a small, nondescript café. He had arrived fifteen minutes earlier from Gorizia, the border town on the very edge of the self-destructing Yugoslav republic. Gorizia was not his home-town, nor was the former Yugoslavia his country.

The man's eyes were special. They held as much life as two round pebbles, a legacy perhaps of too much killing, too many times; or perhaps they were always thus. Either way, it mattered little to the man, to whom killing was simply something he did. He was not a soldier.

The man nursed his single cup of coffee for a further three minutes when the person he was meeting approached and took a seat at his table.

"You are on time, I see," the newcomer began. "Early, in fact. That is good." He spoke English, but with an accent that belonged to the Mediterranean shores of Africa.

"I am always early," the man replied in the same language.

The dark eyes of the newcomer surveyed him, as if searching out a soul. The search would have been in vain.

"Being careful?"

"Of course," the man replied in a voice that was totally devoid of warmth.

"A wise precaution. My men are around. I, too, take precautions. I have been watching you for five minutes."

"I know." The man was unimpressed.

There was a pause, then the newcomer smiled without humor. "I think I shall have a coffee. Then we will talk."

As he raised his hand to attract the waitress's attention, two solid-looking men were suddenly at the table.

"You can die here," one of them said to the North African, "or you can come with us. No harm will come to you if you cooperate."

The newcomer's eyes were poisonous as he glared at the man he had come to meet. "You have betrayed me!" he hissed with venom. "You dog! My men will—"

"Your men have been . . . neutralized," interrupted the solid man who had spoken. "Please come." His partner had taken up station behind the cold-eyed man. "You too, comrade. There is someone who wants to see you."

The cold-eyed man rose without fuss. He knew he would have had little chance, even in broad daylight in the innocuous coffee shop.

Aberdeen, Scotland, 1406 Local Time

As the two men were bundled into separate cars and driven away from the little café, Morven Selby drove her putt-putting metallic green Citroën 2CV along the quiet street in the old part of Scotland's granite city. Presently she stopped outside the neat little two-story house where she lived. The engine gasped unconvincingly into silence as she turned it off. The sound of the motor belied the car's true state of health. It gleamed and was well cared for.

She picked up a couple of thick, hard-backed files from the front passenger seat, a copious shoulder bag, and squirmed her way out of the car, the keys in her teeth. With some difficulty she locked the car, then went up to the house.

Morven Selby was the type of woman some people— usually men who should have known better—tended to call untamed. Certainly there was an undercurrent of wildness about her, but not in the accepted sense. She was not the type of person who made herself the center of attention at social gatherings. The opposite was in fact true. Well disciplined and clever, she knew her goals and set out to achieve them.

The wildness could be seen in her eyes, if one knew where to look. There was a warmth about her, too, that was readily shared at different levels, with those for whom she had a high regard; and for the one person she loved intimately, that warmth was limitless.

Her body, curving and strongly built, was firm yet maintained a softness about it that urged one to caress it. Dark hair, lustrously thick, normally fell past her shoulders. That afternoon she had chosen to secure it with a large bow, so that a single plume hung from the back of her head. She had luminous green eyes, a heart-shaped face with a firm chin, and a high and curving forehead. She possessed a strong nose and, in complete contrast, a mouth that was soft and vulnerable. When she smiled her eyes seemed to light up, as if an intense fire burned within the green depths. Axel von Hohendorf was crazy about her.

Today she was dressed in a thick black polo-necked sweater, a very short denim skirt, thick black woolen tights, and soft ankle boots of black leather, topped by the Barbour she wore almost constantly. For a moment she paused to check her keys, then inserted one into the lock and turned it. She entered, calling as she kicked the door shut with a heel, "I'm home!"

There was no reply.

"Zoë!" she called once more, and when there was still no answer, she gave a little shrug and went up the stairs to her bedroom. She dropped the files and the bag on her bed, removed the Barbour and tossed that, too, on the bed.

The house was not hers. She shared it with a fellow undergraduate, Tricia Balcombe, whose family had owned it for generations. The Balcombes had originally purchased the small building for the very purpose for which it was being used, and as Tricia was currently the only Balcombe at the university, Morven had been invited to share. As a nonlocal student, the chances of finding such a well-appointed accommodation was normally infinitesimal.

But Tricia had gone off to Africa on a field trip for a

year and had left it to Morven to choose a temporary sharer.

Morven had another reason for feeling fortunate. Meeting Tricia Balcombe had started a train of events that had led her to Hohendorf. A ball in London, to which she had been invited by Tricia and had been escorted by her brother, Mark, had led to his inviting her to the very first mess ball at November One. Or, as he had put it: "I had to suffer at that dreadful ball in London, now you can come to mine."

But at the mess ball, she had met Axel. And Mark had not done badly out of that ball in London, either. He had met the incredible Kim Mannon, who had pursued him with breathtaking single-mindedness and who had wrung out of him passions he had never suspected resided within him.

Morven frowned as she thought of it. There were other passions, too, where she and Hohendorf were concerned. Even after all the time that had passed, Mark was still unhappy about that relationship.

The phone rang just as she shook her head in mild irritation, as if chasing an unwelcome thought out of her mind. There was an extension close to the bed.

She picked it up eagerly. "Hullo," she began.

The familiar voice said: "So how is the marine biologist today?"

"Axel!" she cried with pleasure. "Where are you?"

"Not in Aberdeen."

"Are you coming over?"

"No. . . ."

"Oh." She sounded disappointed. "I miss you."

"And I miss you. Can you take some time off?"

"Are we going somewhere?" The eagerness was back.

"I'm going home to Germany for some days. Would you like to come?"

"Yes, please! I can arrange to have the time."

"Good. Then I will see you at the weekend."

"Axel?"

"Yes?"

"I love you."

There was a slight pause. "And I . . . love you very much."

She put the phone down slowly, knowing he could not say what he really wanted to. He had obviously called from the base, to judge by his reticence. He never liked saying much on the phone when calling from there.

She wondered whether he was going to see his parents. She had accompanied him once before and had stayed at the family schloss near Tecklenburg. She had got on very well with his mother, whom she liked, but had not yet met his father, who had been away at the time. She'd discovered that Axel had been pleased by this. He did not get on too well with his father.

Then it had all been spoiled. The visit had been soured by the unexpected arrival of Anne-Marie Gräfin von Ettlingen und Hohendorf, Axel's very blond patrician wife. Anne-Marie had not stayed when Axel had made it plain she was not welcome. But the damage had been done, and Morven had never been back since.

She now began to wonder at her eagerness to return there with him. It was not as if she had forgotten the embarrassing scene. Would Anne-Marie turn up again? And what about Mark? He had been angry with Axel, blaming his squadron colleague for placing Morven in such an unpleasant situation. She wondered whether Mark would again give Hohendorf a hard time.

She hated it when Mark became angry about her involvement with Axel. Those two had to work together when they flew their aircraft as a combat pair, and as Mark had himself told her often enough, you needed to know you could depend on the man who flew the lead or as your wingman. His mistakes could kill you.

She shivered slightly as her hand went to the phone in a halfhearted attempt to cancel the arrangement she had just made. The hand rested upon the instrument but did not pick it up.

"No," she said firmly. "I'm going."

A Day Later, 1445 Moscow Time

The sound of the knock on Kurinin's door was pitched at just the right level.

"Yes?" he called.

The door opened and his staff colonel stood there. "They've arrived," he began.

"Let's have them in."

The colonel motioned imperiously with an arm and stood back to admit the two solid-looking men from Italy, together with their captive, the cold-eyed man. The men entered respectfully, but their prisoner was defiant and had to be pushed in.

Kurinin looked at the man neutrally. "Comrade Yevgenyi Fedorovich Poleskov, you have deprived us of your presence for several months. We have scoured the world for you. For an unbelievable moment, we believed you had taken capitalism to your heart and had defected westward. But you hid yourself well, and now we all know better. You have taken to the new entrepreneurial spirit, it would seem. Attempting to sell Soviet technology and weaponry to all and sundry without specific authority is not a good idea. In fact, it's a very *bad* idea. A serious health hazard." Kurinin paused, waiting.

Poleskov remained stubbornly silent.

"No explanation?" Kurinin asked mildly.

There was still no reply.

"When that little adventure that the late Comrade Colonel Stolybin and his superior officer, the equally late comrade general, had embarked upon failed disastrously, you simply vanished when the pieces came tumbling down, so to speak." Kurinin's voice had grown perceptibly harder. "Yet you were involved, up to your neck. Why did you run?"

After a long moment Poleskov deigned to reply. "Self-preservation."

"At least you're frank. Do you know who I am?"

"No." Kurinin waited. "No . . . Comrade General."

"Are you afraid of me?"

The cold eyes fastened upon Kurinin. If they were capable of sneering, they would have done so. "No . . . Comrade General."

"A brave man . . . or a foolish one. I need brave men. Which are you?"

"I'm sure you have my file. The answer is in there."

Kurinin stared at Poleskov. The stone eyes did not waver. "Leave us," Kurinin said to the escorts.

"But, comrade," one of them began.

"I can take care of myself. Wait with the colonel."

The men hesitated.

"Go!" Kurinin ordered. "I appreciate the concern, but it is not required at this moment. So what are you waiting for?" he finished in the mild but very dangerous voice.

Reluctantly the men left. Immediately Poleskov, with a knowing smile, looked for a convenient chair.

"You will sit when I tell you to." Kurinin had not looked at Poleskov as he spoke but was busy turning the pages of a file. "Impressive," he went on, still studying the file. "Very impressive. So you once waited for a target for a whole week, *within* his fortified grounds, killed him, and while the country was put under martial law as the assassin was hunted, you remained within the grounds for another week until the hunt was called off. By the time you had left the country, a government more to our liking had been installed. Good work, Poleskov."

Poleskov did not seem interested in praise. "It's what I do best."

"When you're not trying to trick our servicemen into selling our military equipment for your benefit, you mean. Equipment sold without the necessary restrictions tend to be used against the seller's nation, or troops, at some time in the future. The West, and ourselves, have discovered this. We must always make sure that what we sell is never the best of the line.

"A MiG-29 sold to a client state, for example, will not be a match for a MiG-29 in the service of the Motherland. So cozy chats with disaffected nuclear scientists and bio-chemists, with a view to marketing their wares and expertise, does not endear you to anyone. Such entrepreneurial behavior can be fatal. Do you understand what I'm saying, Poleskov? There is enough on you to guarantee your very rapid demise one cold night out in a lonely wood some-where."

Poleskov remained silent.

"But I have an even better fate for you. Your North African is alive. Oh, yes. We set him free. As for his body-guards . . . they were somewhat unfortunate. He has gone back to his principals, convinced you have betrayed him. I do not believe you will be able to make another deal . . . ever, anywhere—bad news does tend to get around— assuming your avenging friend's people let you live long enough to try. Even you, Poleskov, cannot withstand the wrath that is about to descend upon you."

Poleskov's lifeless eyes danced briefly. For him, that was frenetic animation.

"You would find it much easier if you were back in the

fold. *They* cannot withstand *us*. Think about it. You have one minute." Only then did Kurinin look up.

"I am at your service, Comrade General."

"I thought you would be." Kurinin did not show triumph. "You'll be traveling again. You're on your way to Britain. Scotland, to be more precise."

Whitehall, London; 1455 GMT

"Ah . . . come in, Charles!" the minister greeted as Buntline strode into the opulent office. "Glad to see you're back from your travels."

"Thank you, Minister," Buntline said smoothly. He was dressed, as usual, in a smart City suit. Anyone seeing him, and not knowing his true profession, would easily mistake him for a successful banker or stockbroker.

"Tea?" the minister suggested. A prepared tray, laden with a freshly made pot and cups and biscuits, was waiting on a low, polished table.

"Thank you," Buntline said.

"Pour, shall I?" Not awaiting a reply, the minister began to fill the cups as Buntline nodded. "Biscuit?" The minister handed over a cup with wisps of steam rising from within it.

Buntline shook his head as he took the tea. "I'll pass, if you don't mind, Minister."

"As you wish." The minister picked up a biscuit and bit into it with pleasure. "Love these things," he went on, chomping as he settled on his chair. "Do take a seat, Charles." When Buntline had done so, he continued, "This affair of the Stealth aircraft is making an awful lot of people nervous. Discover anything on your travels?"

Again, Buntline shook his head. "Nothing has seeped through as yet. However, we did come across an odd little incident in Italy."

The minister dunked a fresh biscuit and popped it into his mouth just before it became too soggy. Buntline hated the minister's habit of doing that in his presence.

"And?" The minister swallowed and picked up another biscuit.

"As you know, Minister, ever since the Warsaw Pact began to dissolve itself, we have been keeping an eye on the movements of sensitive materials. One of the trails we were following led us to a small town not far from Trieste. It had been a very tenuous lead, and we had no idea who the players were. Our information had merely indicated that a meet was taking place, and the location."

Buntline drank some tea and tried not to look at the minister dipping a fourth biscuit into his own cup.

"We got there just in time," Buntline went on, eyes darting briefly to the darkening biscuit on its way to the minister's mouth, "to see a third party move in. They picked up the Soviet seller, as well as his customer. The customer's bodyguards were efficiently and quietly taken out."

"So who stepped in?"

"No trouble with that. They were KGB."

"And the seller?"

"Puzzling," Buntline replied, "but I believe Soviet. As we do not as yet possess hard identification, we're not certain which of the Soviet states he does come from. I tend to say 'Soviet' because in the scheme of things, it makes life that much simpler, despite the fancy new names. The customer was easier. Let's just say the Mediterranean washes the shores of his country, though of course, it may not be the eventual recipient."

"Surprise, surprise," the minister remarked dryly.

"They let him go."

"What?" The minister stared at Buntline. "Now *that* is

surprising, especially after having killed the bodyguards. What about the seller?"

"Still alive, and taken back home."

"A quiet termination?"

Buntline shook his head slowly. "I can't see it. They could just as easily have dumped him in Yugoslavia with a bullet in his skull. No one would have paid much notice. With no papers on him, he'd just have been another victim of that nasty little war."

"How can you be certain he was taken back?"

Buntline was staring at his nearly empty cup. "A feeling, Minister. Just a feeling. I'm hoping for reports of a sighting in Moscow." He looked at the minister. *"Plus ça change, plus c'est la même chose."*

"Reduced to speaking French, are we, Charles?"

"The more things change, the more they remain the same," Buntline translated loosely.

"I do know what it means," the minister said testily.

"I'd like to know why they lifted that man," Buntline carried on, ignoring the minister's feelings of imagined offense. "Is he to be punished for creating his own dirty little black market? Or is there a more serious reason? There was something about him. . . ."

"A seller is a seller, surely. . . ."

"In my line of work, Minister, you either learn to recognize your potential adversary very quickly, or you're dead. That man has another function. He's not just a peddler of redundant arms to small, power-hungry countries."

"What then . . . *who* is he?"

"That's what I intend to find out. He's a strange itch, and itches I can't scratch make me very uncomfortable."

The minister poured himself another cup of tea. Though he did not always see eye to eye with Buntline, he knew well enough that the man was good at his job. Once Buntline found an anomaly, it was best not to interfere.

"More tea, Charles? I see your cup's just about empty."

Buntline moved a hand briefly. "Thank you, no, Minister. This will do."

The minister sat back, then leaned forward to reach for a biscuit. He decided against it and relaxed once more on his chair.

"The November people are being briefed," he said to Buntline.

"And how is the turbulent wing commander taking it?"

"According to Air Vice-Marshal Thurson, very well indeed. He's naturally worried about the crews' chances of survival, but there it is. Tailor-made job for that project of his. If all he says about its intended role is true, how better to demonstrate its usefulness?"

Buntline did not comment on the minister's obvious relish, or on the fact that Jason's November crews had already been twice bloodied in combat. It should not be necessary for them to prove anything. They had already displayed their astonishing professionalism and formidable capabilities to anyone who possessed the wit to recognize that. It was not the minister's skin, after all, that would be on the line.

"Got to be done, of course," the minister was saying. "Imagine if such a radar had existed on the other side during the Gulf War. Can't afford to let the damned thing reach full operational status. There may well be snags with it . . . always is with developing technology . . . but you never know whom it might be sold to. After all, they're desperate for money. I daren't think of the consequences. Ah . . . incidentally, General Bowmaker has come over from America with some of his people. You may want to liaise with them from time to time."

Buntline could tell the minister was not too happy about having Bowmaker involved. He clearly felt that

Bowmaker's sympathies would lie with Jason, thus ensuring the wing commander retained a certain degree of autonomy. It didn't help that Bowmaker was American, of course. AVM Thurson, though capable of being extremely wily, was still British and, even if not susceptible to bullying, could still be made to toe the line now and then. But Bowmaker was a different case altogether. Bowmaker would ignore attempted interference, if it got in his way.

The minister seemed to have forgotten it was an American aircraft that had been shot down and its pilot killed.

4

The Super Tornado F.3S Air Superiority Variant
owed its genesis to the first of the variants, the IDS
Tornado ground attack aircraft. It was on this airplane
that Hohendorf had begun the long process that had
turned him into a highly skilled exponent of the art of
Tornado flying.

The ASV, however, was a very different type of beast.
To begin with, it was longer, giving it a svelte, feline
appearance that made the IDS look stubby. Its variable-
sweep wings—controlled automatically or manually—
were larger as well as having extra length, thus giving it a
greater wing area. Its LERXs, well-blended leading edge
root extensions that began at the upper intake lips of the
engines and gradually disappeared into the airframe at
the point where the radome of the sleek nose began, completed its metamorphosis.

These aerodynamic modifications gave it an agility that

not only went far beyond the capabilities of the IDS, but also served to make it a dangerous opponent to other contemporary fighter aircraft. The revised engine intakes, made to increase airflow to new engines that were a good 30 percent more powerful than those of even the standard F.3 aircraft, gave it a thrust-to-weight ratio that surpassed unity. This better than 1:1 ratio meant that the F.3S, with the weight-lightening composite materials that had been strategically incorporated into its construction, had more than sufficient power to cancel out its own weight by the sheer thrust of its twin engines.

Hohendorf thought of all this as he went through the walk-around checks of his particular airplane, in preparation for flight. His hand lingered perceptibly on each part of the airframe that he inspected, as if saying a temporary farewell. He hoped it *would* be temporary. He had no intention of perishing out in the desert. The beauty of the aircraft, he had always thought, was the potential for further development in its design. Since his arrival at November One several updates and improvements had already been made, continuing to enhance its performance in various regions of the flight envelope.

He glanced up briefly at Flacht, who was already settled in the backseat, warming up the electronic systems that formed part of the heart of their fighting machine. Flacht had his head down, occupied with setting up everything correctly. He knew Flacht was thinking about the crew changes. They had spoken at length about it.

Neither liked being split up, even temporarily. Theirs was a well-coordinated team, like many others. But this was a special requirement, and though they trusted Jason completely, it still felt uncomfortable having to fly a hot mission with someone else in the other seat.

At least, Hohendorf thought as he continued his walk-around, I'll be flying with Johann again. Poor Wolfie has to break in a new pilot just before a mission.

Johann Ecker, married to Hohendorf's cousin, had been his long-standing backseater in the Marineflieger. He remembered ruefully how he had been reluctant to accept the posting to November One if Ecker did not accompany him. But Hans Wusterhausen, the squadron CO, had bluntly refused his request, saying that Ecker's experience was needed to break in newer pilots. Flacht had been selected to go instead.

"And now," Hohendorf said to himself, "Wolfie has Johann's problem."

A member of the ground crew with headphones whose long cable was plugged into the aircraft saw Hohendorf's lips moving. He shifted one headphone long enough to say above the continuous whine of the ASV's internal equipment: "Beg pardon, sir?"

Hohendorf stared at him for a brief, puzzled moment. "Just talking to myself." He winked at the crewman.

"Yes, sir," the crewman said uncertainly, and slid the headphone back into place.

Hohendorf completed his visual checks and climbed the ladder to enter the aircraft. As he settled into the spacious cockpit, he reflected that among all the things he would miss most when he returned to the IDS was the choice of auto wing sweep. The IDS's variable geometry could only be selected manually. Many pilots, he knew, actually preferred the totally hands-on control of manual sweep. For his part, he felt that having auto as well manual served to extend the control envelope. Being able to override the system in a fight could win you the sorts of points that might mean the choice between life and death. A good opponent would read your wing position and make a judgment based upon what he'd extrapolated you intended to do.

Giving him the wrong signals at a crucial time was all part of it.

If he saw your wings spread and thought you were preparing for a tight turn into him, he would be getting ready to counter. If, however, you were holding the wings in that position with burners on and trying hard to momentarily ignore the attention getters flashing red and screaming at you as they warned of the wrong configuration for the speed; and if he read that incorrectly and began his move just as you reverted to auto; then the sleek beast would be sweeping her wings and rocketing out of the way, giving you the separation you needed to curve back onto his tail and give him a very bad day indeed.

Hohendorf knew the trick worked because he had caught out many fellow pilots with it. But the IDS was itself no slouch, if you knew how to use it, especially low down, where its arena existed. Even the ground could be used as a weapon, if you were able to harness its services in your cause. Dragging an overfixated adversary low enough to sucker him into forgetting the proximity of terra firma, was just as terminal as a nicely locked missile shot or a few judiciously placed cannon shells.

With the aid of another member of the ground crew who had followed him up the ladder, Hohendorf strapped himself to the ASV and connected all communication, oxygen, and pressure systems to his person. Helmet secured, and he was ready.

The crewman went back down the ladder as Flacht's voice sounded in Hohendorf's headphones with the cockpit checks. Wolfie sounded distant, he thought. Then he decided he was looking for problems where there weren't any.

Checks complete, he started the engines and watched the digital power readouts on one of the three multifunction displays. Each display held several pages of information about the operating and tactical state of the aircraft, which could be called up at the touch of the button and were interchangeable as desired. He then made a quick check of the standby analog dials to the right of the main panel as they counted up the power in confirmation and settled at idle thrust. The warning horn sounded as he lowered the canopy. It clamped itself shut, and the world was suddenly quieter.

He eased the throttles forward, and the ASV began to taxi out of its hardened shelter. Looking like some trunked, alien life form as he turned his head from side to side, checking the wings were clear, he maneuvered the Tornado along the yellow taxiing line that would eventually lead to the runway threshold, for the takeoff. On the headphones, Flacht's voice was in conversation with air traffic control, requesting and receiving clearance. Hohendorf acknowledged.

The day's training mission was an air combat exercise with Selby. He knew Jason had selected Selby as his opponent because Selby and McCann were the crew most able to give him the hardest fight. It was openly known throughout November One that the crews of Hohendorf and Selby were the ones to beat, and no one would ever take the risk of gambling on which was the better of the two.

To make life even more difficult for Hohendorf, he was being deliberately handicapped in an attempt to simulate the conditions he might encounter if forced to defend himself against attacking aircraft during the strike against the radar. The idea was that the handicap would help him evolve tactics that would work for him in the IDS.

He would thus not be using the helmet sighting system, though Selby would; and the unfinned missile acquisition rounds he was carrying would simulate the standard AIM-9L "Lima" Sidewinder short-range infrared missile. The IDS would be carrying the real ones, for self-defense over the desert. Selby's aircraft was armed with simulated rounds of the ASV's standard fit: the highly advanced short-range Krait, itself an agile weapon whose kill distance extended well into medium range, and the extreme long-range Skyray B, which was capable of taking out targets beyond visual range at distances in excess of 130 miles at speeds reaching Mach 6.1, or over six times the speed of sound. No other air-to-air missile, anywhere in the world, was faster.

The Skyray B's closest range merged deeply within the Krait's longest, leaving no gap in the ASV's offensive envelope. For extreme close range, the F.3S possessed a specially fitted gun. This single but exceedingly accurate six-barreled rotary cannon completed the weapon fit. Fully tooled up for trouble, the ASV would normally carry a mix of ten of its lightweight missiles plus the gun with full ammunition, and still it would weigh less than the standard F.3 with its own war load.

Hohendorf decided he would drag Selby to low level. It was not going to be easy, because the ASV was just as capable at the lower levels as the IDS. It was also far more maneuverable, with a massive power advantage.

To simulate this underdog situation, Hohendorf would not be using any stages of afterburner throughout the combat, for even at MAX DRY the ASV outpaced the IDS. It was going to be tough work.

"We'll have to be very smart today, Wolfie," he now said to his backseater.

"You mean you're going to do things that will frighten me," Flacht said calmly.

"Wolfie, Wolfie! Would I?"

Flacht made a noise that could have been a snort of derision.

Up ahead, another aircraft was making for the same threshold: Selby and McCann. Call sign for the mission was Warlock, with Hohendorf's Tornado as Warlock One giving him the lead.

They joined up at the threshold and, with clearance given, took off in tight formation. Both sets of wheels came up smartly, the two aircraft seemingly barely off the ground. Then both were reefing skyward, to point straight up as they accelerated in the climb.

"Very stylish," a female voice said on the headphones.

"We aim to please," McCann returned.

There was a sound that might have been restrained laughter, but it could have been extraneous noises during transmission. From the ground, the two aircraft were already out of sight. Only the sound of their passage remained. Soon they could no longer be heard.

In Warlock Two, Selby said to McCann: "Breaking procedures to chat up your girlfriend again, Elmer Lee?"

McCann's supposed "girlfriend" was an air traffic controller, Flying Officer Karen Lomax, a slim and outwardly demure beauty. Unfortunately for him, Karen Lomax was someone else's fianceé. Worse, the person in question commanded an engineering section on the November flight line and was a man of fearsome physique who was also a services rugby star.

But McCann had decided he was in love, though to most people he was suicidal as well. Everyone had already come to the conclusion that the only reason McCann's head was still attached to his body was because Flight Lieutenant "Geordie" Pearce had come up against a player whose tackle during an interservices game had been even more brutal than his own. Pearce had suffered a broken leg and was on extended convalescence.

McCann and Karen Lomax had initially crossed paths after he'd heard her voice on his headphones for the first time, and he had responded in a manner not unlike the one he had recently used. The wing commander, however, inbound from a training flight with a new pilot as his wingman, had picked up the transmission. McCann had been ordered to apologize, and had also been given a week as duty aircrew officer in the control tower. As a result of this very first meeting, he had subsequently announced to Selby afterward that he had fallen in love.

Selby had treated this news with a weary skepticism. McCann was always falling in love. But McCann, it seemed, was serious.

"I'm going to ask her out to dinner," he now announced as Selby leveled the aircraft out at the mission's prescribed altitude of thirty thousand feet. "And I'm going to do it when we get back." They were tucked in close to Hohendorf's aircraft, with the wings of both ASVs now at midsweep as they settled into the cruise to the fight area.

"It's not going to last, Elmer Lee," Selby cautioned. "You can't expect Geordie Pearce to be away forever. And when he returns to hear what you've been up to, he'll have your guts for banjo strings."

"Garters."

"What?"

"Garters," McCann repeated. "Guts for garters. Isn't that what you guys say?"

"In your case, it going to be banjo strings."

"I'm not scared of him."

"Ignorance is truly bliss," Selby remarked despairingly. "You may *think* you're not scared of him, but I want your limbs in all the right places in that seat behind me. Thank God he's not going to be on the unit before the mission. We'd have to lock you away out of reach otherwise."

"Warlock Two," came Hohendorf's voice, ending further conversation.

"Warlock Two," Selby acknowledged.

"Thirty seconds to the break."

"Roger. Thirty seconds."

The two ASVs would be separating, and exactly one minute from that time it would be up to Selby and McCann to try to ambush Hohendorf and Flacht. They would endeavor to do this without warning and from any quarter.

"All right, Elmer Lee," Selby began. "I expect you to do your stuff."

"Don't I always?"

"You do. You do. But I want him today. I want to nail him."

Something in Selby's voice made McCann say: "Hey, we're not going to shoot the guy down. This is a workout. We make him sweat, sure, but—"

"Just do it, Elmer Lee."

"You're the boss." There was resignation in McCann's voice.

"Up here, that's exactly what I am."

McCann wondered what had gotten into his crewmate.

What had gotten into Selby was the fact that the night before Morven had called to say she would be going over to Germany with Hohendorf. He found it difficult to understand why she had agreed to go, after what had happened the last time. He had tried to dissuade her, to no avail. Deep within him something seethed, and he wanted to beat Hohendorf well and truly today in the air combat practice arena, as if this would somehow serve to purge what he now felt.

The greater part of him, the true professional, reasoned that up here, what went on between Hohendorf and Morven had no place. But Morven was also his only sister, and he couldn't help the way he felt about the relationship. As long as he didn't endanger his aircraft or his crew, or anyone else, he decided, he could channel his feelings into an aggressiveness that would give him an edge in the coming fight. The boss always insisted that all November pilots be totally aggressive in air combat training. It was the way to win in a real fight; and winning was the only thing that mattered in air combat. It was life.

"Because dead crews, gentlemen," Jason was fond of saying, "are of no use to me. So stay alive, and *win.*"

"That's what we're going to do today, Elmer Lee," Selby now said. "We're going to win."

McCann was watching the digital clock, set in its small rectangular display, next to the right-hand MFD in the backseater's cockpit.

"I always like to win," he said, still watching the figures. But within the secret world of the lowered visor of his helmet, and his oxygen mask, he frowned at the strange undercurrent in Selby's voice. "Five seconds," he went on, counting down. "Four . . . three . . . two . . . one . . ."

"*Fight's on!*" came Hohendorf's voice.

"*Shit!*" Selby exclaimed, banked hard left to a startled squawk from McCann, rolled upright, kicked in the burners, and hauled back firmly on the stick.

The ASV leapt for the upper reaches, sweeping its wings as it went.

At the instant that Hohendorf had spoken, Selby had been treated to a flashing glimpse of Warlock One rolling onto its back, to plunge seaward and disappear. The sod had moved quickly, he now thought grimly.

"Don't lose him, Mark!" McCann was saying, grunting against the crushing onset of G-forces as Selby again changed direction, separating them farther from Hohendorf and Flacht's last position and giving himself room to counter whatever move Hohendorf had in mind. "Don't lose him!"

"Do you think I'm doing this for fun?" Selby squeezed out between his own grunts. "Anything on your box of tricks?"

"They're down on the water and spoofing. My returns are crazy. They could be anywhere."

"Shit," Selby repeated.

While the ASV's systems could burn their way through known adversary countermeasures, Warlock One was using the Super Tornado's own systems against it. Hohendorf was allowed that one capability, because the original version was already on the IDS. The ASV's was a much improved, advanced upgrade, which Jason had said was being incorporated into the systems of aircraft selected for the strike mission.

"All right, Elmer Lee," Selby continued. "Find the sod for me. I'm not going to be in a good mood if he nails us first, especially as he's pretending to fly an IDS. Otherwise you'll think Geordie Pearce is the best thing that ever happened to you."

McCann chose to make light of the situation. "When you put it like that, it's an offer I can't refuse." Something was really eating at Mark, he thought as he began countering Warlock One's spoofing.

However, McCann was well aware that Flacht, in the other backseat, would expect such a response and would be prepared. Having commenced the duel first, the advantage was with Flacht. It was definitely not going to be easy, a fact that would not improve Selby's temper.

Up front, and despite the way he felt, Selby was nevertheless in full control of himself and his aircraft. He flew with all the power of his considerable skill, never maintaining the same position for more than a few seconds, always scanning the air about him for the slightest warning of a pending attack or evidence of a target waiting to be taken.

But he knew Hohendorf would not be waiting patiently. Hohendorf would be planning something totally unexpected, hoping to catch him out.

"In your dreams," Selby heard himself mutter, using one of McCann's favorite sayings. He had activated the helmet sighting system; but the directional arrow, focused on infinity and always so eager to point out the location of a target in an apparently empty sky, was conspicuous by its absence. So where the hell was Warlock One?

Warlock One was doing 450 knots, twenty feet above the cold gray waters of the North Sea.

In keeping with November policy of continually upgrading its aircraft to maximize operational effectiveness, the ASV was capable of visually altering its appearance to blend with its particular surroundings. On this particular occasion it had matched its color to that of the water above which it now appeared to be skimming. Crystals in the paint applied to the airframe were excited via electrical impulses, to cause them to change color. This could be triggered automatically by sensor programming or manually through a repertoire that was accessed by a keypad on the right-hand console, in the backseater's cockpit. The crews had already dubbed the process chameleon.

Hohendorf had suggested that Flacht engage the system, for though the IDS did not possess it, the strike aircraft would be camouflaged to blend with the desert landscape. Merging the ASV with the uniform gray of the sea would have the same effect in a visual engagement, if they managed to evade long- and medium-range missile lock and succeeded in dragging Warlock Two down.

Flacht glanced with apparent equanimity at the surface of the rushing water, so close beneath his feet. At their current speed, hitting it would be as devastating as slamming into a mountain. Hitting it at *any* speed would not be much fun either.

He checked his displays. Warlock Two was still trying to burn through his spoofing.

"How are we doing, Wolfie?" Hohendorf inquired with the sort of calm that Flacht had grown well accustomed to.

"They're still trying. They know where we're *supposed* to be, because of where our spoofing and jamming is coming from, but they can't distinguish us from the sea returns. It is difficult for them. Burning through a kit like this is not supposed to be easy. We might as well be a school of whales." As he finished, Flacht again glanced at the hurtling water. Not far from the truth, he thought. We're nearly swimming.

On occasions like this he sometimes found himself wondering whether Hohendorf had any nerves at all. He understood what the other was doing. On the mission to come, survival would depend upon how low and how fast the approach to the target was made. Here, over the open sea, with not even a ship in the area to create a sudden obstruction, it was hairy enough. But in the desert, even though outcrops of terrain would be of great use for masking, hiding the approach until the last moment, it would be even more terrifying.

And it was all going to be done at night.

Flacht glanced at the water for a third time. How many pieces would be found if they did make impact? The question drifted in and was out of his mind as quickly. It was a detached query, almost as if part of him were sitting out there on one of the wingtips, working out probabilities.

Not for the first time since being told, he wished he had been chosen to go with Hohendorf. True, Johann Ecker had been his predecessor in the backseat; but that had been a long time ago. Ecker would have to learn to fly with Hohendorf all over again.

"I should be going with you," Flacht said now.

"It is useless to think about it, Wolfie. Besides, you won't really be sitting this one out. You'll be with the escort. You'll be watching my back."

Though partially wishing the crew changes had not been made, deep down Hohendorf was relieved that Flacht would not be on the strike mission. The last time they had been in combat together, Flacht had nearly been killed. A single fragment from the near miss of an air-to-air missile had lodged in his chest, perilously close to his heart. Somehow they had made it back to base, and the doctors had performed the delicate operation that had saved Flacht's life.

Despite emotionally wanting to work with his back-seater, he was thus reluctant to take him on the strike mission, where the danger was likely to be considerable if things did go badly wrong. On the other hand, he thought, I would not like to face Erika to tell her Johann had died on a mission with me.

"They had better give me a good pilot," said an unmollified Flacht, breaking into Hohendorf's reverie.

Hohendorf put thoughts of anyone dying out of his mind. "The boss will make sure you get one. Now let's wake up those two upstairs."

Even as he spoke, Hohendorf was putting a gentle backward pressure on the stick. There was no direct linkage between Hohendorf's control commands and the ASV's flying surfaces. Instead the computers of the fly-by-wire system interpreted his inputs and told the surfaces what to do.

Instantly the Tornado fled away from the eager sea and hurled itself toward the sky, hunting for prey.

"Well, well," McCann uttered softly as he stared at one of his screens.

"Something?" There was anticipation in Selby's voice.

"They've broken cover. Coming up. Bearing two three zero. Passing through . . . aah, *dammit.*"

"What? . . . What! Talk to me, McCann."

"Just as they passed nine thousand feet, they spoofed us again." McCann sounded disgusted with himself. "They've got some nerve. They're trying to take us, man. Move it. Go to two one zero."

"Two one zero," Selby confirmed, reefing the aircraft past Hohendorf's last known bearing. "Where are they now?"

There was a pause as McCann tried to pick out the elusive Warlock One from the crowded returns on his screen. Every so often, a square box glowed briefly.

"Elmer Lee, come on. Come *on.* Give me some trade."

"Hell . . . they're back on the deck." McCann was puzzled.

"Of course they're back on the bloody deck," Selby remarked sharply, understanding exactly what Hohendorf had done. "That was a feint. He probed us, and we responded. Sod it! He wants us down there with him. In the IDS, that's his arena. I would have done that myself." It didn't make Selby feel any better.

"So what are we going to do? We can't stay up here all day, and it sure as hell looks as if he's not going to come up to us. On the mission, the defending fighters—if any— will go down after him. They'll be forced to, because they must stop him if they can't take him out at long range. The way he's playing, I don't think we're going to get lock, man. We're going to have to work hard for this one, Mark."

Selby had no argument to give to McCann, whose reading of the tactical situation was correct. Hohendorf was making all the right moves. Ingress to target for the IDS would be low all the way, air combat to be avoided at all cost, if humanly possible. The best result for any interceptor would be to terminate the attack mission well before target. If that failed, it would have to be a knife fight down on the deck.

"All right, Elmer Lee," Selby said. "We've got to grant that so far, he's escaped interception. Let's go visual, and take the fight to him."

Flacht said: "They're coming down."

"So they could not achieve lock-on," Hohendorf said. "Well done, Wolfie. You've forced them to come for a look. Looks like a knife fight on the deck, after all. We have them, Wolfie. We have them! I want your eyes out of the cockpit, and checking our six."

Flacht was already at it, head turning constantly, searching the area of sky about them, but especially checking the rear of the aircraft. This was the vulnerable six, still the best position from which to down an opponent, in a close tangle. Flacht had no doubt that Selby would be setting up for a quick kill, always preferable to a long, drawn-out turn and burn. He was equally certain that Hohendorf would not oblige. It was going to be a nerve-stretching, low-level scrap. No doubt about it.

Warlock Two was now about a hundred feet above the gray sea.

"I've got them at twenty miles," McCann announced,

"bearing zero-four-zero, at . . . Je*sus* . . . *twenty* feet! You hear me there, Mark? Two zero goddamned feet."

"I hear you."

Selby saw the designator arrow of his helmet sight pointing toward the target box, marking Warlock One's position. Satisfied that they had successfully countered the long-range interception, Warlock One had stopped spoofing and were making no further attempt to mask themselves. Hohendorf had moved into the second phase and was clearly ready for the fight.

McCann watched as Selby took their own aircraft lower, and he checked the altitude readout on one of his multifunction displays. They went past fifty feet and continued to descend.

"I'll get out and walk, if you like," he remarked to Selby as nonchalantly as he could. "Looks like a nice day for it. Hey. Look at that wave. Looks close enough to touch."

There was no comment from the front.

McCann tried again. "They must know we're down here, but they're not evading."

"Of course they know we're here. Hohendorf thinks he's going to sucker me."

"Ah-ha! It speaks. And what's all this about 'Hohendorf'? Gone formal, have we?"

"Shut up, McCann."

McCann fell silent, mildly perturbed. His eyes strayed toward the sea. It wasn't a problem. Mark Selby knew his stuff. One of the very best pilots around. It was okay. No sweat. Selby could handle all the low-level stuff anyone could throw at him. Even so.

He returned his scrutiny to his systems. Twenty rushing feet above the deck was not the place to start worrying about your pilot. Then a trace on the screen claimed his undivided attention.

"There they go!" he warned Selby as the data on the

boxed target began to change rapidly. "They're heading for the angels." He kept the sense of relief out of his voice. He wanted some space between himself and the cold gray sea.

But Selby remained at the ultralow level.

"Hey, Mark! They've gone up, man. Axel's going to pull one of his tricks and flip over to come down and nail our ass. Are we going to get out of here, or what?"

"Or what," Selby replied, then brought the nose up slightly before banking into a steep left turn.

McCann felt his eyes widen involuntarily as the tip of the lower wing seemed inches from the surface of the water. He knew his mind was tricking him; but even so, at this height there was no margin for error.

Shit, he thought. The guy's going to play Axel at his own game.

"They're not coming up," Flacht said. "He didn't go for it, Axel."

"I half expected it, Wolfie . . . but I'd hoped he would. Let's give him something else."

Having noted Selby's countermove, Hohendorf rolled the ASV onto its back and plunged seaward once more, curving in the dive to place him behind Warlock Two and in a good position for a short-range missile shot. Deprived of the use of his helmet sight, he had to rely upon the basic IDS air-to-air HUD configuration that he had selected. It was vital to simulate the IDS working environment as far as was possible. If he could hack it against an opponent of Selby's caliber, then he stood a very good chance against whatever put in an appearance in the skies above the desert. He checked the concentric rings of the circular threat display screen, tucked into the top right of the main panel. A red diamond glowed at 090 and on the twenty-mile ring. He adjusted his turn, to bring the target on the nose. He kept descending, arming the acquisition round as he did so.

"I'm going for the shot, Wolfie," Hohendorf said. "He won't be expecting that so soon. Let's see if we can give him a surprise."

"Go ahead. It's looking good."

Flacht had verified the target position on a display. Now he kept his attention out of the cockpit, scanning for any anomaly Hohendorf might have missed. His probing eyes noted that the sea was again very close as they hurtled toward the other aircraft.

Then the Sidewinder's growl began. The target had been acquired.

"We've got the growl," Hohendorf said with satisfaction. "Just a little longer for a good lock, and we'll have him."

"Do you hear that?" McCann said to Selby as the infrared warning sounded. "They've got some heat on us."

"My ears are working perfectly."

From fifty feet up, Selby rolled the ASV into a ninety-degree bank, initiated a left turn, then suddenly rolled through a further 180 degrees, pulling hard into a right-hand turn.

During the roll, McCann had looked up through the canopy to observe the sea rather unnervingly close to his head. But now the ASV was upright once more and climbing. The warning tone had gone.

"They've broken lock," Flacht said. "That was a good move."

"A very good one," Hohendorf agreed. It was the sort of thing he would have done.

Warlock One was on a wingtip, at full sweep and trailing vortices of air superheated by the force of its passage as it pulled into a wide turn, staying low.

"They're coming back down," Flacht began, then his voice tensed suddenly. "Speed is a bit high for the altitude at which they started. He's cutting it fine."

Hohendorf had completed the turn and had reduced his own speed rapidly by bringing the throttles back and selecting the air brakes. The wings went to midsweep, and as the speed continued to drop he reversed the turn.

He brought in the brakes as he saw Warlock Two plunging down and curving toward him to deny the chance of another lock. Soon it was past minimum range and into the gun arena. But Selby had planned well, and Hohendorf had to tighten this new turn even further, to continue to foil Selby.

Warlock Two seemed to pull yet tighter. Both ASVs, like angry predators whirling ferociously about each other, were now inexorably approaching the sea.

Flacht, who had been keeping the other aircraft in view by turning his head constantly to follow its movements, said urgently, "His speed is still too high. He's descending, and that water is too close. . . ." Then Flacht's words ended in a sudden gasp as he saw what happened next.

Hohendorf, still in the turn to counter Selby, had a view of the opposing aircraft over his left shoulder, enabling him to witness the entire sequence of events as well.

Warlock Two wobbled out of the turn suddenly to roll upright and leap skyward, as if Selby had only just realized how close he had come to crashing into the sea.

"Knock it off! Knock it off!" Hohendorf called urgently, signifying the end of the engagement. As lead, it was his prerogative to do so.

"Roger. Knock it off," came the acknowledgment. It was McCann who answered. He sounded strained.

Hohendorf said to Flacht, "That was very close, Wolfie. What was Mark thinking about? It looked as if he had become target-fixated. This is not like him."

"The boss will have seen all of it in Ops Control. It's not good."

In the underground operations center, known by just about everyone at November One as the Hole, a vast screen showing all aspects of the fight—relayed via the instrumentation pods carried by the two ASVs—would have been studied avidly and every detail analyzed.

Hohendorf was thoughtful as they rejoined formation for the return to base.

"Perhaps Mark is not well," Flacht ventured.

"Perhaps," Hohendorf said, unsure of what to make of the incident. "Let's hope that was not the reason. The boss might drop him from the mission. I want him up there with you, watching my back. You'll need him, too, otherwise you and Elmer Lee will be going out with green drivers."

"It doesn't bear thinking about."

"My feelings exactly." As they drew closer to Warlock Two, Hohendorf spoke to the other aircraft. "Warlock Two, are you all right?"

"We're fine." It was McCann again. "No problems."

The landing was carried out in perfect formation.

As they walked toward the squadron buildings from the hardened shelter, McCann, face pale, the indentations of his oxygen mask still etched strongly upon his features, strode next to Selby. Hohendorf and Flacht were some distance behind.

Eventually McCann could hold back no more. "What the hell was going on out there, man? I know you can hack it at low level better than any jock I know . . . except Axel, and *no* one in his right mind goes up against Axel on the deck, if there's a choice. That's his specialty.

You're king of the high walk, and he the low. That's why we four are so good in combat together. Any suckers caught in the same patch of sky with you two guys up front are in deep shit. So I find it kind of difficult to understand what happened back there."

It was first time he could remember being truly angry with Selby. It was also the first time he could remember being really frightened; and that included combat. Selby had always been in control, but a for brief instant Selby seemed to have lost it.

"You listening to me?" McCann continued. "You nearly splashed us." He took a few steps ahead and turned to stop in front of Selby. "You nearly splashed us, *dammit.*"

Selby halted but remained silent.

McCann's eyes narrowed. "I don't get it. A guy like you doesn't get fixated on a target, and especially not when the water's so goddamn close you could drink it. So what's going down, Mark? Do I get some answers here?" McCann paused. "I see," he went on when there was still no reply. "I'm just the guy in back. I don't get told. Right?"

McCann glanced past Selby's shoulder to see Hohendorf and Flacht drawing closer but still out of earshot. A sudden thought hit him.

"You wanted to nail Axel so badly," he began softly, "you lost it for a while back there, didn't you? Jesus, Mark." His eyes widened as he stared at Selby. "That's it, isn't it? I'm right. It's all to do with Morven and Axel. What *is* it with you?"

Selby moved past McCann and continued walking.

McCann kept pace, trotting alongside like an eager puppy. "Come on, Mark. This is me. Ol' Elmer Lee. Regular pain in the ass, but the best guy in the backseat you've ever had working with you. Talk to me, for chrissake. If not . . ." McCann paused, groping for inspiration. "If not . . . then go see Kim. She might make you see some sense about this thing. You two should get back together. It might make you human again. . . ."

Selby had paused for a second time, eyes hard. "Are you quite finished? Stay out of it, Elmer Lee. This is no concern of yours."

"Are you kidding?" The puppy had gone, and the other McCann, the bane of pilots who in his eyes had got it wrong, was back with a vengeance. "It sure as hell does concern me. It's my neck, too, man. You know? My *neck*. If you screw up when we're up there . . ."

"You'd like a change of seats? Fine."

Selby strode away, leaving McCann to stare at him openmouthed, eyes displaying a feeling of deep injury. "God*damnit!*" he said in frustration after a while, swinging his helmet as if to toss it away, then thinking better of it at the last moment.

He was still in the same spot when Hohendorf and Flacht eventually reached him.

"What's up, Elmer Lee?" Hohendorf inquired, staring after Selby's retreating figure.

"You tell me, guys. You tell me. I don't know what the hell's gotten into him. Well . . . part of it, I guess."

They were looking at him now in some surprise. They had never seen the famously laid-back Elmer Lee so agitated.

"We nearly lost it out there . . . no . . . we *did* lose it out there," McCann said. "You know that? Mark, of all the jocks on this base, nearly put us in. It doesn't make sense. The boss is going to chew acres of carpet over this, and he's going to ask me some hard questions. What do I say?"

"Tell him what you think," Hohendorf advised, "and let him judge. I would expect Wolfie to do the same if it had happened to us. . . ."

"Hey, come on, Axel. I can't dump Mark in the shit."

"You're not dumping him into anything. If there's a

problem, we've got to sort it immediately. The boss will not appreciate it if you try to be clever with him. I know what I am talking about. Ask Wolfie here. On my old unit, I tried to keep a situation from my CO. It nearly cost Johann Ecker—the backseater who's going on the strike with me—his life. My CO was not pleased, and he let me know it. He was right. Think about it, Elmer Lee. You will not be doing Mark any favors."

McCann was looking at Hohendorf. "Part of it is to do with you."

"What?"

"Morven," McCann told him quietly.

Hohendorf stared at McCann for some moments before looking away to where Selby was just entering the main squadron building. "This is something we do not need at this moment," he remarked softly.

"I thought everything was okay with you guys," McCann said.

"I thought so, too."

"I have an idea." McCann addressed them both, then hurried on before either could comment. "Kim Mannon. It's not just this thing with you and Morven, Axel. It's Kim, too. I'll give her a call to—"

"And what do you think he would do if he knew you had done that?" Flacht asked with his usual directness.

"Try to take my head off." McCann was quite unperturbed by the possibility. "But he's my buddy and my pilot," he went on. "I've got to help him." He grinned. "Besides, I need my chauffeur."

5

Kimberley Mannon was totally different from Morven Selby, and in the normal scheme of things it was unlikely that they would ever have met. The small, neat body that had so single-mindedly seduced Mark Selby gave in repose the impression of utter vulnerability. Nothing could have been farther from the truth, for she shared with Morven a degree of strength that served her well.

Her gleaming black hair was worn short. Thick eyebrows were set above wide-apart eyes that were dark and full of mischief. A small, sharp nose was countered by an unexpectedly generous mouth, and when she walked, it was with the flowing, assured gait of something dangerously feline.

In tight jeans and a lightweight sweater that seemed far too big for her, she lay sprawled upon her stomach on her large bed. Her feet were bare. She looked almost childlike as she lay there, eyes closed.

But she was not asleep.

A faint sound brought her eyes open. She did not move for long moments, then with startling suddenness she got off the bed to walk across the vast rug that covered her bedroom floor, to stop at a large window. As she stood looking out, she moved her toes absently, playing with the edge of the rug.

The view of the extensive grounds, in a secluded part of Buckinghamshire, was one of the more beautiful ones of the English countryside. It was certainly the best at Grantly Hall, the Queen Anne mansion that was the family home. At least, she thought so.

She studied the long, meandering drive that threaded its way through gently sloping wooded hills, past the bends of a fast-flowing stream, before eventually reaching the house at the end of a long straight. The sound she'd heard came from the drive. Coming fast up the straight was a silver Bentley Continental Turbo R. It came to a snappy halt, and Sir Julius Mannon climbed out from behind the wheel. A uniformed man got out sheepishly from the passenger side. Tom, the family chauffeur.

Instead of the white Rolls-Royce Corniche parked nearby, Sir Julius preferred to drive the Bentley most of the time, on road journeys back from the City. A short distance away from the Rolls-Royce was Kim's own car, a bright red, new Mercedes 500SL.

Given his daughter's height, Sir Julius was taller and younger-looking than expected. A major power in the financial circles of London, he was chairman and chief stockholder of an international conglomerate, Mannon Robinson. His economic, financial, and political connections were substantial, as was his influence. It was said that the yearly gross earnings of the company was such that they far outstripped the GDP of many a small nation. Sir Julius neither confirmed nor denied this.

His full head of silver hair was neatly trimmed, with tiny wings curling above and behind the ears. In his well-tailored navy blue pinstripe, he looked every inch the man his image makers presented to the world: the highly successful magnate. But there was more to him than image. An incisive mind and a quite ruthless manner in business made him a formidable and feared competitor.

Kim watched as he looked up at her window to wave. She returned the greeting as a young and fit-looking man in a butler's uniform came out of the house to take a briefcase from the chauffeur. Jarvis. She had never liked Jarvis, who had joined the Grantly Hall staff on the death of his own father, the original butler. Old Jarvis had been with the hall since her infancy. The younger Jarvis looked like a well-groomed thug, she'd always felt; but her father liked to have him around.

Sir Julius entered the building, followed by Jarvis.

Grantly Hall was home to just two members of the Mannon family: Kim and her father. Lady Mannon, her mother, and her brother, James, an only son, had died in a helicopter crash in Portugal a couple of years before. Unlike many in his position, Mannon refused to use a helicopter for transport since the accident, not out of fear, but out of anger. There were those who claimed this had made him even more ruthless and fiercely protective of Kim, for whom he had mapped out a suitable future. This included the man he expected her to marry. It was not Mark Selby.

Kim moved back from the window to sit on the bed. Then she got up again and, still barefoot, went out of the bedroom. No point delaying the inevitable, she decided. She would have to tell him.

She made her way down the wide central staircase, heading for her father's study. She knocked as she came to the solid oak door, employing a pattern she had used since childhood.

"Come in, Kimberley," Mannon called cheerfully.

She wondered what he would say when she told him. The cheerfulness would be soon gone, to be replaced by . . . Too late to worry about that now.

He had come home early to discuss arrangements for important guests he was having down for the weekend, and she was expected to be the hostess, as usual. But this weekend she didn't want to do it. She had other plans.

Briefing Room Alpha, November One

The crews of Warlock One and Two, plus Jason, were the only people in the room.

"The ground rules, gentlemen," began the wing commander, "are quite simple. You tell me exactly what happened out there." His eyes seemed to penetrate to their very souls. "Forget any idea of trying to pass me a fairy tale. It won't work." The eyes fastened upon McCann. "You first, Captain."

McCann opened his mouth to speak, but it was Selby who said, "My fault, sir."

Jason turned to him. "Is your name McCann?"

"No, sir."

Jason again looked at McCann. "If you please, Mr. McCann."

McCann seemed to be marshaling his thoughts. Jason waited in silence, watching him closely.

"You'll have seen from the screen in Ops, sir," McCann began, "that we did not succeed in getting a good lock. We went down after Warlock One, who was holding at low level. We did not fall for the feint when they gained height to come round on our tail, and broke *their* lock when they acquired us with the Sidewinder round. It then turned into a low-level knife fight . . . during which we got too close to the water and pulled clear. Warlock One then called knock it off."

Jason nodded, eyes seemingly glued to McCann. "That much was evident from the screen. Radar height warning was on, was it not?"

"Yes, sir. Set at fifty feet, and operating."

"So you ignored the attention getters . . . flashing lights, warning tone, *and* voice warning."

McCann gave a dry little cough. "The voice warning was disabled, sir. It's distracting in a low-level furball."

Hohendorf felt he ought to intervene. "Sir, if I may . . ."

"You may not, Mr. Hohendorf. Please await your turn."

"Sir."

"Did you warn your pilot?" Jason went on to McCann.

McCann paused, glanced at Selby, who did not meet his eye. He glanced at both Flacht and Hohendorf. Their faces were expressionless.

"Did you warn your pilot, Captain?" Jason repeated in a mild voice that carried greater impact than any shout.

"Yes, sir," McCann replied at last.

"And?"

"There . . . there was no reply, sir."

"Your warning, and the attention getters, were ignored."

"Sir, it's not so—"

"They were ignored and a multimillion-dollar aircraft, plus its expensive crew, were put in jeopardy."

"Yes, sir." McCann sounded miserable.

Jason turned to Hohendorf. "Now it's your turn, Mr. Hohendorf. Let's have your opinion."

Hohendorf went straight to the heart of the matter as he saw it. "We were fighting the way you would expect us to, sir . . . at the edge. Our task was to evade the defending

fighter and to also engage in air combat with him if the
tactical situation demanded it; to make life as difficult as
possible for the defender. We set out to win, and as the
defender, Warlock Two had to use any means to stop us;
which is what Mark tried to do."

"You dragged him low."

"Yes, sir."

"Therefore it was up to him to judge his altitude and
and speed, and decide upon what action to take, given the
circumstances."

"Yes, sir," Hohendorf agreed.

"And would you say he made the right decision?"

"I was not flying the aircraft. It is impossible for me to
judge accurately, without knowing all the facts. I might
have acted differently. I might even have gone lower. It is
hard to tell from another cockpit."

"You are a highly skilled fighter pilot, Mr. Hohendorf.
You know how to read your opponent. You dragged
Warlock Two low in order to give its pilot the extra pressure of worrying about height off the deck. I find no quar-
rel with that. It's up to the adversary to sort himself out.
Your ruse worked. I also know you're well capable of judg-
ing whether there was an error in the decision making of
your opponent. It is, after all, necessary to recognize such
moments, in order to succeed in air combat. Was there an
error in judgment?"

Despite the advice he had given to McCann earlier,
Hohendorf found himself reluctant to answer.

As if knowing what was going on in Hohendorf's mind,
Jason added, "I know your work. I know you can interpret
very accurately, indeed, what your opponent's up to.
Don't try to fob me off with a vague comment."

"Not an error, sir," he replied at last. "Perhaps keenness.
Warlock Two was going for the kill, and was very aggressive. Which is as it should be."

"Aggressive." Jason repeated the word thoughtfully, as if tasting a wine masquerading in the wrong bottle. "I like aggression in my pilots, but not when it endangers both aircraft and crew. Little point in scoring a kill, if you kill yourself and your backseater in the process. It then becomes a kill for the enemy. All right. Thank you, gentlemen. Flight Lieutenant Selby, you'll remain."

"Sir," Mark acknowledged in a voice that showed no emotion as the others filed out with uncertain, rearward glances.

Jason waited until the door had shut before saying to Selby, "While I admire solidarity among my crews, it's patently clear you lost it out there, for however brief a moment. Under such circumstances, even the briefest of moments can be fatal. Would you care to give me a plausible explanation?"

"There isn't one, sir. I blew it."

"I know you blew it. I want to know why. This is not the sort of performance I expect of you, Mark. You've been successful twice in combat, and I'm quite certain had this been a real fight, you would not have got into such a fix. If your capabilities as a combat pilot are not in question, then what is? Target fixation is not something I would have accused you of being prone to. You're not a baby pilot out on his first ride; and you're well aware of the additional dangers of a low-level fight. All in all, a pretty poor show, don't you think?"

"Yes, sir."

Jason stared at him. "I don't like mysteries. When one of my best pilots allows himself to be pulled into a dangerous situation, I want to know why. I also do not like problems being kept from me. Little problems become big ones that kill pilots and, invariably, their backseaters as well. Do you have a problem?"

"Not that I'm aware of."

"Are you sure?"

"Yes, sir."

"Yet you nearly put that aircraft into the drink."

"I . . . I misjudged it."

"You're not one of those pilots who makes a habit of 'misjudging,' Mark. Try another. Something's nagging at you, and I'm going to find out what it is. If I ground you, Flight Lieutenant . . . yes, *ground* you . . . if I ground you, it means I shall have to select a second pilot without combat experience, to fly the escort mission. This may put both Flacht and McCann in unnecessary jeopardy. So if there is anything . . ."

"It's Axel Hohendorf, sir."

Jason was puzzled. "Hohendorf? What's his role in all this?"

Selby heard himself say with some reluctance, "Morven, sir. My sister."

"I know who your sister is," Jason said firmly. "And I know she's been seeing Axel von Hohendorf for some time. The entire unit is aware of that. It's no longer news."

"I just don't like it, sir," Selby told Jason bluntly.

Jason stared at his subordinate. Something began to blaze in his eyes. It was a warning of the end of tolerance. "Good God, man!" he said eventually, virtually emphasizing each word. "I thought all that had been settled a long time ago. Are you expecting me to believe that you've been harboring a grudge . . ." Jason stopped, eyes showing the steel that made him the tough commander he sometimes could be, when the situation demanded. "So you went after Hohendorf up there and overcooked it? What were you playing at? World War Two revisited? I do hope you're not expecting me to believe that you were so childish . . . Yes! Flight Lieutenant Selby, *childish!*"

Jason stopped again, his anger out in the open, his eyes remaining fastened upon Selby, who dared not blink.

"You," Jason went on, "are one of the best pilots I am fortunate to have on this unit. Hohendorf is another. McCann is our top backseater, and Flacht is second only to him. Now, Mr. Selby, am I to understand that because you choose to be unhappy about your sister's involvement with Hohendorf, you were prepared to put at risk *two NATO aircraft and my best crews?*" Jason's eyes were cold and unforgiving. "Is that what I'm to understand?"

The wing commander had finished with a sudden mildness that was unnerving.

"No, sir."

"No *what*, Mr. Selby? No, you did not put them at risk? No, you're not worked up about your sister and Hohendorf? No, you did not allow yourself to lose it up there, even for the slightest moment? Which is it to be?"

Selby remained silent.

"I'll tell you what, Flight Lieutenant," Jason continued in his familiar, even tones, turning away from Selby to pace a short distance before reversing his steps like a sentry. "I shall pretend I did not hear that pathetic excuse you've just given me as a reason. I shall further assume that Hohendorf's version makes more sense. You were aggressive, and you were on the edge, pushing. It is well known that I demand this of my pilots. I therefore give you a solemn warning: there will be no more of this. Have your differences with Hohendorf on the ground, if you must, but they must not and *will not* interfere with your duties, either down here or up in the air. Am I getting through?"

"Yes, sir."

Jason stopped before Selby once more. "You're a good officer, and an excellent pilot. That's my opinion of you. Don't you dare prove me wrong. And another thing . . . if you do pull a stunt like this again and you kill yourself, I shall come to your grave and drag you out to tell you what I think. Got it?" Jason was not smiling.

"Sir!" Selby acknowledged.

"Thank you, Mark." It was over.

"Sir," Selby repeated, and made his way out of the briefing room.

As he tended to do on occasion, Jason removed his cap and wiped his forehead with the back of the same hand. He replaced the cap, feeling certain there was more to Selby's apparent lapse of concentration during the fight. He wondered whether the incident was stress-related. Both crews had seen combat twice before and, each time, had been given counselling. None of the four had displayed any symptoms of trauma-related disorders. But you never knew. With the new mission coming up, it was better to be safe than sorry.

Jason decided he would have a word with Doc Hemelsen about it. It was the doc who had spoken to the crews on their return from the previous missions. Definitely worth having a word, just in case.

Jason left the briefing room, a bemused expression upon his face. Doc Hemelsen might have some answers.

Grantly Hall, Buckinghamshire

"No!" Sir Julius Mannon said explosively. "I won't hear of it."

The huge study was as spacious as his City office, though it was much more intimate, with deeply upholstered furniture in oxblood leather; a large, inlaid antique desk; rich carpeting; and bookshelves that took up every available wall space, from floor to ceiling, and were filled to capacity.

Mannon moved to a tall window to stare out at the

countryside. Kim remained where she was, leaning against one of the mahogany bookshelves. She watched him, determined not to give in.

He turned to face her, his expression displaying an equal refusal to submit.

"Did you really expect me to agree to this, Kimberley? These are people of great importance to our economy. Why, of all the weekends, does it have to be this one?" Mannon waved an arm at the desk. It was covered with documents. "Do you think I'd have had these here instead of at the office, so early on a Thursday, if I did not think this gathering of sufficient importance?"

She said nothing but watched him unwaveringly. Let him make his case. She had no intention of being swayed this time. It had happened too often in the past.

"It has taken me the better part of a year," he went on, "to get these people together from Europe, and farther afield. In the current economic climate, it was very difficult to find those in this country who shared my belief: that the best way to take advantage of a recession is to *invest*. This leaves you well ahead of any competition, because while you're busy preparing, they're going to the wall. By the time the recession has ended, you are streets ahead of the overcautious investors and, therefore, the competition. You benefit, and the nation benefits.

"Many of my contemporaries think I'm mad. But I'm not the one in trouble, while each day they try to make the books balance. I have found some people, from Europe and beyond, who share that same ethos. It is not by accident that they, too, own successful businesses. The trick is to invest without unnecessary risk taking because some risk, inevitably, needs to be taken. To succeed successfully, one must go beyond the edge.

"There will be wives here this weekend, and I want the atmosphere to be as congenial as we can possibly make it. I need you with me."

She eased herself off the bookshelf to walk slowly over to him. She looked out of the window as she spoke, the low pitch of her voice seeming at variance with the neat packaging of her small body.

"I've lost count of the number of times I've played the hostess for you, Father. I've always put your business interests ahead of my own personal life. . . ."

"Are there not compensations? Look out there." Mannon pointed in the direction of the red Mercedes. "How many other young women of your age can afford to change their cars every year, or twice, or three times if they felt like it, as you have done? And how many credit cards do you hold? How many golds and platinums? In the past six months you've been to Hong Kong, Bermuda, Australia, California . . . I've lost count. And this house, your wardrobe . . ." Mannon paused, looking at her. "For whom do you think I've done all this? In the end, it's all yours, Kimberley."

Her face had grown tight with both frustration and anguish. "You cannot hold that over my head forever! I am not denying that I've been very fortunate. I was born into this family. I had no choice in the matter. It was a random thing. Luck. That was all." She wrapped her arms about herself, shutting him out. "And I know and understand that, because of Mother and James, you have focused everything on me." Her voice softened. "But I want some of me, too, for myself, Father. You—"

A knock interrupted her.

"Yes!" Mannon called out impatiently.

The door opened and Jarvis stood there. "A call, Sir Julius." He glanced at Kim. "For Miss Mannon." His eyes seemed to hold a message.

"Who is it?" Mannon inquired before she could speak.

Jarvis hesitated for the briefest of instants. "A Captain McCann, sir. He sounds American." Jarvis spoke as if that fact mitigated against the caller.

Kim became suddenly animated, arms falling to her sides. "Elmer Lee!" she cried. "I'll take it—"

"In here," Mannon cut in. He went over to the desk and picked up a black phone from its large base unit. Grantly Hall had several lines, and all could be routed via that particular instrument. He tapped a button, and a red light began to blink. He passed the receiver to Kim, who did not look pleased.

"Thank you, Jarvis," he said to the butler, who withdrew backward, shutting the door softly.

Kim said tentatively: "Elmer Lee?"

"Hey, kid. How're you doing?" the familiar voice said in her ear. "Long time no see. No hear, either."

"I know," she began sheepishly. "But it's all been rather difficult." Very aware of her father's eyes upon her, she went on: "Is he . . . is he . . ."

"No sweat. He's all right. Nothing's happened to him . . . but you're wondering why I called. Right?"

"Well . . . yes."

"Could be I just wanted to have a talk. . . ."

"I know you better than that, Elmer Lee. What's really wrong, and where are you calling from?"

The voice at the other end paused. The telephone hummed. "That obvious, huh?" McCann eventually said. "I'm up here, at the base. Look, Kim . . . you've got to promise not to tell him I called. The guy would take my head off."

"You're beginning to worry me. . . ."

"You've got to promise or this conversation ends right now. Do I get that promise?"

He was so serious, she said quickly: "I promise."

"Okay." He sounded relieved. "Let's meet. I've got to talk with you."

"Now I'm really worried."

"There's nothing to worry about . . . not really."

"A worry's a worry, Elmer Lee."

"Yeah, but . . . Look, why not wait till we meet?"

"All right. Where?"

"Can you get to Edinburgh?"

She gave a strange laugh.

"I'm that funny?" he said puzzledly.

"I'll tell you when I come up. When?"

"Er . . . Sunday would be good."

"I can make it. We've got a place on Princes Street. I'll give you directions and a time." When she had done so, she added, "Will that be all right?"

"I can find it okay. I'm a navigator."

She gave another little laugh. "Oh, yes. How could I have forgotten? I'll see you then."

"Yeah."

The line went dead, and she turned to find her father's gaze still upon her.

"This Captain McCann," Mannon began immediately, "a friend of your Flight Lieutenant Selby, I take it? I thought all this nonsense had ended months ago."

"I tried to end it, Father," she said coldly. "Just as you had hoped. That was what my globe-trotting was all about. But places that used to excite me became unbelievably boring. I used to have great times in California. I thought I could never be bored there; but I was. God knows I tried not to be. That's when I knew something was very wrong." A determined expression was now upon her face. "I'll stay till the dinner on Saturday, and I'll be the perfect daughter. You'll have no complaints, but Sunday belongs to me. I expect Reggie will be coming?"

"Naturally."

"Naturally," she repeated wearily and with a deep lack of enthusiasm. "Well, just keep him away from me."

She went out before he could say anything.

At November One, McCann let himself out of the public telephone booth in the officers' mess, looking guilty and hoping he'd done the right thing.

At the medical headquarters, Jason walked along a pristine corridor until he came to his destination. MAJOR H. HEMELSEN, MD, read the sign on the door. Jason knocked and entered.

Major Hemelsen's closely cut hair was of a fine gold that tended to gleam in sunlight. Delicate features and a slim body gave her the appearance of a teenaged girl, and her pale blue eyes seemed larger from behind the glasses she wore. Her lips were also pale because she never wore lipstick, even of the most subtle hue. When she smiled, people claimed it improved their mood, no matter how foul. She was very good at making people feel better, which wasn't surprising. She had perfected the trick as a defense mechanism, since childhood. Major Hemelsen was six inches under six feet and was Danish. Before she was poached by Jason for the November program, she had been serving in her country's air force.

She stood up from behind her desk as Jason entered.

"Please sit down, Helle," he said. He removed his cap, tucked it under an arm. "This is an informal visit. I'm here to pick your brains, and to seek advice."

"Of course, sir. Anything I can do to help."

"We'll dispense with the 'sir' as well."

She nodded and regained her seat. "If you'll just excuse me for a moment." Her voice was soft, with a warm, cozy feel to it. She picked up her phone. "No calls or visits, please, Jenny." She glanced at Jason, who had found himself a chair. "I'm not sure for how long. I'll call you. Thanks." She hung up and gave him her undivided attention. "So . . . how can I help?"

The person she had spoken to on the phone was her noncommissioned secretary. Using first names was her way of dealing with her staff. It did not affect discipline, and Jason had never interfered.

"I'm preparing some crews for a mission," he began. "You've had dealings with them before."

Again she nodded. "Hohendorf, Selby, and so on?"

"Yes."

"Are there problems with them?"

"That's what I need to learn from you."

"When I last saw them, they were very stable. I put that in my report."

"Yes. I know. However, I'm after something else . . . I'm not even sure what it is, to tell you the truth. Can you give me a general . . . impression of how you see them?"

She settled herself more comfortably on her chair. "A general impression is just that: a very loose comment on the subject's general state. Not very specific."

"I appreciate that, but please go on."

"I shall begin with Hohendorf. Very, very stable, despite his own personal complications with his wife. There was mild trauma when his backseater was nearly killed, but he has handled that very well.

"Selby is also stable, though I feel there may be something else he controls, perhaps a little too rigidly. In his first combat he spoke to the man he had killed . . . the MiG pilot who was dying, unable to eject as his plane fell to the sea. Selby was very shocked when he realized for the first time the true nature of his profession. But he handled the resultant stress very well."

"Something else happened to him," Jason said, "prior to his coming to this unit. He lost a good friend in a crash.

Burned to death in the mountains. The friend had taken Selby's slot when Selby's aircraft became unserviceable during a preflight. Selby blames himself for the crash."

Hemelsen nodded. "I've read the report on the accident, but there were no fine details. He has never spoken of it to me, and I have never asked him to. However, I find the omission intriguing." She gave a tiny smile. "I believe he is the type of person who would not consider telling this to someone he sees as a mere shrink. Not done. Very British."

"I'm afraid I can identify with that attitude," Jason said. "In small measure, of course."

The smile deepened briefly. "Of course."

"Oh, no, you don't. We're talking about Selby. Has he been hostile to you?"

"The exact opposite. He is always very correct. I believe he sees counseling as a necessary evil, awaiting his return from combat. He obeys the order to come, but that is it. He cooperates under silent protest."

"But he is stable."

"Oh, yes. Nothing to worry about there."

"And the others?"

"Flacht," Hemelsen continued, "despite the fact he has a family, manages to control his anxieties about their well-being, should something happen to him. He does not worry about himself. Considering how close he came to dying, I find that quite remarkable.

"Then we come to McCann." Hemelsen again smiled, this time almost fondly. "Elmer Lee McCann is either so stable that nothing can touch him, or he is so completely unstable, he has met himself coming the other way and again, nothing can touch him. McCann appears to have come to the conclusion that if the world is itself a crazy place, there is no point in worrying about it. Take everything as it comes, and adjust to the given situation. He is an emotional chameleon.

"Nico Bagni sometimes worries about Richard Palmer's death, but he would be abnormal if he didn't. It does not affect the way he performs his duties. Do you want me to list more? Or will that do?"

"Those are the people I wanted to know about," Jason replied. "Thank you, Helle. Nico Bagni once had a fear of killing his backseater due to bad flying, particularly during landings. But of course time has shown this to have been pure nonsense. The man lands his airplane like a feather coming to earth."

"There is one fear they all have," she said.

"Oh?"

"Fear of being grounded. That is the one thing that would destroy their self-esteem. They are, without exception, in love with their airplanes. Do not misunderstand me. They are not tech-loving, high-speed . . . er . . . freaks. Your men are not automatons. They are thinking, feeling people who will have a host of fears and anxieties, but who will control them because of the one thing they love almost more than anything else . . . and that is flying. Each will have been altered in some way by his experiences. This is natural. They would not be human otherwise. They are also, of course, in the final analysis, killers."

"They would be useless if they weren't."

Helle Hemelsen's eyes looked bigger as they regarded Jason from behind the glasses. "So which one is causing you such worry?"

"Selby nearly went in today."

"Ah."

"He seems rather unhappy about Hohendorf's involvement with his sister and during air combat training became overkeen to nail Hohendorf. He came very close to the water. By all accounts, he briefly lost it. I've chosen to give him a personal roasting rather than make a big issue of it at this stage. He's too good a pilot to lose."

"How did he react?"

"He accepted blame without hesitation. He was very annoyed with himself. That was quite obvious."

"A healthy reaction. It would have been more worrying if he had tried to pretend he had not made the mistake. Do you want me to keep an eye on him? Or perhaps talk to him?"

After some thought, Jason said: "No. I think we'll leave it at that for now. But if I feel there's a problem, I'll call you in. Is this all right with you?"

"I am at your disposal."

Jason got to his feet. She followed suit. "Thank you, Helle," he said once more.

"My pleasure, sir."

Jason put on his cap and went out.

6

General Kurinin had carefully studied the highly secret, dark brown file he had taken out of his safe. The colonel in the outer office had no access to it, and only Kurinin knew of its existence. The others who had known—Stolybin and the general who had been his direct boss—were both dead.

Stolybin and the general. Kurinin closed the file slowly and passed a reflective hand across the name on the cover. It was a single word: TOKAREVA.

She was good, he thought. Very good.

Born in the former autonomous Soviet Socialist Republic of Udmurt, according to the file, she was the daughter of a Finnish mother and a Russian father. Ostensibly she had been promoted through the ranks to lieutenant in the KGB; but she was more, much more, than that.

The file held many official reports on her, but what interested him most were the personal annotations appended therein, by both the late general and Stolybin. For example, her height was given as 180 centimeters, but the bald description was enhanced by a scribbled note in Stolybin's handwriting. "Glorious body," it said. "Pneumatic whirlwind."

It gave a clue to what duties Tokareva had been earmarked for. Unfortunately, subsequent investigations showed that both the general and Stolybin had been rivals for that same body. It had cost them dearly in the end.

Kurinin had seen Tokareva just once, and the impression she had made was still with him. The Russo-Finnish parentage had given her the best of both worlds, in his opinion. The blond hair, almost translucent skin and fine features of her mother had been complemented by the sturdy peasant genes of her father, resulting in a tall woman of classic bearing, on the fine edge of voluptuousness. In her job, however, she was very dangerous. To their cost, neither the general nor Stolybin had known until too late just how dangerous. She possessed, he now remembered, the most incredibly black eyes.

He rose from his desk to put the file away, then went over to a wall upon which was hung a large framed map covering Europe, Scandinavia, and the former Soviet Union. New borders were etched in black, with the original boundaries marked by double rows of red dashes. He stared at the Udmurt capital of Ishevsk. Or should it be Ustinov? National schizophrenia was spreading like a virus, with namings and renamings going on everywhere. Udmurt wanted independence.

Where would it end? The Russian Federation, with its seventeen states of which Udmurt was one, could well go the way of the union itself. Myriad tiny nations, all shouting their disparate, nationalistic slogans. It was madness. Whose defense forces would defend whom? And who would eventually pay for it all?

"We are insane," he murmured to himself. "We brought it upon ourselves."

He returned to his desk. To one side was a selection of current Western journals and newspapers, among which were two from Britain. It was some consolation, he thought, that they were having their problems, too, with Scotland apparently wanting to secede.

It made him feel better. Scotland was home to the first, and so far only, November base. A seceded Scotland might well demand its closure. He would keep an eye on those events. Meanwhile he had a more active part to play in jeopardizing the base's continued existence.

He rose once more from the desk and went through to the outer office. The colonel came to attention. Kurinin waved to him to sit.

"Tell me, Vladimir . . . how well do you know your Gibbon?"

The colonel looked at him blankly.

"You should read more Western books," Kurinin admonished in a mild, almost pensive voice. "What he has to say about rampant, petty nationalism and states splitting themselves this way and that is perfect for our time. No one is spared. He says it all. Our task, Vladimir, is to halt the disintegration of our own Motherland and bring it back from the country of beggars to which it has been sent." Kurinin's voice had lost all its mildness. "As if that were not enough, we now have *religion* rearing its head once more. A sure sign we're in serious trouble. I'm reminded of those cowboy movies from the West. Look for the flock of vultures. You know there are dead bodies beneath. Our land is turning into carrion. Religious fanaticism and zealous ideology of any kind are the enemies of reason."

"We had our own ideology, Comrade General," the colonel pointed out with remarkable bravery. "For seventy years."

Kurinin stared at him as if with new eyes. "Did you believe *all* of it? I took only that which was useful to the integrity of the Motherland. Everything else was secondary."

A knock on the colonel's door saved him from having to make a reply. He looked to Kurinin, who nodded, giving permission.

"Come!" the colonel ordered.

A lieutenant, somewhat old for the rank, entered with a folder beneath an arm. He stiffened when he saw Kurinin.

Kurinin waved a hand at him, indicating he should carry on. The junior officer went over to the colonel, handed him the folder, and left smartly. The colonel opened the folder, read a couple of papers briefly, then again looked up at Kurinin.

"Poleskov's in place, Comrade General, and the *Karelia*'s on its way to station. There have also been no overflights—either by satellite or aircraft—of the radar site." The colonel handed the folder to Kurinin.

Kurinin skimmed through the report, looking pleased. He returned the folder when he had finished. "Good," he said. "But lack of overflights does not mean a lack of interest. The West is not going to take the destruction of the Stealth aircraft lying down. We remain on full alert. They might try anything. And let us hope Comrade Poleskov proves worthy of the lenient treatment he has received," Kurinin added.

There was a barely veiled threat in the last comment. It was unmistakably clear that Poleskov's continuing good health depended heavily upon his success in whatever task he had been set by Kurinin.

The colonel said nothing.

*   *   *

**Early Friday Afternoon the Same Week,
November One**

Hohendorf, in civilian clothes, left the officers' mess
with two pieces of soft luggage to put into the back of his
red Porsche. The car was parked at the rear of the building, and as he came up to a corner, voices, and the subject of their conversation, made him pause.

". . . and it was really unbelievable," one of the voices
was saying. "This black friend of mine was walking along a
street in Berlin with another friend and his girlfriend,
both white. A bunch of those Nazis came toward them
and started giving the black guy a hard time, one of them
accusing him of staring at *his* girlfriend. My friend told
them to shut it, and that's when the trouble started. Next
thing, those bastards were laying into all three."

"And?"

"Well, some Berliners at least had the balls to have a
go, otherwise God knows what might have happened to
them. They told me when they got back that in some
places over there, people just watch while they beat up
foreigners. You'd have thought they'd have learned from
history. My granddad was in Lancasters during the war,
you know. Tailgunner. Eighteen, he was. Used to sit in
that turret on night raids, watching all the fires burning
below. He says he hopes never to see anything like that
again in his life. You can imagine what *he* says about
what's going on. He thinks they'll never learn."

"That bloody wall came down too quickly, if you ask
me. It's leaking poison into Germany."

"Yeah, mate. God knows what's going to happen over
there . . . or to Europe, for that matter. Worries my grand-
parents something awful. They think it's going to be the

old problem all over again. You know the sort of thing . . . the ghost of old Adolf coming back to claim the German people. They're seeing Nazis everywhere. They're remembering the thirties and forties all over again. Personally, I don't believe it's that bad, but . . ."

Hohendorf had decided to make his appearance, and the speaker now stopped in shock on recognizing him.

"Umm . . . er . . . sir! I . . ." The man had come to attention, looking embarrassed. He was one of the squadron drivers. "I . . . didn't mean . . ." He stopped once more, in confusion.

His companion, unknown to Hohendorf, looked at once apologetic and defiant.

"It's all right, gentlemen," Hohendorf said easily. "I happen to share some of your sentiments. I am glad that at least some Berliners behaved with honor and decency." He walked on, wondering how many such conversations were being held throughout the EC-NATO nations. Certain memories would take a long time to fade.

Flacht was waiting by the car, a 944 Turbo SE that was two and a half years old. Hohendorf put the luggage in the back and pulled the cover out of its roller housing behind the rear seats to clip it in place. There was plenty of room left for Morven's gear. After lowering the large glass hatchback and clicking it shut, he turned to Flacht. The two men shook hands and gave each other a brief embrace.

"Hals und beinbruch," Flacht said softly. "See to it that Johann takes good care of you. Good pilots need better navigators to tell them where to go."

"You backseaters always think you're the ones flying the airplane."

"You've only just found that out?"

Hohendorf smiled. "And you take care, Wolfie. Before you know it, we'll be back in our old ship."

"It cannot be soon enough for me."

Just then McCann came hurrying up. "Hey, guy!" he

said to Hohendorf. "Going without saying good-bye?" He offered his hand. "Don't go hitting any rocks."

Hohendorf shook hands again. "I have no intention of doing that. See you soon."

"You bet your ass you will. You're going to need us up top. Uh . . . look . . . about Mark . . ."

"It's okay. We had a little talk."

"Yeah. Yeah, I know. He feels sort of stupid about the whole thing. Anyway, for his pains the boss has made him aircrew duty officer for a few days. Which means when he's finished the day's training schedule, he's still got to go up to air traffic control. We four work so well together, I wish this thing between you two guys would, you know . . . work itself out one fine day."

"It will . . . eventually."

"Yeah. And pigs might fly."

"Oh, I don't know. . . ." Hohendorf looked at him pointedly, with a straight face.

"Get outta here!"

Hohendorf grinned and climbed into the car, started the engine, and pulled away. Their images remained in his mirrors until he turned a corner, on his way to the main gate. He hoped he would be seeing them again.

"How could I have been so stupid?" Mark Selby asked himself quietly as he got ready in his mess quarters for his ADO shift. He'd lost count of the number of times he had uttered those same words since the incident.

There was no other way to describe it. He had allowed emotions to cloud his reason. For the barest of dangerous instants, he had become so determined to get the constantly shifting aircraft in a solid lock that he had ignored one of the prime rules of air fighting and had lost awareness of the deck.

"I nearly totaled my aircraft." Certainly both McCann and himself would have perished. "Moron," he added disgustedly.

But Morven would still be going to Germany with Hohendorf, though he knew his colleague and squadron rival would never tell her what had happened. It was not Hohendorf's way.

Selby was in many ways a contradiction. A little under six feet, he had a compact body that made him seem shorter than he really was. His dark hair was closely trimmed, and he had a square sort of face, with a sharply defined jawline. A neatly cultivated mustache graced his upper lip. His eyes were a piercing blue and seemed to be looking into a great distance. His hands, broad and strong, coarse almost, would delude an observer into believing they belonged to someone who did heavy manual work; a peasant's hands, would have been the first thought. But they were the hands of a true craftsman. Those who knew his flying appreciated the gentleness of his touch with the aircraft and the utter skill with which he flew. He danced with the airplane while becoming, at the same time, part of it.

Selby put on his cap. The blue eyes stared back at him from the mirror.

"You'll do," he said, and went out.

The access road to the base joined the newly widened coastal road in a T-junction about a mile from the main gate. Hohendorf stopped, then turned left onto it, heading for Portsoy and eventually the A97 that would take him on to Aberdeen.

He felt a thrill of anticipation, knowing Morven would be waiting at the end of his journey. They'd be spending the night in Aberdeen before setting off early the next morning on the long drive south to Harwich on England's east coast, for the ferry to Hamburg. From there it would be just an hour's fast drive to his former unit. Johann and Erika, who lived nearby, had insisted they stay with them.

So eager was Hohendorf to get on his way that he took little notice of the small group of people leaning against their parked cars a short distance from the junction. There were always some people there, mainly aircraft enthusiasts hoping to get an exciting photo of the ASV Tornadoes as they took off and landed. The junction was the closest that spectators were allowed to come to November One without specific invitation.

Sometimes the aircraft, usually in pairs, would scream past at low level on their way out to sea. On other occasions, they could be seen rising vertically, afterburners glowing. This was a favorite with the plane spotters.

Among the small crowd was a man in a thick weatherproof jacket. He leaned against a Range Rover, a pair of binoculars to his eyes, as he watched a pair of ASVs doing the sort of climb their crews described as ballistic. All about him people gasped with pleasure. The February day was bright, though cold, without a single cloud to be seen. It was a good day for photography.

After the aircraft had disappeared, the man lowered the binoculars. A short distance away, an enthusiast with a huge lens attached to his camera turned and smiled with satisfaction.

"Aren't they beautiful?" the photographer began with a bright eagerness. "I could watch them do that all day."

"Did you get some good shots?"

"Perfect ones. Of course, I'll have to see how they come out, just to be sure."

"Of course."

"But I think I've done well this time."

"Good."

"Well, that's my lot for today. You?"

"Oh, I'll stay a little longer, then I'll push off."

"Fine. See you around."

"Yes. Okay."

The photographer put his equipment away in a small, battered-looking van, climbed in, and drove off.

Poleskov lounged against the Range Rover and watched expressionlessly as the van went noisily down the road. His accent had been regionally perfect when he'd spoken. It was one of his many skills, vital to the successful outcome of many of his previous missions. He was a consummate linguist and mimic. Those attributes had kept him alive in a profession where mistakes were usually terminal.

He put the binoculars carefully away some minutes later, then climbed into the Range Rover. He had studied the traffic to and from the base for some hours now but had seen no one who had looked remotely like the man in the photograph that had been given to him by Kurinin. Many people had passed with laden cars, clearly going on weekend leave.

He had seen the red Porsche but had given it only cursory attention. Another member of the base off for the weekend. He wondered how many of the people he'd seen were flyers and how many the ground staff. It was not possible to gauge people by the cars they drove, though some virtually shouted their positions by the way they held themselves.

But they were of little interest to him. He had just one man to kill and to find out whether the base was being readied for special missions. From what he'd seen so far, and from careful eavesdropping on conversations, nothing out of the ordinary seemed to be happening. So far. You never knew what could turn up out of the blue.

Poleskov decided to go into the mode for which he was justly famous in the circle of his peers.

He would wait in the local area, bide his time, and see what developed.

One hour into his journey, Hohendorf continued to wrestle with three matters that sought domination in his mind. The thought of Morven was foremost and with it, inevitably, Mark Selby's attitude toward the relationship. On several occasions he had tried to put himself in Mark's place. He had some sympathy with Selby, knowing that had he been the brother of an only sister, he might well have reacted with at least some caution, given the same conditions. However, he still felt the matter really concerned only Morven and himself. He sighed. Of course, there was also Anne-Marie, a real missile on the loose when her temper was raging. He would not tell Morven, he decided, about Selby's narrow escape.

The next item on his mind was the coming mission. The pleasure of working with Johann Ecker again in the low-level arena was tempered by the thought of Wolfie Flacht having to fly with a combat novice—no matter how good a jock—in what might well develop into something quite nasty if the slightest thing went wrong. It was axiomatic that no matter how careful the battle plan, the actual battle itself tended to dictate the outcome. Historically, those who went into combat had learned that lesson, some in the harshest of ways. The prospect of Wolfie getting hurt a second time or, worse, dying because he and his pilot were not perfectly in tune at a crucial moment was not one he wanted to contemplate.

He came to the third subject: the conversation he had inadvertently overheard behind the mess. He was conscious of a slight frisson of fear for his country and hoped his fellow citizens would not allow it to fall, yet again, into the hands of those who would eventually destroy it. The world would never forgive them. *He* would never forgive them. The measure of a nation's level of civilized behavior and its humanity, he felt, was whether it displayed a willingness to allow itself to fall prey to the demagogue. Throughout history, nations had betrayed themselves in this manner, and the results had inevitably been catastrophic, both for their neighbors and for themselves. One had only to look at Yugoslavia.

"No!" he heard himself say with some intensity. "I would *not* forgive you!"

Hohendorf allowed the sounds of the Porsche to soothe him as he drove on toward Aberdeen. Morven would be waiting.

When he arrived, he held her tightly until she gasped.

"Hey," she said softly, arms about his waist and leaning slightly away to look at him. "I'm glad you're pleased to see me . . . but can I breathe a little, please?" Her eyes studied his face. "Is everything all right?"

He kissed her soft mouth for a long moment.

"Well?" she insisted against his lips. "Are you going to tell me? Or do I have to keep asking until you give in?"

At last he spoke. "There is nothing to tell."

Her eyes remained fixed upon the countenance she had grown to love so deeply, searching his face with rapid movements as if probing for the answers she felt were certain to exist there.

When she had first seen him at the mess ball, she'd been immediately intrigued by the tall, slim man standing quietly to one side. The aura of strength she had sensed then was still with him. His crop of blond hair and his unlined face had made him look far younger than his age. Then she had looked into the pale blue eyes and had seen within them a far greater life experience. His self-assured stillness had drawn her like a magnet; and when they had locked eyes for the very first time, each had known in that instant—almost like the old cliché—that they wanted each other.

What had followed, she had thought ever since, had been inevitable. Whatever Mark wanted to believe, Axel von Hohendorf had not seduced her. The opposite was closer to the truth. Axel had not stood a chance from the moment she had set eyes upon him.

"Are you going to tell me or not?" she demanded for a third time. "I know something's bothering you, Axel. So give."

He decided that of the three matters that had exercised his mind on the way down, only one could be safely discussed. He chose the least complicated.

"I overheard two of the ground staff today," he began. With an arm about her waist, he steered her to a sofa and they sat down, remaining close. He relayed the conversation he had accidentally eavesdropped upon. "You know," he continued, "in Germany, especially in Berlin, everyone is talking about what is happening. They are very, very worried . . . and disappointed, too, after all those years of hard work. They know all the other nations are watching Germany like hawks, waiting for us to put a foot wrong. After the nastiness of the hostels—the burnings and killings—many non-Germans are again beginning to think the only really good German is a—"

"Oh, Axel . . . surely not . . ."

"Oh, Axel, surely yes. The reality is that memories of Germany's past are still very strong. You have only got to listen to what is being said here, in the U.K., by some prominent people. I've actually heard one of your members of Parliament say he's not going to take orders from any German." Hohendorf smiled ruefully. "Good thing he's not at the base. There are Germans who give orders up there. Our deputy commander is German. *I* sometimes give orders. At times I even begin to wonder whether Mark thinks I am some kind of secret Nazi. . . ."

Morven was horrified. "*No,* Axel! You can't believe that. Mark has his differences with you about me, but that's it. He'd be very upset to hear you say such a thing. He respects you completely as a professional, and as a man."

"Perhaps." Hohendorf was unconvinced. "Except where his sister is concerned."

"That's something we're just going to have to live with. He'll come round in the end."

"I hope so. Now come here. No more about Mark, or Germany's problems. I want to . . ." Hohendorf paused and looked about him. "Zoë?"

"She's off to a party tonight, so when she heard you'd be coming, she very diplomatically decided to make a whole day of it. She won't be back till tomorrow. It's just us chickens." She licked playfully at his earlobe. "We can do whatever we like. By the way," she went on, "she's been asking about Elmer Lee. She's taken a fancy to him, seeing Mark's got Kim in his blood."

"Elmer Lee McCann likes living dangerously," Hohendorf said. "He thinks he's in love with another man's woman."

"Still? Mark told me about that. Not . . . what's her name . . . ah yes, Karen Lomax . . . whose boyfriend is the rugby person who likes hurting people. . . ."

"That's the one. The mouse trap was invented for Elmer Lee. All you need is the right kind of cheese."

"Poor Elmer Lee," Morven said. "One of nature's true optimists. Just a minute," she went on, and got up quickly to draw all the curtains, plunging the room into a warm twilight within which they could still see each other. There was still some daylight outside. She returned to the sofa and snuggled close to him. "Let's forget them all. Let's get really close. I want you."

They began slowly to undress each other, each taking great pleasure in revealing the other's body as the items of clothing came off.

"You have," he murmured against the erect nipple of her left breast, "a wonderful body, and I love every inch of it."

Both breasts were now bare, and he moved his face slowly against them, kissing each in turn. He felt her shifting beneath him each time he did that, readying herself to receive him when the time was right. Long, slow gasps, punctuated now and then by soft moans, came out of her. His hands caressed her gently, stroking her thighs and legs, running up and down her body with a sensitivity that drew tremors from her.

"I can't wait anymore," she began to say, repeating this with increasing urgency.

When at last he went into her, time seemed to stretch and his entry seemed to go on forever, enveloping him in a cocooning warmth that served to make him feel safe. Safe and free of Mark Selby's disapproval, of Germany's nascent social problems, of the coming mission. And when Morven's heaving body began to tremble, he found himself wishing this would continue without limit, that he could stay here, free and safe, indefinitely, where the madness of the world could not reach him.

But even as his body was seized by the urgency of its own passions, straining against hers—as his arms tightened about her on the large sofa, as she squealed and whimpered and he groaned and grunted hoarsely in response—even as he felt his whole being pouring into her, he knew he was being given only a short time to forget.

But he was grateful, for even this might have been denied him. The advent of Morven Selby into his life had been one of the most fortunate events to come his way.

As their moist bodies relaxed against each other, he kissed the top of her head. She snuggled closer in response, pressing her warm face against his neck.

"I love you," he told her softly.

"I should think so," she said.

Far to the south, one of the people Hohendorf would eventually be coming up against in combat was standing partially out of the commander's hatch of a desert-camouflaged armored personnel carrier.

Lieutenant Anatoly Tikov scanned the desert horizon for intruders and saw nothing to cause any new anxieties of his own. He had managed to obtain permission to accompany one of the small patrols that routinely went out on search missions, to ensure that the continuing security of the area immediately beyond the radar site was maintained. They were now a hundred kilometers out, the limit of the imaginary boundary.

The three fully air-conditioned APCs were parked beneath the low overhang of a centuries-old eroded rock face that gave them both some shade and protection from air and spaceborne prying eyes.

Back at the site, a sense of relaxation had returned. The majority of people now seemed to have little fear of an impending attack as time went on. With no apparent evidence to the contrary, and made buoyant by the total destruction of the Stealth aircraft, they seemed to think it was all over.

Tikov did not believe it.

A thorough search had failed to find any debris of use. The aircraft's self-destruct systems had effectively added to the destruction of the surface-to-air missile launched at it, shredding the machine as if it had been paper. Already the strong desert winds had farther dispersed and covered the fused shards that had once been the high-tech airplane.

But Tikov was not happy about the speed with which his comrades had returned to feeling invulnerable. Something was coming, he knew.

We'll be reaping the whirlwind, he thought as he continued to scan the horizon. I am sure of it.

"Satisfied, Lieutenant?" a voice said beneath him.

He moved the binoculars away from his eyes, almost guiltily, and looked down. Standing next to the APC was the Russian captain in charge of the patrol.

"Yes, sir," Tikov replied with the right level of respect.

The captain grinned. "Enjoying the patrol?"

"Yes, sir," Tikov repeated.

"Tell you what, Tikov," the captain went on, patting at his face with the sand-colored sweat rag that hung about his neck. "It may be hotter than an overworked whore's fanny out here, but the way things are back home, this is the place to be. We live well, and from time to time we have a little action. Better than freezing your balls off in a pathetic tent full of holes, eh? At least we're proper soldiers doing a soldier's job."

The captain, promoted from the ranks, was, like Tikov, a veteran of Afghanistan. The desert deployment was, to him, a perfect posting. Who wanted to be spat upon by all those ungrateful nations in Europe that had been happy to take soldiers' money during the days of the Soviet Union, to finally end up living in a tent on the return home? It was scandalous.

Tikov fully understood what was going on in the captain's mind. Now that it seemed inevitable that agreement would not be reached on what to do with the armed forces, Tikov was equally certain he knew what would happen next. The forces themselves would eventually take matters into their own hands.

Would the various armies degenerate into fighting each other? he wondered as he looked at the Russian. Or would the fight be among those who had caused the disintegration of the union?

Tikov was quite prepared to take the fight to the politicians, the idiots responsible for the screw-up. But it would mean, in his particular case, fighting with the Russians against Ukrainians, if matters deteriorated to that level. He hoped he would not be forced to choose. He wanted the union reestablished. Equally, he did not relish the idea of killing fellow Ukrainians who thought differently.

Something had to be done soon, or the bloodshed would be horrific. It was best to be away from all that.

"I like being here," he said to the captain.

"So do we all." The captain patted the APC's flank briefly. "Time to go back and report our area's clean. You can be the lead vehicle, if you like."

"Thank you, Captain."

"Nonsense, Anatoly. You and I, we know what soldiering's really about. We've seen the fire." The captain gave the APC another pat. "Whenever you're ready." He returned to his own armored personnel carrier with a parting wave.

7

Hohendorf and Morven set off at daybreak the next morning, heading south for Harwich and the ferry to Hamburg. By 2200 that same night they were asleep in a cabin on the ship after some quiet lovemaking, as it made its way across a mildly choppy North Sea.

While they slept, Kim Mannon was having a far less enjoyable time at Grantly Hall. For her, the day, and the subsequent dinner that had followed in the evening, had been sheer hell. She had played the dutiful daughter, charmed her father's guests, and had even managed to be civil to Reggie Barham-Deane.

Barham-Deane was her father's protégé. Sleek and slightly overweight, he was considered a financial bar-racuda by Sir Julius. When Kim had once pointed out that Barham-Deane looked less like the predatory silver lance of the deep than an overfed goldfish, it had in turn been pointed out to her that Barham-Deane's financial capabilities were indeed predatory.

For all that, every time she looked at him she could never resist the mental picture of a slug trailing slime across a garden. Her father hoped she would eventually marry Barham-Deane and, indeed, was doing all he could to make it so. More as a dare to herself than compliance with her father's wishes, she had actually gone out with him on occasion, using him as a barrier to other hopeful suitors. Unfortunately this had led to his mistaken belief that he had some sort of right to her. Then she had met Mark Selby. The evening of the Mannon Robinson annual bash had not impressed him. Looking obviously bored and wanting to be somewhere else, he had clearly attended under sufferance. Deliberately she had decided to chat him up, only to be greeted with a bluff response. And though she had sensed that he had found her very attractive, she had been intrigued by a man who would not play her game. Instead, showing complete indifference, he had left the ball with his sister, for whom he had acted as escort for the evening. But the very next morning she had tracked him down to the flat he and Morven had borrowed for the weekend in London. Within a short time of her arrival, they had engaged in one of the most frantic bouts of sexual gymnastics she had ever experienced. She had dared, and he had called her intended bluff. Each had been surprised by the result.

Kim now found herself savoring the memory, then tried to put it out of her mind as an involuntary response was suddenly triggered within the lower regions of her body. She kept an interested smile fixed upon her face while someone babbled to her about exchange rates within the coming months. She knew far more about exchange rate fluctuations than the person trying vainly to impress her could have possibly imagined.

That's all I bloody need, she thought. If this dinner doesn't end soon, I'll scream.

Deep within, the frustrated screaming had already begun. What more did her father want? She had done her duty. She had saved the weekend for him. He could handle it from now on. She wanted to leave the table.

But she knew she couldn't and would have to go the distance. So she smiled at her guest, and let her mind roam elsewhere. She just wished her body would not betray her with its excitement at the prospect of meeting up with Mark again.

At least, not at a table full of diners.

Kim smiled as she caught Barham-Deane's gaze upon her once again.

Next morning found Kim with a small suitcase, ready to leave. She'd had an early breakfast on her own and was standing near her car but would not be using it. A short distance away, resting silently on the big H of the helipad, was the company helicopter. Despite Sir Julius Mannon's personal antipathy toward the machine, he did make it available to his guests. The eight-seat Agusta 109 would be taking four of the previous night's diners to Heathrow, and she intended to hitch a ride.

Footsteps crunched on the drive, and she turned to look as her father approached. He was dressed for a long walk about the grounds in warm clothing and sturdy shoes, and he carried a bone-handled stick. He stopped before her and glanced pointedly at the suitcase.

"Eager to be off?" he began. "Where to this time? Paris? Florence? You haven't got much, so it can't be out of Europe."

She looked at him steadily. "I'm catching the helicopter to Heathrow."

"Is your destination a secret?"

"Edinburgh," she said.

Mannon's eyes hardened. "When are you going to stop this nonsense? The man's not right for you!"

Kim did not want a confrontation. "Your guests will be out soon, Father. You wouldn't want them to see us going at it hammer and tongs, would you? Especially after all the good work I put in last night. I deserve this time off, don't you think?"

Mannon seemed to hold his breath, as if trying to control an outburst. "And what about Reggie?" he said at last.

"What about him?"

"He hoped—"

"No, Father, *you* hoped. I'm certain Reggie can find things to do without my being there to hold his hand."

"I could curtail your activities," Mannon warned.

"The only thing you can do is close my account. But even that won't help. I've been using the account Mother left me. I haven't used the one you gave me for over a year now."

Mannon seemed surprised and, strangely, a little hurt.

"So you haven't been checking on the accounts," she said into his silence. "At least that's something."

The arrival of the departing guests ended further conversation. Mannon, the genial host once more, hurried over to escort them to the helicopter. Two of the male staff brought up the rear with luggage.

Kim was about to follow when Barham-Deane came quickly out of the house to join her. She stopped, suitcase in hand.

He eyed the suitcase casually. "Early, and leaving."

"Yes."

"May I ask where? Or is that a military secret? Doesn't need the brain of Britain to work that one out," he continued, noting her mild surprise. "When you're going far, you usually take more substantial luggage. This little bag tells me you're going where you've already got the things you need. So it's got to be Edinburgh."

"We've got other homes."

"None close to where a certain pilot flies. He's not right for you, you know, whatever you might think."

She began to walk purposefully toward the helicopter, where the guests were climbing in. Barham-Deane followed.

"How cozy. Both you and Father singing the same tune." There was a barbed edge to her voice. "Strange as it may seem to such a pair of sages, I can actually think for myself."

"We're only telling you—"

"What's good for me? Oh, do spare me that, Reggie."

"So why is it taking you so long to make up your mind about him? What's holding you back?"

"Nothing's holding me back."

"Of course." Barham-Deane was skepticism itself. He stopped suddenly, forcing her to slow down. "Perhaps he'll solve the problem for us all by running into a passing mountain. They do tend to do that from time to time."

She felt the blood drain from her face as she halted now, and she turned to stare at him. Her eyes had narrowed, but the pupils had so dilated that for a terrible moment there seemed to be only dark sockets where the eyes should be.

Despite himself, the supercilious smile that had appeared upon Barham-Deane's face when he had spoken faltered uncertainly.

"You bastard!" Kim spoke in a low, deliberate voice. "You prize shit." Then she turned her back upon him and walked toward the waiting helicopter. "I'll be back whenever," she said to her father. "You know where I am if you need to reach me." One of the staff took her suitcase and stowed it aboard.

He looked at her silently. In the helicopter, curious eyes were turned upon them.

"But keep Reggie away," she added firmly.

He still said nothing.

She kissed him on the cheek. "Bye, Father." She climbed in and took her seat, looking back at him as she secured the seat belt.

He stepped back to a safe distance, and the pilot started the engines. He watched as the blades began *whupp-whupp*ing up to speed until they disappeared in a blur.

The aircraft lifted off. Mannon remained where he was, a solitary, unmoving figure within the expanse of his grounds. Beyond him, Barham-Deane was walking back to the house.

Then Mannon waved his stick once as the Agusta wheeled, heading for Heathrow.

At the airport, Kim said a polite farewell to the guests and then went on to the domestic flight terminal to take the shuttle to Edinburgh. By 1330 she was at the Princes Street house.

The doorbell rang half an hour later. Kim hurried to open the door. McCann, in casual civilian clothes and looking furtive, stood there.

She smiled a welcome. "Elmer Lee! How nice to see you after so long. Do come in out of the cold." She kissed him near the corner of his mouth.

"This is probably not such a hot idea," he said as he entered.

"Too late now to worry about that. Drink? Or something nonalcoholic? I can make fresh coffee. The real stuff."

"Er . . . coffee will be just fine."

"Come through and take a seat while I get it ready."

McCann followed her to the big lounge, looking about him as he did so, taking in the expensive furnishings, decoration, and pictures that graced the walls. "Some place," he said appreciatively. "You look after this all by yourself?"

"Oh, no. There's a couple who've been taking care of it for as long as I can remember. They live not far from here. But when Father comes up or has business guests, then some staff come as well. But I like being up here on my own. Now do sit down and relax. Wait till we're having coffee before you tell me anything."

"Okay."

During the coffee, he gave her a brief version of the last stages of the fight over the sea, making no mention of the reasons for that particular training mission. As far as she would know, it had been just another routine training flight.

"I'm not kidding here," he added. "We were that close to saying good-bye." He held up a forefinger and thumb with barely a space between the tips.

Kim's heart lurched with each disclosure, her eyes widening with a strange sense of foreboding. She tried not to think of Barham-Deane's taunting, parting shot; but the words seemed to echo on the periphery of McCann's own recounting of the near disaster over the North Sea.

"I thought if I talked to you," McCann was saying, "you might be able to do something for him. You know . . . sort of"—he paused, shrugging—"anything. . . ."

"He may not want to see me."

"You can change his mind. Go to work on him."

"It's been a long time, Elmer Lee."

"Come on, Kim. The guy's nuts about you, even though he tries to pretend he isn't. If he's got a problem, you're just the person he needs right now. I look after him up there. Down here, you take over."

Kim was silent for some moments, then she said: "On the phone, you wondered why I laughed when you said meet you here in Edinburgh. You see, I had already decided to come up before I received your call."

"There you go. You must've known something was wrong."

"I wouldn't put it quite like that. I just felt I wanted to see him again."

"Whatever the reason, you're here. Call him today. He's pulled some extra duty because of what happened, but he'll be free for the evening. He's not confined to base."

"What if he refuses to come?"

McCann smiled at her. "You ever take no for an answer?"

"Not very often. In fact, practically never."

"There you go." McCann stood up. "Got to leave. Er . . . I've got someone waiting at her friend's apartment. . . ." He stopped, looking strangely ill at ease.

She brought her head forward a little as she looked up at him. "Elmer Lee, if I didn't know better, I'd say you were about to blush. Are you?"

"Who me? Never!"

Kim stood up, looking amused. "You should have brought her with you."

"Not exactly the best of moments."

"Given the situation, perhaps you're right. Another time, then."

"Yeah. Well . . . er . . . she's not really a girlfriend. Just a friend . . . sort of."

"Of course."

"We're just checking out the museums and sights. Stuff like that."

"It's all right, Elmer Lee. You don't have to give me explanations."

"Uh, sure. Look. You won't tell Mark about this, will you? I mean, I've got to fly with the guy."

"You have my word."

"Okay."

They began walking to the door. When they had reached it, McCann halted, needing to say more. "He needs you," he said to Kim.

"I know," she told him softly. She again kissed his cheek, then opened the door.

"Bye, Kim. Thanks for the coffee. I'll see you around."

"And you. Take care of yourself, and of him."

"You bet," he said, and went out into the cold, windy afternoon.

She stood at the door to watch as he climbed into his stone gray Corvette, hugging herself against the chill. The powerful V8 engine growled into life, and McCann drove the car slowly down the wide street, the exhausts rumbling as if sending a challenge to the cold sides of the buildings.

She waited until it had turned a corner before quietly closing the door, a thoughtful expression upon her face.

While Kim Mannon was wrestling with the problem of how best to persuade Mark Selby to come to Edinburgh, the *Karelia* was making her way across the top of the world toward her assigned station.

By any standards, the *Karelia* was a very special vessel. As a submarine, she was also most unique. Based upon the design of the monster boats of the former Soviet navy, she was much bigger even than ships of the Typhoon class, which were the biggest in the world. Yet her displacement was, at thirty-three thousand tons, rather less than would have been expected for her gigantic size, and only two thousand tons more than the standard Typhoon.

Part of the reason for this relatively small gain in weight, despite the great increase in size, was the total lack of the Typhoon class submarine's usual warload of twenty huge ballistic missiles—at thirty tons each—and ancillary equipment. These would normally have been carried upright, in parallel lines of ten individual silos in the vast forward section of the vessel. Their omission from the *Karelia*, plus the subsequently enlarged vacated space, gave the submarine its very special role.

The *Karelia* was a double-hulled boat and, at 212 meters long, was nudging 700 feet, while its width of just over 30 meters made it exactly 100 feet across. Powered by twin, massive water-pressurized nuclear reactors, its turbines delivered 150,000 horsepower to two huge multi-bladed propellers. These were mounted within stream-lined rings that neutralized the cavitation caused by the myriad bubbles of air, which would normally have surged hissing from the whirling tips of the blades as they forged through the water. The reduced cavitation so lessened the noise caused by the passage of the vast, submerged body that the vessel's soundprint was far less than that of boats half its size. The *Karelia* could make fifty knots submerged and could outrun any torpedo currently in service.

Since the existence of this particular submarine was a closely guarded secret to all but a relatively small group of people, there was no signature for any potential adversaries to identify it by. Tests had shown that its sound-print was consistently mistaken for that belonging to other subs. It had been repeatedly misidentified by operators, even by those who—for the purpose of the tests—had deliberately been alerted to its presence in a given area. There was thus very little chance of an operator aboard a potentially hostile boat being able to know what he was listening to, should the *Karelia* happen to pass within sensor range.

A special coating of the enormous hull and an outer skin of anechoic tiles also further reduced the noise it made beneath the water. But something else made her special and unique.

The *Karelia* was an aircraft carrier.

Within her cavernous hulls, in the space that would have been filled by missiles, she carried six Yak-142 advanced vertical-and-short-takeoff-and-landing aircraft, their wings folded for ease of storage. Despite the inclusion of full support equipment, maintenance crews, and aircrew necessary for the viable operation of this onboard aviation unit, the weight penalty was still far less at 350 tons than the 800 tons the normal complement of missiles and equipment would have needed in the comparatively smaller Typhoon class boat.

The Yak-142's, updated versions of the world's first supersonic VSTOL aircraft, the Yakovlev-141, were the only ones in existence. Special funding had been supplied to develop them, despite the starvation of finance affecting many other projects. Kurinin and his group had ensured this. Fast and highly agile, the Yaks also possessed a good combat range and were sufficiently versatile to be able to operate as both fighters and strike aircraft.

The *Karelia* as yet had no sister boats, though planning existed for more. She had still to prove her worth, and sending her on station was Kurinin's way of finding out just how effective a weapon she could be. Her sea trials had been completed without the knowledge of the outside world. The time had come to test her potential, as an opportunity was soon expected to present itself. An aircraft carrier that could move fast and could hide beneath the waves was a fearsome military asset.

Berthing for the submarine was the most secure yet devised. The *Karelia*'s lair was deep within a semiartificial peninsula on the shores of the Barents Sea. Developed within an active dockyard for merchant shipping, all of it was undersea and underground. Work had been carried out in such a way that even spy satellites had missed the construction, deliberately fed as they had been with photo opportunities to observe other naval ships being built at different locations.

Entry to the pen was always made submerged and at night. A channel had been dredged and lined with steel and concrete, beneath an existing dock. Its point of entry consisted of two ninety-degree turns, before a five-kilometer-long straight led to the pen itself, a huge underground cavern deep beneath the peninsula. Only then would the *Karelia* surface. Exit for the crew and other personnel was via a pair of three-kilometer-long tunnels that led away from the dockyard and were spacious enough to accommodate vehicular traffic. These ended in a complex of innocuous buildings that gave no outward clue to what lay behind them. The personnel were always in civilian clothes when they left the complex, ostensibly a cluster of commercial warehouses.

Torpedo- and submarineproof double-skinned doors secured the entry channel at strategic points. Though the pen itself possessed one, it was not expected that any hostile submarine would get past even the first of the doors without being totally destroyed. Thrusters enabled the *Karelia* to negotiate the ninety-degree turns with unexpected agility. In the open waters of the world's oceans, she could use them for better maneuverability under combat conditions.

The submarine was currently forging beneath the ice of the Arctic Ocean before she would eventually change course to head south to the warmer waters of her station, nearly eight thousand miles away. Throughout the mission she would make no communication with the outside world, unless in dire emergency. Such an event, in any case, would mean that the mission had itself already been compromised.

Like a great leviathan from prehistoric times, the *Karelia* went on her way, silent and deadly.

Aboard a Los Angeles class hunter/killer submarine of the U.S. Navy, a sensor operator momentarily held his hands against his headphones, as if trying to identify more clearly a faint noise he could hear. Before him were two displays. His hands moved to the buttons that controlled their functions and began to operate them, then he turned briefly to look at an officer standing nearby.

"Got something strange here, Lieutenant," the operator began.

The lieutenant leaned over to study the displays. Nothing showed. "I don't see anything, Tollini."

"On the phones, sir," Tollini said.

The lieutenant picked up a spare set of headphones and put them on. He frowned. "Very faint," he said. "What do you make of it?"

"Small sub, sir. Smaller than an alpha class, but faster. . . ."

"I didn't know they had anything faster than an alpha *and* smaller."

"Neither did I, sir. 'Least not on any recognition chart I've seen. No soundprint comparison."

"Range?"

Tollini made some adjustments to his displays. On one of them the range to the sounds appeared, but this fluctuated constantly.

"We've got some sensor decay, but I can do a little augmentation. We're picking up a lot of other stuff, but I think I can isolate it before it goes out of range . . . There we go, sir. One hundred miles. Oh, hell." The range had blinked out. "Sound's gone, sir."

"Yeah, it's gone off my phones, too. Any ideas?"

"Either it was a fast-moving whale, sir, or the other side has got a hot rod of a little sub out there."

The lieutenant stared at him, not certain whether Tollini, noted for his dry comments, was joking. Tollini, however, was a good sound man. One of the best.

"You being funny, Tollini?" the lieutenant asked.

"No, sir, Lieutenant. It was either a big, fast whale or perhaps a shark no one's ever heard of, or it's a small, very fast sub. Faster than anything we've got, that's for sure. Just look at that calibrated speed. Nearly fifty knots, plus or minus a few knots for error. Hell, that thing can outrun any fish we've got aboard."

"We're not here to fire torpedoes, Tollini."

"No, sir. Suggestion, Lieutenant?"

"Go ahead."

"I know we're doing only passive listening, sir . . . but why don't I try a quick, active sweep?"

"And let everybody know we're here?"

"Not of the target, sir. Of the water, to check the wake profile. If we link that with the temperature changes, the computers can come up with something. Maybe."

"I'll check with the exec. Meanwhile, log the incident. I'll come back to you."

"Sir."

Tollini got permission to sweep the water in the immediate area for the briefest of moments. Water, a highly effective transmission medium for both sound and motion, could retain a wakeprint for long periods and distances, depending on the size and speed of the object concerned. When Tollini at last got his computer images, he showed the lieutenant.

"Something a hell of a lot bigger than a small sub made that, sir. Of course the computer's only giving us an idea of what it *thinks* made it, but the strength of the wake for the distance . . ." Tollini shrugged. "Could be several boats in close formation. . . ." He shrugged once more.

"But what for? Why put a whole group of boats out to sea?"

"Who knows these days, sir? The way things are over there, no one seems to know who's in charge of anything anymore. Kind of dangerous. Maybe they're defecting. You know . . . like those guys who flew their MiG-29's from the Ukraine, or the Iraqis who took their airplanes to Iran during the Gulf War. Perhaps this is the submarine version."

The lieutenant glanced at Tollini suspiciously. "Okay, okay. I've got the message."

Tollini kept a straight face.

"All right," the lieutenant said at last. "Make a report. I'll pass it on to the exec, for the captain. He'll take it from there."

"Yessir."

Autobahn A7, Just Past Neumünster, Germany, 1430 Local Time

Hohendorf drove the Porsche at a steady 160 KPH, heading for Schleswig. There was very little traffic and no sign of the rain that could at times swamp the far north of Germany at this time of the year. There was no ice or snow on the road. Driving conditions were perfect.

"Are you glad to be back?" Morven asked. Once they had cleared Hamburg, they had been lulled into a comfortable silence by the background sounds of the car. Now that the end of their journey was getting closer, she began to feel slightly unsure of herself. How would his old friends react to her? He had once shared a home with his wife up there. That fact made her feel uneasy, despite her having stayed at the family home in Tecklenburg. If anything, memory of her experience when Anne-Marie had unexpectedly turned up at the schloss added to the unease. She hoped Anne-Marie would stay away this time.

"Yes," he replied. "I am."

She knew there was more. "But?"

"I have a new life now. I have shared intense and sometimes frightening experiences with the guys at the base. And I have you. I am a very different person from the one who left here all those months ago. But of course, I am also looking forward to seeing my old *Staffel* colleagues, especially Johann."

"Because he's married to your cousin?"

"That, yes . . . but more because we used to fly together. This is a tie you never forget. My God. Look at that."

They were approaching another car and about to pass.

"What on earth is it?" she asked, turning with a smile to look at the strange vehicle as they went by.

"A Trabi."

"You mean that funny little car we saw in droves all over the telly when people came from the east, during the opening of the border?"

He nodded.

"But it doesn't look like it at all."

The Trabant had been modified with spoilers, large wheels, and expanded wheel arches. The whole had been painted a violent green.

"Somewhere underneath," Hohendorf said, "is the same old, wheezy Trabi. It's a new sport. People buy them cheaply and transform them into play objects." He paused to glance in the mirrors. The Trabant had receded in the distance. "We in western Germany are also trying to transform the eastern part, but . . . there's plenty of work to do underneath. There is a growing antipathy between us," he continued, "and the Ossies—those from the eastern *Länder* . . ."

"Yes. I know who you mean."

"Well, you'll also know it is not what people had expected when the wall came down. Now, many western Germans are not so happy about paying so much to the east, especially as everybody can see how bad it really was over there. It has created bad feelings . . . on both sides. We resent paying, and they resent our resentment.

"It is not going to be easy," Hohendorf went on. "It's like having a twin brother you never knew about. Suddenly, you are united. You may not necessarily like everything you discover about him, some of which might frighten you. But he is of your blood, and you've got to hope that the things you dislike are not to be found in you. Making just the surface pretty is not going to be enough. Have you heard of Martin Niemöller . . . Pastor Niemöller?"

"I'm afraid not," she said.

"No need to sound apologetic. Not many people outside Germany have, except perhaps those with a particular interest in our history. He was well known internationally. He's dead now. In Germany, there are many who would prefer to forget about him."

"Why? Was he . . . someone embarrassing?"

Hohendorf gave a brief, rueful smile. "There are those who would say yes. My father, for example, thinks he was a demagogue and at times a great danger to Germany."

"And you?"

"I think he was a remarkable man; even a contradiction.

A warrior and pacifist, he was honored and reviled, admired and hated . . . sometimes even by the same people. Perhaps I have a soft spot for him because he was navy. He had his own U-boat during the First World War. In the Second, he hated the Nazis but wanted to fight for his country. He didn't in the end, because he spent that time in the camps. I am being very vague about this, but that's the basic story. No matter what people think about him, one thing he said still resonates in my mind."

Hohendorf began to quote:

> "When the Nazis came for the Communists,
> I was silent.
> I was not a Communist.
> When they jailed the Social Democrats,
> I was silent.
> I was not a Social Democrat.
> When they came for the Trade Unionists,
> I did not protest.
> I was not a Trade Unionist.
> And when they came for me,
> There was no one left to protest . . .

"I am translating loosely from the German, but that is the essence of his words. They always send a chill down my spine."

Morven nodded. "I think I understand. 'And therefore never send to know for whom the bell tolls . . .'"

"'It tolls for thee,'" Hohendorf finished. "John Donne. *He* understood, all those centuries ago."

The silence descended upon them once more.

8

Kim Mannon stared at the telephone. "You might as well," she said to herself, and picked it up to dial the unrestricted direct line to the officers' mess at November One.

"Flight Lieutenant Mark Selby, please," she requested when mess exchange had answered. She waited, her entire body in a state of heightened tension, as the connection was made.

"Flight Lieutenant Selby."

The voice, full of military correctness when it came, was still unexpected. She twitched involuntarily in surprise, and for an irresolute moment, found she could say nothing.

"Flight Lieutenant Selby," he repeated. "Hullo?"

"Mark. It's me."

Now it was his turn to be silent. His own surprise was

so profound, she could almost feel it coming down the phone line.

"Kim."

There was a whole mixture of emotions in that single utterance, and not all of them were loving. She could sense his reserve. She'd hoped for a little more warmth; but all things considered, perhaps she'd been expecting too much.

"Where are you calling from?"

"Edinburgh."

"Oh."

"Just 'oh'?" She had regained her equilibrium and was not going to give up without a fight. "I've come all the way up here to see you and all you can say is 'oh'?"

"Are you in Princes Street?"

"Yes."

"If I remember, the last time we were there was not an entirely auspicious—"

"I'm not going to talk on the phone about how I feel and how I've been. Speaking of which . . . wouldn't you like to know how I've been, where I've been, and what I've done since we last saw each other?"

"Well . . ."

"I'm all by myself up here, and I'm cooking dinner. I'll never forgive you if you ruin it by not coming. I hope you're off duty tonight."

"Well, yes, I am, but—"

"Great. I'll see you at nine-thirty. You're staying the night, so you'd better be off duty tomorrow as well. And get your skates on. If you leave now, you should make it in plenty of time."

"Now just a minute—"

"If you don't, I'll come and park myself outside the main gate. I've already booked a car from the company that supplies us when we're up here," she continued, lying, "so it's going to be a long drive in the dark for me. . . ."

"That's blackmail."

"Really?" she said, and hung up. "I think I handled that rather well," she congratulated herself as she hurried to the kitchen and began hunting frantically through the cupboards, praying the housekeeper had stocked up with food.

She checked the freezers and the fridge. In the end, she heaved a sigh of relief. She need not have worried. Stocks were always kept up; but it was always prudent to make sure. She got out a small apron, tied it firmly about her small waist, and started raiding the fridge.

"You'd better turn up, Mark Selby," she said warningly.

Despite himself, less than twenty minutes later Selby drove his pale blue, four-wheel-drive Ford Sapphire Cosworth along the access road away from November One. A thin rain was falling, coating the early darkness and sparkling in the bright glare of the headlights. There was the barest sheen on the road surface, but this held no terrors for him. The car, surefooted even in far worse conditions, could easily handle the fast drive across country to Edinburgh.

A multiple roar traversed the air above his head as he turned off the access and onto the main road. Two ASVs off on night training, he decided. Zero Two squadron was scheduled for night exercises to bring the newer pilots up to speed.

As Selby accelerated into the night, he was the unknowing focus of attention from a pair of infrared binoculars. His unseen watcher had been studying the access road traffic for quite some time.

*　　　*　　　*

The MD500 Defender helicopter was making a routine security sweep of the area around the November base. It moved slowly, sensors scanning the ground. It was fully equipped with advanced avionics and a powerful Nightsun searchlight attached beneath its nose. The MD500 was also armed with a six-barreled, rotary Minigun of 7.62-mm caliber and a 40-mm grenade launcher. As part of the airfield defense system, its primary intended use was against heavily armed, infiltrating specialist troops.

In the current international climate, however, its routine duty was to patrol the base environs for intruders. Its crew were under the strictest of orders not to use weapons unless fired upon. No such incident had occurred since November One had become operational. There were six such aircraft on November strength, and from time to time they had picked up nothing more sinister than enthusiastic plane spotters, overzealous journalists, and the odd protester trying to climb the perimeter fence. On this night they were due for a little excitement.

In the left-hand seat, the gunner/weapons operator was staring at his infrared display. "Shit," he said. "I've got a target."

"What?" the pilot demanded. "What target?"

"Three three zero. Man on the ground by those ruins, in the firing position. I'm magnifying. Range . . . two miles."

"Is he aiming at us?"

"No. He's pointed toward the airfield. . . ."

"Are you certain he's got a weapon? We don't want to blow away anyone unless he's popping off at us. Think of the stink we'd cause if we took out some poor innocent. So be very careful with that shiny new gun and that grenade launcher, won't you? The press would have a field day, and I don't think the powers-that-be would like us very much after that, either."

The gunner, a sergeant, was more hard-nosed. "Nobody lying out here like this in the rain and the dark, freezing his balls off, is an innocent . . . Ah, shit! He's heard us. He's moving. Let's go!"

"Roger. Powering up." The pilot then spoke to November Ops Control. "Sentry Omega to November Ops."

"Go ahead, Omega."

"We have a contact and are in pursuit."

"Roger, Omega. You have contact and are in pursuit. We're alerting a team."

"Roger. Omega out."

The helicopter gathered speed quickly as its nose canted down, heading for the castle ruins. The searchlight was not turned on.

"What the bloody," the gunner began in astonishment. He had the display on full magnification. Clearly shown was the ghostly infrared image of the man, artificially given a reddened highlight by the computers on the otherwise monochrome unit. The man was standing now, looking upward and in the direction of where he thought the sound was coming from. The shape of his face was clearly visible, as if on a rouged negative. The object in his hands was quite easily identified. Calmly, he'd raised it to his eyes.

"What? What is it?" the pilot demanded.

"The bastard's not got a weapon at all. He's pointing binoculars at us, for Pete's sake!"

"Cool customer. If he really can see us, those are not ordinary binocs."

"Not much of an innocent, then," the gunner remarked with satisfaction, pleased to have read the situation correctly. "What kind of innocent would have been out here with infrared glasses stuck to his face?"

"Not the kind we should let get away."

"Don't worry. I've got the bastard well framed. I'm going to put some light on the proceedings."

"Do it."

The gunner switched on the Nightsun. The darkness seemed to flee as the searchlight bathed the ruins in a stark luminance that gave an unnerving impression of being more daylight than daylight itself.

"Fuck!" the gunner said. "Fuck!"

"Am I going to hear more than your wishful thinking?" the pilot queried mildly.

"That bastard's gone!" The gunner sounded both chagrined and furious.

The pilot said nothing. The helicopter was now above the ruins, at the hover.

"There's nowhere for him to go," the gunner insisted.

Just beyond the ruins was a disused quarry. There were plenty of hiding places.

"He must be down there, in the quarry. I'll call for the defense guys to do a search while we wait up here. November put one on alert after our last call." The area defense troops were November's special forces.

"They'd better find the bastard."

But they didn't. A thorough search of the area about the ruins, even with dogs, failed to find the man with the binoculars. Had the gunner not recorded the incident on infrared film, Omega's crew would have found it difficult to prove the man had actually been there.

Poleskov had come well prepared.

As soon as he'd heard the helicopter and had verified its intentions, he had raced to the shallow trench he had dug on the edge of the quarry. Though the helicopter had prowled around with that searchlight turning everywhere it touched into a sunrise, the trench had remained undiscovered, secluded as it was beneath slabs of discarded stone. There had been plenty of time to pull the dirt over him before the searching troops had arrived.

He breathed through a small tube, carefully hidden beneath an apparently haphazard spread of soggy earth. Its outlet was virtually invisible among other chunks of stone, some distance from where he lay. Once, he'd had a close call when one of the more enterprising dogs had sniffed at the tube, although it had been unable to reach it. The mouth of the tube had itself been coated with a neutralizing gel that had repelled the dog.

Poleskov felt the tread of boots all around him, but his hiding place remained secure.

It was to be a good two hours after the last footfall before he'd decide to move.

Blissfully oblivious of the excitement at November One, Mark Selby made it to Princes Street a good eighteen minutes early. He had driven fast across country, along roads that had been deserted save for a lone vehicle every so often.

He climbed out slowly, locked the car with his overnight kit still behind his seat, and paused to look at the house. Almost immediately the door opened, and silhouetted against the light from within was a barefoot Kim with the shortest of dresses on. The material of the dress, though not transparent, seemed as thin as gossamer and looked horrendously expensive.

"So you're here," she said in greeting.

"I'm here."

She made a great show of looking from one of his hands to the other. "Brought your invisible stuff, I see."

He cleared his throat, buying time. He'd almost forgotten how frighteningly attractive she was in the flesh. Against the light her silhouette, in that wafer-thin dress, teased at him.

"Still in the car," he said awkwardly.

"Hedging your bets? Are you going to get it, or are we going to stand here all night and freeze?" The wind had dropped during the afternoon, but it still blew with sufficient strength to create a marked chill.

He'd only just arrived, and already she was winning. I'm soft in the bloody head, he thought. But he unlocked the car to get his kit and shut it once more.

"It's okay to come in," she said. "I won't bite."

He could almost hear the unspoken "yet" as he climbed the short flight of steps, feeling slightly annoyed for allowing himself to be wrong-footed so early in the game.

"Thank God for that," she said with relief, shutting the door. "Brrr! My toes were beginning to lose all feeling."

It was a wonder her body was not already in the advanced stages of frostbite, he thought. A dress like that.

She was standing very close, looking up at him, her eyes wide with anticipation. "It's good to see you," she added softly.

Backed against a wall near the door, he heard himself say: "Good to see you, too." There was a very faint smell of something delicious being cooked, mixed with the smell of her. And that starved piece of red-and-black cloth that passed for a dress seemed to move sensuously over her body, as if making love to it.

Dear God. Barely inside the house and already he was desiring her.

"I'm glad you came."

"Are you?" He was certain she had moved closer, though she had not appeared to have done so.

But she must have because her body, in the thin dress,

was warm against his. She might as well have been naked.

"Can't you tell?" Her voice had become perceptibly husky, and her eyes seemed about to engulf him.

His own body was betraying him.

"And *I* can tell you're glad," she went on with a distinct note of triumph. She kissed him fully on the lips, arms going about his neck, body pressing hard.

After some halfhearted resistance, Selby dropped his bag to the floor and put his own arms about her, squeezing her to him, putting all his months of longing for her, all his fears and frustrations, into the embrace.

It was a good minute before they paused to look at each other, eyes slightly wild, breath coming in short gasps. They still held on to each other tightly, their bodies seemingly glued together.

"My God," she said in a low, throat-tight voice. "I must have been mad to let you convince me to stay away."

"Not me. Your father convinced you. I reacted to his attitude. He's never going to give up. You might as well accept it. He's determined you should marry someone *he* thinks is right for you. I can remember his telling me how much he admired fighter pilots while at the same time making the point about how unsuitable I was for you. A man who can praise and insult in the same breath."

"I don't want to talk about him. Not tonight."

"I agree." A hand stroked her on the cheek. "You've got me hooked," he said. "And you know it." The hand shifted position to stroke the delightful curve of her back.

She rubbed her body against his. "I'm . . . I'm hooked, too. So we're . . . we're . . . aaah . . . that's nice . . . we're both in the same boat." She shifted some more, feeling the excitement in him.

The hand moved farther down her back, paused on the

accentuated curve of a buttock. There was no subtle ridge beneath the smooth feel of the dress.

"That's right," she said. "I haven't got one on. Took it off when I saw you arrive."

"Hussy," he said.

"Yep. Now you'd better let me go, or our dinner will be ruined."

"To hell with dinner. Let's—"

"Oh, no. I've worked hard on this, and we're going to do it justice. Now go upstairs to our room . . . I'm sure you haven't forgotten . . . dump your bag, freshen up if you want to, then go into the drawing room and help yourself to a drink. And the kitchen's out of bounds." She prised his arms away and wriggled out of his embrace.

"Any more orders?"

"That's enough for now." She kissed him quickly and hurried off before he could detain her farther.

At November One, Jason was in briefing room alpha studying the infrared film taken by the helicopter crew. Morton and Macallister were with him.

As soon as Sentry Omega's call had come through, Jason had been alerted in his quarters. He had then ordered the two Americans, who had returned earlier from a short trip to one of the coastal villages, to the briefing room.

The brief length of film had already been run three times and was now coming to the end of its fourth.

"Any ideas, Major?" Jason asked as the lights came up.

Morton shook his head. "None, sir. That man may not be connected to the Pale Flyer mission at all. This is a special unit. There'll always be interest in what goes on."

"Granted. On the other hand, we'd be wise to assume he is hostile, until we're absolutely certain he isn't. It does not help that he got away. He is skilled in evasion techniques. That makes him rather more than an ordinary snooper. Copies of the film will be made. The AVM, and General Bowmaker, will want to check it out with some people. Sergeant Macallister."

"Sir?"

"Can you do your enhancing magic with the shot of the face with the binoculars? There's only the briefest of moments on film before he puts them to his eyes, almost as if he *knew* he was being scanned. The real close-up is with the binoculars in place. I'd like an enhancement with the glasses removed. We might get an idea of the face then. Can you manage it?"

"I'll scan the shot into the computer," she said, "then go to work on it. After I've got a face, I can get the computer to give it proper flesh tones. That should give us something, sir."

"Magic," Jason said. "I'm afraid I must ask you to have a go right away. It could be a long night."

She smiled at him. "What's a long night?"

"That's the spirit. Thank you, Sergeant."

"No problem, sir."

Princes Street, Edinburgh

"It's ready!" Kim Mannon called.

Selby stood up, carrying the drink he had nursed for the last half hour. She had left him to himself while she'd hustled away to prepare the meal. All offers of help had been firmly rejected.

He now made for the dining room and paused in the doorway to stare. The lights had been dimmed, and a pair of silver candlesticks holding two lighted candles each were on the table. Two chairs had been placed on either side, opposite each other. In the middle of the table was a large dish, and resting upon it was the biggest salmon Selby had seen for a long time. Placed about this central piece were various side dishes that she had prepared. A bottle of Chablis Grand Cru, already opened, was waiting in a chiller. The wine came from the Mannon stock, specially imported for years from the same, minute vineyard.

He was glad he had decided to come. She had indeed worked very hard, and it would have been terrible if he had stayed away. She would never have forgiven him.

She came up to him, looking strangely shy. "See? The little rich girl can actually cook. I've decided to cut out the first course. Not enough time."

"I couldn't have handled a first course. The size of that salmon. I don't know what to say. Where . . ."

She put a finger to his lips. "Shhh! Don't say anything. I hope you'll like it," she added, a little anxiously, he thought.

"I'll love it," he assured her, and kissed the soft lips gently. "Thank you for going to all this trouble. It's marvelous." He held out her chair, and when she had sat down he picked up the wine to fill their glasses. He then took his seat and held up his glass. "What shall we toast?"

Her eyes were dark pools in the candlelight. "A long and happy life," she said.

And Selby found himself thinking how close his own had come to being cut short—McCann's, too—because of his own stupidity about Hohendorf. Yet despite knowing this . . .

"A long and happy life," he said.

The dark pools gazed at him.

A second bottle of wine later and the salmon reduced to its bones, they stared at each other with satisfied smiles.

"I don't believe we've polished off that fish," he said.

"No one else around," she said, waving a slightly uncontrolled hand. "Must be us."

"You're drunk."

"Me? Never. You're the one who's drunk."

"And I'd forgotten how much you can eat. Where do you put it all?"

She waggled a finger at him. "Mustn't ask such questions, but I'll show where the energy goes to . . . later." She got up, slightly unsteadily. "Coffee should be about ready."

Selby stood up. "Here. Let me."

"No. You sit down. I'm in control of this seduction."

He feigned shock. "Is that what this is all about? Seduction?"

"Of course. Why should it always be the man who seduces the woman with a candlelit dinner?"

"It's always like that on the television," he said, gazing at her with some amusement.

"Television," she scoffed, and walked with a slight stagger toward the kitchen. "It's all right," she continued, raising a hand briefly as she went. "I'm not going to pour it all over me. So stay right where you are."

She was as good as her word and came back with a laden tray. He still thought she looked unsteady but allowed her to do as she wished. She poured the coffee into fine bone china cups, then sat down.

As he sipped the hot coffee, Selby said, "Kim, that was a fantastic dinner."

The dark eyes studied him carefully, with more control than would have been expected of someone who was drunk. Four points of candlelight were reflected within them.

"I am worth something, after all."

"You're worth . . . everything."

"You'd better mean what you say," she said in a suddenly quiet voice. Her eyes held him fast.

"I do mean it." Abruptly he gave a sheepish smile and took something out of a pocket. It was a tiny expanse of red silk. "I carry this with me every time I fly."

She stared at the cloth. "My knickers! You've been carrying them all these months?"

He nodded. "And don't you ever let Elmer Lee know. I'd never live it down. It would be all over the station before you could say McCann."

She giggled. "Who would have thought it? Imagine what my father would say if he knew." The giggle suddenly degenerated into an unbridled cackle. "And I can just see Reggie's face!" She laughed even louder, unrestrained and ribald, until tears began to course down her cheeks. After a while the laughter subsided. She wiped at her eyes, suppressing the giggles that threatened to erupt once more.

"I didn't think you'd find it so funny," Selby remarked, uncertain of how to react to this display.

She left her chair to come over to him. "Oh, darling," she said, leaning over to kiss him gently. "I'm not laughing at you, but at those two joyless people . . . though to be fair, in Father's case . . . now I'm breaking my own rule. We're not talking about him tonight," she stated firmly. "And," she went on, "I think carrying my knickers up there with you is wonderful. It's . . . very romantic. Not like your outward self at all. I'm glad you've let me in on the secret, and I feel a lot better knowing you were thinking of me even when we weren't seeing each other. Now move your chair, Mr. Fighter Pilot, sir. I want to sit on you."

He eased the chair away from the table. She moved round, opened her legs, and sat down, straddling him. He felt the heat of her, burning at him. She hadn't bothered to put her knickers on.

She maneuvered herself even closer, understanding the look in his eyes. "No point putting something on that's soon going to be removed," she murmured as her arms went about his neck and she kissed him. "It's wastes valuable hmm-hmm time."

"And what's hmm-hmm time?"

"If you have to ask, no point telling you." She kissed him even more thoroughly.

"We'll . . . we'll topple over," he said against the soft, mobile lips. "This chair . . ."

"I'm relying on you to make sure we don't." She had begun to make soft noises within the far depths of her throat. Her body squirmed sinuously. "Your jeans," she said, pausing briefly.

"What about them?"

"They're in the way. I can tell you think so, too." She raised herself off him, to work at his belt.

His hands stroked her body beneath the dress as he watched her attack the zipper of his jeans with some urgency. Then, when she had pulled it down, he moved his hands away just long enough to slip the jeans and underpants to his ankles.

"Ooh," she whispered eagerly, glancing down. "Oh, yes."

Slowly she lowered herself upon him, the glowing dark of her eyes holding him in their gaze as she descended. Then they shut for the briefest of moments as her mouth opened slightly, and a barely audible gasp came out of her.

He felt the heat of her gradually enveloping him as she continued her descent, until it appeared she could go no farther. Her body stretched and arched against him as it swayed and writhed and plunged.

In a sudden motion she moved her arms from about his neck, grabbed at her dress, and pulled it off, throwing it to one side.

"It was in the way," she said, placing her arms about his neck once more.

Then she was moving again. This time she brought her hands down to grip each side of the chair, using it as a lever to impale herself upon him as her writhings grew in intensity.

The noises in her throat were escaping now. The cords on her neck stood out. Her eyes had closed, and a thin film of moisture cloaked her entire body.

Selby felt himself being swept along by the force of his own passion, and his hands gripped at her, pulling her down. Her movements had now become so vigorous, it seemed as if she would indeed topple them to the floor. But he was past caring now. His whole body had been taken over by an increasing tremor. Kim was bouncing up and down, gasping squeals coming out of her partially opened mouth, her breath panting tremulously with mounting urgency.

Then she gave a long, quavering shriek as her arms pulled at the sides of the chair, as if trying to pin herself even farther down upon him. Her muscles clutched at him even as his lower body lurched at her in great spasms, his arms tightening about her waist, gripping until it seemed they would pass right through her. They remained thus, straining against each other, for long glorious moments, almost teetering off the chair, until at last their bodies relaxed.

She collapsed against him with a long sigh, her damp head falling upon his shoulder, her arms wrapped loosely about his shoulders. His open shirt, the only remaining garment from his ankles up, was soaked and hung wetly upon him.

"We didn't topple," she said weakly. "Did . . . did we?"

"No. We didn't."

Then she was moving against him once more and sensing a response.

"Umm," she said. "More. Oh, yes! I like that."

*   *   *

Monday, 0105 Hours, November One

Macallister was alone in briefing room alpha, working at
the face on the infrared film. She had successfully
scanned the shot into the the computer, eliminated the
binoculars, and was now about to put definition on the
grid-patterned, wire-frame head that appeared on the
monitor. As yet, she had not given it eyes. The head
rotated slowly.

After she had viewed the image for some moments, she
halted the rotation and continued with her task.

The four borders of the screen were full of paint and
construction icons, and she used what looked like a com-
bined mouse and lightpen to touch various icons as she
worked. Each icon produced either a shade of color or an
alteration to the shape and features of the head.

An hour later she had the makings of flesh tones, but
the head did not as yet look natural. There were eyes
now, but they were closed. She continued to work.
Another thirty minutes, and she had finished. She tapped
a command on the computer keyboard. The eyes suddenly opened and seemed to stare directly at her.

She could not restrain a gasp of surprise.

"And well you might," a voice said.

She turned quickly to look at Jason as he came up to
her. "Quite remarkable," he said, staring at the head. "Is
this how he really looks?"

"Next to seeing him in person . . . yes, sir. We can make
it into a photograph, if that will help you more."

"It most certainly will. Sergeant Macallister, you're a
genius. I think I'll poach you from General Bowmaker."

Macallister looked pleased. "Thank you, sir. It would be
interesting to work here permanently."

"I'll see what can be done when this is all over. Have you had anything to eat or drink?"

She waited for the sound of aircraft passing overhead to subside. "I've had a few snacks, sir, while I've been working. Major Morton's gotten me some stuff. I'm okay."

"Fine. Secure everything, then close down for the night. Get some rest. We'll need the photographs in the morning."

"Yessir." More aircraft passed overhead. She glanced up at the sounds.

"November never sleeps," Jason explained. "You get used to it."

"Oh, I've been in some real noisy places, sir. I'm already used to it. I'll sleep like a log."

Jason stared at the face of the intruder once more. "Quite, quite remarkable. Has Major Morton seen it?"

"No, sir. You're the first, after me."

At that moment Morton entered.

"Ah, Major," Jason began. "See what your sergeant has done."

Morton came to look. He stared in silence for long moments. "This is really something," he said at last. "Mac, you're one hell of a genius."

"That's what the wing commander said." She did not say it smugly.

"You're right there, sir," Morton said to his superior. He leaned forward to inspect the head more closely. "That really the guy, Mac?"

"As near as possible, Major."

Morton straightened. "What now, sir?" he asked Jason. "What's the next move?"

"As I've said to Sergeant Mac, we'll need photographs in the morning. Then we'll see. All right, you two. Very good work. See you in the morning. Major . . . Sergeant. I'll say good night."

"Night, sir," they said together as Jason went out.

* * *

Edinburgh, 0310 hours

In the Princes Street house, Selby was sleeping deeply on his side with Kim lying partially across his back, her arm hooked beneath his armpit and across his chest.

Then his body twitched briefly. Moments later it twitched again, this time severely enough to awaken Kim. She drew her arm away carefully and sat up in bed in the darkened room, to study him. The twitching increased, and he began to mumble, his voice rising and lowering in pitch intermittently.

Suddenly he was shouting, *"Pull up! Pull up,* for God's sake! You're going in!"

Just as suddenly, he was quiet again, and his body once more relaxed into undisturbed sleep.

Kim remained sitting, studying the shape in the bed, her knees drawn up, arms clasped about them. Thanks to Elmer Lee, she had some idea of the terror that had come to them out there, over the North Sea. She moved a cautious hand, to touch him gently on the shoulder. Her touch did not wake him. She clasped her knees once more and kept her eyes on the quietly sleeping shape. She had understood. She'd understood only too clearly the shout from Mark's dream.

It was what he must have been screaming in his mind when he had realized he was staring into the face of disaster.

9

Kurinin was already in his office while Selby was doing battle with his nightmares. He had chosen to come in early, wanting to have to himself the two hours before his aide and the remainder of the day staff came in. There was a sealed message on his desk, left by the night staff, who were collating countless items of information that had been picked up from around the globe during the hours of darkness. He looked at the sealed item thoughtfully, then began to open it.

The brief message had come from Poleskov. So far there were apparently no indications that the November units were preparing for anything special. He had also not yet been able to locate his target.

Kurinin fed the message into the small shredder attached to one side of his desk. He was tempted to send a backup to Scotland, to put some speed into Poleskov, but decided against it for the time being. Poleskov preferred to work alone; but one day the entrepreneurial assassin would have to understand he couldn't always have it as he wished.

Kurinin decided he would wait a while longer, to see how matters developed. He would, however, keep his options open about the backup.

There was the usual small collection of Western newspapers and journals on the desk. These were weekend issues. He picked one up at random and studied it, turning the pages with leisurely interest. He smiled, more with satisfaction than with humor, as he read.

Britain was having more problems with its regions. Now Wales seemed to be wanting its own form of independence. The more the merrier. Another article went on at length about the withdrawal of the UN weapon destruction team from Iraq, in protest against that country's refusal to comply with UN resolutions. It was the considered opinion of the correspondent that it was only a matter of time before combat was resumed there, as continuing obstruction of the teams would become a matter of deliberate routine. Only a new and perhaps ferocious trial by combat would settle the entire affair once and for all.

"I agree with you, my friend," Kurinin said to the paper as he folded it and replaced it on the pile. "Such a development was obvious."

Anyone who had cared to read the signs would have come to the same conclusion months before. All the necessary ingredients had been there on the day the war was officially halted. This current situation now made the value of the radar unit out there in the African desert even greater.

The new union that would eventually grow out of the ashes of the old would not be hidebound by the ideology of dinosaurs. Lost territory would be reclaimed, former partners would rejoin the fold—since being out would be infinitely worse—and this time a lean and powerful system would be in place.

In such an environment, stealth-defeating radar would be not only of prime defense importance, but a high-value asset. Its export version—necessarily devoid of the most sensitive items of equipment, but still deadly—would be for sale to approved customers, an asset whose time had come and whose foreign revenues would be extraordinarily bountiful.

Already he could think of many potential clients.

At 0615 hours Schleswig time, Hohendorf opened his eyes slowly to look at Morven's sleeping face. Her relaxed breathing fanned him softly. She was so close, he barely needed to move to kiss the tip of her nose.

Her eyes opened sleepily, and she moved away slightly, trying to focus upon him in the gloom. "What are you doing awake?" she asked, her voice drowsy. "It's still dark."

"No, it's not. Anyway, I must get up. It is time to get ready. I have a simulator test today. I shall be leaving with Johann, but I shall be back by lunchtime. Will you be all right?"

She nodded. "I should be angry with you."

"You should?"

"Yes. I thought we were coming for a holiday."

He put an arm about her. "We will have a little holiday. . . ."

"But you've got work to do as well."

He paused, not knowing precisely what to say to her.

She put him out of his difficulties by kissing him lightly on the lips. "Don't worry. I'll be all right. Erika's determined not to let me get bored. I like her."

"I feel terrible," he said contritely. "Perhaps I shouldn't have asked you to come. . . ."

"Of course you should have. I want to be with you, and besides . . ." Her body moved beneath the duvet. "I've been enjoying the trip. The question is, will you have enough strength for the simulator—" There was a sudden and sharp intake of breath. "Oh, wow! You didn't let me finish. . . ." Her voice faded into a long sigh of pleasure.

"Does that answer you?"

"Oh, yes," she murmured.

Forty minutes later, Hohendorf in his Marineflieger uniform—deliberately without the November One shoulder patch—stood before her. Morven propped herself up in bed to look at him.

"Very smart," she said. "All the girls love a sailor."

He leaned over to kiss her. "A flying sailor," he corrected. "Umm. You smell very nice."

"I smell of bed and—"

"That's what I mean."

She pushed him gently away. "Off you go flying, sailor . . . and don't crash the simulator."

"That," he said, "would be very embarrassing."

He gave her a parting smile and went out to meet Ecker, who was already waiting, having also left Erika in bed. They made themselves a very light and quick breakfast and within minutes were climbing into the Porsche to head for the base. They placed their caps behind their seats.

"She's a very nice girl, Axel," Ecker said in German as they drove. "You are very lucky."

"I know."

"And Anne-Marie has seen her?"

"Unfortunately, yes."

"Ah." The small word spoke volumes.

"She came to the schloss unexpectedly while we were there."

"I would have liked to see that."

"No, you wouldn't."

"That bad, was it?"

"Terrible."

They fell silent as the car turned into the road that led to one of the entry gates to the base. They put their caps on as they approached it.

"How does it feel, coming back . . . even though it's for a short while?"

"Like a new boy."

"But a very special new boy. We know you've been in combat."

Hohendorf glanced at him but said nothing.

"Come on, Axel," Ecker said. "News like that gets around the circuit. Details are sketchy, but that's only to be expected. But the grapevine knows that the unit you've joined is doing some very special jobs."

"And now you're going to be part of it, Johann."

"Only for this one mission."

"Yes. I don't think the Seeadler would like you to be with us permanently."

The Seeadler, Hohendorf's former boss, Korvetten-kapitän Hans Wusterhausen, would certainly not agree to a permanent posting to November One for Ecker.

"God knows how my new boss persuaded him to give you up, even for this one," Hohendorf continued. "What pressure did he use, I wonder?"

"No pressure," Ecker replied. "Just friends in high places."

"You mean it was an *order?*"

"Nothing so blunt. More like heavy persuasion."

"It certainly worked. It will be good to do the low-level stuff with you again, Johann," Hohendorf added.

"And here I was, thinking I had enough gray hairs to last a lifetime." Ecker touched his fingers to his jet black hair.

They looked at each other and laughed as they reached the gate. They showed their passes and were saluted by the armed guard, and then Hohendorf drove the Porsche through.

The November Base, 0800 Local Time

Jason was in the briefing room, where Mac was already at the computer, looking as fresh as if she'd had a full night's sleep. Morton stood to one side. The image of the intruder's head was on screen.

"All right, Sergeant," Jason began. "Send it down the line."

"Yes, sir."

She tapped a key, and via a scrambler-protected modem the image was transmitted to another computer in the air vice-marshal's office in Whitehall. Half an hour later Jason got a call from Thurson.

"We're on our way," was all the AVM said, giving no clue to the identity of his traveling companion or companions.

At 1035, the BAe HS 125 CC military executive jet came in to land. Fifteen minutes later Thurson, accompanied by an immaculately attired Charles Buntline, was shown into the briefing room by the wing commander.

"Mr. Buntline," Thurson began by way of introduction. "Major Morton, USAF . . . Sergeant Macallister, U.S. Marines."

Buntline nodded at Mac and Morton as he went straight to the computer. Mac had brought the imaged head back on screen.

Buntline stared at the image for long seconds while everyone else waited for his reaction. "Very good work, Sergeant," he finally said. "Now I want every copy you've done, including photographs, and then delete this entire file."

Mac turned to stare at him, her eyes unwavering.

"You've got to be kidding." She turned to Morton. "Major?"

Buntline's face had begun to stiffen.

Jason said quickly: "Er . . . Sergeant, you may look upon Mr. Buntline as an officer of Air rank. In your terms, a general."

Mac looked determined. "With respect, sir. General Bowmaker . . ."

"Is not here," the air vice-marshal put in quickly. "I'll handle this," he continued to Jason. "Sergeant Macallister," he went on, "I appreciate your adherence to procedure, but in the absence of General Bowmaker, I have command over both yourself and Major Morton, as long as you're involved with the November program. In *my* absence, the chain of command of this unit takes precedence. General Bowmaker must have advised you both of this."

"Yes, sir," Mac acknowledged. She pointed to the screen. "This is a different ball game, though, isn't it, sir? This man might have something to do with the desert radar unit. . . ."

"That is what we're going to find out. Mr. Buntline's avenue of work, so to speak."

Mac favored Buntline with a neutral stare. "So I do what the . . . General says?"

"I'm not a general, Sergeant," Buntline said in a voice several degrees cooler. "But I do carry the same weight. You may address me in the civilian manner."

"Yes, Mr. Buntline." Mac stared at him just long enough to avoid being considered insolent, then turned back to the computer. "File being deleted." The image disappeared, and a caption appeared upon the otherwise blank screen.

FILE DELETED, it announced.

Mac pointed to a tray. It held a large brown envelope. "All existing printouts and photos are in there. I cannot account for the one we sent down the line to the air vice-marshal." Her voice held no warmth.

"Let me worry about that," Buntline said. He picked up the envelope. "Thank you, Sergeant." He turned away from her and walked out of the briefing room, followed by Thurson.

Wing Commander Jason paused just long enough to give her a neutral glance before he, too, left the room.

Morton looked at her. "One of these days, Mac . . ."

"That man was a rude, goddamned son of a bitch."

"Yeah, he was. But you don't let him know it. The guy's equivalent to a *British* general, for crying out loud. You don't mess around with him, Mac . . . even if you are a marine."

She smiled tightly. "I can take orders like anyone else, so long as it's not dumb. This was dumb . . . and rude."

Morton sighed. "You don't choose the orders you like. Since when was being in the military a democratic pastime? You've heard the air vice-marshal. Buntline's a spook. He's got ways to handle this thing, and we don't want to know about it. I used to fly F-16's for a living. That's what I want to do again. This spook stuff's not for me. We leave Buntline to do his business. Anyway, he's bound to have connections with *our* spooks."

"Well, he didn't get it all his own way."

Morton stared at her. "What do you mean?"

She tapped swiftly at the computer. The head was back.

"Jesus, Mac. I saw you delete that thing."

"You thought you did, Major. So did everyone else. I hid it. I compressed it and logged it into high memory. Let's call it a secret compartment."

"But the computer acknowledged the deletion."

"Sure. From the previous file."

"Mac, you're going to get us into trouble. Correction.

You're going to get *my* ass reamed. This assignment's my ticket back to flying. Don't do this to me."

"Don't worry, Chuck," she said soothingly. "You'll get your F-16 again, or perhaps something even better. Who knows? And as for this"—she pointed at the head on the screen—"I want to show it to General Bowmaker personally." She tapped once more at the keyboard, and again the FILE DELETED caption showed on the newly blanked-out screen. "See if you can get it back."

"Hey, you're the computer whiz kid around here."

She tapped the keys. A long list appeared on screen. "I've given you some help," she said. "That's the file directory. Now find the head. Its file is titled IRMAN . . . infrared man." She moved from her seat to make way for him.

Reluctantly Morton sat down. "I'm no good at this."

"Good enough. Try."

Ten attempts later Morton accepted defeat. The computer kept beeping at him with the same message: ERROR—FILE NOT FOUND. DELETED.

He stood up. "Looks like you did a good job hiding it. But the general might not thank you for bucking our British allies, especially on this base. Besides, he likes the wing commander."

"I know. But did you notice? The wing commander didn't look like he enjoyed having Buntline stomp all over us."

"So what's the new file?"

"Better if you didn't know, Major."

"Mac," Morton began warningly. "I am your superior officer."

"You wouldn't have known if I hadn't told you," she pointed out.

Morton decided to leave it. "Well," he began, a note of caution in his voice, "just remember that when a sergeant

comes up against a general, it's no contest . . . even if you
have slugged a senior officer before."

"He can always bust me to private, I guess," Mac
retorted.

In the room where Thurson had previously talked with
Bowmaker, Buntline was explaining his actions.

"So, Wing Commander," he was saying to Jason, "you
consider my behavior high-handed."

Jason frowned. "I did not say—"

"You might not have said it, but your expression was
quite eloquent. As I've already outlined to the air vice-
marshal," Buntline went on before Jason could make comment, "my . . . er . . . people have got observers on the
ground in your general area. Ever since that affair over the
Mediterranean—which has given me good cause to appreciate the prowess of your men, since their actions undoubt-
edly saved our lives—I have had people on the lookout for
those with unnatural interest in this unit. Never can be too
careful, especially these days, end of the cold war or not.
It's turning into a damned free-for-all out there, what with
old animosities resurfacing from the Caspian Sea to the
Baltic, and lunatics venting their spleen upon each other
with the aid of lethal weaponry. Yugoslavia, for example, is
right on NATO's doorstep. Its people seem quite determined to turn it into a terminal basket case, and with each
passing day, they appear to be succeeding.

"Now that we in the West have made the mistake of
recognizing some of these 'new' so-called republics, it
may only be a matter of time before the Russians decide
to recognize a few of their own: Serbia and Macedonia, for
instance. That would not make the Greeks very happy.
Your November idea may well be seen as of increasing
importance, both by those currently slow to appreciate its

value and by those who would like to see it terminated, for a variety of reasons. I make no apologies for confessing that in the early days, I was also skeptical. Air Vice-Marshal Thurson has always been ferocious in your defense; but you're not out of the woods yet. There's still a growing appetite for defense budget cuts. You therefore cannot afford to rest on your laurels."

"I never do," Jason said.

"Somehow I didn't think you would. I am impressed with your security arrangements, but for this—" Buntline tapped one of the photographs he'd taken from the envelope—"we need to employ different methods."

Jason glanced at the air vice-marshal before addressing Buntline. "Do you know him?"

"It would not appear so, but there is something familiar about that face."

"I don't understand."

"Let us just say I recognize the type. Now I'd like to have that infrared film, if I may."

Again Jason glanced at the AVM. Barely perceptibly, Thurson nodded. He did not seem bothered by Buntline's demand.

At the Schleswig base, Hohendorf had visited his old squadron to pick up full flying gear from the spare kits. He had been greeted warmly by those he knew and had been looked upon with some curiosity by new faces he did not recognize. Wusterhausen had been there.

"So, Axel," his erstwhile commander had begun, "the great man comes to steal my best backseater."

"Only for a short while."

"And have they paired Wolfie?"

"Yes, but I don't know who with. I left before the boss told us. Johann and I will know when we go over."

"Don't get him killed, Axel," Wusterhausen had then told him seriously. The eagle eyes had been piercing.

"I'd have to be killing myself, too, and I'm not about to do that."

Wusterhausen had given a fleeting twitch of the lips that might have been a smile. "I suppose not. So you like it over there?"

"It's . . . interesting."

This time, Wusterhausen had smiled. " 'Interesting,' he says. For a man who has been in combat twice . . ."

"The grapevine reached you, too?"

Wusterhausen had given a sideways glance. "I asked a price of your wing commander, for the theft of Johann."

"Johann knows, too."

"He didn't get it from me. There's a network. You know that. As usual, there are no details, of course. I don't suppose you could . . ."

"You know I can't, Chief."

"Of course you can't. But just remember, Hohendorf, your soul belongs to me, and to this squadron."

"As always, Chief," Hohendorf had responded, grinning.

"Now off you go, and try not to make the simulator think it's used for plowing the ground."

Remembering the conversation, Hohendorf smiled to himself as, fully kitted up, he sat strapped into the front cockpit of the Tornado IDS simulator. He had spent the last few minutes reacquainting himself with the instruments and controls of the aircraft he used to fly.

The fixed-base simulator was a faithful replica of the actual aircraft, and it would behave in precisely the same manner, except fly. However, with the panoramic visual display and the motion cues of stick shaker, seat bladders, and pressure feed for the G-suit, the brain would soon adjust to the environment and believe it was actually flying. Even the hum of the equipment and the sounds of the engines were authentic. Both crew members wore full oxygen kit.

"All right, Johann," Hohendorf said, "takeoff checks."

They went into the routine with practiced ease.

"Wings to twenty-five . . ."

"Wings twenty-five."

"Flaps to mid . . ."

"Flaps mid."

"Nosewheel steering to low . . ."

Hohendorf checked the square button tucked at the top left of the main instrument panel. The green LOW showed. "Nosewheel steering low . . ."

The checks continued, and then it was time to release the parking brake and to take off. Hohendorf reminded himself that he had much less power to play with than in the ASV as he opened the throttles, holding the IDS on the brakes. Just as in the real aircraft, the engines roared and the nose dipped.

Before him, the black swath of the runway stretched into the distance, in an artificial world that was the exact image of the one he inhabited. He released the brakes and pushed the throttles firmly into afterburner. The aircraft began to move, slowly at first, then with a rush of acceleration. He felt the surge and sensed the vibrations that would have been mirrored in the real world. On the left side of the HUD, the green numerals began to count the knots upward. Soon takeoff speed was reached, and he eased the stick back, feeling the Tornado take to the air. He brought the wheels up quickly and got the three reds of the status lights, confirming they had retracted cleanly.

He canceled the burners and began a gentle turn to the left. Though the IDS was very different from the high-speed flick knife that was the ASV, he was pleased to find he did not find it cumbersome. Already he was merging into the older aircraft, once again beginning to understand it. He had not forgotten anything. It was as if that part of him that had whirled in the dance of death was resting for the time being while he carried out his current task. It was a very different aircraft, but he had again become one with it; and by the time the training period was over, he knew, he would be ready to take it into battle.

It was almost like coming home.

"Well, Johann?" he began. "How was that?"

"As if you hadn't left."

"Flattery will get you everywhere."

"Always knew it would."

In Edinburgh, Selby opened his eyes to the sound of music.

"What the . . ." He rolled in the bed to find the source.

A small compact disc system was at the far end of the bedroom, attached to two smallish but very powerful speakers. He recognized the song: "Keep Coming Back," by Richard Marx. Kim was not in bed, but she soon appeared, naked and carrying a full tray of freshly made coffee and hot croissants. She placed the tray on a low table near the bed.

"It's awake," she said at him.

He pointed to the stereo. "Not much chance of sleeping."

"I thought you liked that song. I bought it especially." She gave him a look that was full of mischief. "Describes our situation perfectly. We both keep coming back to each other."

"It says there's a devil in the woman."

"But of course there is. Would you have me any other way? Come on. Up, up. It's eleven o'clock."

"You're wicked, Kimberley Mannon, and by the way, did you prepare breakfast like that?"

"Like what?"

"The way you are. What about the windows?"

"What about them? Anyway, I had an apron on. Out of bed. Let's dance to the music."

"What? You're—"

But she had moved forward to pull the bed linen off. "Out," she commanded, then stared down at him. "Hmm . . . I like."

Deciding to humor her, he got off the bed and they began to dance to the sensuous beat of the music, bodies moving gently against each other.

Before long she said, "We're . . . we're not going to finish this dance, are we?" Her voice was barely audible.

They had come up against the bed.

"Doesn't look like it," he said, and swung her round as they slowly collapsed upon it.

She put her hands to his face, dark eyes looking up at him. Then the eyes widened and her mouth parted slightly as he entered her. She closed her eyes slowly, her lips coming together as she arched beneath him.

"I love you so much," she whispered to him. The words were almost like a prayer.

The music continued to play, their bodies undulating within its rhythms. She had put it on repeat.

In the simulator at Schleswig, Hohendorf had carried out a series of maneuvers and was reasonably satisfied with his performance.

"Good stuff," Ecker commented from the backseat of the enclosed cockpit. "You haven't forgotten anything."

"I can do better," Hohendorf said.

Ecker chose to let the remark pass. He knew from

experience that nothing he said now would convince Hohendorf. "Would you like to try the pop-up?" he suggested instead.

"Let's go for it."

The pop-up attack was the method chosen for the coming mission. It was a fast, low-level approach that was displaced from the actual target, followed by a rapid pull-up, a reversal, a steep dive back to low-level, and a roll-out onto the target, all happening in quick succession. The maneuver served to confuse the defenses; but every part had to be spot-on. Get it wrong and you were dead; for if the defenses didn't get you, the ground would. And the target would still be intact.

Hohendorf considered the options as Ecker searched for a likely object in the artificial landscape that would make a good aiming point.

"We'll take the lighthouse," Ecker said. "See it on the map?"

Hohendorf changed the scale of the central moving map display. The map whizzed through before settling into the new mode. He identified the lighthouse on one of the smaller Frisian Islands.

"Got it." Altitude on the head-up display glowed 1,000 feet. "Going down to two hundred feet."

"Roger." Ecker began setting up the run-in on his displays, placing the marker cross on the target. "Select Late Arm to hot."

"Okay," Hohendorf began. "Master's Live. Late Arm coming to hot. Will you give me steering to target?"

"Yes."

"Okay. Go ahead with the attack plan, I'm still selecting." Hohendorf's left hand worked swiftly as he carried out the selection procedure. Then he called out range to target and course. "Twenty-one miles, zero nine two."

"Roger," Ecker confirmed.

"Stick of three?" Hohendorf suggested, meaning three simulated bombs on target. "Autorelease?" His voice was crisp, professional. Simulator or not, he was playing it for real.

"Stick of three, autorelease," Ecker agreed.

"Do we have SAMs or triple A to deal with?"

"Did you want them? I thought this being your first time back . . ."

"We do it for real, Johann. Call them in control and ask for defenses."

"We copy that," a voice from the control center interrupted. "We'll give you defenses. How tough do you want them? We can give you a ring of triple A and some outer SAM batteries."

"Do it."

As they'd not be carrying antiradar missiles on the real mission to take out or shut down troublesome SAM radars, Hohendorf decided it was pointless asking for a weapons change for the simulated attack. However, he intended to ask for ALARMs on the mission itself, despite what had been said at the original briefing. Even if the radar wavelengths were unknown, the defenders would not be certain and might well shut down for a while, just in case. A blind SAM was a useless SAM, whatever the reasons for the shutdown. It would give a breathing space, space enough within which to continue living.

"How about some ALARMs?" the voice suggested. "This mode is very accurate, Axel. It's a lot to take on at this stage."

"I might as well find out. No antiradars. Do it, Jurgen."

"As you wish." The voice addressed as Jurgen sounded as if it didn't think Hohendorf would make it. "I'm going to pause the simulator while I reconfigure. All your setups for the attack will remain, so you can continue when we're back online." Jurgen tried again. "Absolutely no weapon change?"

"No. We're okay."

The pause was a short one, and Hohendorf was still sharp as the mission continued. The aircraft was moving again.

"All right," he said to Ecker. "One hundred fifty feet, five hundred knots, eighteen miles to target . . . eleven miles. We'll take a ten-degree starboard offset, left roll-in." His own breathing seemed suddenly loud in his oxygen mask. "Do you go with that?" The symbology for the bombing run had appeared on the HUD.

"Yes. Looks good."

Two horizontal dashes had now made their appearance on the left side of the head-up display. In the center, a long vertical line had also come on. The bombs would release when the line dissected the bars.

"Bomb fall line and target bars," Hohendorf announced. "Target bars to the left. You call the pop-up."

"That's a go," Ecker acknowledged.

"Pop-up distance three point three miles. Altitude now one hundred feet. Confirm?"

"Confirm. Watch that heading. At this height and speed, we should be past the SAMs without waking them up."

Hohendorf glanced at the threat warning receiver. "No lights. Nobody's painting us."

That meant the SAM radars had not picked them up. Yet. And there was still the antiaircraft artillery. The threat warning remained mercifully dark.

Then a green box suddenly appeared on it.

"SAM launch!" Ecker called. "I'm spoofing," he added as he released a decoy. "Do you want a change of heading?"

"No. Call the pop-up."

"Roger. Hold it, hold it . . . Ah! Good. We've lost that SAM. Stand by for pull-up. Pull-up . . . *now!*"

"Roger. Going up." Hohendorf pulled firmly on the stick, feeling the G-suit squeeze at him. The aircraft reared skyward. "Thirty degrees nose-up."

To one side, a stream of light flashed past. Then another. Then a third. Each came from a different direction.

"Triple A," Ecker said calmly. "We're okay. They haven't got the range. Stand by for reverse. Reverse . . . *now!*"

The altitude readout said 3,100 feet.

"Reversing!" Hohendorf's left thumb flicked at a switch on the inner throttle lever, then he pushed both throttles forward. The maneuver slats that aided agility were extended. Wings were at forty-five degrees sweep. The afterburners came on as he rolled the aircraft through 130 degrees. "Maneuvers out, burners in. Going down. Twenty-degree dive." Another stream of tracer went past, but it was nowhere near them.

He rolled the IDS level and began to pull out. "Rolling out. Target's on the nose." The radar altitude attention getter began to go berserk, flashing red and beeping. Altitude was just below one hundred feet, the bomb fall line neatly separating the target bars.

"Pickle-pickle *now!*" Ecker was saying.

Hohendorf's right thumb squeezed the uncaged bomb release button on the top of the stick.

"And recover!" Ecker said.

"Recovering."

The aircraft swept over the target, and Hohendorf banked steeply away, reversed the turn, and went low, afterburners roaring. About them, tracers lanced the sky, but again nothing came close. No other SAMs had fired. Then they were out of the danger zone. The whole thing, from pull-up to recovery and egress, had taken mere seconds; but within those seconds, in the real arena, getting it wrong meant dying.

"Not bad. Not bad at all!" said Jurgen. "Target was wiped out, and you took no hits. Any lower, and you might have been taken out by your own bomb blast. You're still on the ball, Axel. All that soft living over in GB hasn't spoiled you after all."

"Flattery from you, too, Jurgen? I cannot believe it."

"You're still the only person who can get through my special. The Seeadler has done it, but he's taken hits. So that still leaves you."

"And me," Ecker complained. "I plotted the path."

"We all know he'd be lost without you, Johann," the controller said pleasantly.

"Just making sure you don't forget."

Jurgen laughed. "Do you gentlemen want to fly the approach? Or do you want to stop?"

"We'll carry out some more attacks," Hohendorf said, "with really hostile defenses."

"Roger. So you'd like some more punishment." The controller seemed to be enjoying himself. "I'll try to make life miserable for you."

After five simulated attacks on different targets—each heavily defended—the target was destroyed each time; but no hits from incoming fire were taken.

"All right, all right, Axel," the controller said good-naturedly at the end of the session, accepting defeat. "For that you can buy me coffee."

"It won't be so easy on the day," Hohendorf later said to Ecker as they removed their flying kit from their damp bodies.

Ecker looked at him with calm eyes. "I didn't think it would be."

"You're not going to die, Johann," Hohendorf said quite seriously. "I won't let that happen."

Ecker's smile was reflective. "You'd better not."

London, Early Evening, the Same Day

Bowmaker was in Thurson's Whitehall office, at the Ministry of Defense. He had arrived from one of the U.K.-based American units, having flown there from the States.

"I tried to convince them at the Pentagon," the American general was saying, "to get an Aurora flight authorized. One fast run, to give us up-to-date infrared shots of the target, or even an attack. Save your boys going into that hellhole."

The Aurora was the much-speculated-upon hypersonic replacement for the SR-71A Blackbird, a super-super-stealthy aircraft that made the Gulf-famous Stealth fighter look positively naked. Aurora was not even supposed to exist. Equally speculated upon was the cost of that particular "black" program, which was said to be exospheric.

Mindful of this, Thurson remarked dryly: "But, sadly, no one wanted to risk such a valuable asset over a target we know so little about."

"Got it in one. It's bad enough that the F-117A went down. Hell, Robert, imagine if they zapped an Aurora as well."

"Panic stations?" the air vice-marshal suggested mildly.

"Oh, that British understatement! Let's just say a lot of stuff would be flying from the fan. And after *that*, I'd be lucky to get a job selling hot dogs. I can just see the fiscal nightmare for defense research after that."

"So it's still up to my November crews."

"I'm afraid so. They're the boys."

"Expendable, you mean."

"Not my words, Robert."

"Never anybody's in such situations, is it? Convenient."

At the Ecker home on the outskirts of Schleswig, Johann Ecker was regaling Morven with some of Hohendorf's past exploits.

"We were upside down over the sea, so low I could see the fish!"

"Oh, Johann," she said disbelievingly. "That's really stretching it."

"I am very serious," he countered innocently. "We were just off Sardinia, and I tell you I saw a shark."

Hohendorf entered with a tray laden with mugs of coffee.

"The only shark I see is the one telling impossible stories."

"Then *you* tell her, Axel," Ecker insisted as he picked up his mug. "We were very, very low."

Morven looked at Hohendorf. "Is that really true?"

"Perhaps we were a little low," he admitted after an amused glance at Ecker. "But I am not so sure about the shark." He passed her a mug as both he and Ecker began laughing.

The sudden ringing of the phone cut into their laughter. Erika stood up. "I'll take it in the kitchen."

No one spoke as they heard her pick up the phone.

"Ecker," she said, answering in the German way. Her voice dropped suddenly. "Where are you?" There was astonishment in the words, followed by rapid, low-voiced conversation.

In the other room, Ecker and Hohendorf looked at each other questioningly. Then Erika was standing in the doorway with a strained expression upon her face. "Johann," she said, and went back into the kitchen.

With a puzzled expression, Ecker got to his feet and followed her.

"What's all that about?" Morven asked Axel after Ecker left the room.

He gave a barely perceptible shrug and glanced toward the kitchen. "Nothing serious, I hope. Erika looked a little worried."

"I'd say she was *very* worried."

Presently Johann and Erika returned. A moment's silence fell upon the room.

"Well?" Hohendorf began. "Is something wrong?"

There was a slight pause before Ecker spoke. "It's Anne-Marie."

"What?" Morven and Hohendorf both exclaimed.

"She's got radar, that one," Ecker commented ruefully.

"Where is she?" A sudden tightness had come into Hohendorf's voice.

"Just passing Rendsburg. . . ."

"About fourteen kilometers from here," Hohendorf explained to Morven urgently.

"She was using her car phone," Ecker finished.

"The way she drives," Hohendorf said grimly, "it will

not be long before she's at the door. What is she doing up here?"

"She was in Hamburg and thought she would visit."

"So she calls when she gets to Rendsburg?"

"You know Anne-Marie," Erika said. "It's her way. She's always been like that."

"She cannot come," Hohendorf said firmly.

Erika looked at her husband uncertainly, then glanced at Morven before turning to Hohendorf.

But before she could speak, Morven said: "Let her. I'm not afraid of her."

Hohendorf was adamant. "No! I will not put you through this. That last time at the schloss was bad enough. *Why* must she always spoil things?"

"To be fair," Morven said, "she didn't know we'd be here."

"Fair? That word is unknown to Anne-Marie. I'll meet her outside. . . ."

"It's all right, Axel," Morven assured him. "I can handle it."

Hohendorf sighed as he looked at her. "Imagine if your brother gets to hear of this. . . ."

"So who's going to tell him? Not me."

"Anne-Marie never does anything without reason," Hohendorf went on. "She was not in Hamburg by coincidence. She knows I am here."

"But how?" Ecker demanded. "She did not get it from us."

"I would never think that of you two. You know that, Johann," Hohendorf said. "Anne-Marie's family has the airline, which gives them plenty of access into the aerospace business. Her father has contacts all over the place, in some very high positions."

"Surely you're not suggesting . . ."

"She's here, isn't she?" Hohendorf countered with more harshness than he'd intended.

Another silence fell, and a pall of gloom, brought on

by the impending arrival of Anne-Marie, settled upon them.

The large four-story hotel gleamed whitely in the cold light of the headlights as the big BMW 850i coupé cruised past in the silence of the sprawling village, to turn the corner that would take it onto the street where the Eckers lived.

"She's here," Ecker said with resignation when they all saw the flash of light as the car swung off the street and onto the wide, paved area in front of the house.

Hohendorf was already moving. "I'll talk to her," he said determinedly. "She is just impossible!"

Ecker went with him.

As they left, Erika looked at Morven. "I am so very sorry."

"What for? It's not your fault. It's for me to handle. Please don't worry, Erika. Not on my account. All right?"

Unsure of what to do, Erika nodded slowly.

Outside, Hohendorf and Ecker reached the car just as the lights were turned off. The driver's door opened, and Anne-Marie got out elegantly. The glow from the street-lamps and the night-light on the house gave the patrician cast of her features a haunting beauty—which, by any standards, she was.

She smiled widely. "Axel! How wonderful! What a surprise!" She came forward to kiss him warmly on the lips, then went to kiss Ecker near each corner of the mouth. "And how are you, Johann? How's Erika?"

Hohendorf's voice was cool. "It's not going to work, Anne-Marie. You're not here by coincidence."

"This is a strange welcome, Axel. Aren't you glad to see me? And what's this? Is no one going to invite me into the house?"

Hohendorf was unmoved. "Who told you I was up here? And please don't try to tell me you came up just because you felt like it. I know only too well how unpredictable you can be; but I also know your methods. So I'll ask again. How did you know I was up here?"

"No one told me." She sounded petulant. "I worked it out for myself." She paused.

They waited.

"I called Wolfie Flacht at his home in Scotland, day before yesterday," she continued with marked reluctance.

"Checking up on me?"

"If you must know . . . I wanted to find out whether you had come to your senses about that ridiculous English girl."

Hohendorf felt his jaw tighten and was aware of Ecker's hurried glance. He said nothing, letting Anne-Marie carry on for the moment.

"I called Wolfie because no one at the stupid base ever gives a straight answer to a straight question. When I asked Wolfie where you were, *he* gave me some story about your doing a flight test. As he's your backseater, I found it strange he wasn't with you. And of course he would say no more on the phone. So I called your mother to see if you were on holiday and had come over to visit her. . . ."

"So now I am supposed to tell you when I take my holidays?"

"I am your wife, Axel."

"When it suits your purposes."

"Your mother didn't know where you were," she went on as if Hohendorf had not spoken. "I then asked *Vati* if any of his contacts knew of anything that might be happening at your base. He called a few people, but no one knew anything . . . or so they said." She had clearly not believed that. "So I decided I wanted a long drive, and here I am. And I was right," she finished triumphantly.

"Are you expecting applause?" Hohendorf's words held the continuing chill of unwelcome. "What's the matter, Anne-Marie? Is it Gerhard Linden's day off?"

Anne-Marie's face had gone pale in the ghostliness of the light. Linden was one of the family airline's senior pilots and the man she had left Axel for.

Ecker cleared his throat awkwardly. "Er . . . perhaps we should go inside. . . ."

Hohendorf turned to stare at him.

"We can't stand out here like this," Ecker went on. He paused uncertainly.

"Some sense at last," Anne-Marie said, and strode past them toward the door. She was entering the house before either had moved.

They hurried after her, dreading the coming explosion, and entered the living room to find a frozen tableau waiting for them. All three women were standing, staring at each other. Morven was defiant. Erika looked as if she wished she were anywhere else. And Anne-Marie's patrician features were so pale with anger, they seemed to have been assaulted by a bleaching agent.

Eyes of diamond blue white turned upon Erika. "My best friend . . . my childhood friend." The voice, deep and sensuous, carried the knell of a death sentence. "How could you do this to me, Erika? How could you have her here? In this house where *we* used to spend so much time together?"

Erika seemed transfixed, but Morven had been simmering ever since Anne-Marie had made her dramatic entrance. The luminous green eyes were now on fire.

"Don't talk about me as if I'm not here," she began, miraculously under full control. "And you can leave Erika out of this. I'm the one you want. Women like you make me sick! You don't marry a man. You want to own him . . . every single part of him becomes a possession to control, according to the whim of the moment. Your kind are never happy until you've got his balls hanging from your neck like a trophy. That's not what I call love. Axel is not a possession. You did a very cruel thing. You walked out on him when he most needed you, because it didn't suit you to remain. But you also miss not having him around. You never really succeeded in controlling him . . . and you can't stand that. The men you can control soon make you bored. When that happens, you go hunting for Axel." The green eyes seemed to stare fearlessly into Anne-Marie's very soul. "I know I'm bloody right about you. Now if everyone will please excuse me, I need some air."

Morven walked past a stunned Anne-Marie to go to the bedroom she shared with Hohendorf.

A full minute passed before anyone said anything. Then Anne-Marie turned and began walking toward the door. "I'll be staying at the hotel," she said haughtily as she went past. She paused. "I don't give up easily, Axel."

No one spoke as she went out. The silence remained as they heard the door of the BMW open and close firmly. The powerful engine started, the lights came on, and the car reversed into the road, then accelerated away.

At last Ecker glanced up at the ceiling in silent thanks. "Morven's got guts," he said, the relief plain in his voice. "You picked well, Axel."

Hohendorf smiled tiredly. "She picked me . . . for which *I* thank God." It occurred to him that if Anne-Marie, working on a hunch, could track him down, then someone with a definite interest in the mission . . . His thoughts came to a halt. Imagine the mission being compromised by an estranged and jealous, resourceful wife.

He wondered if he should mention that to the wing commander when he got back.

*　　　*　　　*

A Coastal Village on the Moray Firth, Grampian, Scotland

The crowded pub was close to the seafront. Many of the clientele were local, but several were off-duty servicemen from the various bases that dotted that particular stretch of the Scottish coast. The village, a thriving fishing port in its heyday, now made its living from tourism.

The dark waters of the small harbor were sparsely punctuated here and there by the speckles from the lights of small boats riding at anchor. Far out to sea, the running lights of a large ship could be seen. A narrow mole that had seen better days jutted out into the harbor, its far end shrouded in darkness. A Range Rover and several other cars stood empty near the edge of the seawall, their owners having abandoned them for the attractions of the pub. The area was totally deserted.

The quiet of the seafront was broken harshly by the arrival of a small, battered-looking van. It parked sloppily at the end of the mole, three cars away from the Range Rover. The driver, whose scruffy dress seemed in keeping with his van, got out, slammed the door shut, and, without bothering to lock it went to the pub.

Poleskov sat in a secluded corner. He had been coming to the pub regularly, making himself blend into the background as much as possible. He would drink unhurriedly, chat with the frequent customers, and sometimes join a scratch team to play a darts challenge. His true purpose was to siphon low-level intelligence, obtained easily merely by listening in on the casual to-and-fro of leisurely conversation. It was one of the many things he was good at. So far he'd heard nothing to excite his interest.

"Hullo," someone said. "Still here, I see."

Poleskov looked up, looked puzzled for a brief moment, then brightened at the sight of the scruffy man. "You are

. . . the photographer from the other day, near the airfield. Right?"

"Yes. That's me." The man grinned sheepishly.

"Didn't the shots work?"

The photographer shook his head. "'Fraid not. I've got to do it all over again. It's so difficult to get a shot that nobody else has done. Well, the best is always worth waiting for."

"It certainly is," Poleskov agreed genially. "Can I get you one?" he added, pointing to his glass.

"That's kind of you. Thank you. I'll have a half of lager. Driving, you know. Mustn't overdo it."

"I know what you mean. I've been nursing mine."

The photographer grinned once more. "Pubs won't get rich on us. Look," he went on, "I'm just going to get something out of my van. Won't be long."

"Fine. I'll get the drinks in."

"Right. See you in a minute."

Poleskov watched keenly as the man made his way through the crowd. Something was not quite right.

Outside, the man was hurrying toward the van. He got in quickly, rummaged in the glove compartment for a penlight. Out of a jacket pocket he pulled a five-by-four photograph and shone the light upon it. A man's head looked up at him.

"Jesus!" he breathed. "It's him! I've found him!"

He switched off the light and put it away, returned the photograph to its hiding place, and took a small communications unit out of another pocket. He pressed a button. "Jackdaw," he said into it.

"Go ahead, Jackdaw," the unit replied.

"I've found him! Jesus, I know him. His car . . . everything . . ."

"Good work! Where?"

Then the unit began to crackle. Reception had deteriorated.

"Shit!" Jackdaw said exasperatedly. "If they gave us decent budgets, we might get equipment that sodding well did the job it's meant to!" He tried again. "This is Jackdaw. Can you hear me?"

Crackles answered.

"Look. I don't know if you can hear this. There's a phone box a short distance away. I'll try that." He cut transmission. "That's always assuming the bloody phone works."

But Jackdaw never got the chance to leave the van. Suddenly the door opened and something at once hot and cold entered beneath his right ear and pierced searingly into his brain. The radio fell out of shuddering, useless fingers as his body stiffened briefly then collapsed across the seats.

"Jackdaw! Jackdaw!" the radio abruptly began to repeat frantically. "Come in. Come in!"

Poleskov calmly withdrew the thin, ice pick–like blade from Jackdaw's ear, wiped it clean on the dead man's clothing, then put the weapon away. The radio was still screaming. He picked it up and stamped it into silence. Then he arranged the body as if the driver had decided to take a nap, shut the door, checked to make sure no one had seen what had occurred, and sauntered back to the pub. No one else was about.

He went round to one side of the pub, up an alley too narrow for anything but bicycles and pedestrians. The window to the male toilets was still open. He waited until he was certain no one was in there, then climbed back in, leaving the window partially open as he had found it.

He went to a lavatory and flushed it, then went to a washbasin, where he made a production of washing his hands. A customer, already well mellowed, entered while the lavatory was still completing its flush cycle, to walk a little unsteadily toward the urinals.

"Good beer in this pub," the man said casually to Poleskov.

"Aye," Poleskov replied. "It's good all right. See you," he added as he went out.

"Aye," the man said in parting.

Poleskov returned to his table to finish his drink. He had not ordered the half pint of lager.

It was 0700 the next morning before anyone decided to look into the van that had stood by itself all night after the pub had closed. As there was no sign of blood, it remained untouched for another full half hour because everyone thought the driver was still asleep.

"Hard night at the pub," a passerby commented.

His companion laughed understandingly.

Jackdaw's people had been trying to find him, but as he had not given any specifics of his routine for the past night, it was not until the local police had been called to check on the van and what was finally discovered to be a dead body that the news eventually filtered its way to Buntline. The police were then astonished by the speed with which the matter was subsequently taken out of their hands.

The Hotel on the Outskirts of Schleswig, 0900 Hours

Anne-Marie was sitting in composed chill to a solitary breakfast.

"I do hope you will forgive the intrusion," a voice said to her in English. "Would you mind if I shared your table?"

The pale blue eyes looked up slowly, surveyed the pleasant-looking, youngish man before her, then pointedly looked round the breakfast room before responding. "There are other tables."

"Well, yes. I know. I merely thought . . ."

She returned to her breakfast. "Are you trying to pick me up? If so, it is very clumsy."

"I'm very sorry," the man said contritely. "I wasn't trying to be . . . clumsy, as you so succinctly put it. I was late in last night, and I saw you come in. You seemed upset. I merely thought you could do with the company. I'm here by myself. . . ."

"Are you English?"

The hostility in her voice took him by surprise. "Well . . . er, yes. Is that a problem? We're not still fighting the last war, are we?"

"The last war? Don't be stupid." Anne-Marie was not one to mince words when she was in one of her moods. "That was before my time. What has it to do with me?"

"Can we start again? Or am I going to have to stand here looking silly?"

"Very well," she said after making him wait. "You may join me. There is the buffet. Or you can have something cooked for you. English breakfast, perhaps?"

"Thank you," he said dryly, taking a seat. "If it's not the war, what have the English done to you? I'm Jerry Craven, by the way."

"And I am Anne-Marie Gräfin von Ettlingen und Hohendorf."

"My word. I *am* in exalted company. Forgive me if I appeared to have been attempting a cheap pickup. I assure you, I was not."

"Are you a pilot? Military?"

He hesitated.

"It is all right," she said before he could speak. "You do

not have to reply. You are wondering why I seemed upset. Are you married, Mr. Craven?"

"No. I'm not."

"You are lucky. My husband is sleeping with another woman . . . an *English* woman." She made it sound like an unpleasant disease.

Craven seemed unsure of how to respond, but Anne-Marie didn't notice. "Worse, he brings her over here, to the house of my close friend, where *we* used to go." Perhaps if she had not been feeling so angry and humiliated, she would not have been so indiscreet.

"Why did you ask me if I was a pilot?" Craven said.

"This is pilot country. My husband is one, but he is stationed in England . . . no, Scotland . . . and he has decided to come back here for a holiday, bringing his little whore with him."

"So he used to fly from here?"

Some inner caution made Anne-Marie pause. "Are you interested in me or my husband?"

"I'm merely offering company."

"Perhaps that is not such a good idea. I do not want to appear rude, but I think I would really prefer to be alone."

Craven gave in amicably. He stood up. "As you wish."

She nodded detachedly at him, and he went to another table.

The Ecker home was a substantial, two-story, four-bedroom house with a steep roof. Internally the overriding impression was of wood paneling and beams. But the proportions were generous, so it all came off with a sense of ease and comfort. On that particular morning, breakfast was a subdued affair.

Hohendorf and Ecker were starting the day somewhat late. A training mission with a real aircraft was scheduled.

This would take them over the Baltic to an outlying island, where the pop-up attack would be carried out with practice ordnance. They had a good hour to kill before they needed to begin preparations for the flight.

It was Erika who voiced what everyone else was thinking.

"I . . . I cannot sit here eating while I know she's by herself in that hotel. . . ."

"If you were the one over there, Erika, I'm sorry to say I don't think Anne-Marie would be worried about you," Hohendorf said.

"She's my oldest friend," Erika protested. "I'd like to think she sort of would . . . you know." When anxious about something, Erika's way of speaking English tended to take on an American edge. "I know what she's like, and yes, I know she's selfish. I still hate to think she's eating breakfast all alone." She gave Morven an apologetic glance.

Hohendorf was neutral. "She'll find company. Never hard for her. Johann, tell your wife to see sense."

Erika kept pleading eyes upon him.

At last Hohendorf sighed. "All right, my soft cousin. If it will make you feel better, go over to the hotel and see how she is."

Erika looked at her husband.

"I'm not standing in your way," he said to her amiably.

"I won't be long. Morven . . . I don't want you to think . . ."

"I'd probably do the same in your place," Morven told her reassuringly. "It can't be easy for you."

Erika smiled in relief. "Thank you."

She left the table and went to get ready. Soon they heard her leaving.

"I won't be long," she repeated, calling out as she left.

"I still think it's a bad idea," Hohendorf said.

Morven stroked his arm briefly, letting him know she didn't mind. "Don't worry," she told him softly.

Ecker smiled at them uncertainly.

* * *

Anne-Marie looked up as Erika was shown to her table.

"Well," she began in German, "I am popular today. Do sit down."

"Popular?" Erika took a chair opposite. "What do you mean?"

"An English pilot tried to pick me up. I sent him away. I don't like the English today. I wonder why."

"What was an English pilot doing here?"

"Who knows? Who cares? Perhaps there's no room in the Fliegerhorst and they booked him in here. So what's the purpose of this visit? To apologize?"

"No, Anne-Marie," Erika replied firmly. "I came to see how you were."

"Guilt?"

"No. No guilt. If you stop long enough to think about it, you were rude to our guests last night."

"Guests!" Anne-Marie was dismissive. "Axel is your cousin. He's family. And as for that English trollop . . ."

"Do you know, Anne-Marie, I am the best friend you've ever had. From childhood I've seen all your moods and all your tantrums; but I stuck with you. I am also the only person who tells you the truth about yourself."

Anne-Marie smiled coldly. "And the only one I'll take it from."

"When you think you're going to lose, you call people names. . . ."

"Doesn't everybody?"

"You left Axel of your own free will," Erika continued relentlessly, "when things got a little difficult. I saw the wreckage you left behind. He was all alone those months in that house, with everyone knowing his wife had walked out on him. But held himself together and continued do his job. God only knows how. But something died in him then. You shouldn't have married him if you couldn't take him for what he is."

"Perhaps I was hoping to be an admiral's wife one day. Or maybe the chief executive of the airline."

"Oh, Axel will be an admiral, but not an executive on your family airline . . . and you won't be the admiral's wife. You threw that away. You can't marry just for the times it suits you, Anne-Marie. Morven loves Axel just as he is. She's made him alive again."

"So she'll become the good hausfrau, with a castle thrown in for good measure. . . ."

Erika was becoming exasperated. "Why must you always do this? She's not interested in any castles or titles. And she is not the good little hausfrau, as you call her. She has her own mind."

"Yes. I got some of that last night."

"Anne-Marie, it would be best for everyone if you went back."

The pale blue eyes regarded Erika unflinchingly. "And I thought you came here for my benefit."

"I did. I am thinking of you."

There was a pause, then Anne-Marie spoke in milder voice. "I do believe you are. Am I not attractive anymore?"

"Oh, come on. This is me. Erika. The modesty line does not work. I wish I had half . . . no, a quarter of your beauty. You know you're beautiful. You don't need an ego polish from me."

Another smile, this time with some warmth. It made Anne-Marie look ravishing. "So. It's Hamburg and dear old Gerhard."

Erika stared at her. "You've got Gerhard Linden waiting for you in Hamburg? And you came up here on a whim?"

"Not a whim. A certainty. Gerhard always does what I say. I'm getting bored with him." Anne-Marie looked away briefly. "Does he love her?" The question was almost fearful.

Feeling kind, Erika said gently, "Yes."

Anne-Marie stared at her cup. "I see."

Jerry Craven had finished breakfast quickly and was approaching Flensburg, on the German-Danish border. It took him a little time to find a parking space, but he made his appointment on the Rotestrasse with thirty seconds to spare.

"Let's walk," said the man he was meeting.

They began to stroll, talking quietly. The language they used and with which they were fluently at ease was neither German, nor Danish, nor English. The man known as Jerry Craven was being addressed by another name by his companion.

"It's interesting what can come your way during an ordinary conversation," Craven was saying.

"You were trying to pick her up, weren't you?"

Craven smiled. "Of course. Woman like that on her own. She was a beacon. Her body language said 'come and get me.'"

"Except that the message wasn't directed at you." There was a malicious pleasure in the remark.

"Snobbish bitch," Craven said without real anger. "'Anne-Marie Gräfin von Ettlingen und Hohendorf,'" he mimicked.

"What a mouthful."

They laughed.

"Rich, though," Craven went on. "You should have seen her car . . . big, metallic gray BMW coupé. Powerful machine."

"So the lady likes power."

"You can believe it. She is furious over the woman her husband is sleeping with. Her face goes white with anger when she mentions it."

"And now we know he's a pilot who's currently based in Scotland, but who was originally over here. From the mouths of babes, and the women who believe they have been scorned. Hell hath no fury."

"A misogynistic comment."

"Which in this particular case happens to be true."

"Well? Do you think there's anything in it?" Craven asked.

"Who knows? It is not our job to try to make sense of it. That's for the analysts. People like us are all over the world, supplying the fodder. It may be useless information. On the other hand, it may fit into whatever jigsaw they're constructing. Incidentally, have you checked out of the hotel?"

"I thought I should, just in case."

"Good. It may be worth following her for a while, to see if we can get an identification on the husband. Or his car, for that matter. They might be able to find out if it was seen anywhere in Scotland. Not you, though. I'd better do that, since I'm unknown to her. Her car's a BMW, did you say?"

Craven nodded and gave Anne-Marie's license plate number.

Hohendorf and Ecker were in their uniforms, getting ready to leave for the base, when Erika returned.

"That wasn't a very long time," Hohendorf commented dryly. "You must have had a lot to talk about."

"I'm sorry. We . . . just got talking."

Ecker said: "No. Really?"

"Stop it, you two. At least she's leaving."

Hohendorf brightened, kissed her on the cheek. "Now you're talking! How did you manage that?"

"A few truths."

"And she took them? I would have liked to hear you."

Hohendorf and Ecker looked at each other. "Then again," they went on together, "perhaps not."

Morven, who had been listening quietly, said, "It feels a bit horrible talking about her like that."

Hohendorf turned to her. "*She* was horrible to *you.*"

"Yes . . . I know . . . but . . ." In victory she could afford to feel some sympathy.

Hohendorf stopped her with a kiss. "Don't make the mistake of feeling sorry for Anne-Marie. Take it from someone who knows."

"Can I have the car, Johann?" Erika was saying. "I'd like to take Morven into Schleswig."

"We're taking the Porsche to the base, anyway," Hohendorf said to Ecker. "Aren't we?"

Ecker nodded to them both.

Then Erika said: "You were right, Axel."

"About what?"

"Anne-Marie having company. An English pilot." She decided to say nothing about Gerhard in Hamburg.

Both Ecker and Hohendorf were suddenly alert.

"What English pilot?" Hohendorf asked. He turned to Ecker. "Are there foreign NATO aircrew on the base?"

"As far as I know, we have no seconded crews at the moment."

"Tell me about this pilot," Hohendorf demanded.

Unsure of his reasons, Erika related what Anne-Marie had said.

"Is that all?"

"That's all she told me. Is something wrong, Axel?"

"I don't know. Come, Johann. Let's see if we can catch her in time."

Hohendorf kissed Morven quickly, gave Erika a swift peck on the cheek, and began to leave, followed by Ecker.

"Take care flying," Morven called to him.

He paused just long enough to answer, "Don't worry. I will."

Outside, they threw their caps behind the seats and climbed into the Porsche. Hohendorf started the car, reversed onto the road, and drove rapidly away toward the hotel in what seemed like a single, fluid motion.

"Do you think we have a problem?" Ecker said on the way.

"I don't know," Hohendorf replied with a sigh. "When Anne-Marie's in one of her moods, anything is possible. God knows what she may have said to this man. When she's persuaded herself she is the injured party, she is capable of anything, as you know. She even once tried to justify her affair with Linden by blaming me because I would not stop flying the Tornado."

They made it to the hotel just as Anne-Marie was about to enter the BMW.

"Well," she commented as they climbed out of the Porsche and came up to her. "The farewell party?"

Hohendorf went straight to the point. "Anne-Marie, you were talking to a man who said he was a British pilot. . . ."

"Jealous? What will your little girl—"

"Listen to me! What did you tell him?"

Her eyes widened, shifted from him to Ecker and back again. "That's none of your business."

"It *is* my business, if you have said anything about me."

"I said nothing about you."

"I can't believe that. When you feel angry, you complain . . . usually about how you wish I would leave the military."

"Well, I said nothing like that," came the defensive retort. "I only told him you were flying in Scotland—"

"*What!* For God's sake, Anne-Marie! Don't you know by now when to keep your mouth shut?"

"But . . . he was a pilot . . ."

"You know that, do you? Sometimes, Anne-Marie . . ." Hohendorf turned away from her in exasperation. "Come on, Johann. Let's get out of here."

They returned to the Porsche and climbed in.

Anne-Marie had raised an uncertain hand, as if wanting to stop him. "Axel," she began tentatively.

He'd left the engine running and drove away without looking back at her.

He had paid no attention to the nondescript car that was parked across from the hotel and thus did not see the camera or hear its soft *click-whirr*, as it had recorded the entire scene.

On the base, Hohendorf went immediately to Wusterhausen, the boss of his former squadron, who confirmed his fears that there were currently no visiting NATO crews.

"Chief," he then said, "I need to make an urgent and secure report to November One. Can you arrange it for me?"

Wusterhausen did not waste time asking for reasons. "Do you want direct contact?"

Hohendorf nodded.

"Leave it to me," Wusterhausen said. "I'll have a squadron driver take you over to Communications. Give me a few minutes to call the base commander for permission."

"Thanks, Chief."

Wusterhausen grunted and picked up a phone as Hohendorf went to wait outside the squadron building. Presently an olive-drab combi van turned up. The driver recognized Hohendorf.

"Nice to have you back with us, Kaleu," he greeted, using the shortened and familiar form of rank as Hohendorf climbed in.

"Nice to be back."

The driver was smart enough not to ask how long Hohendorf would be staying. He drove swiftly around the airfield to the communications block.

"I was told to wait for you, Kaleu," he said as Hohendorf got out, "to take you back."

"Thank you," Hohendorf said hurriedly, "I won't be long."

"I'll be here, Kaleu."

Hohendorf nodded.

He had to wait briefly for someone from inside the building to come and open the secure door, with its warning sign forbidding unauthorized entry, then he was escorted to the section where he would make the call. A junior security officer was waiting for him.

The officer glanced at Hohendorf's name tag. "Please come with me, Kapitänleutnant. Do you want us to send your message?" he continued as they walked. "Or would you prefer person-to-person?" His own name tag read BRÜNST.

"Direct to Wing Commander Jason, please."

"Very well. Here we are. Please go in there."

It was a small booth, with a single black telephone that had no dialing control. A red button was on the main body.

"When the light comes on," Brünst was saying, "pick up the handset. Your wing commander will be on the other end. I shall secure the booth. No one will hear. Not even me. I am forbidden to record your conversation. You must have powerful friends, Kapitänleutnant." He gave a tight, brief smile.

Hohendorf stared at Brünst.

Brünst got the message. "Of course." He shut the booth and left Hohendorf to it.

A short time later the red button glowed. Hohendorf picked up the handset as he'd been told.

"Jason," he heard with astounding clarity. There was not even a hum on the line.

"Sir," Hohendorf began, "this is—"

"Yes, Mr. Hohendorf?"

Hohendorf quickly related what had occurred with

Anne-Marie while Jason listened in silence. "Do we abort and return to base, sir?" he said when he'd finished his report. "And are we compromised?"

"The answer to your first question is no. As for the second . . . there's no such thing as one hundred percent security at all times. There's always the unknown factor. We've had our own excitements on this side of the Channel." Jason did not expand on this. "Continue with your workup unless you hear to the contrary from me. Concentrate on your part of the mission. There are others whose job it is to handle extraneous problems."

"Yes, sir."

"Thank you for informing me, Axel. Good show."

The red light went out. Communication had ended.

Hohendorf replaced the receiver slowly. The booth hissed, and the door opened. The security officer was waiting.

"Was that all right?"

Hohendorf nodded. "Very clear. Quite amazing."

"Satisfied customers," Brünst said. "That's what we like."

"So how does it feel?"

The words had come from Ecker in the backseat as the Tornado IDS hurtled low over the Baltic on its way to the small, uninhabited island for the day's target practice.

"Feels good. No problems."

In the front, Hohendorf held the aircraft with a light but precise touch, at five hundred knots. He'd had no trouble adjusting.

"Like the old days," he now said.

"Well, let's see how you do with this," Ecker said. "Target's at thirty miles."

Hohendorf acknowledged and began the arming sequence while Ecker set up the attack.

"Going for an offset pop-up like in the simulator?"

"Yes. A left roll-in again. That will be the best way for the mission target, so we'll stick with it."

"Just remember the ground and the sea are real this time."

"Johann, Johann. Not worried, are you?"

"Me? Of course not."

Hohendorf smiled in his mask. Same old Johann. It would be good doing the real attack mission with him. Wolfie Flacht was a brilliant backseater in air-to-air combat, but the low-level attack arena belonged to Johann Ecker.

"Ten miles," came the word from the backseat.

There was a fine haze over the water. The tiny island could not yet be seen. The Tornado was now at a hundred feet.

"Five miles," Ecker called. "Stand by for pull-up." Pause. "Pull-up . . . *now!*"

"Roger. Going up."

Hohendorf brought the stick back and held the nose at precisely thirty degrees as the Tornado climbed to preattack height.

"Reverse . . . *now!*"

"And reversing," Hohendorf confirmed, straining against the G-forces.

The aircraft went partially onto its back and plunged toward the sea, afterburners glowing. Hohendorf rolled out dead on target, the bomb fall line bisecting the bars neatly. He began to ease the nose up as altitude decreased rapidly. The water seemed perilously close, but the target area on the island was perfectly straddled by the attack symbology.

"Pickle, pickle now!" Ecker shouted. "Bomb gone. Recover."

"Recovering." Hohendorf hauled the Tornado away.

"Perfect attack. Want to check visually?"

"We won't be able to go around on the real thing, but let's indulge ourselves."

They circled the island once. It was indeed a direct hit. They carried out three more attacks until all the practice ordnance was used. There were no misses.

Morven and Erika had walked through the Altstadt, the old part of Schleswig, and had paused by a footbridge to look out across the Schlei, the town's harbor. A strong breeze came from the east, bringing with it a perceptible chill from the Baltic.

Morven thought she could hear the sound of a fast jet and glanced up involuntarily, absently tucking some strands of hair behind her ears.

Erika noted the movement. "He'll be fine."

"Yes. Yes, I know."

"Has he ever told you about what happened with Anne-Marie?"

"He did mention the breakup when we first met, but no real details."

"She hurt him very badly." Erika paused, as if not quite sure she ought to say more. "One of the things she did after she . . . um . . . had left for some weeks with an excuse about wanting to think about things, was to ask him to a restaurant. In the middle of that place, while they were *eating*, she told him, without any feeling or warning, that she was having an affair. It was as if she had asked for a glass of water." She paused again, seeing the pain for what had happened to Hohendorf in Morven's eyes. "We women," she went on, "well, some of us . . . can sometimes be really very cruel, as you said to Anne-Marie, especially to the men who love us. Anne-Marie, on one of her days, can be terrible. When we were at school . . . but

I have already said too much. I wanted you to understand a little. Now, it is up to Axel."

"He doesn't have to tell me anything. I'm not with him to hand him a questionnaire, you know. I love him as he is, and that's it. I'm not one of those people who needs to dissect a man first, so that every part of him is laid bare before me. I wouldn't like him to do that to me, so I've no intention of doing it to him."

Erika smiled at her. "Then Axel is a very lucky man. After Anne-Marie . . . and I say this even though she's a childhood friend . . . he deserves a little good luck."

"I'm the lucky one," Morven said, and glanced once more at the sky. The sounds of the fast jet had faded. "Very lucky," she added softly. She regarded Erika with a new respect. Like Axel's mother, Erika effectively hid an inner strength and sense of understanding beneath a seemingly vulnerable exterior. Johann Ecker, she decided, was also a very lucky man. "Come on," she said, linking her arm with Erika's, who seemed pleasantly surprised by this unexpected display of intimacy. "Show me some more of this town."

As they walked on, Morven hoped both Axel and Johann would indeed be all right. She did not want to suffer one day the fate of Charlotte Newton, chief player in her brother Mark's nightmares.

November One, the Same Day

Wing Commander Jason stood by one of the two staff cars and watched expectantly as the military executive jet came to a halt. Its twin engines spooled down, and the forward door raised itself open. Charles Buntline, followed by the air vice-marshal and Bowmaker, came down the steps and approached.

"You ride with me, Chris," Thurson said. "Mr. Buntline and General Bowmaker will take the other car."

"Sir," Jason acknowledged, and waited for his superior to enter through the door that the driver was holding open before following suit.

The two cars sped away.

"Would you care to expand on this matter of Hohendorf?" Thurson said.

As Jason gave him the full story, the air vice-marshal listened attentively. A partition in the car prevented the driver from eavesdropping on what was being discussed.

"Are we compromised, sir?" Jason asked when he'd finished. "Hohendorf asked me that same question."

"Only Buntline can answer that with any degree of certainty. The killing of his man, coming so soon after our mysterious observer on the infrared film . . . and now this incident, does rather point to the fact that we're being deliberately targeted. Not surprising, but we'd hoped to gain more time. However, I'm not prepared to state categorically that we have been compromised. I'm inclined to believe that the Hohendorf incident was sheer bad luck. One of the unforeseen things that sometimes occur. I very much doubt whether our potential adversaries had placed his wife under observation as a matter of routine. Or that they knew Hohendorf or any of your other crews. I think one of their fishermen—as Buntline would term it—simply struck lucky. Bad news for us, of course."

"Should we advance the mission? Personally, I'd prefer not to."

"That, Christopher, depends on several factors. We need to know how both Buntline and General Bowmaker appraise the current situation. We talked on the aircraft, but everyone agreed we should first see how you're getting up to speed."

"We're doing very well, sir. The selected crews are

working up effectively, and when Hohendorf's ready, we'll send the tanker for a rendezvous over the North Sea where with Bagni's ASV, he'll practice the ultraclose formation tactic. The object of the exercise will be to get close enough to spoof any snooping desert radar into believing it's looking at a single aircraft, until the time comes for separation."

"You'll be pleased to know we've located a charter airline which flies a cargo route that's perfect for our requirements. On the day of the mission, they'll be persuaded not to make a flight. We'll be using the route. Your tight formation will be taking the place of that cargo airplane."

Jason thought it prudent not ask what methods would be used in order to coerce the airline into playing ball. "Very good news, sir," he said. "Incidentally, the special mods for the IDS in the secure hangar are virtually complete. Hohendorf and Ecker will not actually fly the aircraft until they take off on the mission itself. This means no one will observe it in flight prior to its departure, which, of course, will be at night."

Thurson nodded his approval.

"They'll be spending the rest of the workup period back here at November," Jason continued, "but in the specially configured simulator. A mission tape is being programmed for installation in the simulator, and it will be in place and run-tested by the time they've arrived from Schleswig-Holstein."

"You seem to have your side of this business thoroughly sewn up, Christopher," Thurson said, sounding pleased. "It now remains to be seen what Mr. Buntline and General Bowmaker have got for us. Ah. Here we are."

The staff cars came to a halt at the Operations block. They climbed out and entered the building while the cars were neatly parked side by side, long hoods pointing outward as if sniffing the air.

They went straight to the small conference room that had already been prepared and took their seats at a polished table. Freshly made coffee was waiting.

"I've ordered that we should not be disturbed," Jason began to the air vice-marshal, "so if that's all right, sir, I'll serve."

"We'll serve ourselves, Christopher," Thurson told him. "Let's dispense with the ceremony, eh?" Then he added to the others: "Whenever you're ready, gentlemen."

Buntline decided to speak first. "Last night's incident in the village, coupled with the report from Kapitänleutnant Hohendorf, is a clear indication that this unit is in the firing line. The man who died last night was not one of my own people, but was attached to my department. Normally his job was counterterrorism on mainland Britain. Unfortunately for him, he came up against someone rather more dangerous than your average man with the Semtex. My own people have extensive experience and operate worldwide. They know extreme danger when they see it and would have acted accordingly. The man last night, whom we shall call Jackdaw, was like a novice when pitted against the adversary he came up against."

Buntline paused to take some papers from the slim, leather portfolio he'd brought with him. He spread one before him and studied it briefly before passing it round. "This is necessarily an abridged report," he continued, looking up. "However, preliminary examination of the body revealed an interesting fact. Jackdaw was killed by a single punctuation beneath the right ear." His eyes studied each man in turn. "A thin bladed weapon that went straight into the brain. Efficient, silent. Jackdaw would have died almost instantly. But that's not the truly important discovery. Our killer has made his first mistake. He's given us a clue to his possible identity, but even better, we know his real trade. He's a top assassin. This method of killing is known to my . . . er . . . people. Unless there are several others in our . . . er . . . profession who favor this particular form of killing—which on the known evidence seems unlikely—he has operated in places as diverse as Africa, Latin American, the U.S.A., the Far and Middle East, and a wide selection of European countries, both east and west. Equally, he has been used within Russia itself. We must therefore assume he is after someone up here."

Buntline's eyes had fastened upon Jason, who was looking somewhat pale. Air combat was one thing; being stalked on the ground by a professional killer was another game altogether.

"You are, Wing Commander, the true guiding force behind the November program. You have fought tooth and nail for it. It's your baby, and given the current world situation, even your most implacable detractors must now begin to see the validity of your ideas. I am, as I've recently indicated, a convert. There will be others, no matter how currently reluctant.

"But there is another side to your particular coin. The November program can be seen as inimical to those who would like to take advantage of the increasingly unstable world situation. The Yugoslavian madness is a perfect example. Had there been several November squadrons already operational when this mess began, they might well have been used in time to prevent the sickness from spreading, as it now has. None of the current hand wringing and intergovernmental scrabbling around for an elusive solution would now be embarrassing us all before the entire planet.

"But to get back to you, Wing Commander. It is our considered opinion that you are in extreme danger. Should you be eliminated, the psychological and material damage to the program would be considerable. For a start, your crews practically venerate you. You appear embarrassed, but it's quite true. You will therefore, for your own safety, be confined to this station until we have run our assassin to ground and the mission is complete. However, I believe that if the mission is successfully completed before we've caught him, he'll disappear . . . for his own health. Failure on his part could be very bad news indeed for him. His own people will hunt him down. You can be certain of that."

Jason poured himself a cup of coffee and took a sip of it before he spoke. "Does this confinement include flying?"

"As long as you land nowhere else, I can see no reason why you should stop flying."

Jason nodded slowly.

"It's quite likely," Buntline went on, "that our man in the picture was specifically pulled in by his masters to carry out this job."

"A sighting somewhere else?" the air vice-marshal asked.

Buntline nodded. "We witnessed a very strange incident in Italy, near the Yugoslav border. A man was lifted out of there by the KGB." He chose not to give any more details. "While we have no positive ID, I believe that same man is actually here.

"And now, to the matter of Hohendorf. It is most unlikely that either he or his wife have been under deliberate surveillance. Unless we have a con man chasing beautiful women in that hotel, I'm assuming a fluke. My own lot have from time to time experienced such windfalls, so one must expect the other side to have their lucky days. Wise counsel, however, to further assume that he is now being watched, just to see what turns up. Instruct him to keep a high profile with that Porsche. Let it be seen when he takes Miss Selby out while they're over there.

"When the time comes for his return, he is to leave the Porsche and use another car for the journey. His backseater for the mission has a car, no doubt? Big enough to take three people?"

Jason gave a brief nod. "Yes."

"Then they can use that. Ecker, is it?"

Again, Jason nodded.

"Ecker's wife will no doubt enjoy driving the Porsche for a while." Buntline gave a hint of a smile.

"Won't she be in danger?"

"We can warn the security people over there to keep an eye on her, but I strongly doubt she will be. Fishermen are not killers. They are low-level gatherers who want nothing more than a quiet life." Buntline glanced at each in turn. "Finally, gentlemen, we must also assume that the fact we were covering our unknown assassin will have alerted the opposition that we're on to them. And now I'd really like that coffee." Buntline reached for the pot and began to pour. "General Bowmaker, all yours."

"The upgrade unit for the simulator visuals came on the airplane with us," Bowmaker said, "and is being incorporated as we speak. We were able to do some enhancing of the terrain to give us a close approximation of the topography at the target's location. We still don't know, unfortunately, the exact positions of the defenses. When your men carry out their attacks in the simulator, Wing Commander, any triple A or SAMs that may come up at them will be from *estimated* positions. It will be up to the fast recce ship on the day of the mission to supply real-time target update by the secure data link.

"Of course, we've applied a certain amount of logic regarding their placement, but we all know there's no telling what the other guy might do. What we think is logical may not appear so to him."

Bowmaker paused, deciding he too needed a drink. "Hell, I could use some of that stuff," he said as he filled his cup. He raised the pot slightly toward Thurson, who declined. He put it down and took a drink of the coffee, holding it in his mouth before swallowing. "Damn."

Thurson looked at him. "Bad?"

"Good," Bowmaker commented with approval, taking another drink. "I've also brought something else with me," he continued, looking at Jason. From a side pocket of his uniform he took out a small square envelope, which he slid across the table. "Open it, Wing Commander."

Jason did so, and extracted a 3.5-inch floppy disk.

"A very special, extra-high-density disk," Bowmaker went on. "All the revised terrain data is on there. Give it to Morton and Macallister so that they can reprogram the briefing computer. This new data will show the same topographical modifications that are being put into the simulator visuals.

"The air vice-marshal here will have told you we've got a route for the mission. The company that has leased the cargo planes to the airline is American. On the day of the mission, that cargo plane will suffer a technical problem and will not make the flight. The mission will be over long before anyone works out why. Two points I'd like to add. . . ." Bowmaker drained his cup before continuing: "Mr. Buntline believes the present Russian regime won't last out a second year, that its demise will come sooner than later, and that the hard-liners will be back. I agree. The second is that Yugoslavia might start a chain of events that could give us World War Three, if we're not all very careful. That's why, Wing Commander, your men *must* take this desert radar out. We don't want it around if our nightmare ever comes true. That radar could be the difference between a containable conflict and one that fries us all."

*   *   *

It was dark when the staff cars made their return journey to the waiting executive jet. This time Jason rode with Buntline, at Buntline's request.

"The air vice-marshal has told me," Buntline began, "that you'll carrying out a few training flights in a Hawk with a former fighter controller who was one of your personnel, Flight Lieutenant Caroline Hamilton-Jones."

"Yes," Jason admitted. "The AVM has approved it. Is there a problem?"

"No problem. How do you feel about women combat pilots?"

Jason sighed. "Everyone seems to ask that question these days."

"And the answer?"

"I have faith in Caroline."

"Nicely hedged. I could not have done better myself." Buntline sounded as if he were smiling. "You are aware, Wing Commander," he continued mildly, "that the other side know what you look like?"

"I don't see how—"

"If you were in Intelligence, you'd know that everything, even the most incongruous, is filed somewhere. In air combat, you tell your crews to note all that's taking place, no matter how apparently unimportant. Know your arena. . . ."

"Situation awareness, we call it."

"Precisely. We have our own situation awareness. Do you remember an incident when this unit was about to achieve operational status? A group of the unwashed—as the minister likes to call them—paid an unwanted visit. You were captured on film."

Jason did remember. A van load of protesters bearing antinuclear placards had arrived with the intention of setting up home outside the main gate. Not wanting an old-style Greenham Common permanent encampment, he had moved swiftly to defuse the situation. His gamble had paid off, and the protesters had gone somewhere else. There had been no trouble since. Unfortunately, he had been filmed carrying a little girl who enjoyed wearing his cap, while he tried to persuade her mother there were no nuclear weapons at November One.

"My God," Jason exclaimed softly.

"Quite. You had a TV audience. Almost certainly, some stills of your performance exist where they shouldn't be. By all means, continue flying, but please do make sure that while all this is going on, the only place you come in to land is at November One."

"I feel like a green, noncommissioned airman on punishment."

"The price of fame," Buntline said.

12

Moscow, Four Days Later

Kurinin sat at his desk, studying a spread of photo-graphs of Hohendorf, Ecker, and Anne-Marie, a few shots of the red Porsche and the BMW. To one side was a photograph that was larger than the others. It was of Jason and the little girl, with the cap virtually covering her face. The child's head was upturned as she tried to peer beneath the peak at Jason.

"The protective warrior." Kurinin spoke with just a hint of cynicism. "Are you planning to attack my radar? Or are you giving air cover to someone else?" He knew the November base housed air superiority fighters; but if the reports so far received were correct, what was one of its pilots doing at an attack base in Germany? Had he been washed out from the unit? He had been seen all over the local area, in civilian clothes, either with his woman or in the company of friends. The plentiful supply of photos of the red Porsche was sufficient testimony. It would be interesting to see whether it eventually returned to Scotland. It would be a very strong indication of the possibility of an attack being planned from there.

Kurinin stared at Jason's photograph. The base knew of Poleskov's presence, even if his identity was so far still unknown. It had been stupid of Poleskov to kill that man. Somehow he had blown his cover and focused attention upon himself. It was definitely time to send a backup. Poleskov, in his belief in his own invincibility, was at last beginning to make serious mistakes. He was becoming a liability.

Kurinin gathered the photographs carefully and placed them in a box file. Something would have to be done about Poleskov when the operation was over.

Five thousand nautical miles into her journey, *Karelia*, the monster submarine, headed south toward her station. The entire passage would be made submerged, and when she eventually arrived on station, a ship would be waiting. Suspended a hundred meters beneath its hull would be a cable that terminated into what seemed to be the weighted version of the drogue at the end of an air-refueling hose. A probe would be guided, with the aid of a TV display, into the basket. Coded signals would be received. The probe would withdraw and the cable would be reeled upward. The submarine would not communicate in any way with the ship, for data transfer would be automatic and no one on the vessel above would see any physical evidence of a submarine in the vicinity. The surface ship would depart, and *Karelia* would remain on station, having received a full update on the state of the operation without having surfaced since leaving her base.

Within their air-conditioned quarters, the pilots kept themselves fit in a well-stocked gym. Each was handpicked for his psychological stamina. So far, the experiment of cooping fighter pilots underwater for long periods seemed to be going well. None had shown evidence of incipient claustrophobia.

Still some distance from her appointed station, the *Karelia* had been completely successful in eluding the lurking Los Angeles class hunter/killer boat that had briefly caught her unfamiliar soundprint. She rushed southward, her massive body plowing through the depths of the Atlantic Ocean.

And no one, except those who had sent her, knew she was there.

In the village pub, Poleskov sat at a table well away from the one he'd previously used. True to his method of hiding in plain sight, he had not quit the scene of the killing. However, he looked different.

Plucking his eyebrows and then judiciously adding new, false strands had effectively altered their shape. He also now sported a thriving mustache. Long ago, four perfectly sound teeth had been removed from the front of his lower jaw, to make way for different sets of secure dentures that he used to slightly alter the line of his lower lip. Contact lenses transformed his eyes. A different and faultless accent completed the metamorphosis. Everything had been done minimally. Poleskov didn't believe in the distortions of pads in the cheeks, wigs, and fake glasses. He no longer had the Range Rover. Instead he now drove an ordinary sedan.

Quite close to where he was sitting was a group of enlisted men with whom he had played a darts challenge on the night of the killing. None recognized him.

Then one man glanced round. "Hey, mate. Fancy a game of darts?"

"I don't play," he replied in a voice whose tones would have been familiar in Glasgow.

"Fair enough," the airman said, and left him alone after that.

The group discussed the main topic for the last few days, the murder of the man in the parked van.

Another airman suddenly remarked, "The wingco must be mad. He's going to go flying with a bint. You wouldn't get me in the same bloody plane with a woman pilot."

"Listen to you, Mr. Macho," one of his companions said. "You do a little service dodging SCUDs in the Persian Gulf last year, and already you're calling women bints. Personally, I have nothing against women pilots. They can play with my joystick anytime."

The entire group erupted in laughter.

"Anyway," the one who had said "bint" began defensively, "I wasn't dodging SCUDs. I stayed right where I was, putting bloody bombs on."

"Ooh, he puts them on and they take 'em off," someone else sang, "poor bloody sod. So he puts 'em on and—"

"Shut it!" they all chorused.

"All right then."

More laughter.

"So what's this about the wingco? He really going flying with a female pilot?"

"Yeah. She used to be up here, you know. Then she put in for aircrew and made it through flying training. . . ."

"So far," a voice said ominously. "It's not over yet."

"You really don't like the idea of women fighter pilots, do you?"

"Bloody men are bad enough. God help us if we've got to service bloody airplanes flown by birds."

"Oh, I like that. Airplanes flown by birds. Very poetic."

"Shaddup!" came another chorus.

"Oh, all right then."

Another burst of laughing.

"So what's she flying? This female ace?"

"A Hawk. She's coming up for a few days in a dinky little Hawk to give the boss a ride."

"Oooo!" they all said in mock horror. "Naughty!"

Listening to their banter, Poleskov stayed just long enough to finish his drink, then quietly left. He had work to do.

November Base

The secure hangar was positioned well away from the perimeter fences and from inquisitive binoculars. Hidden within a complex of buildings in the main engineering area, it was well secluded. Inside, the sounds of instructions being given and acknowledged, the whirr of machinery, and the hum of electronics were all mixed in together.

Dressed in flying overalls, Jason strode into this cacophony. He walked across to the Tornado IDS that would be used to fly the attack phase of the mission. Painted in the desert "pink" color the world saw on television during the Gulf War, it stood on chocked wheels, front and rear sections of its canopy raised open. As though wounded, great spaces in its airframe were displayed by missing or hinged panels. Its nose cone, hinged open to the right in two segments like sliced fruit, bared the mass of the electronic wizardry of its on-board systems. To the rear, its tailpipes gaped open, its engines reclining on trolleys beneath them.

Like surgeons, a number of men and women in work overalls were heavily occupied within, around, and about it. They were unfussed and attended to their particular area of interest with the professional calm of people who knew precisely what they were about.

Jason did a slow walk-around of the Tornado. Some paused only briefly to acknowledge his presence. They knew he was not there to disturb them. He halted and stooped beneath the aircraft to look at a man whose head was turned upward into the Tornado's belly. It was the engineer officer in charge.

"As usual, Manfred," he began, "you like getting your hands dirty."

The head turned and lowered, showing a broad, smudged face. The man squatted on his heels and grinned. On the shoulders of his work overalls were the barely visible badges of the rank of major in Germany's Luftwaffe.

"And the face," Manfred Dormer said. "Don't forget the face. Wasn't that what you expected when you made me boss of this little outfit?" Dormer spoke with a strong American accent.

Jason made no reply to that. Dormer was the kind of engineer officer who *liked* getting his hands dirty. He knew his stuff and believed in leading by example. It was why Jason had picked him in the first place.

"What I really want to know," Jason began, "is whether it will fly on the day."

"It will," Dormer said positively, "and it will also do anything asked of it."

"Anything?"

"Well . . . it won't swim." Dormer gave another grin.

"All right, Manfred, you've made your point."

"Don't worry, sir. Everything will be working on the day. The new data-link equipment is already in place, and we're concentrating on the revised weapon connectors right now. The engines are out for a routine check but in reality, there's nothing wrong with them. Just making sure."

Jason nodded, knowing that indeed there was no cause for anxiety on that score.

Dormer glanced at Jason's flying overalls. "Going up?"

"I'm taking someone up for a check ride."

"An ASV?"

"No. A Hawk."

"Ah."

"What does that mean, Manfred?"

"The lady pilot."

The way Dormer had spoken made Jason say, "Not you as well."

"I would not fly in a jet with a woman pilot. But what do I know? I'm just an engineer. Now go away and let me do my work."

"Yes, sir," Jason said dryly. He gave Dormer a friendly pat and left him to it.

As Jason left the hangar to enter the small utility car for the drive back to the squadron, he recalled Caroline Hamilton-Jones's approach to the airfield earlier. The brightly colored Hawk had swept fast and low along the main runway to go into a stylish fighter break in preparation for an impressive landing. Many people had watched and, despite themselves, had been forced to give her full marks.

She certainly knew how to fly. Whether she'd make it to a frontline fighter squadron was another matter altogether.

Poleskov watched as the two-seat Hawk tucked in its wheels and banked steeply toward the Grampian Hills to the southwest. Like the other plane spotters who came almost every day to watch the aircraft movements, he followed its progress with his binoculars. He was able to read its serial number before it disappeared from view in a valley between low foothills.

He lowered the binoculars, working out his plan of action.

During the course of the day, the Hawk made two flights, once with just the front seat occupied. Poleskov's binoculars were powerful enough to enable him to note the difference. On both flights, the Hawk had taken the same route.

Poleskov checked a road map and a civil aviation chart with low-flying areas indicated and made his decision. He left his vantage point and drove toward the foothills. All he needed was already in the car. He found what he was looking for just over an hour's fast drive later. He parked the car in some woods and kitted himself out in attire suitable for mountain walking. Then, taking a rolled backpack from the car, he locked the vehicle and began to climb a steep path through the woods.

He had surveyed the area before, though he had not previously taken that particular path. On each occasion of his visit, he had heard and seen low-flying aircraft. He knew he was taking a long shot despite the fact that, according to the chart, this was a favorite low-flying corridor; but if, as his instincts were telling him, he had chosen correctly, this would be the only chance he would have of carrying out his mission. He had considered other options. None seemed likely to produce results under the present circumstances. This was his only window of opportunity.

It took Poleskov another thirty minutes to reach the spot he was making for. It was an outcrop with a thick screen of bushes that would serve as good cover, while giving him an unimpeded view of the valley below. Perfect for his purposes. He lowered his pack and began to prepare. All he had to do was wait.

The car that had followed Poleskov cruised slowly past the wood until its driver spotted the car's route of entry. A few minutes later, the car was found.

The driver slowly checked the sedan, being very careful not to touch it. Then the almost hidden path up the mountain was discovered, but the newcomer did not take it. An aircraft, flying low, roared past in the distance. The driver of the second car took no notice, scanning the leafy floor of the wood instead with probing eyes. Seemingly satisfied, the newcomer returned to the car and drove away.

November Base, Early Evening in the Officers' Mess

Selby and McCann had returned from their debrief after their latest air-to-air combat training sortie with Flacht and Cottingham. Cottingham had been selected to be Flacht's pilot for the mission.

"I'll say that for him," McCann commented. "He'll never be as good as Axel to work with, but he's okay."

"I'm sure that will cheer him up, Elmer Lee, knowing you've given him such an accolade."

There was a razor-edged relationship between McCann and Cottingham. To begin with, both were American. Cottingham had been an F-15 Eagle driver before Jason, impressed by his air-to-air capabilities, had poached him from the USAF. Cottingham had been with a flight of F-15's that had tangled with ASVs flown by highly capable crews during one of Jason's searches for suitable personnel. Cottingham's had been the only Eagle to take the ensuing fight to a draw. All the others had lost.

McCann was supremely envious of anyone who had flown the Eagle. In his dreams of becoming a pilot, the cockpit of the Eagle was nirvana. Washing out of pilot training had served only to make that now distant dream a painful one. Cottingham was also black, and in an excruciating attempt to show solidarity at their very first meeting,

McCann had greeted Cottingham with the words "Yo, bro" and a palm turned upward.

The expected slap of palm on palm had not come, and Cottingham had stared at him with cold disdain. After a long pause, Cottingham had finally put McCann out his embarrassing misery by eventually slapping the offered palm. Later, Cottingham, then a captain to McCann's lieutenant, had quietly warned McCann never to do that again. McCann was himself now a captain, but still junior to Cottingham.

"I cannot believe that guy still thinks about our first meeting," McCann said in an aggrieved tone of voice. "I was only trying to welcome him."

"The road to hell, Elmer Lee, is paved . . ." Selby paused. "Look, it's Caroline."

They were passing the anteroom but did not enter. Mess dress code forbade the wearing of flying overalls in the room during the evening. They paused by the door.

"Yo, Caroline," McCann greeted. "How did it go?"

She had been reading a paper. She put it down, brightening as she saw them. "Elmer Lee . . . Mark . . . hullo." She stood up and came toward them.

She was of average height and had crisply cut hair of a rich, dark blond that reached just past her ears. Her body was full without being voluptuous, with a firm, flat stomach and small waist. The pale brown eyes in the smooth, roundish face had lost some of the pain suffered by the death in the mountain crash of Neil Ferris, the November navigator she had fallen in love with. It was an attractive and warm face, with a firm chin that showed her determination to get over the tragedy and to pursue her goal of becoming a fighter pilot. A smile lit up her features.

"Well?" McCann said eagerly. "Tell us. Don't keep it a secret."

"I think the boss was pleased."

"You think!"

"At least he didn't say I should be grounded."

"She's being modest, Mark. What do you think?"

"I think you're right," Selby answered.

"Madam," McCann said with exaggerated courtesy, "we think you should dine with us tonight."

"I'll accept, provided it's not off the base. I've got one more flight with the wing commander tomorrow before I get back to my own unit. I want to be spot-on . . . so no late night."

"Your wish is our command. We dine in the mess."

"Just give us time to get out of these things," Selby said, "then we'll join you."

"All right," she said. "By the way, I see the poem's still there."

"The one in the kitting room? You know of it?"

"I should. I wrote it."

She smiled once more at their consternation.

In the briefing room, Macallister was busy at the computer. She had installed the new program that Bowmaker had brought with him and was using it to update the graphics of the target.

Morton entered to look in on her. "Still at it, Mac? Aren't you going to eat tonight? It's twenty-one thirty. Why don't I get something brought in?"

"I'm nearly done, Major. Want to look?"

Morton stared at the screen as she ran the program. As before, there was the run-in to target. But this time a deep wadi afforded good cover for terrain masking, enabling the approach to be made unseen. Then the dried canyon ended abruptly in a sudden cliff face that had to be cleared. The unseen "camera" swept upward, then leveled out over a baking plateau. This continued for several computer miles, before the ground suddenly disappeared and plunged sickeningly.

"That's a drop of twelve hundred feet," Mac said, "and there's the target."

The central disk of the target area was clearly marked out in a horseshoe depression, surrounded by its SAM batteries. There was just one exit: through the narrow mouth of the horseshoe. Everything else was high ground.

She tapped at some keys. The peaks and high ground that made up the horseshoe were given height markings. The lowest, at 1,200 feet, was the point of entry to the target. Some of the peaks scaled 3,600 feet.

"There must be triple A," she went on, "but the programmers didn't know where to site them."

"Jeezus!" Morton remarked softly. "I don't envy the guys who've got to do this. They've got to fly down that cliff. They'll never make it."

Mac stared at the image and said nothing.

That night at the Ecker home on the outskirts of Schleswig, Morven held on tightly to Hohendorf as they lay in bed.

"I'll never walk out on you," she vowed sleepily to him, "no matter what. Promise me you won't crash your plane."

"I promise," he said, kissing her eyelids. "Now go to sleep."

She was getting jumpy, he thought, although she knew nothing of the mission. He wondered if she would one day change her mind about loving him unconditionally. He hoped not.

Hohendorf did not really believe in omens. All the same, it wouldn't hurt to be extra careful on the mission.

*   *   *

Though it had rained, the dawn came bright and clear in the Grampians, promising a perfect day. The steep flanks of the surrounding peaks, made dark by the earlier downpour, seemed to gleam as if polished. Poleskov had spent the night on the mountain but had constructed his hiding place so well, he had remained quite dry throughout. Sleeping on the mountain had been no hardship. Compared to some places he'd spent other nights, this was almost luxury.

A hooded thermal oversuit, ultralight and easy to stow with a zip that reached to his chin, had been pulled on over his clothes to keep him warm and dry. That had been sufficient. He now removed the suit and put it away neatly, then chewed at a high-protein biscuit as he began to make his preparations. It was all the sustenance he required for the time being.

When he had finished, he inched forward on his stomach to the edge of the outcrop. The valley was spread out beneath, giving him a full 180-degree view along it. Pleased with his choice of position, he moved back into his hiding place to wait.

An hour later he heard the roar of jet engines. Two attack Tornadoes swept past on their wingtips in tight formation, so low that he nearly missed their fleeting shapes against the backdrop of the valley. Vortices, like fluttering ghostly shrouds, streamed from the leading edges of their wings and the four tips. He followed them with the binoculars as they reversed bank to thread their way through the valley. They leapt up a steep slope to fling themselves over the other side and were gone, the noise of their passage fading swiftly.

It had been beautifully done and despite what he was there to do, Poleskov admired the skill of the flying.

A substantial pause followed, then a single Jaguar shot past, following the route of the Tornadoes. It did not breast the hill with similar aplomb, as if the pilot did not quite trust himself to do it.

Poleskov sat still, prepared and waiting. It was clearly going to be a busy day.

It was the better part of an hour before a heavy roar filled the valley. A USAF F-15E, the two-seat version of the Eagle, came hurtling through. It banked steeply, displaying its vast wing plan. It seemed positively huge by comparison with the Tornadoes and Jaguar that had gone before it. However, instead of flinging itself over the ridge as the Tornadoes had done, it cut in its afterburners, rolled level, and stood on its tail. It tore for the heavens almost vertically, its thunder seeming to shake the entire world.

Poleskov turned away from it. Would the Hawk ever come? Had he misjudged after all?

November Base, 1020 hours

Jason, in full flying gear, accompanied by a similarly attired Caroline Hamilton-Jones, walked out to the flight ramp where the little Hawk awaited them. He watched approvingly as she carried out a thorough preflight walk-around of the aircraft.

"If you'd like to get in, sir," she said to him, very crisp and professional.

Aware that the male ground crew were watching her movements avidly, Jason placed a booted foot upon the extending step, to lever himself upward along the left side of the aircraft. He placed his other foot in the toe-in step, eased himself beneath the side-hinged canopy, and hoisted himself into the rear cockpit. A member of the ground crew helped him secure his harness to the zero/zero ejection seat. Like those of the immensely more powerful Tornado ASV, the Hawk's seats permitted ejection at zero speed and zero height.

Caroline completed her checks and entered the front cockpit, went through her start-up checks swiftly, checked that communication with the backseat was clear, and then started the engine. Canopy closed, she requested taxiing permission.

"Roger, Kestrel Zero One with November Boss aboard," the tower said, "you are clear to taxi."

"Kestrel Zero One," she acknowledged. "Do they sound amused to you, sir?" she asked Jason.

"I wouldn't have thought so," he replied. An incipient smile, however, was safely hidden in his oxygen mask. "You have nothing to worry about, Caroline. You're a very good pilot."

"Thank you, sir."

She taxied toward the runway threshold, stopped, did her pretakeoff checks, then pushed the throttle firmly forward. Takeoff was clean. She pressed the button that raised the wheels and, when they were safely tucked in, banked smoothly to head toward the Grampian valley for the low-level section of their flight.

In the backseat, Jason noted her flying abilities with continuing approval.

The car that had followed Poleskov the day before was on the way back to the woods where his car was hidden. It traveled along a stretch of twisting road, almost too fast for the prevailing conditions. The surface had not yet quite dried out in places from the night rains. On bends, the car used the whole road, powering through the apexes, straightening the line it took through them.

* * *

Poleskov thought he could hear something. The noise was sharper, by a smaller, single-engined aircraft. Was his wait at last over? He began to get ready.

Well hidden within the shrubbery was a small loop antenna. A cable led from it to a hand-held unit with a screen like a tiny pocket-size television set. There would not be much time for what he intended to do. There would also be one chance only.

To one side on a small ramp was what looked like a plastic, one-piece model of a comic-book rocket ship, about twelve inches long. It was in reality an inert missile, powered by a miniature jet engine of the kind model plane enthusiasts used. A tiny rod aerial protruded from its spine. Its range was limited, but sufficient for requirements. Provided, Poleskov knew only too well, he could succeed with the single attempt. He was about to carry out his own birdstrike.

He moved along the outcrop, to look up and down the valley, ears tuning themselves toward the faint sound. Something was definitely coming.

The range of the loop aerial was also limited, but he had positioned it so that it would give him the widest-possible coverage of the entrance to the valley.

He switched on the handset. The screen came alive but remained blank. Then a red button glowed. Almost immediately a small dot appeared at one edge of the screen and began to inch across it.

Poleskov grabbed his binoculars for a quick confirmation. The powerful glasses picked up the aircraft almost immediately. Still some distance away, but coming fast, was a Hawk.

Poleskov almost flung the binoculars down as he decided to chance the strike. He pushed a sliding switch on the edge of the handset. With a high-pitched whine that was almost inaudible, the miniature jet started and worked itself up to full thrust, and the model streaked off the ramp and into the valley. It had its own seeker, and it immediately curved toward the approaching aircraft.

Poleskov watched in satisfaction as a box appeared on the screen, framing the dot of the incoming Hawk. Then the handset gave out a continuous beeping. Lock-on had been achieved.

Poleskov relaxed and waited for the inevitable. There was nothing else he had to do.

Caroline, visor down for the low flying and feeling good, was just reversing bank to follow the track of the valley when something struck the canopy behind her with explosive force. The Hawk felt as if it had been stopped in its tracks, and the rear section of the canopy seemed to disintegrate into a million fragments.

The plastic model, doing 200 knots, had met the Hawk's own 350 knots head-on, to give an impact speed of 550. Luckily it was a glancing blow, and instead of entering the rear cockpit, the model had skimmed over the aircraft in a multitude of shards. The damage, however, was still considerable.

The shattering of the rear section of the canopy produced a devastating chain reaction. Pieces were immediately ingested by the engine, causing surge. Others, in big chunks, had entered the rear cockpit to slam into Jason's face. Only the fact that his visor was down protected him from death-producing disfigurement. In the event, his visor was itself shattered, though it had remained more or less intact, leaving him blood-soaked but still alive.

Horrendous noises were coming from the engine, and in the front cockpit Caroline felt her heart freeze.

Get hold of yourself woman! her mind screamed at her. *Fly the aircraft.* Everything had to be done almost simultaneously. The recovery procedure shot through her memory.

Fly the aircraft . . . remain in control. Check height, speed. Consider immediate actions to deal with the emergency. Find somewhere to land, if possible. Do a backup check to see if actions taken are correct. For landing, consider weather conditions, fuel state, fuel leaks, airframe and/or engine damage, control problems, low-speed handling checks.

All of this sped through her mind even as she called urgently: "Sir! Are you all right?"

No reply came from the backseat.

"Sir!" she called again. "Are you all right?"

There was still no reply. The engine was dying on her. She pulled into a gentle climb to 3,500 feet, converting speed to height, then shut down the engine. From that altitude she had six miles to glide at 180 knots, provided there was somewhere to land. She could not bring herself to eject until she was certain Jason also could. Command eject activation was in the back, so she couldn't punch him out.

She called him a third time but still got no reply. He was either totally incapacitated or the cockpit intercom was out.

Oh, God! she thought. I've killed him!

Horror filled her mind as she looked out of the crippled aircraft for somewhere to set down. She attempted a relight, but that only made things worse, and she shut down again quickly. She could forget the engine for all the use it now was.

She called her emergency to November base: "Mayday Mayday Mayday! This is Kestrel Zero One. We have a birdstrike . . . repeat, birdstrike. Damage severe . . . possible serious injury to rear occupant. Mayday Mayday Mayday . . ."

"We have you, Kestrel. State conditions."

"Flame out. No stores." That meant she had nothing to

jettison to lighten weight. "Control satisfactory." For the moment. The central warning panel was showing a host of failures, and the attention tone was going mad on the headphones. She pressed one of the flashing buttons, and the noise stopped. The CWP continued to glare balefully at her.

She had checked the twin hydraulic systems. Number one had failed, but the automatic ram air turbine had extended into the airstream to supply sufficient power to number two to continue power to the controls. All she had to do was find somewhere to land within six miles.

On the mountain, Poleskov had the satisfaction of seeing the effect of his missile and was doubly pleased when, in the attempt to right itself, the afflicted Hawk had displayed the number beneath its wing. He had struck the correct target and was certain both seats were occupied.

In the binoculars, his eyes mercilessly followed the aircraft, watching the pilot's attempts to survive. They were brave attempts, he conceded, and if that were truly a woman flying, he was suitably impressed. But there was no remorse.

On the ground, the other car had arrived but was parked well away from Poleskov's, out of view. The driver had not gone up the path but was nowhere to be seen.

At the November base, the crash teams were rapidly getting ready. The news had spread, and people were in a state of shock. The rescue and crash teams could not believe the urgent message.

"November Boss is going down!" the speaker system

had blared at them. "Repeat . . . November Boss is going down! Crash teams scramble! Scramble!"

"November Base!" the tower heard suddenly. "Landing site found! Repeat . . . landing site found!" The coordinates were given.

"Roger, Kestrel. Teams are on their way. Good luck. Stay open for communication."

"Kestrel."

"This is November Rescue, Kestrel. We are monitoring your coms and are on our way."

"Kestrel," she acknowledged for the second time, feeling a little better.

She had seen the likely spot when all hope was nearly gone: a disused grass strip near the edge of a wood that seemed reasonably suitable. In any case, it was her only choice. She lined up and prepared for the most important landing of her life.

She went through her checks. Throttle high-pressure cock . . . OFF. Fuel pump switch . . . OFF. Low-pressure cock . . . OFF. Engine start switch . . . OFF. She selected the gear, heard them come down, and hoped they would stay locked during the landing. The checks continued. Harness . . . TIGHT and LOCKED. She checked number two hydraulics yet again and the brake pressure, remembering *not* to test the brakes. That might use the only pressure left to her.

On the mountain, Poleskov lowered his binoculars in consternation. That pilot was stubborn. It would be a forced landing, possibly terminal; but he had to be certain. He would have to finish the job at the crash site.

He raised the binoculars for a last time, noted the distant aircraft's direction. It was clearly on its final approach. Quickly he picked up his already secured backpack. A swift check showed he had left no evidence of his presence. He began to hurry down the mountain.

Caroline lowered the flaps and felt relief as they came down. Speed was now down to 160 knots. Her minimum approach was 150. Below that, and the Hawk, having performed valiantly so far, would run away from her . . . and that would be that. Both she and the wing commander would be two more fatal statistics.

"It's not going to happen!" she heard herself say.

At precisely 150 knots, the Hawk touched down on the grass trip and ran along it, nicely controlled. For a while.

The night rains had softened the ground on a length of strip that had once been really suitable only for light, propeller-driven aircraft. The Hawk's speed, despite Caroline's pressure on the toe brakes, soon caused it to use up the available space. She nearly made it, but the soft ground, though slowing the aircraft perceptibly, was also making it increasingly unstable. Worse, a low ditch, hidden by the grass from the air, ran directly across the end of the far threshold.

The Hawk's nosewheel slammed into the ditch, and all the gear collapsed upward. This fired the ejection mechanism of the rear seat, punching Jason out. The seat separated cleanly, but there was not enough height, and Jason landed heavily, breaking both legs. He lay unconscious, a tangled, bloody heap.

Caroline was badly shaken and bruised but otherwise unhurt. Quickly she snapped off her harness and climbed out of the aircraft to race to where Jason had fallen, more certain than ever that he was now dead.

He groaned as she reached him, and she felt her heart lift. But his injuries seemed horrific. She dared not raise his visor for fear of what she would see and of the damage she might farther cause. Pieces of it seemed to be stuck to his flesh. His oxygen mask had come undone and was hanging off, still attached to one side of his helmet. Either he had somehow managed to unclip it instinctively or it had detached itself during ejection. The lower part of his face was almost spotless, where the mask had been. Nose, mouth, and chin seemed uninjured; but slowly congealing blood was seeping from beneath the helmet and visor. She did not want to move him either in case that, too, made his injuries worse. She decided the best thing to do for the moment would be to keep him warm. Leaving the parachute harness still attached to him, she gathered the canopy and made a protective cushion about his broken body.

She settled down to wait for the rescue teams while she kept her anxious vigil and contemplated the end of her career as a pilot.

"I'm . . . I'm so sorry, sir," she said softly, feeling guilty and helpless. "So very sorry."

Incredibly, she heard a low sound come from him. His lips were moving. "That . . . that was a very good landing, Caroline. We walked away from it." A hand moved slowly to hold on to hers.

"Shhh. Don't speak, sir."

"You . . . you giving a wing commander orders?"

"Yes, sir."

"Very well."

At the far end of the strip, the Hawk did not catch fire.

Poleskov had reached his car and was about to open it.

"Hello, comrade."

He whirled and froze. *"You!"*

"Me."

He felt a sudden anger. "So they sent you to check up on me. Didn't they think I could do it? Well, I have. I've done it!" He paused. "You've changed a little. Plastic surgery? You're slimmer than I remember, but still sexy. And the hair . . . that's different, too."

"You look different."

"That's our job, isn't it?" he said. Then he went on with some urgency, "We can talk about old times later because before long their rescue team will be at the crash. It's not far, so let's go, just to make sure. Since you are here, you might as well come, too. Then you can tell the suspicious bastards who sent you that Poleskov has done the job again, as usual. We'll still have time to get well away before the team arrives, if we leave right now." His eyes widened suddenly. "What the hell's this?"

A silenced automatic was pointing at him. There was no reply to his question.

"I get it. I do the job, then they send you to take me out. You shits! Well, Poleskov's not that easy. . . ."

Even as he spoke, he was moving; but he was already too late. For the first time in his career, Poleskov had been caught off guard. Perhaps it was a small feeling of euphoria at the success of his strike against the Hawk that had made him less alert. Perhaps it was the unexpected appearance of a backup. Whatever the reason, it was to prove fatal.

The automatic coughed twice at him, the heavy bullets striking into his chest with deadly accuracy. The force of the blows flung him against the car, where he remained upright for brief seconds, then slid untidily to the leafy floor.

"Tokareva!" he said hoarsely. "You bitch!" he added as he died.

She walked away without looking at the body, climbed into her car, and drove off.

13

November Base Hospital

Jason's facial injuries had looked far worse than they actually were. He had lost plenty of blood, but, miraculously, the damage to his face was relatively light. It was the stronger, lightweight ASV helmet—its targeting system disabled for the Hawk flight but with a compatible connector for communication—that had saved him. Its equally stronger visor had been more resistant to the flying shards of the canopy, and that had saved his sight. Only the slightest scarring would remain when his face eventually healed.

His legs had been reset. Again, he was fortunate in that the breaks were clean. He would walk and certainly fly again; but it would be some time before he would be able to do so.

At the moment of impact and the shattering of the

canopy, something had sliced through the coms cable, but he had been in no condition to notice as his world had dissolved into pain and intermittent unconsciousness.

Now he slept deeply in the hospital bed, heavily sedated against the waves of pain that would be waiting to break through. In the corridor outside his room, it seemed the entire personnel of both November squadrons—aircrew and nonaircrew—were waiting.

"Gentlemen . . . ladies," pleaded a harassed doctor, "you cannot see him for at least two days, and then only in the strictest of rations." Caroline was there, too. "Flight Lieutenant Hamilton-Jones, *you* should be in bed. You're still in a state of shock. I've examined you, and you're all right; but I insist that you remain here for further observation. Your home unit has been informed. Now off you go. I'd hate to make that an order." The doctor was a Royal Navy commander.

He looked at Selby and McCann, who were standing close by. They took the cue.

"Up you get," Selby said to her gently. "You're serving no purpose here."

McCann accosted the nearest nurse and brought her back to Caroline. "Come on, ma'am," the noncommissioned nurse said with kind politeness. "Let's be having you."

Caroline allowed herself to be led away. "I nearly killed him," she said to the nurse.

"Nonsense, ma'am," the nurse said firmly. "You did no such thing."

That night in the pub, the same group of airmen that Poleskov had eavesdropped upon were having a subdued drink.

"Bloody women pilots," one said. "Didn't I tell you? Nearly kills the wingco."

"Shut it, mate," another said. "Word is she did bloody well. Anyone can be caught by a birdstrike. Mr. Hohendorf had a very nasty one when this unit first started up. Blood and bird guts all over the canopy. Engines chock full of gulls. He couldn't see out, but he put it down nicely. And the reason *she's* a pilot and you're not is because she showed guts, kept her nerve, put that Hawk down on a postage stamp of a grass strip, and *still* walked away."

"Yeah . . . but the wingco didn't, did he?"

"Christ. Get him a drink, somebody, if only to shut him up. We'll be hearing this record forever otherwise."

"I've got a bloody drink."

Buntline's people were all over the crash site and its environs. They eventually found Poleskov a day later and immediately put a tight security seal upon the incident. That same afternoon he met with Bowmaker and Thurson—who had flown in the night before—in the conference room.

"Well, we shan't be worrying about our assassin anymore," he began immediately. "We've found him . . . dead."

"How?" This from Bowmaker.

"Shot, General. Very cleanly. A pro hit."

"Are you saying there are *two* of them?" Thurson asked.

"Either that, or the second one was meant to eliminate him anyway."

"Doesn't make sense."

"Oh, but it does. I believe he had outstayed his welcome and was turning into a maverick. In the present climate, they obviously thought he would soon be selling his services to the highest bidder. After all, he had been caught attempting to sell arms independently. And just to clarify something . . . it was not a birdstrike that downed the Hawk," Buntline added.

They stared at him, waiting.

"We found some metal pieces in the rear cockpit," he told them. "Not from the aircraft. They have been identified as coming from a miniature jet engine. The sort that model enthusiasts put in their radio-controlled aircraft. Our man's body was found not far from crash site."

"Good God." Thurson's voice held astonishment as well as a subdued anger.

"We're still searching," Buntline went on, "but I'm certain he was responsible. He was thorough. I'll give him that. When he realized he could not get Jason on the ground, he tried the air and damned well nearly succeeded. It was only the young lady's remarkable flying that saved them both."

Bowmaker said: "But how did he know the wing commander would be flying in the Hawk?"

Buntline smiled grimly. "Low-level intelligence. He listened to gossip. Their cherished wingco flying with a female pilot must have set the tongues wagging. There's ostensibly no security risk in discussing such matters. The media is full of comment about the pros and cons of female combat pilots. Why should your personnel be any different? As I've said before, unless we're prepared to live in individual fortresses, there's no such thing as one hundred percent security. If there were, no one would ever have succeeded in assassinating a monarch, a president, or a prime minister. Each of these things, as we all know, is recorded in history. Equally, if we are going to live like that . . . we might as well give up now. I don't think I'd like the kind of society it would produce. The Iron Curtain gave us a glimpse of one kind of nightmare. This would be another."

"So what will this second killer be up to?" Thurson asked. "There are guards at the hospital. . . ."

"Unnecessary. He can't get in. As a matter of fact, something puzzles me about the second killer. There was time enough before the crash teams arrived to make it to the site from where the body was found. If the killer had wanted Jason dead, he had sufficient opportunity to get there to administer the coup de grace and still make a clean getaway. Yet he did no such thing. I believe he was after the first man, and not Jason at all."

"Trying to stop him?"

"Too late for that."

"A deeper mystery," Thurson said. "We have an agent, not belonging as far as we three can ascertain, to either of our governments. Whose, then? Surely not one of theirs."

"A rebel faction, perhaps," Buntline said. "There are all sorts of groupings jostling for power. All is confusion, and their particular bloodletting is far from over. It's still very early. The best—or worst, if you prefer—is yet to come over there."

Two days after the crash, Jason was propped up in bed to receive visitors. His bandaged face was swollen, and his legs hurt; but he insisted on seeing people.

Thurson was on a visit. "You're driving the medical staff crazy, Christopher. Your visitors are clogging up the corridors. Try not to do this too often, will you? Or you'll give the docs multiple breakdowns."

"Don't make me smile, sir. It hurts. How's Caroline?"

"You ask that of almost everyone who comes in, I gather, and receive the reply I'm about to give you. She's fine. Off back to her unit tomorrow. A new Hawk's coming in. She'll be flying the return journey."

"Good. Best thing for her. She deserves a commendation,

sir. That was . . . bloody good . . . flying . . ." Jason's voice began to fade. "Bloody . . . good . . . indeed . . ."

"You need more rest," Thurson said quickly. "I'll see to everything. She'll get her commendation."

"Th-thank you, sir. The mission . . ."

"Is in good hands. You have a rest. I'll see you tomorrow." Thurson went out just as the doctor entered, giving him a severe look.

This particular commander was apparently not fazed by air vice-marshals when his patient's welfare was at stake, Thurson thought dryly.

"That's the navy for you," he said to himself.

The next day, the national papers carried a story of the crash. A birdstrike, so the story went, had caused the crash of a Hawk advanced trainer aircraft, severely injuring Wing Commander Jason, who was not expected to live. Thurson showed a newspaper to Jason, who tried to laugh but stopped when the effort hurt too much. His face had begun to lose some of its swelling. The doctored description of events was Buntline's idea. He wanted to send the wrong message to those who had sent the man who had been found in the woods.

All November personnel were strictly forbidden to discuss the matter off the base.

In Schleswig-Holstein, Hohendorf was told of the crash just before the story broke. Despite himself, he counted it as the second omen and waited for the third.

"I don't believe in such things," he muttered, trying to convince himself.

*   *   *

Moscow, Twenty-four Hours Later

In his office, Kurinin read the usual selection of Western papers. Many carried a photograph of Jason similar to the one already on file.

He had not heard from Poleskov but it didn't matter. The job had been done. Poleskov could indulge himself for a short while.

Three days later Hohendorf received orders to return to November One with Ecker. His constant flying of the Tornado IDS had brought him up to speed, and working with Ecker had once more made them into an instinctive and cohesive combat attack crew. Further instructions were that they should make the return journey in Ecker's car and leave the Porsche until after the mission had been carried out.

With Morven on the backseat, they set off at night for the Channel port selected for the crossing.

"I hope Erika takes good care of my Porsche," he said worriedly as they left.

Ecker grinned in the gloom of the car. "She's a better driver than you are."

"Smile when you say that."

"I am smiling."

The next morning, "Jerry Craven's" colleague drove past the house and glanced idly at the red car parked at the front. He later reported that the Porsche was still in Germany.

The *Karelia* had made her way southward via the northwest Atlantic basin. Testing the flexibility of her enormous engines, she had cruised at speeds ranging from a pedestrian twenty knots right through to sustained dashes of fifty knots plus. On one occasion she had maintained maximum speed continuously for over twelve hours, with no adverse effects. No surface ship, no submarine, and no torpedo currently in service could ever hope to keep up with her. She would be able to strike anywhere at will, her aircraft giving her a long reach, her ability to escape unmatchable.

She had traveled at various depths, at times pausing silently upon a plateau near the mid-Atlantic ridge, at depths that approached ten thousand feet. And though at those times her crew had listened anxiously for ominous creakings in her double hulls, nothing had occurred to disturb their peace of mind. Then she had turned eastward, threading her way though a canyon in the ridge to enter the Cape Verde basin, her assigned station. Her orders had been specific.

Now, for the first time, after ensuring that not even a weather satellite was surveying the area, she surfaced. This was an event in itself. Like a great leviathan from prehistory, she rose out of the depths, a colossal presence that sent huge waves of displaced water rushing away in all directions. It took the immediate sea area some time to return to equilibrium.

Karelia was about to carry out another stage of her trials. She was about to launch her aircraft.

The great clamshell doors unsealed themselves with a hiss loud enough to outdo several whales blowing in concert; then, with uncanny silence, they began to open, first sliding outward, their curvatures disappearing into the body of the ship. The lower lips met and stopped, half retracted to reveal the planform of the long area of the flight deck.

The six Yak-142's were already prepared and waiting,

pilots strapped into their cockpits. The wings began to unfold, giving the unnerving impression of huge, predatory insects getting ready for the hunt.

Soon two of the aircraft were moved forward by catapultlike strops to the empty section of deck near the bows. The strops retracted, and engines were started. Before long, the Yaks lifted off the deck and, at a selected height, went into forward flight, the power of their engines hurling them into steep climbs. The process was repeated with each remaining pair. All six aircraft had become airborne within less than three minutes.

For an hour the pilots reveled in the first freedom of the air they had experienced since leaving base. They engaged in mock combat, the more skilled scoring several "kills." Of the six, who were themselves all highly capable air-to-air practitioners, three came out as high-scoring winners. Then the hour was up, and the birds returned to the roost. Deck recovery was faultless.

Karelia retreated to the depths to await a satellite-free night, for night launches were next on the program.

The opportunity came forty-eight hours later. She surfaced without lights, for in those latitudes any light would be seen for miles. The aircraft were themselves without lights. On a normal ship, such an environment would have been extremely hazardous; but in the case of *Karelia*, the launch would be carried out automatically.

Before surfacing, all the aircraft had been attached to their individual strops. Once on the surface, the launch sequence would begin, with no deck crews having to expose themselves to any danger.

The launch went off without a hitch. It would be up to the pilots to find their way back using their instruments and the infrared sensors that would enable them to see the deck almost as if it were daylight.

The Yaks disappeared into the night, and their base

waited in the vastness of the dark ocean, a silent monolith upon the water.

Klaas de Glind loved the sea so much, he frequently made long solo yachting voyages in his prized teak-hulled ocean racer. On this night, on a trip from Portugal to the West Indies, he was dozing on a calm sea, his yacht at sea anchor.

A sudden roar had him clambering off his bunk. He rushed on deck but could see nothing. The sound faded, and he was about to return to below, when another roar was upon him. This time he thought he barely observed two fleeting shapes. There were no more sounds, though he thought their fading wake lasted longer than expected. Perhaps there were more of them out there.

He went back to bed, wondering about it. Probably the Americans at it again, he thought, on some sort of night exercise. Ascension Island was some way to the south, but these days military jets, thanks to air refueling, had long ranges. De Glind had once been in the Dutch air force, though he had not been a pilot.

To break the daily routine on his Atlantic journeys, he sometimes chatted from time to time with a radio ham friend on one of the islands. He would have something new to say when they next made contact in forty-eight hours, he decided. Fast jets way out in the middle of nowhere. A man could not find peace, even on the ocean.

De Glind sighed wearily, yawned, crawled into his bunk, and went back to sleep.

He was not disturbed again.

On the day that Hohendorf returned to November One, visitors had not been allowed to see Jason, who'd been in great pain. On the morning after Klaas de Glind's interrupted sleep, he was able to gain admission. He took Ecker with him.

"See what happens when I'm away for a little while," he greeted Jason.

"You're being insubordinate, Mr. Hohendorf," Jason said weakly.

"Yes, sir."

"And this, I take it, is the famous Johann Ecker?"

Ecker came forward. "Sir."

"Well, Mr. Ecker. Think you can do it?"

"Yes, sir."

"Good. Pity I can't . . . poach you . . . for good. We could use you here. But Wusterhausen . . . promised he would fight tooth . . . tooth and nail . . . to keep you. I think he means business. Don't . . . don't you? Aah! Damn! I hate this pain."

"We'll leave, sir," Hohendorf began solicitously.

"You'll leave when I tell you . . . Mr. Hohendorf!"

"Sir."

"Well, Mr. Ecker? Will . . . Wusterhausen fight?"

Ecker nodded. "Yes, sir."

"Thought so. Oh, well . . . can't have it . . . all I suppose. Things working out . . . for you two?"

"They're working fine, sir," Hohendorf answered. "We've got our tactics sorted."

The bandaged face nodded fractionally. "And Flacht. How's he . . . feel about . . . Cottingham?"

"They're working well together, but I think he wants the old team in the cockpit again."

"Only to be expected. Once this . . . is . . . all over, you'll be back. Now . . . if you gentlemen . . . don't mind, I think I need some . . . sleep."

"Yes, sir."

Hohendorf glanced warningly at Ecker, and they left as Jason shut his eyes.

"He really got hurt," Ecker said in the corridor.

"Don't let that fool you. The man's an ox. He'll be back in no time."

"And you can't fool me, Axel. All of you are worried sick about him."

"He's a good boss."

"Like Wusterhausen?"

"Like Wusterhausen, but different."

That afternoon they were in the mission simulator, which had been reprogrammed with the full updates, and were low over the computer-generated desert landscape on the final leg of the run-in to the target.

Hohendorf was holding fifty feet above the wadi floor. So far, they had escaped the attentions of the defenses. Fully aware that the positions in the computer world, based as they were upon available knowledge and thus only approximate, they did not take the lack of offensive fire as an expectation of what the real thing would be like. Such an assumption could lead to a quick demise.

"High ground, three miles," Ecker announced.

"Okay," Hohendorf acknowledged.

They hurtled up a steep cliff face. Almost immediately the radar warning receiver went berserk, telling them a SAM was on its way.

"Chaff!" Hohendorf demanded.

"Going out."

But the warning tone was still there.

"It's hanging on to us, Johann. I'm going to evade."

"Roger. I'm still spoofing."

Hohendorf flung the aircraft into a hard left turn, then broke hard right. All the while the computer terrain seemed perilously close.

The warning tone stopped.

"We've lost it," Ecker said with relief.

On the threat display, Hohendorf saw the symbol vanish. He returned to his course and stayed low.

"We must hope that doesn't happen on the run-in, Johann. We don't want to warn them. If a SAM fires at us when we're still some distance, it gives them time at the target site."

"Then we must get as close as possible before they know. Target is now thirty miles. Usual offset?"

"Yes. We've been practicing it. Let's do it that way."

"Roger. Remember our height here is fifty feet, but the drop to target is twelve hundred. You want a climb to thirty-one hundred over the *target* elevation, not this ground level. We'll be exposed for too long otherwise."

"Okay."

"Target twenty miles."

"Okay. Selecting. Master's LIVE. Steering to target's all yours."

"Roger. Target now ten miles. We'll be going over the edge soon. And here we are. . . ."

Hohendorf brought the nose up to give him clearance, rolled the Tornado onto its back, and pulled the stick toward him to plunge down the cliff face. He rolled upright and had begun to level out at one hundred feet above the floor of the depression for the run to target when an enormous explosion shook the simulator. The visuals were replaced by a vivid red glow, and then everything went dark. The simulator stopped.

Hohendorf and Ecker sat in their respective cockpits, feeling shock. The simulated mission had ended in their deaths. For long moments they found they could not speak.

Then the lights came on and the machinery whirred back to life.

"What the hell happened?" Hohendorf asked.

"I . . . I . . . don't know." Ecker was at a loss. "We were doing well. . . ."

"Obviously not, Johann. We're supposed to be dead." Hohendorf realized he had spoken curtly. "Sorry."

"No problem. I'm baffled as well. I'm sure we didn't do anything wrong."

"Sorry, gentlemen," an embarrassed voice said in their headphones. "The problem's on this side. The new program got excited. It fired off a SAM when you inverted. In the scenario, there are no SAMs in that position."

"Maybe it knows something we don't," Hohendorf said.

The voice laughed. "This is a computer, not a psychic. Give us a few minutes to reset."

"Roger."

Hohendorf found himself thinking that the third event had occurred. He tried to discount the whole idea as nonsense, but it wouldn't leave him.

"Johann."

"Yes?"

"On the real mission, let's alter the approach. Move our route a few miles."

"Are you telling me you actually believe there's a SAM at that location?" Ecker asked.

"Why take chances? Could be man-portable, shoulder-launched."

Ecker said nothing for a while. "Frightening, wasn't it?" he said at last.

"I don't know about you, but my heart stopped."

"In the real thing, it would have."

Alone in his room that night, Hohendorf lay back on his bed with his hands clasped behind his head and stared at the ceiling.

Further attacks on the simulated target had been

successful, without any hits being taken from the air defenses. But Hohendorf did not feel at ease. His mind kept returning to the incident at the edge of the cliff. He could not explain to himself why he felt so strongly that mortal danger lurked there. It was just an incomplete computer program, after all. . . .

He sat up suddenly. Suppose the program had *not* been wrong? Suppose whoever had done the original programming had in fact *included* the SAM location, based either upon tactical thinking or upon actual knowledge? And suppose during installation in the simulator someone had got the installation sequence screwed up and had omitted the SAM or inadvertently logged it into some hidden part of the memory? Perhaps the way he'd taken the leap over the edge had somehow activated the path that allowed the SAM to become enabled.

Hohendorf sighed in frustration. Whatever the reasons, he was going to take the incident seriously. If there were no SAMs and he was only being jumpy . . . fine. But if there were . . .

He owed it to Erika not to get Johann killed. He owed it to Morven not to get himself killed. And he owed it to himself to complete the mission successfully.

Dawn in the desert was beautiful. Lieutenant Anatoly Tikov had again persuaded his superiors to let him go on another patrol. The same captain commanded the three armored personnel carriers. They had been out for a day but would not be back for another three.

The APCs had just arrived and had parked side by side, snout pointing toward the cliff edge. Tikov stood in the hatch and trained his binoculars on the radar site down below.

"How far do you think it is, Lieutenant?" a soldier,

yawning and stretching, called up to him from the ground.

"Fourteen kilometers," replied Tikov, who'd already checked it. "Or if you prefer, just over eight and a half miles."

"Imagine," the soldier said. "Only fourteen kilometers away, but we'd have to go one hundred and fifty to get back there."

Which was true enough. The surrounding landscape was not kind, even to tracked vehicles. The detour to reach an accessible route to take them back to base traversed a great distance. The only way to the site by a short route was on foot and down the twelve-hundred-foot cliff.

But to a bomber, Tikov thought, it was no distance at all.

He swung the binoculars round in a 360-degree search of the horizon, then raised them up to the sky. Far in the distance, a silver shape was twinkling in the early light.

"You're not thinking that cargo plane is a bomber, are you, Tikov?"

He looked down hastily. The captain was smiling up at him. "Come down and have some breakfast, Anatoly. We'll be on this patch for a couple of days, so relax. A few sweeps of the area, then it's back for nice cold showers."

The captain moved away to where some of the men had already put out the remarkably appetizing field rations. Even on patrol they ate better than their comrades in the former Soviet Union.

Tikov made another sweep of the wide horizon. Something was definitely coming. He could feel it in his bones. Afghanistan had done that to him. He could almost smell the advent of an attack. Trouble was, he didn't know how or from what quarter.

Worse, he wouldn't dare tell the SAM battery commander, his colonel back at the site, who would only see him as an upstart Ukrainian. The colonel had still not forgiven him for being right about the Stealth aircraft and shooting it down. The colonel would probably want to shoot *him* for daring to bring up the subject of a possible attack.

Tikov put the binoculars away and paused. Almost absently, he stroked the twin-barreled, antiaircraft heavy machine gun that was mounted just ahead of the hatch. Based upon the old 12.7-mm DShK, the twin barrels effectively doubled the weight of firepower it could bring to bear. With day and night optical sighting, it was not limited to good visibility. It had a serviceable range—1.5 kilometers horizontally—and was effective up to one thousand meters when firing upward. Its rate of fire had been improved and could match the quadruple ZSU-23-4 at one thousand rounds per minute, from each barrel. Within each APC was also a supply of portable surface-to-air missiles.

At least, Tikov thought, if something hostile were to come from the far horizon, they would not be helpless. He climbed out of the hatch and went down to breakfast.

14

November Base: The Mission; 0130 hours, Zulu

The special briefing room was full, its doors
secured. The eight men who made up the four Tornado
crews were in the front row. Behind them were
Bowmaker and Thurson, who would be staying on the
base for the duration of the mission, and Jacko Inglis, the
overall commander of November base. Farther back sat
Morton and Macallister. Bowmaker's aide was conspicuous by his absence. For some time now the general had
seemed to prefer traveling without his supercilious ADC.

To one side were the specialist officers who had
already given Intelligence updates, meteorological fore-
cast for the route, and so on. Near the podium were
Jason's deputies, Helm and da Vinci. As the last specialist
officer stood down, Helm took the podium.

"This, gentlemen, is it," he began. "You have your

orders, and you are as familiar with the mechanics of the mission as you are ever likely to be. You know where the refueling tankers will be positioned and the emergency escape routes and recovery airfields should anything—God forbid—go wrong. Search-and-rescue teams are fully briefed and will be in position, should you need them. Let us hope you will not.

"I know Wing Commander Jason would like to be here with you tonight but, if not in person, he is still with you. I know he will be listening to your takeoff from his hospital bed. You will be in the saddle—as my old American instructor used to say—for many hours . . . but I do not have to tell you to remain alert. Just be careful.

"Since the mission was proposed, there have been diversionary activities going on at many locations: deployments in the North and South Atlantic, the Caribbean, the Persian Gulf, off the Yugoslav coast, military exercises with friendly African nations, and so on. Many are deployments in response to world crises. Others have been with deliberate purpose in mind . . . a cover for the mission.

"Mr. Hohendorf and Mr. Ecker, Mr. Bagni and Mr. Stockmann . . . you four will be the ones to stir up the hornets. You will arrive over the target at dawn. You know the precise timings, so get in there and get out. Fast. Mr. Selby and Mr. McCann, Mr. Cottingham and Mr. Flacht . . . your job is to make sure they are covered against any air attack on the way out. Gentlemen, there is not much more to say. Good luck."

Helm drew himself to full height and saluted them. Da Vinci did the same.

McCann turned to Selby and whispered, "Do we get salutes because they think we're going to die? Wait a minute, it's the other way round. We who are about to die salute—"

A sharply prodding elbow drew an involuntary "Aah!"

from him. Helm paused as he was about to step down, eyes riveted upon McCann.

"Captain McCann, you are in pain?"

"No, *sir!* Well, sir, it was my foot. I caught it in—"

"Look after that foot, Captain. You'll need it."

"Yes, sir!"

Helm did not smile as he got down. The air vice-marshal left his seat to stand before them.

"You've heard all there is to know about the job in hand. It remains for me to wish you good luck, gentlemen. As I expect to count you all back in, I'd hate to be disappointed. Got it?"

"We'd hate to disappoint you, too, sir," McCann said.

"Captain McCann, I just knew you would."

The air vice-marshal shook hands with each.

The Desert Cliff Top, 0235 Hours, Local Time

Tikov sat on the ground, leaning against the APC. He stared out into the darkness at the radar site, then put his night glasses to his eyes. They were light-intensifying lenses that enabled him to see the radar structures with sufficient clarity. Much of the system was now aboveground with very few lights showing. By the time dawn came, he knew, the whole thing would again be hidden underground.

Tikov shivered. It had nothing to do with the desert's night air. He felt a strange unease.

A footfall made him turn alertly.

"Take it easy, Tikov," the captain said mildly. "Don't shoot me. Who do you think is going to sneak up on you in the middle of this great desert?" The captain came to stand next to him and looked out into the darkness of the horse-shoe canyon. "So . . . you can't sleep? It's not your watch."

"I'm okay."

"What are you looking for with those glasses? No one can sneak up on the site. We've done a very wide sweep." The captain checked himself and shone a pen-light with a red filter on his watch. "I nearly said 'today,' but it's . . . two hours and thirty-eight minutes into the new day. So yesterday, we did a sweep of totally empty desert."

But Tikov was not worried about an attack by ground forces or even paratroops. Paratroops would be slaughtered before they'd even landed.

"I'm thinking of aircraft."

"Not that again. Don't you think we've got people all over the world making sure we get warning? You got that Stealth aircraft, didn't you?"

"What about all those reports of military maneuvers?"

"The world's going mad, Anatoly Grigorievich. There are military maneuvers everywhere. Our own army has to go into the republics to stop idiots killing each other. Don't worry. If there's a fight, I'll make sure you're in the thick of it."

But Tikov would not be deflected. "It's an itch. I used to get it in Afghanistan before the Afghanski sprang their nasty little surprises. We lost less aircraft on the ground than other units because we were waiting for those attacks."

"I still think you should get some sleep," the captain said. "I want you alert in the morning for another sweep. Is that all right with you?" The tones of an unmistakable order were in the voice.

"Yes, sir," Tikov acknowledged.

As the captain walked away, Tikov had one last look at the sky. Perhaps they were on their way, even now.

*　　*　　*

Hohendorf and Ecker, in full flying kit including immersion suit, walked into the hangar and looked at the Tornado IDS that had been painstakingly prepared for them. Its desert paint gleamed eerily in the light. Its weapons hardpoints on spread wings were fully laden, giving it a powerful air of menace.

Hohendorf walked around, checking each item, while Ecker made his way up into the rear cockpit. Under the belly, slung from a preloaded stores carrier, were four identical bombs of a very special type. They were deep penetrators with an experimental high explosive warhead. Two would be used on the first pass, with the other two as spares for a second. Hohendorf did not believe in second passes. The defenses would be waiting eagerly to pay you handsomely for your folly.

He was pleased to note that he had got two antiradar missiles, sharing the underwing tanks pylons with two short-range, air-to-air Sidewinders. One Sidewinder, and an electronics countermeasures pod, were on the outer pylons. The twin Mauser cannon made up the rest of his tool kit.

Satisfied with his inspection, Hohendorf signed for the aircraft and shook hands with the crew chief, then climbed up the ladder. He paused at the top. Ecker was already strapped into the back pocket, warming up the systems. Hohendorf held out his hand.

"Johann."

Ecker's eyes were serious as he smiled briefly. "Axel."

They shook hands.

"Let us hope we can do that again when it's over."

"We will," Ecker said.

Hohendorf climbed into the front cockpit and began to secure himself to the machine. A member of the ground crew had followed him up to assist. Hohendorf wriggled briefly on the seat to make himself more comfortable, then leaned forward to check that the harness moved freely. He gave an experimental forward jerk, and the harness locked, then eased freely again when he moved gently. He nodded at the crewman.

"Luck, sir," the man said.

"Thank you."

The man patted the cockpit rim and descended.

Hohendorf and Ecker went rapidly through their checks, and the engines were started as the hangar doors opened out onto the night. The loud warning tone sounded as the canopy began to come down, ending abruptly as it clamped shut.

The IDS began to roll forward, edging out into the darkness.

Across the airfield near the squadron hangars, Bagni and Stockmann's Super Tornado ASV was already taxiing to the takeoff point. The IDS and the ASV would be leaving together, Hohendorf's aircraft in the lead. The second pair of Tornadoes were timed for three minutes later.

In another hangar, Selby and McCann were walking toward their own aircraft.

"Boy, I hope Helm never gets to be boss of this outfit," McCann said. "Did you see that look he gave me? If looks could kill . . ."

"There's a line, McCann, and I'm at the head of it. Helm can have your bones as consolation."

"Aw, c'mon, Mark. What did I say back there?" McCann seemed impervious to censure. There was a beatific look upon his face.

"Nothing would have been a good start. And what are you looking so pleased about, anyway?"

"What's it to you?"

Selby made a noise that sounded like a groan. "Not Karen Lomax. Please, not Karen Lomax."

"She kissed me good-bye yesterday."

"'Good-bye' is the correct word. When Geordie Pearce finally makes it back, we'll all be kissing you good-bye."

"That's where you're wrong, my man. I know something you don't. Pearce is not coming back. She told me. He's been posted to the States. Checking out some new kit for our birds. He's on liaison for a whole year!"

"With your luck," Selby said, "he'll be back with a promotion, and you'll be dog meat. Meanwhile, put Miss Lomax out of your mind and get up there." They had reached the ASV. "We've got work to do."

McCann winked at him. "You got it."

"Lord preserve me," Selby muttered. He watched McCann climb upward and settle into the back, then commenced his walk around the aircraft.

He had told McCann to forget about Karen Lomax, but in his own mind, visions of Kim Mannon floated. He hoped he would be seeing her again.

"Pale Flyer One and Two, clear for takeoff," the tower said.

"Roger."

Hohendorf held the laden Tornado IDS on the brakes as he opened the throttles, released the brakes, and almost simultaneously shoved the throttles into combat burner. Slowly at first, and totally unlike the greyhound leap of the ASV that he had grown accustomed to, the IDS began to gather momentum. Just a little to the right and behind, the other aircraft kept pace. Bagni was clearly doing a low-key takeoff so as not to overtake.

Hohendorf eased on the stick, and the IDS lifted

cleanly. His left hand swiftly reached over to move the undercarriage lever to the UP position.

"Gear traveling," Ecker announced, "and locked."

Hohendorf eased the IDS into a gentle climbing turn to the required heading for the long journey south.

The mission profile was hi-lo-lo-hi—a high, fast transit, followed by a low approach, low escape, and a high return to the recovery airfield in the Azores. There would be refueling points throughout the entire route.

As they climbed to transit height, he could hear Ecker checking with the other aircraft, leaving him to concentrate on the flying. They were now into cloud, and the pinpricks of light that had betrayed human habitation below were blanked out. Fleeting shadows, cast by the navigation lights, danced upon insubstantial backgrounds.

His mind went back to the corridor after the briefing. Selby had come up to him.

"We'll be watching your back all the way," Selby had said. "Just make sure you stay in one piece. Morven would never forgive me."

"I would not forgive myself. And just remember," Hohendorf had added, surprising himself, "today's Germany is not the one of the thirties. It belongs to our generation, and we know the dangers."

There had been a nascent understanding in Selby's eyes as they'd shaken hands. Then McCann, inevitably, had approached Ecker.

"Hey . . . you look after that guy, Johann. We don't want to lose him."

"I'll do my best," Ecker had said, somewhat bemused. He was still trying to work McCann out.

Remembering, Hohendorf smiled in his mask. "So, Johann, what do you think of our Elmer Lee?"

"He's crazy."

"But brilliant."

278 ■ JULIAN JAY SAVARIN

"Crazy people can be brilliant."

"How would you know?"

"I'm flying with one."

"Ah, Johann, Johann. Remind me to complain to my cousin about you."

They broke out of the cloud cover and headed for forty thousand feet, in clear sky. At altitude, Hohendorf opened the throttles slightly, swept the wings fully, and headed at supersonic speed for the first refueling waypoint over the Bay of Biscay. Less than half a mile to the right and slightly to the rear, Bagni and Stockmann's ASV kept perfect station. At the second tanker rendezvous, they would be holding the tight formation that would make any vigilant radar think it was looking at a single aircraft.

"Axel?"

"Yes."

"Are you thinking of Morven?"

"I was. She's out of my mind until this is over."

"I am thinking of Erika."

It was understandable. Ecker had never been in combat.

"Don't worry," Ecker continued. "She won't be there when the time comes."

"I'm not worried, Johann."

There was a long silence as each checked through his systems yet again, making certain that everything was working properly. They immersed themselves within the many sounds of the aircraft. It was as if it breathed its own life about them.

"Those things that are happening back home in Germany," Hohendorf began suddenly as he pondered his parting words to Selby, "it's not good for us. It won't be like the thirties, you know. This time, the people who are being attacked will fight back eventually. And it won't be a small response. Arms will flood into Germany for the purpose, and before long they'll be hitting back with things like rocket-propelled grenades and perhaps even mortars."

"You're talking about a civil war," Ecker said. "Are you trying to frighten me?"

"I hope so, because it's frightening *me*. We could lose everything. This could rip Germany apart for good, Johann, and I mean the total end of the German nation as an entity. Those damned politicians of ours should have seen this coming and acted a long time ago. Sometimes I despair about the voters who put such people in. They won't be able to hide their shame like last time, by pretending they didn't know what was going on. It won't be a case of 'following orders' anymore. The rest of the world won't accept that. It will simply finish us off. It's not as if we haven't got history to warn us."

Ecker, stunned by Hohendorf's passionate expression of his fears, found he could say nothing. Another silence descended upon them.

Moscow, 0455 Hours, Local Time

Kurinin turned restlessly in the bed of the small duty flat that was next to his office. No disturbing news had come to him, yet he could not sleep. After fifteen minutes of trying, he got up and went to the phone. He rang a duty officer.

"Bring me the latest reports."

"Yes, Comrade General. At once."

If the man at the other end was surprised by the call, he gave no indication.

Presently there was a knock.

"Come!"

It was the lieutenant who seemed too old for the rank. He carried a full box file.

"Thank you," Kurinin said. "What do these represent?"

"The last five hours, Comrade General. I've brought everything that might be of particular interest to us."

"Thank you," Kurinin said again. "That will be all."

"Comrade General."

The man went out.

Kurinin spent nearly an hour sifting through a wide selection of low-grade information, but nothing appeared to set off alarm bells. There was even a routine coded signal from the radar site. Nothing wrong there. All was well. There were the usual bursts of coded signals that would require some—perhaps even considerable—time to break down, if at all; but even that traffic showed no increase in volume. Nothing special seemed to be happening. The various deployments of Western forces were being closely monitored, as a matter of routine. Still nothing. Even the nighttime trawl of the world's signals and telephone conversations showed no anomalies—at least, for the time being. There should be *something*.

Kurinin shut the file wearily, grudgingly accepting defeat, and gave an involuntary yawn. *Karelia*'s location was also secure. Yet again, no worries.

"So why can't I get to sleep?" he asked himself softly.

Something was wrong. He could feel it. He would have liked to check with the desert site, but there were strict periods for communication to minimize the risk of eavesdropping. Precise adherence to these had helped keep the site totally secret until the rogue satellite had made its unscheduled observation. Breaking the embargo could well have dangerous repercussions, but there were at least another twelve hours to go before the next window.

He would just have to sweat them out, he decided. But he didn't like it.

*　　*　　*

Kurinin was sharing his insomnia with others whose identities he would have been chagrined to learn. About the time that Pale Flyer One and Two had completed their first refueling and were on their way to the next tanker rendezvous, Bowmaker and Thurson were down in November control watching the wall-size tactical screen. Deliberately sparse, secure data-link messages had been translated by the mainframe computers to show the respective positions of the Pale Flyer flight, together with ancillary aircraft.

Bowmaker was nursing a coffee while Thurson kept his eyes on the big operations screen. Morton and Macallister were there, too, wanting to be in on a mission sanctioned by their discovery.

A telephone next to Morton began to ring. He stared at it, expecting one of the Ops Control personnel to pick it up. No one came, so he began to look around and saw one of the operators at the bank of telephones at a far end of the vast room, motioning to him to pick it up.

"Morton," he said as he did so.

"Major," she said to him, "there's a Major John Elmore topside who claims he knows you and wants to see you right away. He says it's very important. He's just come in from the States."

"Elmore? Yes, yes. I know him. I'll go up."

"Thank you, sir. I'll relay the message."

Morton put down the phone and went over to Bowmaker. Noting the urgency of his movement, Mac watched him interestedly.

"General, sir. Something really important may have turned up. When we were at JOSIS, I got to know a USAF major, John Elmore, pretty well. . . ."

"Elmore? Do I know him?"

"I don't think so, sir. But he was one of the few people in the other departments who bothered to take us—Mac and me—seriously. Before we left to come over here, I asked him to look out for other anomalies and, if he found any, to try to let me know even if he had to do it himself. He must have found a way to hitch a ride across to one of the bases down south and somehow got authorization to fly up here to November."

"With the base closed down tight because of the mission, he must have some powerful friends."

Morton cleared his throat. "He does, sir. You."

Bowmaker straightened and fixed his eyes upon Morton. "It had better be a good explanation, Major."

Thurson had now come up to listen and looked on with great interest.

"I told him if he had problems"—Morton cleared his throat for a second time—"to say it's urgent for you."

"Go on, Major." Bowmaker looked at his subordinate steadily.

"Sir. Major Elmore would not have risked coming over unless he thought it really important to the mission, sir. He knows it's both our tails if we screw up, and we might have to start thinking about new careers."

"Then you'd better go and see what he's got."

"Yessir!"

Elmore was waiting in the reception area of the low building, which housed the guarded access to the underground center. He was in flying overalls and forage cap. "Hey, buddy," he greeted as Morton joined him, then glanced around. "This is some real estate."

"John." They shook hands. "How did you get up here?"

"Someone lent me an Eagle. I said the magic word." Elmore grinned. "Bowmaker."

Morton shut his eyes briefly. "This had better be good, Johnny, or we're out of here so fast we'll be rocket-assisted. We'll be lucky to get jobs driving trucks. Have you any idea how badly I want to get back to flying?" It was a heartfelt plea. "I can't afford to screw up."

Elmore unzipped a copious side pocket in the flying overalls and took out a large envelope. "Then this ought to help."

Morton took the envelope and opened it to find copies of two transcripts inside. He read them swiftly. "Jesus!" he exclaimed in a shocked voice. "The general had better see this right now." He looked up at Elmore. "John . . . you need special clearance to go down the Hole. Let me see the general. . . ."

Elmore held up a hand. "Hey, hey. I don't need to go down, unless he needs to see me. Personally, I prefer to keep away from generals except when I need a name to get an Eagle, of course. I hate sitting at a desk just as you do. But tonight I'm just the messenger boy. Besides, I'm bushed. I've got a bed in the officers' club, and—"

"Mess, Johnny. Officers' mess. This is a NATO unit, but a British base."

"Whatever. I need my beauty sleep. So? Did I do right?"

"Oh, you certainly did right. This is hot stuff. Look, I'd better get back down there. See you when it's all over. And thanks for bringing this."

"Anytime, buddy boy," Elmore said as they again shook hands. "Any excuse to fly the Eagle. Say one thing, though. They've got some sweet-looking ships here."

Morton hurried back to the operations room and handed the information to Bowmaker, who read it silently, eyes widening.

"God almighty," he uttered softly, and handed the sheets of paper over to Thurson.

The first transcript carried two reports. One was about the crewman aboard the Los Angeles class submarine. It detailed Tollini's discovery of the fast soundprint that did not tally with the subsequent wakeprint. The captain of the submarine had concurred with Tollini's opinion that either a close formation of boats had formed the giant wake or a single craft. Someone had appended "Impossible!" in a margin.

The second half of the transcript was about an eavesdrop on a conversation between a lone yachtsman and his radio ham friend on a Caribbean island. The yachtsman had complained about American fighters disturbing his sleep, mentioning at least four but possibly more in the area. The coordinates were given. Again, someone had written in the margin: "No U.S. aircraft belonging to any of the services in that area. No seaborne deployments of any kind."

The next transcript was short, but its information was devastating. It merely stated that Intelligence sources had confirmed that a vast submarine—based on the Typhoon class boats—was at large, believed to be an experimental aircraft carrier. Again, there was a note in the margin: "Not impossible, after all, if true. It fits!" Thurson looked up and silently handed the papers back to Bowmaker.

The general turned to Morton. "These notations by your friend Major Elmore?"

"It's his writing, sir."

"Where is he now?"

"Gone to the mess to sleep, sir. He's bushed."

"Tough. Get him back here." Bowmaker turned to Thurson. "Can we give him special clearance if I run a check on him from here?"

Thurson nodded. "I'm sure we can."

Coded signals went back and forth—some by land line—and within fifteen minutes Elmore was ruefully contemplating the fact that he would not get his sleep as he was hustled back to Operations Control center, in the company of two solid-looking military policemen. The MPs were at pains to assure him he was not under arrest.

As soon as he arrived, Bowmaker said, "You can sleep later, Major. This is Air Vice-Marshal Thurson, overall boss of this outfit. You know Major Morton and, I believe, Sergeant Macallister. I am, of course, Bowmaker."

"Sir," Elmore said.

"Suppose you tell us, Major," Thurson began, "in your own words, exactly how you came to be here?"

Elmore glanced toward Bowmaker as if awaiting permission. A barely perceptible nod came from the general.

"Well, sir," Elmore began to the air vice-marshal, "I work in a department that sometimes sends stuff down to JOSIS—that's where Chuck and Mac—er . . . the major and—"

"I know what you mean. Do please go on, Major."

"Er . . . yes, sir. You see, sir . . . sometimes, the other departments made fun of JOSIS, there being just the major and the sergeant. Most people saw it as a dead end. Major Morton and I used to meet from time to time, and after the discovery of the radar site, he told me to look out for anything that didn't seem right, no matter how small.

"I suppose," Elmore continued apologetically, "if it hadn't been for the fact that they discovered the site after we'd all missed it, I would not have paid serious attention. Er . . . sorry, Chuck. You know how it is."

"Tell me about it," Morton said dryly.

Elmore gave an embarrassed shrug. "The first anomaly," he went on, "was the report from the L.A. class boat. No extra attention was paid to it by my colleagues, but because of what Major Morton had said I decided to look some more. When the intercept on the radio ham arrived, another check showed there was no deployment by any of the Western forces in that patch of ocean. It was then that someone who had done the check on the navy report for me thought I'd be interested in a piece of intelligence that had come in a long time before and had not been taken seriously."

"So those are your comments in the margins?" Bowmaker asked.

"Yes, sir."

"I see. Go on."

"I decided that it seemed important enough to let Major Morton know immediately. Putting it through normal channels would take forever. . . ." Elmore looked at Bowmaker. "You know how that is, sir," he said, approximating his earlier comment to Morton. "And I didn't want to risk a signal. So I invoked your name and got permission to join a deployment of F-15's coming over to Europe. And that's it, sir.

"I'll say one thing," Elmore said ruefully, addressing Thurson. "You've got a hell of an outfit there, Marshal. Your guys were on to me when I was still way out. I didn't even know I'd been corraled. They were just there. Great-looking ships, too. I guess I'd have been dead meat if I'd been a hostile."

The comments pleased Thurson. "You would have been. We never sleep."

"Ah . . . sleep," Elmore said involuntarily. "Umm . . . sorry, General, er . . . Marshal," he added quickly to Bowmaker and Thurson.

"Not to worry, Major," Thurson said. "There are bunks in here, or would you prefer the mess?"

"The mess, please, sir . . . if you and the general are finished with me."

Bowmaker nodded. "All right, Major. You did well bringing this information to us. Good initiative, but watch how you use my name in the future."

"Sir!"

"Now you go get some sleep. Major Morton, take him up."

"Yes, sir."

Bowmaker turned to Thurson. "What do you suggest?"

"If we contact the Pale Flyer flight," Thurson began, "we risk an eavesdropper noting the sudden burst of coded traffic. It could alert anyone with connections to the site."

"I agree. But it means they could be heading for an ambush."

Thurson nodded slowly. "We can't do anything that might jeopardize the attack itself. We wait until we've received the signal confirming a successful attack, then we warn them."

"And if there's a combat air patrol over the site?"

"Then the lads must do the best they can."

Bowmaker turned to stare at the screen. It had changed to show a map of Western Europe and North Africa. Traces, showing the Pale Flyer positions, were moving across it.

"God*damn!*" he said. "Who would have thought it? A *submarine* aircraft carrier."

"According to your Major Elmore," Thurson said calmly, "some corner of Intelligence did get wind of it, but as is so often usual with these things, it was not taken seriously. Not a new idea, of course," he went on, "but very difficult in the past to make viable."

"Looks like they've succeeded, and well before us. Goddamnit!"

"Perhaps," Thurson said.

Bowmaker stared at him. "Do you know something more?"

"I know my men," was what Thurson replied.

There was a knock on Kurinin's door.

"Come!" He was lying on a utility couch, partially dressed, and had still not been able to get to sleep.

The old lieutenant entered with a single sheet of paper. "Please forgive this intrusion, Comrade General . . . but I know you want to see anything that's out of the ordinary."

Kurinin sat up immediately and took the paper. "Coded traffic, from southern England to the Pentagon. To do with Yugoslavia? The Gulf?"

"We're still trying to break it, Comrade General. We don't know."

"Bring me answers, man! Not riddles."

"Yes, Comrade General. I'm sorry. . . ."

Kurinin relented. "It is I who should ask your forgiveness. Not your fault. Thank you for showing this to me. Do your best to break their wretched code."

"Yes, comrade. . . ."

"All right. You may go."

The lieutenant went out, and Kurinin got to his feet to pace about the room. If only he could work out what was happening!

But he dared not break the twelve-hour embargo on communications with the site. It would be like lighting a beacon. Not very difficult to work out what kind of attention that would attract.

15

The IDS and the ASV had made rendezvous with the second tanker and were tucked in so close, anyone staring at a radar screen would have seen just the one blip.

From the backseat of the IDS, Ecker glanced upward at the great expanse of Tristar above him. An error of judgment on Hohendorf's part and all three aircraft would explode in a huge ball of all-consuming fire. The bombs they were carrying would create a conflagration that would probably be seen for hundreds of miles, given the altitude at which they now were.

Don't think about it, Ecker told himself. You've flown close formation before.

But never like this. This was a real combat mission.

He looked over to his right to where Bagni and Stockmann, in their ASV, appeared to be tucked in even closer. Stockmann, in the backseat, raised the circle of forefinger and thumb to signal that the formation was perfect.

Ever since they had left the previous tanker, no communication had taken place among any of the aircraft. The refueling procedure had been carried out by a series of cockpit illuminated warnings and electronic blips. Each plane's crew knew precisely what had to be done.

Farther west and low down over the sea in order to avoid detection were the other two ASVs, their air cover. Farther yet, flying a conventional airline route, was the Sentry E.3A aircraft—a highly specified and modified version of the Boeing 707 airliner—that would be acting as the airborne communications relay for the mission.

Ecker glanced eastward, to his left. Dawn was already approaching at altitude, though the earth below was still in darkness. Soon it would be time to begin the descent, and the moment of truth would be upon him.

In the tanker aircraft, the crew were dealing with a normal air traffic control interrogation.

"Roger. This is AfriCargo flight 611. . . ."

"AfriCargo 611 . . . squawk 2376. . . ."

"Roger. Squawking 2376. . . ."

The copilot selected the requested code on the transponder.

"Roger, AfriCargo 611," the air traffic controller acknowledged. "We have your squawk 2376. Have a nice day."

"Thank you. AfriCargo 611." The man who had been replying to the interrogation now said to the flight deck crew: "That seems to have worked okay. I think they recognized my voice."

He was the actual pilot of the aircraft whose place the tanker and the pair of Tornadoes had taken. Somehow, perhaps because he was a former U.S. Navy pilot, Bowmaker had managed to get him to agree. The crew did not question how that had come to pass.

"After this," said the pilot, whose name was Gleeson, "I don't think I'd better work this route anymore." He did not sound particularly distressed by the thought.

"Hope they made it up to you," the captain of the tanker said.

"They did," Gleeson told him, but said no more.

Just over two hundred miles away in the deeply buried control center of the radar site, there were those who had listened in on the entire conversation between the aircraft and the traffic controller. All such transmissions in the area were listened to and taped as a matter of routine.

The officer in charge of the shift, a captain, removed the tape and slotted it into another machine. Another tape was already in a second slot. He switched on the machine and a small monitor screen came to life. He ran both tapes. Two waveforms appeared on the screen. They matched. He stared at them for some moments. They still matched. He turned off the machine and picked up a telephone.

"The voiceprint matches," he said into it. "It's the cargo plane. We're secure." He laughed. "I know it's always the same each time, but if we didn't do it, we might find ourselves trying to stop the Azerbaijani and the Armenians from killing themselves. . . . What?" The captain gave a chuckle. "Exactly. They'd both start shooting at us. Log the report, will you? Thanks."

He hung up and yawned prodigiously. It was all routine.

In Pale Flyer Three, McCann watched one of the multifunction displays that was his infrared window on the gloom. They were at very low level over the sea, but dawn would soon be reaching with its early light for them, even this far down. Once the attack on the radar site was in progress, they'd head for the higher levels in case any hostile aircraft came out to do battle. With the extralong reach of their Skyrays and the 150-mile-plus range of their radars, they would be able to sniff out any potential attackers that chose to threaten Pale Flyers One and Two.

Out there in the darkness with no nav lights showing, Pale Flyer Four was keeping perfect station. Despite himself, McCann had to admit that Cottingham in Four was shaping up nicely. Wolfie Flacht, as Cottingham's backseater for the mission, had seemed happy enough. Cottingham would never be able to replace Axel Hohendorf, but he seemed to be getting on with Flacht.

McCann slipped a tape into a spare channel of the cockpit coms. Bob Dylan and the Band's "This Wheel's on Fire" came flooding on the headphones. That particular cover version had a female voice spiced with a ferocious Hammond organ sound.

"Off, Elmer Lee!" Selby ordered.

"Hey, Mark. C'mon. I'm cooking. I'm not gonna miss anything."

"Like the missile that might be on our six?"

"No missiles down here with us fishes."

"Where did you get that thing, anyway?"

"Thing?" McCann was scandalized. "This is rare stuff, my man. I heard it at Karen's. . . ."

"No, no. Not again. . . ."

"An old record of her uncle's," McCann charged on. "She liked it, so she taped it to bring back to the base with her. I liked it, so she gave me a copy. I especially like the part where it talks about notifying your next of kin. Appropriate, huh?" He began to sing with the chorus. "Yeah! I'm gonna explode! And listen to that organ! Wow! Some pounding."

"I'll pound *you* in a minute, you demented, warped, Kansas City gnome. Off!"

"That's a lot of adjectives, but you got it."

The sounds died in Selby's helmet. It had been too easy.

"McCann," Selby called suspiciously.

"Yo."

"Have you switched channels?"

"Would I?"

"Would a cutpurse cut purses? Off!"

"Your wish is my—" McCann stopped suddenly.

"What is it?" Selby's voice was sharp. Alert. "Talk to me, McCann!"

A light was blinking on McCann's panel. "It's started, Mark," he said, all trace of levity gone. "They've begun their descent."

The light had stopped blinking, programmed as it was to illuminate only at various stages of the attack mission, thus maintaining the communications blackout. When next it came on, it would mean that the attack was actually in progress and that it was time to head for high altitude. All need for subterfuge would by then no longer be necessary.

"This Wheel's on Fire" had stopped playing. McCann had once more become what he really was: the highly skilled combat veteran.

He was indeed cooking.

After having tanked up to maximum fuel capacity, Hohendorf's IDS in company with Bagni's ASV had broken away from the Tristar at twenty-seven thousand feet. They were now in a steep spiral, heading rapidly toward the darkened earth below. They stayed close together, still giving the impression of a single trace should they be picked up by radar.

With his eyes on his instruments, it seemed to Ecker they were plunging toward the desert in a vertical dive.

The steepness of the descent was to give as rapid a loss of height as possible, while the spiral minimized displacement so that instead of covering several miles, they were virtually above the same area. A normal dive, even at great speed, was in fact a powered glide that tended to traverse a large patch of sky, leaving the aircraft exposed for a considerable length of time. The spiral was rapid but had the added advantage of appearing to be static for a brief moment on a radar screen before disappearing altogether. It was a dangerous maneuver if not done properly, but Hohendorf and Bagni knew precisely what to do.

As they hurtled earthward, Bagni kept closely tucked in to the infrared image of the IDS that filled his head-up display. In the backseat, Stockmann was already programming the chameleon, the "intelligent" crystals in the special paint that was the self-altering camouflage system of the ASV Tornadoes. By the time they reached operational height above the desert the ASV would, like Hohendorf's IDS, be dressed in desert "pink."

Three turns, and it was time to level off. They settled at one hundred feet, very carefully, since they had switched off the radar height warning to minimize any radar broadcast. At five hundred knots they streaked toward the target.

In the control center of the Stealth radar site, a bored operator who was glad to be coming to the end of his shift had turned briefly away from his screen. Thinking he'd seen something out of the corner of his eye, he had turned back to look, frowning.

The captain who had checked the voiceprint of the transmission between the traffic controller and the supposed cargo plane glanced in his direction. "What?"

"I thought I saw something, Captain."

The captain moved over to look. "It's still just that

cargo plane, following its normal route." He gave the operator a hard stare. "Were you sleeping?"

"No, Captain!"

The captain continued to pin his subordinate with cold eyes as if he didn't believe it. "Just keep your attention on that screen."

"Yes, Captain."

The captain glanced up at the ceiling, as if expecting to see an answer there.

On top of the cliff that overlooked the horseshoe canyon, there was leisurely activity as preparations were made for the coming day's sweep. Overhead, the sky was beginning to show signs of lightening.

Tikov had not slept at all. The captain in command strode to where Tikov had again sat on the ground, leaning against his APC.

"So you didn't get some sleep, Anatoly Grigorievitch," the captain began. "I don't want you nodding off while we're out there, in charge of one of my APCs. Better have some strong coffee." The captain grinned suddenly. "It's American."

Tikov rose slowly, almost tiredly, to his feet. His binoculars were again hanging from his neck. Once more he brought them to his eyes and slowly panned the ever-lightening horizon.

The captain sighed with exasperation. "This is an obsession, Tikov! I've humored you . . ."

"Then please humor me a little longer, Captain. If nothing happens today, I vow not to bring the subject up again. Ever."

The captain stared keenly at Tikov, peering at him in the gloom. He then turned to look out at the horseshoe. The radar structure would still be up, but soon it would be retracting underground.

He turned back to Tikov. "Why today?"

"I don't know. It's a feeling."

The captain paused. "You are serious, aren't you?"

"Yes, sir."

The captain sighed once more. "All right. I will humor you a little longer . . . but not for the whole day. We'll take our time over breakfast. But when the sun begins to get really hot, I want to be inside the APC with its air-conditioning . . . not baking out in the desert. Once I give the order to embark, we begin our patrol. There will be no arguments. That's my deal."

"I'll take it, sir."

"Very well. Now by all that used to be holy, let's have something to eat."

The captain had once been an Orthodox Christian.

With one last look at the northern horizon, Tikov followed him to where the coffee was being brewed.

Pale Flyers One and Two were still in close formation, almost hugging each other as they swept along the floor of a wadi, barely fifty feet above the ground. High ramparts of dark red, their vicious rock faces still hidden by the remaining night's shadow, towered over them, making them seem like fragile toys. Against those ancient battlements they certainly were, for neither would have survived a collision. Ecker marveled at how calm he was as Hohendorf banked steeply to negotiate what seemed like an impossibly narrow gap. Jagged cliff faces cast their fleeting cloaks of deeper gloom over the cockpit, as they flashed past.

"Are you okay, Johann?" came Hohendorf's voice on the headphones.

"Yes."

An impenetrable wall of rock was suddenly before them.

"A box canyon?" Hohendorf queried. "Will we have to go over?" He did not want that, as it could mean exposure to radar.

Ecker was looking at one of his displays in infrared. "No. There's an opening. Over to the left. One five zero."

"Roger. One five zero." Hohendorf trusted Ecker implicitly, and although he could not as yet see the opening, he turned onto the new heading.

And there it was. The tiniest of cracks, it seemed.

Hohendorf stood the IDS on its wingtips and pulled very gently on the stick. The Tornado threaded its way through. Almost as if tied to it with a rope, Bagni's ASV was right there with them.

They were now two hundred miles from where they'd descended from the tanker. It was time to make the split. Soon, they would be arriving at a fork in the wadi. Hohendorf and Ecker would be going left along the planned attack route, while Bagni and Stockmann would break right and increase speed slightly. The ASV would overfly the target thirty seconds before the IDS, sending back target update information by data link. This would give Ecker enough time to make fine adjustments for the attack itself. Any longer would give the defenses too much of a window within which to react. Pale Flyer Two would be still be exposed rather longer than was desired.

Ingress to the target area would be from different directions, to catch the defenses unawares.

The waypoint light began to blink in both Tornado cockpits. Without communicating, both aircraft banked on cue and went their separate ways. They were now 160 miles from target: just under twenty minutes.

"There they go," Hohendorf said.

Each of them silently wished Pale Flyer Two good luck.

At November base, everyone's eyes were glued to the big screen. Although there was currently no actual information being transmitted—in the interests of security—

the mission data had been fed into the computer. It was thus displaying where each aircraft ought to be and would instantly update when the Sentry E.3A began transmitting via its allocated satellite. By then, even though the transmissions would still be in code, there would be no further need to keep the act of communication secret.

Bowmaker and Thurson watched as the traces identifying Pale Flyers One and Two diverged to begin the final run-in.

No one said anything.

Tikov was twitching. He had eaten very little and almost in rude haste had returned to the APC. Absently his hands stroked the twin machine guns, as if telling them to wait, wait, their time would come.

The captain had come up to the APC and was staring at Tikov. "You look as if you're expecting an attack."

"There's going to be one," Tikov said with absolute certainty. He looked about him, traversing the gun mount as he did so. His eyes narrowed, trying to see beyond the horizon. "I know it." He let go of the guns to put the binoculars to his eyes yet again.

The captain, still keeping to his bargain, laughed good-naturedly. "Don't you think our radar would have picked something up by now? What can your glasses do that radar can't?"

Tikov did not reply.

The captain took no offense, and shaking his head, went back to his own vehicle.

"Baleninov!" Tikov called to one of his men.

The man poked his head from the back of the APC. "Yes, Lieutenant?"

"Get a couple of SA-7As out. Give the second to Darievskiy. Be ready to use them when I tell you."

The SA-7A was a man-portable SAM, an improved version of the old SA-7.

"Yes, Lieutenant."

There was a question in the man's voice, as if he were wondering whether Tikov had finally taken leave of his senses. However, he also knew, as did everyone else on the site, that it was Tikov's SAM team that had taken out the American Stealth aircraft. He was thus not about to argue, whatever his own misgivings.

The captain was not so circumspect. After watching in disbelief as the men brought out the weapons, he strode angrily back toward Tikov's APC.

"What the devil do you think you're up to, Tikov! Since when did you assume command?"

Tikov was calm. "You gave me till the sun got hot, Captain. I merely gave instructions to two of my own crew."

The captain stared at the men, who waited expectantly. Do we keep them or put them back? their eyes asked of him. "You're making me regret this, Tikov," he said. To the men he went on, "All right. Keep them with you . . . until we move. Then it's back in they go." He looked up. "Is that fine with you, *Comrade* Tikov?"

"Yes, sir."

"Oh, good."

The captain stomped back to his APC.

In Pale Flyer Two, Bagni and Stockmann would soon be breaking cover to curve toward the entrance of the horseshoe canyon. It was going to be a fast dash, with the sharp pull-up at the end to clear the high ground on the way out.

"Time to go public," Stockmann said in a neutral voice. "Ready?"

"Ready," Bagni said. They would be curving left so that their approach would be from the west.

"Okay, here we go. Standby for zero nine zero ten seconds from . . . *now!*"

They left the concealment of the last wadi, traveling at over five hundred knots low down on the deck with afterburners unlit. Bagni had rolled the ASV into a steep bank as he pulled onto the new heading, lining him up nicely with the entrance, and there on one of the multifunction displays was a perfect image of the site, in all its glory. Surprise had been achieved.

"Right on the button!" Stockmann was saying. "I've got it on my MFD. Data link with Pale Flyer One established . . ."

Instantly the target information was relayed to Hohendorf's aircraft, giving Ecker all he needed to update his attack plan.

"And complete!" Stockmann finished. "Let's get the hell out of here, Nico! Move it!"

"Roger," Bagni said, not requiring encouragement. "Burners going in and we're away." He moved the throttles into combat burner, and as the twin prongs of blue-white flame surged from the Super Tornado's tail, the aircraft hurled itself into the canyon. He hauled on the stick, and it leapt vertically for the heavens.

Then all hell broke loose.

On the cliff top, Tikov had been scouring the horizon with his binoculars. He had turned toward the radar site when a swift movement, almost invisible in the still weak light of the new day and against the desert background, had made him stiffen like a gun dog.

"They are here!" he bawled, galvanizing everyone into action, even if they had no idea of what he was going on about.

Then the thunder of the ASV was filling the canyon as

the aircraft stood on its tail, and no one was left in any doubt about what he meant.

Triple-A fire was rising from the canyon floor, reaching for the fleeing aircraft, but it had suddenly rolled ninety degrees, cut out the afterburners, and was hauling itself back to earth. The tracers fired uselessly into empty sky.

Tikov followed it with his binoculars, praying that its maneuver would bring it into range of his SAMs. He noted that the aircraft was making good use of the confusion it had sewn. Then, suddenly, it seemed to lose definition; but he could still hear it. What was going on?

"Baleninov! Darievskiy!" he shouted. "SAMs ready! Fire at my command!"

He could barely see the aircraft as it headed for the deck. They were going to lose it! Already the triple A from the canyon had become hesitant, and not one of the SAM batteries down there had fired. None on the outer periphery, either. Tikov wanted to weep with frustration. He should have been down there. What was that stupid colonel doing?

"Fire!" he yelled at the two men.

Nothing happened.

Tikov pounded at the APC with an angry first. *"What are you waiting for?"* He could still hear the aircraft. Why were they so *slow?*

"We can't see anything, Lieutenant," one of the men protested. "Nothing to aim at."

"You can hear it! And it's still got a nice fat heat signature for the missile to home on to." But with afterburners out, the signature was lessening by the second. "Fire both! They will achieve their own lock-on."

Baleninov and Darieskiy fired the SAMs in the general direction of the aircraft's last position. Like strange beasts off the leash, the missiles seared off, trailing plumes of

white. They rose briefly before veering sharply toward the
ASVs last known position.

In the ASV, hurtling low above the desert, Stockmann
watched the symbols on the threat display. Missile tracking information came up on an MFD. SA-7A, very short
range and at the ASVs current altitude and speed, there
was zero probability of a hit.

"Two smokers on our tail. I'm countering. No sweat."

"I have them," Bagni confirmed. Stockmann had
patched the same display to him.

"That was a good maneuver back there, Nico. They
were throwing some hot stuff up."

"Yes. I am pleased we are out."

Stockmann watched the missile traces as Bagni went
into a series of hard turns close to the ground. The attitude
direction indicator in his own cockpit seemed to be going
crazy as it tried to keep up with the aircraft's gyrations.

"One's gone!" he announced. "Two's gone!"

Pale Flyer Two regained equilibrium. Then Bagni went
into a wide turn.

"Hey!" Stockmann said. "We should be heading for the
next refueling point. What gives, Nico?"

"This turn will put us behind Flyer One, who'll be coming in soon." Less than twenty seconds had passed since
they had overflown the radar site. "They may need a
diversion."

"This is crazy, Nico. Let's follow the plan."

"We were told to adjust our tactics," Bagni insisted,
"according to the prevailing conditions. Flyer One is going
to pass right over that cliff where those APCs are. That
threat was not in the briefing."

Stockmann stifled his objections. "Okay. But let's not
play around out there."

"Don't worry. I don't intend to."

In the canyon, the radar structures were being retracted underground.

Tikov was furious. The aircraft had escaped. He forced himself to hold the binoculars to his eyes calmly as he focused on the site. They had started the retraction, but it seemed agonizingly slow.

The aircraft that had flown over had not attacked. That meant a reconnaissance mission, which meant a prelude to an attack. But when? Immediately? In a few days?

"My God, Tikov," someone was saying from below. "You were right!"

Tikov looked down. The captain was looking at once harassed and sheepish. "How did you know?"

"I didn't. I've told you. It was just a feeling." Imperceptibly, Tikov had grown the stronger.

"So what next?" the captain asked.

"I think we should wait . . ." Tikov paused suddenly. *"Get ready!"* he yelled to the men. *"As many SAMs as you can!"* He'd heard engines.

Pale Flyer One's track had described an elongated "S" at an extremely low altitude, hiding behind the dunes and the precipitous walls of the dried river beds. On the final run-in, right on time, it had been heading east.

Hohendorf now reefed the IDS into a hard turn westward.

This is it, Ecker thought as he swiftly set up the attack. Then he thrust all extraneous thoughts out of his mind to concentrate on carrying out the mission.

"Four miles to the cliff edge," he said, "and another eight miles to target."

"Okay. Master's LIVE . . . and Late Arm is HOT," Hohendorf confirmed. "You've got steering to target—"

"*APCs!*" Ecker shouted suddenly.

"Yes. I see them." Hohendorf's voice was calm, his mind swiftly assessing this new but not entirely unexpected threat.

"My God, Axel! It's just as you thought!"

They swept past the armored personnel carriers so low, it seemed the commander in the hatch of one was looking *down* upon them. Then they were at the cliff edge.

Hohendorf rolled the aircraft onto its back and plunged steeply down the rock face, bracing himself for the first scream of the threat warning.

But nothing happened.

Then a voice spoke. "We're in, Flyer One!"

Hohendorf had rolled upright and was heading for the radar at fifty feet.

"It's Bagni and Stockmann!" Ecker exclaimed. "They've come back. That's crazy. . . ."

"Forget it for now, Johann. Let's get the target."

"Roger." Ecker pulled himself together and began to work swiftly. "You're on course. Hold that heading."

So far, the defenses appeared to have been caught out. That state of affairs would not last for long.

"One pass," Hohendorf said. "Stick of two."

"Roger. We go for autorelease. Yes?"

"Yes. Where's that triple A?"

"I can do without it, Axel."

"So can I . . . Ah!"

A vicious stream of tracer snaked overhead.

"You were saying?" Ecker commented.

"Sorry I spoke. Five hundred knots, fifty feet. We'll do the ten-degree starboard offset with left roll-in."

"Roger." Ecker's breathing had grown perceptibly in frequency.

Another stream of tracer shot by, then another and

another. Ahead of them the radar site seemed to be turning into a firework display. Still no hits. Even as he set up
the attack, Ecker had the countermeasures systems
working overtime. The guidance radars of the guns were
having a hard time of it.

The bombing symbology was now on the head-up display, with the two target marker dashes appearing on the
far left.

"I have the target," Hohendorf said. It was time to
change direction, before the tracers latched on to them.
"Call the pop-up, Johann."

There was no radar warning. They were still too low for
serious acquisition by the defenses. It would be a different story altogether during the pull-up; but if he did
everything right, those same defenses would still not have
the time to acquire. He hoped.

"Standby," Ecker was saying. "Standby for pull-up.
Pull-up . . . *now!*"

"Roger . . . and we're going up." Hohendorf pulled firmly,
straining against the onset of the G-forces. The IDS reared
into an antiaircraft hell, it seemed, as the tracers fought
each other to land on the fleeting target while the radar
warner started to go berserk. "Thirty degrees on the nose."

"Standby for reverse." Ecker was very calm now.
"Reverse . . . *now!*"

"Reversing!" Hohendorf called as he flicked the maneuvers switch and pushed the throttles all the way to the
stops. "Maneuvers out, burners are in . . . and we're going
down, twenty degrees in the dive."

The traces were left groping uselessly, at the empty
space suddenly vacated by the IDS. The SAM radars, and
those of the guns, had still not been able to achieve lock-
on. The heat seekers were a different matter, and
Hohendorf was well aware of the dangers they posed.

He rolled the IDS level and started the pull-out. The

target bars were perfectly sliced by the bomb fall line. The IDS was now at one hundred feet. Once the attack had begun, he had activated the radar altimeter. It was now giving off its characteristic rising hoot.

"Target's right on the nose! They haven't got it fully down! We've really caught them!"

"Pickle-pickle *now!*" Ecker's voice was showing excitement.

Hohendorf squeezed at the uncaged bomb release button.

"Bombs are gone! Recover!" Ecker seemed to be shouting both with relief and with a sense of real achievement.

"Recovering."

The IDS hurtled over the still only partially retracted radar and fled for the opening in the canyon, staying low and pursued by the still inaccurate fire.

"I think we got it," Ecker said.

"Let's hope so. I don't want to go back in there."

Ecker turned to look. All above them, it seemed the canyon was streaked with triple A. This tilted unnervingly as Hohendorf engaged violent evasive maneuvers to carry them to safety.

"My God!"

"What is it?"

Above the canyon, Bagni's ASV seemed to be playing thread-the-needle with the ribbons of tracer.

"It's Bagni. He's diverting the defenses to let us get through."

"Call him. Tell him to get the hell out!"

"I'm doing it. Flyer Two, Flyer Two. Get out. Get out!"

In the ASV, Stockmann said, "Hear that, Nico? We've played around enough. Let's go, man. Hit it!" Stockmann, like Ecker, was employing the much more powerful and comprehensive set of countermeasures of the ASV to full effect. Electronically, the systems automatically attacked anything using radar guidance while he programmed blooms of radar-confusing chaff and blazing, sunburst flares for release behind the aircraft to spoof any missiles that had actually managed to launch.

"On my way," came Bagni's voice, glacially composed, it seemed.

Stockmann hoped Bagni was not thinking back to the time of the accident in the Scottish mountains, when Palmer had gone down with Ferris during the air combat practice. You never knew during which conditions of stress such trauma could come back to haunt. Bagni had a clean bill of health from the head doc. But doctors didn't always know everything.

Suddenly Stockmann felt a rush of guilt, as if he had betrayed the man in the front cockpit. Bagni was flying with consummate skill, and it took real guts to go back into that hellhole to help Hohendorf and Ecker . . . despite the fact, Stockmann knew, that Bagni must be dreading his greatest of all fears: getting his backseater killed.

But even an aircraft with the capabilities of the ASV and a pilot like Bagni, having deliberately remained in such an intensely hot antiaircraft environment, could not prevail forever by itself. The inevitable happened. A savage bang rocked the aircraft. A puff of smoke appeared on the right wing, then dispersed to show a large hole with jagged edges. The ASV seemed to teeter before recovering itself. The attention getters were at it again.

"Nico! You okay?"

"Yes, yes. We should get away from here, I think." The warning sounds stopped as Bagni pushed at one of the red flashing buttons, confirming to the systems that he was aware of the malfunctions.

"And I think, too," Stockmann remarked dryly. "It's

kinda warm in this holiday resort. My panel's showing some lights. Yours?"

Bagni had seen the unwelcome caption lights on the central warning panel as he sent the aircraft screaming for the lower levels, heading west toward the rendezvous point. Fortunately, the self-sealing fuel bag in the wing, protected by solid structures, had not ruptured. Though the fuel stored there had by now been used, resident gases were still within and just as prone to ignition by a hot splinter from missile or cannon shell.

"I have got some lights," he said to Stockmann.

Some, but not all, captions for the warning systems were repeated in both cockpits. Stockmann could, however, call up a failures page on one of the MFDs and repeat that to the front cockpit.

"I've got amber AP trim and CSAS," Bagni added.

That meant autopilot trim had failed and a first failure in the command stability augmentation system had reduced its redundancy options. The ASVs many redundancy channels, however, still meant that control of the aircraft was fully retained. It would need at least another three channel failures before Bagni would begin to experience any deterioration of control performance. Even so, complacency did not come into the equation.

"We've taken a hit in the maintenance panel," Stockmann said, "and we've also lost some weapons-aiming capability. But we'll still be able to fight if we've got to." He did a swift check of the missile systems. "We can still shoot."

"That is what I like to hear. Now give me a heading for the tanker. I am happy to leave this place."

"You got it," Stockmann said, and brought the next waypoint on screen.

16

Pale Flyer One was skimming low over the desert
as it made its escape, so Hohendorf and Ecker could not
see the devastation they had wrought.

They had delivered their weapons with deadly accuracy.
The delayed-action bombs had plunged down the central
shaft of the radar, bouncing from time to time off its structure as they went, sending ominous echoes through the
entire underground complex. People fled for their lives.
Others, mesmerized by shock and fascinated horror, stood
and listened as the sounds of doom reverberated about
them with a terrible, rhythmic clanking whose very
inevitability appeared to have a mind of its own.

All sounds of the retraction machinery had stopped, as
if those responsible for operating it knew further movement would be pointless. Perhaps some hoped against
hope that the bombs would prove to be duds. A dreadful
silence, broken only by the inexorable clanking, had now

descended. People far along the radiating arms, from the central core of the many-storied subterranean construction, paused by monitors, waiting. They fully understood what the frantic messages that had suddenly appeared on the emergency screens had meant. Some had already left their posts in their attempts to save themselves.

Those who remained—fearful, dreading, hoping—could only wait. They had been caught at their most vulnerable. It was not the bombs that would do the destroying, but the volatile fuels and explosive missile warheads in the bowels of the desert with them. The bombs would merely be the triggers. They knew that those who had gone would not make it. It was already much too late.

Tikov stood in the hatch of the APC, a sickening feeling coming upon him. Though expectant, he had still been taken aback by the ultralow approach of the second aircraft. It had been so low, he could swear he had looked down at the cockpit. The impression, though illusory, had been very hard to dismiss.

He had watched, astonished, as the aircraft had rolled onto its back and disappeared down the cliff; he'd wondered whether the pilot had gone mad. Then he had seen it again, low down in the canyon right side up, a barely distinguishable, fast-moving object heading directly for the radar. Only then had he understood the pilot's maneuver. Not one gun or SAM had by then fired, including his own.

Further, when everything had erupted, the first aircraft, with its strange ability to alter its visual aspect, had returned. It had then begun to distract the defenses, preventing them from concentrating on the priority threat, baiting them by putting itself in considerable danger.

Despite the circumstances, Tikov had admired the pilot's bravery, while ordering his men to fire on the dancing, prancing aircraft, hoping its removal would make the defenses turn their full attention upon the bomber. He had fired his twin machine guns as well, but more in frustrated anger than with any real expectation of a long-range hit. Then had come a powerful feeling of satisfaction—not unlike the time when the Stealth aircraft had gone down—when a burst from one of the SAMs fired by his men had struck a wing. Unfortunately the damage had not been sufficient to bring down the hard-maneuvering airplane. The burst had not been close enough. To his intense chagrin and foreboding, both aircraft had escaped. Yet he could still admire the way in which it had all been done. The surprise had been complete because no one had deemed it important enough to listen to him. His fears had been ignored. What could a lowly Ukrainian lieutenant know that his senior officers didn't? And one promoted from the ranks at that.

Tikov thought of the colonel with an all-consuming hatred. "I hope you roast, you stupid bastard!" he snarled as he stared out at the canyon. On his headset, he thought he could hear snatches of panicky instructions from the SAM and gun batteries below. A lot of good that would do them now.

He was aware of, but did not look down at, the captain, who had come to stand by his APC.

"Do you mean me?" the captain asked diffidently now that Tikov had been proved so comprehensively right.

"No. That stupid colonel down there. He's going to roast, and I'm glad, the idiotic son of a whore. He should have done his job. Any minute now the place is going to be blown sky high." Tikov's anger and frustration made him sound tired. "They used delayed-action bombs."

After the incredible noise of the firing, the silence that had followed was unnerving. It was as if the desert itself were waiting to see what happened next. All the men from the vehicles were standing in an unconsciously choreographed line, facing the canyon. They, too, some carrying their weapons loosely, were waiting.

When it began, it was barely perceptible. A distant rumble, faint, like the far approach of thunder. Then it swelled rapidly, filling the canyon with the power of an earthquake. Suddenly they saw, even from the distance of their vantage point, huge, fast-moving protrusions begin to run along the canyon floor. It was as if some prehistoric monster were trying to break free of the confines of the earth but couldn't quite work out how and was searching for an exit.

The watchers knew with dread that multiple explosions were occurring within the many tunnels radiating from the center, consuming warheads, fuel, and people. Their faces showed the nightmare of their visions as their minds thought of friends and colleagues perishing down there.

Then, from the center, a gigantic explosion hurled debris skyward, exceeding the height of the canyon rim by several thousands of feet. Sympathetic explosions began as the tunnel areas themselves at last erupted into the open. Then the ground upon which the APCs stood began to shake.

Tikov tore his eyes away from the enormous dark and constantly evolving cloud that grew above the canyon. Glancing down, he saw the danger immediately.

"Into the cars!" he yelled above the noise. "We must get away from here. Come on, come on! Move! Captain . . . that means you!"

His men obeyed quickly, climbing into the vehicle with alacrity. Some of the others took too long to react. The captain was swift, but the crew of one APC were still not all aboard as the other vehicles began to move.

These did so just in time, for the cliff top had begun to crumble as the explosions in the canyon grew closer, with mounting intensity. The horseshoe was now almost entirely obscured, and a great pall of smoke and debris was settling over the fast-retreating APCs.

The third armored carrier was unlucky. Just as it began to move, the ground collapsed beneath it. It fell, tumbling down the twelve hundred feet of disintegrating cliff face, bouncing its occupants against its hard metallic insides, beating them to death as it went. By the time it hit bottom, a great blazing fissure had opened, swallowing and consuming it at the same time.

The two surviving APCs stopped a safe distance from the raging canyon, and Tikov once more opened the hatch and propped himself up to look upon the disaster. Next to his vehicle, the captain also stood out of his own hatch.

Both turned to look at each other with grim faces and said nothing.

At November base, everyone in Operations Control had been energized by the sudden burst of code from the E.3A Sentry. The wall screen had swiftly updated itself as the information had come in, showing the real-time traces of the various aircraft. Then had come the one-word mission success signal:

PALE FLYER

It glowed in huge letters on the screen. Grinning with relief and pleasure, Thurson and Bowmaker shook hands with each other and with Morton and Macallister, as the rest of the information had continued to come in. Hohendorf and Ecker unscathed, Bagni and Stockmann hit but still flying.

Then Bowmaker said, "Major Morton, I think it appropriate that you rush to the hospital to give Wing Commander Jason the good news."

"Yes, sir!" Morton acknowledged eagerly, and hurried off.

"And now," the air vice-marshal said to Bowmaker, "we

send the bad news about that submarine. It's not over yet."

Urgent transmissions began.

0740 Hours, Moscow Time

The colonel who was Kurinin's aide had come on duty early. He now rushed into Kurinin's office, face very pale.

Kurinin, sleep-deprived, looked up irritably at the unannounced intrusion. Then he registered the expression on the colonel's face. "What is it?"

Wordlessly the colonel handed him a printout. A burst of code had been intercepted in the area of the site.

Kurinin felt his stomach congeal but displayed no outward sign of this. "Contact the site," he ordered. *"At once!"*

As the colonel rushed out to give the necessary orders, Kurinin remained perfectly still at his desk, somehow knowing it was already too late. At every step an operation had been run counter to his, matching his moves and creating diversions. His lips tightened grimly. He may have lost this skirmish, but he was not beaten. The fight had not ended. There was a long way to go before his plans for a new union would come to fruition, and the current instability that was abroad in the world was a valuable asset. The West's seemingly unending confusion, ineptitude, and inertia would continue to serve his purposes. They were missing all the chances they were likely to get.

He stood up suddenly. *Karelia*, however, must be saved.

At forty thousand feet, in Pale Flyer Three, McCann stared at the data-link message.

"All right!" he exclaimed. "Yeeharrr!"

"Care to tell me?" Selby queried mildly.

"Patching it over to you."

An MFD in Selby's cockpit briefly went dark to show the glowing words—PALE FLYER.

"Yes!" Selby cried. "Good stuff. Good stuff!"

"Are those guys brilliant, or what?"

"Brilliant, Elmer Lee. Absolutely brilliant."

"So what do you think of Axel now, huh?"

"What I've always thought. The man's a great flyer."

"And?"

"And what?"

"You know . . . Holy shit!" McCann said, interrupting his own trailing questions abruptly. "Ooh . . . hell . . ."

"Which is where you're going if you don't share the secret, McCann," Selby told him.

The signal light had come on at the time of the attack phase of the mission, and both air cover ASVs knew that Pale Flyer One was all right, but that Two was hit, though still flying. They were now heading at speed toward the area, fully prepared for action. So far, brief radar sweeps had shown no hostile aircraft within 150 miles.

"Better tighten your harness, buddy," McCann said. "Get this . . . there's a submarine in the area. . . ."

"So? It's hardly going cross the desert. . . ."

"A monster of a submarine, based on the Typhoon class, but bigger. A humungous . . ."

"That's the description sorted out, Elmer Lee. What's the meat?"

"Hey, I'm glad you said meat, because that's what we're going to be if we don't do this right. The sub is an aircraft carrier."

"*What?*"

"Yep. I like the way bad news concentrates the mind."

"But that's impossible," Selby protested. "There's no such animal."

"Tell that to the jokers who sent it down here. And just to add to the fun, it's got six—count 'em—*six* aircraft aboard. Yak-142's. Supersonic, agile bastards. Nice news, huh? This is going to be a fun day."

"Shit," Selby said.

"Took the word right out of my mouth . . . Hold. There's more coming in . . . Aha. Flyer One's to attack the sub . . . seems he needed to use only half his bomb load . . . and they've given approximate coordinates. Bet Axel's going to love that."

Just then they heard from Cottingham in Pale Flyer Four. "You guys get the news?"

"Yep," McCann answered.

"You believe it?"

"We believe it." McCann had been reaching out with the radar even as he spoke. His voice now took on a sharp edge. "Better believe it, Flyer Four. Either somebody's lost way out here or I've got me a bogey at one fifty-five miles. . . ."

"I have him, too," came Flacht's voice almost immediately.

"Your lead, Three," Cottingham said to Selby, suddenly crisp and professional.

"You go high. Let's check this out."

"Roger. Going high."

In the near distance, something streaked for the upper reaches.

McCann had turned to look. "There he goes in that Eagle climb of his. He still thinks he's flying that bird."

"The ASV can do better," Selby commented, "so he ought to be happy. Okay, Elmer Lee. Let's see what sort of company we've got. We must keep them away from One and Two, especially as Nico and Hank in Two took some hits."

"We're in," McCann said eagerly. "So it's a-weavin' an' a-duckin'. Let's go, buddy boy."

"Give me strength," Selby muttered.

* * *

In Pale Flyer Two, Bagni and Stockmann were startled by the sudden noise of the attention getters. Bagni immediately pressed one of the red flashing buttons to stop the sound and glanced at the warning panel. There was now a red CSAS warning. That meant a critical failure in the control systems. Either all channels but one had gone and the system was on direct link or they were in what the November crews liked to call pig mode. This was full and final reversion to the mechanical mode whereby the aircraft was controlled without fly-by-wire assistance. It was like driving a bus with bald tires on ice, as one of the newer November pilots had described it while compulsorily practicing the condition.

"I've got critical CSAS up here," he said to Stockmann.

"Repeated on my panel. We must have taken worse hits than we thought, or this is a gradual deterioration from the original."

"Unless something's caused the rudder to center and lock." Bagni gently tested the rudder pedals. There was movement, but only just. "Not locked, but very stiff. Partial jam, I think. Perhaps a splinter. Call the news. We'll go as far as we can toward the emergency strip . . . but we may have to punch out."

"A little desert walk? Simplicity itself." Stockmann began to warn the rescue teams of their predicament.

"Roger, Flyer Two," one of the teams responded. A French voice. "Your status and current position noted. Will maintain constant monitoring. Can you make the strip?"

"We'll try, but may have to eject."

"Roger . . . we copy that. Stay airborne as long as possible. Closer you are, the sooner we can get to you."

"Understood. Well, Nico?" Stockmann went on. "How do we look?"

"I can make the strip if nothing else happens to the system," Bagni replied. He checked his fuel readings and the central warning panel to make certain that at least their fuel state gave them enough of the precious juice to make it to the strip. There was more than enough to reach the tanker; but tanking with the controls in their current state would be asking for trouble. It was the strip or a walk to one of the designated pickup points until the rescue team arrived.

Then, without warning, the attention getters were at it again. The CWP showed dreaded red captions: L FIRE, R FIRE. Fire or overheating in both engine bays. The automatic extinguisher systems had immediately gone to work as Bagni brought the throttles right back to idle. The wings rapidly adjusted themselves to give the best lift possible as speed decreased. He pushed at the flashing buttons, and the noise stopped only briefly before starting up once more.

The extinguishers had failed to do the job.

Bagni decided there was little point in staying too long and getting roasted. The aircraft was finished. It was time to go.

Stockmann was calling the emergency. "Mayday! Mayday! Mayday! Fire in both engines. Ejecting."

"Eject! Eject! Eject!" Bagni called.

Both seats left cleanly, and neither man sustained any injuries. The stricken ASV flew steadily for a few moments before nosing down toward the desert, where it exploded on impact 210 miles from the destroyed radar site.

Had he been there to see it, Lieutenant Anatoly Tikov would have felt a certain degree of satisfaction.

The remaining three Pale Flyer aircraft were immediately informed of the situation, their crews relieved by

Bagni's and Stockmann's survival. At November base, Pale Flyer Two's trace had vanished from the screen.

"That move took guts," Bowmaker said, looking at the spot where it had been, "even though he deviated from the mission plan."

"He succeeded in diverting the antiaircraft fire long enough to give Hohendorf and Flacht a better chance," Thurson said. "And while it was not strictly according to the mission plan, it did serve its purpose. Brave indeed. Chris Jason expects initiative from his crews. He picked them for the very qualities you saw displayed. All things considered, a very fair exchange . . . especially as we have not lost our crew." On the screen, the trace of the rescue aircraft had appeared, heading for Pale Flyer Two's last position.

Pale Flyer One had made it to the tanker and was now heading toward the suggested position of the submarine.

"This will be more like old times, Johann," Hohendorf said. "We'll be back over the sea."

"If there is such a thing as a submarine aircraft carrier. Six aircraft, too. Let's hope Three and Four can find those birds."

"They will, if that big submarine really is out there. And if its aircraft are up, that's good news."

"Oh, yes?" Ecker did not sound as if he thought that was such good news.

"Look at it this way, the sub can't dive unless it expects the pilots to swim home. It will be vulnerable."

"Unless it sees us coming and lets loose with everything it's got."

"It won't see us. We'll do our Baltic trick," Hohendorf said, referring to his times with Ecker on his former squadron when they went on training missions over the Baltic. The Baltic trick was an ultralow approach.

"You should have told me. I'd have brought my water skis, if I'd known we were going spray-hopping."

Hohendorf grinned tightly in his mask. Johann was doing all right. "We'll go for a straight pass," he said. "With the two bombs left, we'll have just the one chance."

The IDS sped low over the desert landscape, heading for the sea, its shadow rising and falling over the undulations, sometimes seeming to come right up to merge with it. The route out had been planned so as to take the Tornado well away from any points of habitation. In the event, they traversed desert all the way to the edge of the ocean.

Hohendorf kept the aircraft so low, Ecker was sure the sea-spray whipped at the cockpit. They sped on, waiting for the data-link signal that would give them the exact position of the submarine.

High above and still some distance away, McCann was saying: "I've got two—repeat, two—bogeys now, and they're coming our way, ol' buddy."

"Let's make quite certain," Selby cautioned. "We don't want to start splashing some perfectly innocent bystander. Interrogate."

McCann went through the identification "friend or foe" routine, electronically asking the unknown airplane to identify itself. A hostile aircraft, not having the codes, could not respond. The Sentry would have already advised of neutrals.

"Zilch," McCann said. "No reply to IFF interrogation."

"Okay," Selby remarked slowly. "Helmet sight's on. What do we have?"

"Still two bogeys, and still not replying to our interrogation. I'm also still getting 'insufficient data' on my screen. Flyer Four has gotten the same problem."

A good twenty miles away, Cottingham and Flacht were positioning themselves for a wide trail intercept. This would give Selby the lead, allowing Cottingham as his wingman to swing behind him in trail, well within the range parameters of both Skyray B and Krait missiles. This gave them a reasonably fluid option to enable them to counter any moves the as yet unidentified aircraft might choose to make.

There was still no news as yet on the submarine's position. If those fighters really did come from there, they would not have traveled very far, for fear of running out of fuel and facing a long glide to the drink. Further, they would be constrained by the fuel problem in any coming fight.

Selby considered that a plus in the ASVs' favor.

"Come on, Elmer Lee. Give me something!"

"Why are you pilot guys so impatient? You'll get it when I've got it. Those bogeys out there are playing hard to get, and . . . hey. Jesus. It's true!"

"I'm waiting."

"The sub does exist! There really *is* a submarine aircraft carrier. We've got a down link from the E.3A. They've found it and are giving a simultaneous patch to Axel and Johann. And . . . Hey!" McCann said again. "We've got movement! The bogeys are running. Their mothership must have picked up the Sentry's transmissions, and even if they can't read what's in them, they're taking no chances. They're calling their boys home . . . or . . ." He stopped.

"They're going after the Sentry!" Selby and McCann said together.

Selby hauled the ASV round to intercept the new course taken by the distantly invisible aircraft, while McCann spoke urgently to Flacht in Pale Flyer Four. Immediately the second Tornado's track moved in concert.

At their current altitude on afterburners, though not

into full, fuel-gobbling combat burner, and with wings at maximum sweep, the two ASVs were hitting over thirty miles a minute and still accelerating. They would intercept within four minutes if the other aircraft continued on course.

"More company," McCann said. "Two more bogeys low down, coming up. Fifty miles. I think those guys were just launched, Mark. They want a fight. Their buddies are definitely going for the Sentry."

In any aerial conflict a big, relatively cumbersome, and unarmed airborne warning and communication systems aircraft like the Sentry would generally be well out of the danger area, with fighter cover to protect it. A high-value asset, it was a prime target. In the current situation there was no real cover, and it was well within the danger area. No one had expected a submarine with aircraft.

It was obvious, the Tornado crews realized, that the submarine commander had weighed the situation and decided to make a fight of it. Accepting the evidence of his radar, he had clearly assumed that there were no other aircraft in the vicinity. Two fighters and one vulnerable AWACS, so his reasoning had apparently told him, would be no match for his own six fighters. He would also have known by now of the fate of the radar site and would be hopping mad. What better way to demonstrate the power of the revolutionary concept of a modern submarine aircraft carrier?

But he didn't know about Hohendorf and Ecker. With luck, he would not find out until much too late.

Voicing those thoughts, McCann said, "Axel must be doing his let's-walk-on-the-water stuff. That sub's boss is thinking we're out here on our own, just to cover the Sentry."

"There is another possibility," Selby began thoughtfully. "The message said six aircraft. Unless the last two are still on deck waiting to launch, they may well be out hunting . . . just in case."

"I'll warn Axel."

"Do that."

In Pale Flyer One, Ecker watched as the secure message came in from Three. Having previously received the submarine's position from the Sentry, Hohendorf had gently altered heading to the new course, still keeping very low. From time to time Ecker had glanced out of the cockpit to make sure that the blur going by had not crept closer. A backseater new to Hohendorf's style of flying would have been involuntarily trying to raise his feet off the cockpit floor, half expecting to see the water come through it.

"Message from Flyer Three," he now said to Hohendorf. "They've got four bogeys on screen, but think we should look out for the other two . . . in case they're out looking for us."

"Let's get their nest first," Hohendorf said calmly. "They won't feel too happy with fuel running out and nowhere to land."

"And after?"

"We'll see."

"That's what I thought you'd say."

Hohendorf, Ecker knew, would engage in air combat—even in the IDS—should they be attacked. With the last two bombs gone and the continuing fuel usage, the aircraft would be much lighter and more nimble. In the right hands, the IDS was no slouch. Ecker had watched Hohendorf win over F-16's, F-15 Eagles, and Phantoms. It would be interesting to see how he fared against the Yak-142's.

Failure, unfortunately, would be terminal. No one would be calling "Knock it off."

*   *   *

The two ASVs were still racing toward the intercept point.

"Still just the four," McCann was saying. "No sighting of the last two by Flyer One. Reckon they must be still on deck, after all."

"Let's hope so. Perhaps they'll go down with the sub when Axel drops his surprise."

Selby had been scanning out of cockpit, looking for the first sign of attack, waiting for the helmet sight to acquire.

"Ah!" McCann said.

"That must do wonders for your dentist. Now what about me? I'm feeling deprived."

"We have an ID. The targeting systems just decided it's picked up a Yak but is giving me the 'No Further Data' sulk."

"Well . . . now we know. Arming Skyray."

"I have confirmation. Flyer Four," McCann went on to their wingman, "we're going hot."

"Roger. Going hot," Cottingham answered.

There was no need for further communication for the time being. Cottingham knew what to do.

Selby's head continued to track across the sky, waiting for the arrow on the helmet sight to start pointing. Seconds later, it did. "I've acquired," he said urgently to McCann.

The targeting arrow on the helmet sight, focused on infinity and superimposed upon the outside world, was pointing toward the still invisible target. As Selby turned his head toward it, the arrow shortened until it became a point. He was now looking directly at the other aircraft. Almost immediately, the targeting box framed the area where the Yak should be. The box began to move, itself tracking across the sky as it stayed with the targeted aircraft.

Selby followed it with his head, keeping it in sight and maneuvering the ASV in preparation for the shot.

"Target range one hundred miles," McCann said. "The sensors have given us a picture. It's a 142 all right." McCann always marveled at the way the artificial image produced by the systems always managed to look so realistic. The image would faithfully mimic all the shifts of plane carried out by the target. "He's still taking it easy. No idea we've got him."

"He's in for a shock."

"Do we fire without warning?"

"He's not here to shake our hands. Our mates have just totaled his radar site. Besides, we can't let them take a shot at the Sentry." Selby glanced at the threat warning display. Nothing showing.

As the range closed, the targeting box began to pulse. The Skyray B, though having a range that was well in excess of 120 miles, could be fired from as little as thirty miles, which was also within the short-range Krait's envelope.

The box glowed. The Skyray had begun its death-knell sounds with rising volume, slavering, it seemed, eager for the kill. The other aircraft suddenly turned violently.

"He knows he's in lock!" McCann cried. "But not where from. Guess his radar must still be blind. Not yet in range."

Then, suddenly, a bloom appeared beneath the wing of the image on McCann's MFD. Almost instantly the missile tracking warner began its manic beeping.

Beep-beep-beep-beep-beep . . .

"Bloody hell!" Selby exclaimed, breaking hard left, rolling right and climbing. "Either he's hopeful or he's got a long-range weapon we don't know about. Well . . . he's still in for a surprise."

Selby had reacquired the Yak on the helmet sight, and the Skyray was again gleeful. He squeezed the release button. The Skyray dropped from the ASV's belly and, with a searing rush, took off after its target.

Beeb-beep-beep-beep-beep . . .

"That thing's still on its way," McCann said as Selby rolled the Super Tornado onto its back to plunge seaward. His eyes were still glued to his displays, even as the world about him pivoted and tumbled in response to Selby's evasive tactics.

"Aha! Now he's beginning to wonder what's coming up his AC. Hey . . . watch my head, guy. Trying to knock me senseless, or what?"

Selby grunted as he hauled the aircraft back up to rack it into a tight right-hand turn. The accelerometer showed a count of 7 g.

"What the hell's AC?"

"Think biology," McCann said.

"I might have known," came Selby's resigned voice.

Beep-beep-beep-beep-beep—

"You ready to get rid of that thing?" McCann queried. "Or are we going to tow it round the sky with us and . . . Oh, yeah! Down he goes!"

The Skyray's slavering had ended abruptly, signifying a hit. On McCann's screen, the computer-generated image had suddenly blinked out.

Beep-beep-beep-beep-beep . . .

Like a demented limb on the loose, the dead Yak's missile was still out hunting, as if on a quest for revenge. There was an eerie feel to its persistence; but, though searching, it had not yet achieved lock-on. The beeping would have changed to a continuous tone otherwise.

"All right, Elmer Lee. It's cruised around long enough now and should be running out of fuel soon. It's feeding time. Give it some chaff."

The gleaming strips bloomed away as Selby took the ASV high and at high speed, giving the incoming missile no choice but to go for easier meat. A sudden flaring about five miles away told the story.

"Thought you were never going to get rid of it," they heard Cottingham say. "I'm engaging."

McCann looked round and up, seeing the briefest of movements. Pale Flyer Four was obviously using the chameleon, for in streaking away, the fleeting visual identification had given the impression of an outline rather than that of a positively defined shape.

Before either Selby or McCann could speak, something flared brightly high above them. There was a silence on the headphones.

Christ, McCann thought. Wolfie.

"Flyer Four!" he called urgently. "You guys okay?"

"Of course we are," came Flacht's voice. "What did you think?"

McCann heaved a sigh of relief. "Well . . . it happened so quick, I thought . . ."

"You thought wrong, McCann," Cottingham put in. "Eagle drivers are naturally quick."

McCann ended transmission and spoke to Selby. "That guy needles me. You know that?"

"Only because you let him. Now let's go after those jokers who've been following us."

"I was worried about Wolfie," McCann said in explanation as he set up the new attack.

"So was I. Now what have you got for me?"

"They've extended, now that their buddies are gone. Range eighty miles. They can't hang around for much longer. They've got to think of fuel, and the nearest gas station is on that tub navy guys call a boat."

"They've still got enough for a fight, and they're a lot closer to their base than we are to our tanker. No tanker captain in his right mind is going to bring his plane into this area until we've made it safe. And don't forget that last pair. They can swap shifts and might be launching even as we speak."

"So let's get these bozos first."

"It may have escaped your notice, but that's just what I intend to do. Tell Cottingham."

"No need." McCann was watching the screen. "He's on his way. The guy's hungry. They've seen him and are countering."

Pale Flyer Four had gone into a modified trail position, away to the right and slightly above. The incoming fighters had decided to split, one going high, the other coming straight on toward Selby and McCann. Both Yaks launched their missiles simultaneously, clearly a deliberate tactic.

Almost immediately the warning tone sounded, and McCann had both missiles on track.

Selby broke into a hard ninety-degree turn, rolling right. He continued the roll and pulled left, rolled again, pulled, and was heading down in a thousands-of-feet plunge toward the ocean.

"He's following us down," McCann said. "So's the missile, in case you're interested. I'm countering." He also programmed the chameleon to give a constantly shifting color scheme. On the MFD he'd selected to track the missile, there was a slight wavering of the trace as the electronic countermeasures confused its brain. But it steadied and continued the chase.

"Hey," McCann said. "This one's smart. Probably additional optical guidance."

Beee-beee-beee-beee-beee-beee . . .

"Different tone," Selby said. He still held the ASV in the dive, watching the altitude unraveling on the head-up display. The missile had not yet achieved full lock.

"I'm not worried," McCann started to say carefully, "but are we pulling out of this dive today?" He tried not to think of the near miss they'd had over another patch of sea when they had been doing the knife fight with Hohendorf. On his own display, he watched the altitude disappearing and hoped Selby was not about to screw up.

Then the ASV was inching its nose upward, losing momentum, wings coming forward as speed dropped.

McCann felt the enormous forces of gravity pressing down upon him as the ASV began to haul itself into the pull-up. He expected to hear the aircraft scream with the effort, as if it were a living being. He strained against the G-forces, giving his body more tolerance to the punishment.

Selby had brought the throttles right back, letting gravity create its own propulsion. Speed was still high, and the sea was still approaching.

So was the missile.

Bmmmmmmmmmmmmmmmmmmmmmmmmmm!

"All right, Elmer Lee! Chaff now!"

McCann needed no further bidding. The chaff bloomed and the missile wavered, hunting for the real target that was now perilously close to the water. Confused, it wavered for too long.

McCann shut his eyes. *C'mon, baby,* he said in his mind. *C'mon. Get up there!* The sea appeared to be reaching for the cockpit. But, no, there was sky on the nose, and the ASV was leaping for the high vaults of the heavens, wings sweeping, engines hurling it upward.

The missile went for the chaff, missed, and plunged into the sea. It kept going down and did not explode.

"Now I want him," Selby said grimly as they passed twenty thousand feet and continued the climb.

The Yak had balked at following him too far down, probably because the chameleon effect had confused and worried its pilot as the water came too close for comfort. It was now some miles away, preparing for another run-in.

Selby turned his head, searching, arrow on the helmet

sight like a sneaky child, pointing toward the hiding place. The Yak was right above the cockpit, a speck within the targeting box.

Beee-beee-beee-beee-beee-beee . . .

"Goddamn that guy," McCann said. "He's just firing off any old how."

"Perhaps," Selby growled, "but it's going to spoil our shot if we evade."

"What are you saying?" McCann demanded in a voice that had a squeaky edge to it.

"He's within Krait range. He's not going to be able to get away."

"You mean we're not evading." To McCann, it sounded like suicide.

"We've got time."

"Hey, buddy. I hope this missile knows it." McCann's eyes fixed upon the missile track on the MFD. It was just thirty miles out. The image trailed a cometlike tail that shortened the nearer it came, as the range closed. "We've got seconds to live, Mark, if you don't do some good shit. This baby's doing Mach three point five. We've got thirty-eight seconds to impact and counting."

"We've got . . . time." Selby hauled the ASV up and onto its back, rolled upright, and curved round to the left. The Yak was nicely locked in the box, a few thousand feet below.

"Thirty seconds," McCann called. "The missile's followed our maneuver, but the turn's given us more time. Still thirty seconds to impact."

The Krait had begun its chilling, modulated hissing tone. It was happy, eager to go.

"Twenty-five seconds. Jesus, Mark!"

Selby squeezed the release. The Krait set off to what sounded like an amalgam of hiss and howl as it seared toward the Yak, now trying vainly to get out of the way.

Selby threw the ASV into a series of violent evasive maneuvers, while McCann worked the countermeasures as the world again tumbled about him. The flares described fantastic patterns in the sky as the ASV fled from the determined missile whose seekers seemed capable of ignoring the bait.

During one of the gyrations, McCann thought he saw a violent bloom of fire far down near the water. He wondered if Cottingham had scored once more or if that had been the Yak they'd just shot at.

Then the missile that had been pursuing them exploded. At first, McCann was certain they'd taken a bad hit. The aircraft had rocked with the force of the explosion, but none of the warning systems had come on. The warning panels in both cockpits remained steadfastly unlit.

"Wooo!" McCann cried. "I guess we're still alive." He did a swift systems check. "All systems are go. You're one lucky citizen, Mark. You know that?"

"Of course."

"Yeah, yeah. Modesty is sure not something you pilots have heard of."

"So did we get him?"

"We did, my man. We did."

"And Cottingham?"

Something bright lived briefly in the distance, and someone died.

"I reckon he's just nailed the other guy."

"Check."

McCann called up a page on an MFD. The image of the second ASV filled the screen. "Flyer Four," he called, "you in business?"

"We're in business, and coming up," Flacht replied.

"Good kill."

"Why, thank you, Elmer Lee," Cottingham said. He seemed to be laughing.

McCann said nothing. After a while he muttered, "That guy's really insufferable."

"I've heard people say that about you."

"Yeah . . . but I'm cute."

The last pair of Yaks never launched. The submarine skipper had been waiting for what he had hoped was his returning aircraft; but having lost four, he was not prepared to risk his last assets. He began to make preparations for a crash dive, to leave the area as quickly as possible. The depths were his cloak of invisibility.

Karelia could disappear and wait in a deep undersea canyon while the West's navies hunted for her fruitlessly.

Klaxons sounded, and deck personnel began to scramble below. Slowly the deck-length clam doors began to move.

Pale Flyer One was approaching the target at five hundred knots and so low that no one on the submarine saw it. They were all too busy with the dive.

Ecker had the target on the imager. The approach was bows-on, and he could see the huge doors. "My God. What is it? There are huge open doors on the deck, almost along the whole length."

"Then she can't dive until those doors are closed," Hohendorf said urgently. "Give me steering and range."

On Ecker's thermal display, the repeated HUD symbology showed the bomb fall line perfectly within the target bars, the whole superimposed upon the target's image. "Maintain heading," he said. "Target three point five miles . . . three miles . . . two point five . . . two miles. Standby . . . Pickle, pickle . . . now! And bombs gone!"

Ecker looked up suddenly as darkness filled the cockpit, totally convinced they were about to hit what appeared to be a skyscraper. But Hohendorf had hauled on the stick, and the IDS hurtled over a huge mass that seemed to go on forever.

Then they were away, hugging the sea once more, tearing away from there, putting as much distance as possible between them and the eruption that was to come.

On the submarine, the men at the inner end of the flight deck beneath the huge tower that was the *Karelia*'s sail could not believe their eyes as the IDS seemed to rise out of the sea to hurl two objects at them.

The bombs came through the closing doors in shallow arcs, propelled by five hundred knots of inertia. One skimmed above the cockpit of one of the remaining Yaks, to embed itself in a thick bulkhead behind. The other took one of the men with it, leaving a disintegrating trail of bone and tissue as it shot through the sole watertight door still open to continue along, carving a destructive path as it went. It finally came to rest just above the main bridge of the submarine.

Neither bomb exploded on impact.

People froze for what seemed an interminable time. Like mindless beasts, the flight deck doors continued to close. The submarine continued with its diving routine. For an insane moment, it was as if nothing had happened.

Then people began to run. Orders were shouted to abort the dive. One man simply stared at the bomb above the bridge, as if inspecting a strange animal.

The flight deck doors closed and sealed shut.

The bombs exploded.

ENDINGS

Washington, Three Days Later

Mac was in the JOSIS offices, putting some of her things into a small service hold-all. There was a knock on one of the doors. General Bowmaker stood there.

She came to attention. "Morning, sir."

"Good morning, Mac." Bowmaker's eyes seemed to hold secrets. "At ease. So you're really leaving us."

"Yes, sir. New unit."

Bowmaker nodded slowly. "The Pale Flyer was a good mission. Wasn't it?"

"It certainly was, General. Everything worked out. It got close sometimes, but the result is what counts. Taking out both the radar *and* the sub was very good work by the November boys."

Again, Bowmaker nodded. He seemed very thoughtful. "Wing Commander Jason is very proud, and of course, he's proved his point once again. The November system makes sense. When these people take something on, they get it done. And how! Beats the UN any day."

"*I* think so. The UN's a mess. Vested interests over reality." Mac was blunt. Then she gave a wistful smile. "I hear Major Morton got his wish, after all . . . back to flying."

"Better than he'd hoped. I've kept my promise. He's now one of Jason's elite. At least . . . he's learning to be. The selection process is tough, but he'll make it." Bowmaker paused, clearly coming to a decision. "A man came to see me yesterday, Mac. Something he thought I should know. He said I should talk to you."

She looked wary. "Oh?"

"It's okay," he assured her. "I've been given the appropriate clearance, but you decide what to tell me. Like your true rank, to begin with."

She took a while before replying. "You still outrank me," she answered, the brief smile coming on. "I'm a lieutenant colonel."

Bowmaker gave a dry whistle. "Some jump from sergeant. Whose army? Ours? Or theirs . . . or should I say yours?"

"Both."

Bowmaker raised an eyebrow. "I'm impressed. Dangerous, though."

"All danger is relative. It's how you cope with it that really matters."

"Jason would have a fit if he knew he'd had a Russian on his base, helping him plan the mission. And of course, you've been in place here, in the holy of holies. There are some people here, too, who'd have a fit."

"Half Russian," she corrected, grinning.

"Half Russian," Bowmaker repeated, shaking his head in wonder. "And I suppose the information about the sub that seemed to come from nowhere . . . that was you, too."

She nodded.

"And that man in the mountains . . . did you take him out?"

Again she nodded. "I was able to go off base and get back without arousing Chuck Morton's suspicions."

"Hell . . . *my* suspicions weren't aroused. I could not believe it when I was told the truth yesterday. What I can't understand is why they bothered to tell me. Your kind of people usually don't even talk to each other."

"I asked them to."

Bowmaker stared at her. "Why?"

"I liked working with you, General. I felt you ought to be told . . . some of it. Though I never expected they'd send you to see me. I think the November system is a very good idea," she went on. "It should be allowed to succeed; which is why the wing commander needs people like you in his corner. Perhaps one day he will have Russian pilots, too." She shrugged. "But that might take a very long time. There is much to do and change over there before that can happen."

Bowmaker held out his hand. "Mac . . . do I call you Mac?"

"Mac will do." She took the hand and shook it.

"It's been a real pleasure," Bowmaker said gruffly.

"Mine too, General."

"So what's this unit they're sending you to? And which general do you get to charm this time?"

"That, sir, would be telling."

Bowmaker nodded. "Sure."

"General . . ."

"Yes, Mac."

"Something I'd like you to do for me."

"Name it."

She handed him a small envelope. "I'd like Chuck Morton to get this."

Bowmaker was surprised. "You're telling him?"

She shook her head. "It's just a card."

"I'll make sure he gets it."

"Thank you, General."

Bowmaker drew himself to attention and saluted her. "Good luck, Colonel."

She returned the salute. "Thank you, sir."

November Base, 0900 Hours

McCann was walking along a corridor in the officers' mess. Someone was following him.

"Wait up, McCann."

He turned warily. It was Cottingham.

"Haven't seen you since the debrief," Cottingham said. "We did pretty good out there."

"We belong to a good outfit."

There was an awkward silence, then Cottingham said, "I've got something to say. When I get my real backseater, if he's as good as you or Wolfie Flacht, I'll consider myself lucky."

Not wanting to believe he'd actually been complimented by Cottingham, McCann stared. Then he nearly spoiled it. With a wide grin, he raised his right hand, palm open in expectation. "Put it there," he began.

Cottingham's own hand remained obstinately at his side. "Quit while you're ahead, McCann. And by the way, there's a lady waiting to see you in the anteroom. Miss Lomax."

Whitehall, London

Charles Buntline entered the minister's office, looking pleased with himself.

"World kind to you today, Charles?" the minister

greeted him. "You do seem rather chirpy." He glanced out of his window. A heavy, windy rain smashed itself against the glass. "I know we need the rainfall, but this is ridiculous. Second day of continuous deluge."

Buntline ignored the minister's querulous tones. "It all worked, Minister," he said of the mission. "No casualties on our side, though we did lose an aircraft. Remarkable thing, that submarine. Glad we got it. Bonus points for Jason's men."

"What of the reactors?" The minister was not interested in bonus points for anyone but himself. "Any risk there?"

"The bombs exploded, forcing the doors open. It sank like a stone. The secondary, truly destructive explosions occurred when it was already very deep down. It's now in nearly twenty thousand feet of Atlantic Ocean. The area is being closely monitored for radioactivity, and so far there's no evidence of a leak. And as for the outside world, a submarine aircraft carrier never existed. No survivors."

"Do keep me informed, Charles."

"As always, Minister," Buntline said, keeping the usual contempt he felt out of his voice.

Never once did the minister ask how Jason was, nor did he express any admiration for the men who had carried out the dangerous work. Had the mission been made public, no doubt the minister would have been effusive in his praise. It would have made him look good.

Buntline left the room, feeling in need of a bath.

In Schleswig-Holstein, Johann Ecker walked into the squadron commander's office.

"The warrior returns," Wusterhausen said. "I'm glad Axel was as good as his word and sent you back in one piece. Well? How was it?"

"Unbelievable, Chief. It's one thing practicing, but to do it for real . . . you never know until the day, how you're going to react."

"Scared?"

"I was."

"Good. I wouldn't want any man on my squadron who didn't feel afraid now and then. But you did the job well."

"We did the job," Ecker corrected. "You should have seen Axel. It was as if we were on a training mission, and no one was really firing at us. It's strange . . . but I never doubted he would get us through."

"It's what I would expect of him. And what are you going to tell Erika?"

"That I'm glad to see her . . . over and over again."

Aberdeen, Midnight

Hohendorf and Morven relaxed in each other's arms. She leaned over to kiss him, then stroked his forehead in the pale darkness of the room. His lovemaking had been strangely gentle, yet she'd felt that he'd wanted more and more of her.

Funny thing, she thought. It was only a few days ago that they had last seen each other. Yet his need of her had felt as if it had been years since that parting.

"I love you," she said softly to him.

Selby entered the phone booth in the November Mess feeling groggy from interrupted sleep and wondered who was calling him at midnight. The duty orderly who had woken him had not given details.

He picked up the receiver. "Flight Lieutenant Selby," he began.

"Marry me," she said.

"Good grief! Kim!"

"Yes or no."

"Yes."

"Oh, good. I'm in Edinburgh. See you in the morning, if you've got the time off."

"I've got the time."

"Oh Good," she said again, and hung up.

Selby stared at the receiver before putting it down and returning to his room. He got back into bed and slept deeply. He did not dream of Sammy Newton.

Northern Russia, Two Days Later

Kurinin stood on a high balcony in a vast submarine dock beneath a mountain and looked down upon the huge keel that was being laid. The loss of both the *Karelia* and the radar had served to convince him of just how valuable both assets had been. That was why they had been targeted so ruthlessly. The West had been mortally afraid of them.

Karelia would not be the last. Neither would the Stealth radar. And as for the November program, it was the most dangerous of potential adversaries, because of what it promised. Currently, the state of confusion and indecision in the West was a good thing. The November program, however, if allowed to become successful, could bring a sense of unified purpose where there was now self-interested chaos.

The November program would therefore continue to be a prime target and merit hostile attention, no matter how long it took.

Another skirmish had been lost, but the battle had only just begun. Meanwhile, the task of rebuilding the union was one of supreme urgency. Already he had detected in the populace—as he had predicted during the crazy nights of the August revolution—the very real fear of the unspeakable consequences that would come in the wake of rampant nationalism. They had seen the early results in the old republics, the madness in Yugoslavia, the stupidity in what was Czechoslovakia. And now, with Russians on holiday being killed in crossfires by the Black Sea in Georgia, they were at last beginning to lose faith and patience with those who had promised them the sunlit uplands of freedom. They should have been smart enough to have thought the consequences through, but as the wars that were springing up like suppurating boils showed, people never are. He felt no sympathy.

Kurinin smiled grimly. It would not be wise to move in haste. Strength had to be rebuilt into the new union. The time had to be picked, preferably when the nation's fear had grown so great, it would sweep the so-called reformers before it with very little prompting. There would be a cry for a new union, one to relieve them of the nightmare that had been visited upon them.

Then would be the time.

A month after Mac had left the Pentagon for good, Chuck Morton was summoned to Jason's hospital room.

Morton looked at the suspended legs in plaster, the propped torso, and the by now lightly bandaged head, and he marveled at Jason's determination to stay on top of things.

"Well, Major?" Jason began. "Are you liking it with us?"

"Yes, sir," Morton replied eagerly. "Great planes you've got there, sir. I've been up for a couple of rides in a two-seat trainer, but no one's given me the controls yet. But I do get plenty of front seat work in the simulator."

"Up here, we walk before we can run, Major. I know you're an experienced F-16 jockey, but to us you're a baby pilot until we clear you for the ASV. And then . . . you'll only just be starting. At November, we fly our way."

"Yes, sir."

"A word, Major, from the older, if not necessarily wiser, head. We are not always masters of our own fates. No one is. However, while we can sometimes prepare ourselves for unknown and unseen events, we can never be fool-proof. Always expect the unknown to be waiting for you when it's going to be the least welcome, and try to counter. Being primed for such action can make all the difference. Remember that in your flying. It may save your life one day."

"Yes, sir," Morton repeated, taking the advice to heart.

Jason tapped briefly at the bandages. "Even I can be caught out."

Morton, unsure of what to say, smiled uncertainly and remained silent. "But not to worry," Jason continued briskly. "I've been hearing good things about you and . . . I haven't thanked you and Sergeant Mac properly for doing such valuable work on the mission. It was a job well done. How is she, by the way? Heard from her?"

"I got a card from Washington, sir. She's doing fine."

"Glad to hear it."

The card had said, simply, "Missing me?"

She had been in position on the hill for two days now. Below her, well within range, was the bend in the road. She watched unmoving as the sniper settled himself a mere one hundred meters away. Then she followed his movements with her own scope, traversing her Dragunov SVD to stop on the sniper's intended first target.

Just at the bend was the leading, beacon-white UN

armored personnel carrier, behind which, unseen, was the food convoy and the rest of the escort. The convoy had stopped because someone had, in his demented wisdom, decided to mine the road. The APC commander, a Swede, was half out of his hatch, looking at the two engineers who were gingerly working a short distance away.

She shifted her own sniper's rifle back to the hopeful assassin's position. He was going for the commander.

She had been well picked for the job. Her aptitude for languages enabled her to speak Serbo-Croat with the correct nuances of dialect so that when she spoke to a Serb, she sounded Serb; and when she spoke to a Croat, she sounded Croat.

Since coming to the region, she had killed ten snipers, two of whom had been women. There were three others like her, all men, operating in other districts. Each worked alone and would not be in contact. Those were the rules.

As she watched the sniper prepare, she wondered grimly when it would begin to dawn upon the outside world that some of these people impersonated each other; that they accused each other of horrors, in order to look the victim and influence for their own ends the sympathy that would result.

It mattered little to her to what so-called ethnic grouping the sniper belonged, for she had no patience with the insanity of their ethnic squabblings. He was about to shoot the UN soldier. That made him a candidate.

She waited, scope now fixed upon her target. From her position she could even see his finger moving toward the trigger. She shifted fractionally. A head shot.

The Dragunov barked sharply just as the sniper decided to shoot. It was a perfect shot.

Down on the road, the engineers paused, fearful. In the APC, the commander traversed his single mounted gun, wondering where the shot had come from and probably wondering equally why he wasn't dead.

The combat engineers, their blue helmets making them look absurdly vulnerable, returned to their dangerous task after glancing about them nervously. They hunched down, carefully working at the mines. Their shoulders betrayed the tenseness they felt, their flak jackets magnetic targets for any lurking gunmen who might be among the trees.

The APC commander peered impotently at both sides of the road, up and down both wooded slopes, searching for a sign of movement. But he saw nothing.

She had left almost immediately, distancing herself from the location, leaving the sniper where he lay for his compatriots, whoever they might be, to find. She had not even gone to check. She never did. Now, she had more hunting to do. As she disappeared swiftly, silently, into the forest, she wondered if Chuck Morton had got the card she'd given the general to send on to him.

There was no evidence left on the hill to betray that she had once occupied a position there.

Except the dead sniper.

Born in Dominica, Julian Jay Savarin was educated in Britain and took a degree in history before serving in the Royal Air Force. Mr. Savarin lives in England and is the author of LYNX, HAMMERHEAD, WARHAWK, TROPHY, TARGET DOWN!, WOLF RUN, WINDSHEAR, NAJA, THE QUIRAING LIST, VILLIGER, and WATER HOLE.